The
Invisible Car Race

By

By Patrick Meservier

Edition
1st 06 01 2018

ISBN
978-0-692-12666-0

Distributed from the United States
Available around the world

In Dedication

For Katrina Meservier, to whom I spun a fine story in
her youth. That was so many years ago now and I'm a
little embarrassed to admit that it took so many years to
actually sit down to put it on paper. I hope it's as good as
you remember.
And to my wonderful wife; without whom I would be
swimming in a sea of pages without form and proper
punctuation. She is the base where my creativity can
spring consistently.

Chapters

Chapter 1

On a computer screen an email application was open.

"Only Multi-Billionaires need apply."

That was the subject line in Harvard Bertrand's email when he got to his office that morning. Harvard stared at the email thinking it was just another of the hundreds of spam emails he had to deal with at his office every morning. He sighed before he hit the delete button. That's when it caught his eye. Elizabeth Champlain's name was in the sender's line.

"Shit." Harvard swore as he tried to find his deleted folder.

Once there he flipped the emails value to unread and sent it back to his inbox. Finally, now that he had things back under control he sat back, he opened the email, took his coffee cup in his hand and read what his friend had to say.

Elizabeth was a friend from Harvard Business School. And yes he had been named after the storied school as both his parents had attended it where they had consequently met and married. As with Elizabeth, he had started his own business after graduating, which had succeeded to a degree that had made him very rich.

In groups of entrepreneurs, the Bertrand family was well known for rampant success. Elizabeth was not family per say but she was considered family because of the close relationship she maintained with Harvard. Harvard opened his eyes wide after reading the email. He was interested in what it said and wanted to discuss it further. He picked up the phone and dialed Elizabeth's personal cell. He turned to face the morning sky out of his office window and waited for Elizabeth to pick up.

His computer screen showed her message.

*"I found this in my
inbox yesterday. Initially I
was going to flush it, but
something made me check it
out. It is not in my business
field but I know it's in yours
and it is real. This
organization is operating at
a very low exposure rate as
it is not legal in the US but
the payout is huge. To get
more information decrypt
the message within.*

*Car, fast, new tech,
big $, only open to the most
dedicated. If you heard of it
before, you'll know what
comes next. >>>!$>>>! Win.
Look to the future and talk
to the commander for more
information."*

~~~

In a small office on the other side of the country, a
phone rang. The three hour difference between Boston
and California meant that the 7:30 Boston phone call
rang at 4:30 in the morning in California. The security
system picked up the call and a message was left.

At 7:10 Darrin Prettiflin came into his office at The Future Automotive Skin Design Company to open up the facility for the day.

It was a small company in San Francisco that specialized in next generation automotive body panels that responded to the elements and converted light into electricity. It was supposed to be the next big thing in automotive tech... if it caught on. Their product never needed to be washed and created power as long as it sat in the sun.

Last year they had invented a specialized auto skin at the request of an underground company. They had been paid six figures for the designs and had been told to wait for a call before they could start producing thirty of them. That morning, the message on the advanced security system was five words. "The trigger has been pulled."

~~~

The nine o'clock classes at MIT were about to begin. Professor Jenkins was running late. His class would be waiting for Doctor Jenkins of the Mechanical Engineering Department, and his latest lecture on "Hydro mechanics and their effect on the new metals."

Doctor Jenkins was still assembling his lecture materials when his watch alarm went off.

"Shoot." He exclaimed.

He knew if he heard this alarm then he was really late. He ran his hand through his thinning brown hair before scrambling to pick up the last of his materials and hurrying off.

He had given up running as a pastime because of a foot injury but he could still move pretty quickly when it was required. He had a thin body profile even after all these years, though not as thin as he'd once been. His students kept him running in a different way and he had turned to swimming as an alternative exercise routine. His tenured colleagues all suffered the effects of age with bulging bellies and the beginnings of medical problems. Compared to them, he felt rather healthy. "Feeling good about your body could go a long way toward stimulating one's mind," he thought.

The good doctor of Mechanical engineering still had a twinkle in his eye at the prospect of teaching, although, at the moment that twinkle had been replaced with the panic of being late. Most of his peers had lost the desire to teach years ago and now did it only as a way to make a living. Instead, he loved being absorbed by the energy that his students reflected back to him. Not only did his eyes still twinkle at the prospect of teaching another day, he held his head high in anticipation at the infusion he would get from it. In a way he saw it as the elixir of life.

Just as he was leaving his office his iPhone rang. The ringtone was an odd one. Technically it was called 'Sci-Fi' and it truly sounded like the sound effect used in many old science fiction movies of the 1950's and 60's. His stomach fell. It was the last sound he wanted to hear. The ringtone was specifically assigned to tell him he was getting a text from an organization that had preyed on his hopes and dreams. He had fallen victim and now they were calling him in on his commitment.

Several years ago Doctor Jenkins had been invited to attend a lecture sponsored by men from several big name companies. The lecture was not been what he expected. It had been held by several men from profitable companies, but their companies had been absent. A sign indicated their meeting location in a small hotel conference room under the name of 'Big $'.

Intrigued, Doctor Jenkins had gone, along with other big names known in the mechanical industry. He recognized many who had attended. Some were friends, others acquaintances from their shared industry of mechanical innovators and professors.

A man from the company 'Driven Motor Innovators' took the stage and introduced himself.

"Welcome. My name is Grant Phyindress. I am the owner of the company Driven Motor Innovators. Today I stand here, apart from my company, as an investor to further mechanical innovation waiting to see the next great race towards creating the next automobile and what the mechanics will look like.

"We have seen in the past that the pressure to succeed will jolt technology forward. War, especially, always produces new and amazing technology. This has been true for every war on this planet. There are some who are bold enough to suggest that there is a secret society out there that works behind government curtains to create war just to advance our technology. I'm sure it's just a legend but that concept has led to the creation of other equally pressured environments in order to achieve specific goals. One such field is in automobile racing. Another is the famed X Prize system. For our little secret society, it will be a combination of several of these ideas.

"To better focus your interest as to why you are here, we are going to discuss a tremendous opportunity for all of you, one that will probably make some turn away, but for others it will pique their interest.

"First off, all of you have been handpicked to be here today. All of you share a similar background in mechanical engineering and have demonstrated great talent in designing the greatest machines of our day. I wanted to bring up a slide show of who all of you are and what great machines you have invented, for those who are unfamiliar with the background of everyone else present, but the day is short and there is much to discuss. If you are interested in learning more about the person sitting next to you, there is a book at the back of the room that lists everyone's backgrounds and accomplishments. After the meeting I will run the slideshow for those who wish to stay on.

"Your accomplishments are the reason we are all here today. Myself and a few other investors have put together a car race. Our goal is to advance automobile technology. We believe that we have been on the precipice of creating new and better cars for years, but for some reason we are stuck in the same technology that we have been using since the internal combustion engine was first invented. The goal of our race is to finally push the auto companies to see the greener grass and finally make the new technologies available to the public.

"Auto companies operate under the absurd notion that they have countless years to keep new technologies bottled up until they are ready to release them, or maybe they believe we are not ready for them. Either way our goal is to find these emerging technological ideas and force them into play.

"At this point our organization has made headway on many fronts. We are now at the stage where we need to recruit master engineers. We are looking for thirty teams to build racecars from scratch to fit exacting specifications."

A hand went into the air from a woman with long brown hair and old fashion glasses. She spoke out without being asked to. "Why not recruit NASCAR engineers? They have all the experience and shops already set up."

"Ah, we knew this question would arise." Phyindress said. He looked to the floor for a moment to insert a dramatic pause then brought it back up with a smile painted on his face. "The point here is to build new designs. The NASCAR people have been drilled into thinking that there is no other way to build a car. NASCAR rules require internal combustion engines, therefore they will never see beyond that ideal. We need fresh ideas, new blood.

"Please understand, we have the greatest respect for all those who have invested time in making the internal combustion engine work so efficiently. Their designs have pushed gas mileage and pollution controls to such a degree that we can see almost one hundred miles to the gallon. Imagine if a hundred years ago, you told an engine manufacturer that his same engine could one day achieve the hallmarks I just mentioned. I'm very sure he wouldn't have believed you. Now we are at that point where we need to abandon the tried and true power plant designs for something new and better."

Grant crossed to the other side of the small stage. He brought his hands up. "Let's focus again on our goals. We are looking for thirty teams to hit the road and race. That's why all of you have been asked to be here. Let me outline some of the specifics we've achieved thus far to help you understand what we're looking for.

"For starters we have the race segregated into groups with an assigned driver. That means an investor has been assigned to a specific team. Therefore the money is already in place to do discovery and prototype testing. The bodies of all of the cars are being built as we speak. All of your final designs will have to fit under the same body style. So what we need are teams of engineers to design and build the cars being raced. The investor for each team will provide direction for his or her dream and fund each project.

"Be aware that this is a commitment. When each team is contacted, they will be responsible for finding the remaining members of their engineering teams and support staff. Money is available to fund all the work. Consequently, finding the shops and vendors to build the final car is also your responsibility. Who among you would like to fire off the first question about our little endeavor?"

Doctor Jenkins remembered that many people had questioned the legality of the race, whereupon they immediately stood and left the room. It was true that to race over the open road in the United States was an illegal activity. Grant had tried to assuage everyone's fears by stating that those issues fell to the investors and to the appointed drivers. But for some it made no difference, they didn't want to be connected to any illegal activity.

"It has been decided that the engineering staff of the teams are to remain anonymous since the whole point of the race is to create new technologies." Grant had said. "The investors have the money to fight any possible legal battles for the drivers."

To Doctor Jenkins, the chance to build a car that illustrated some of his automobile engine designs made his heart soar. He knew that it may be his only chance to finally build his invention. And if so, then he should consider becoming part of a team. He wasn't getting any younger. If the engineers were to remain anonymous, then he could decide later whether or not to remain unidentified.

In the past his designs had been shot down by all of the major auto companies. He knew it all had to do with the oil industry. They pulled all the strings and didn't want see a car that didn't use gas or oil to find its way onto the roads in the U.S.

So he stuck it out for the entire meeting and signed himself up as a senior individual engineer. In the back of his mind he wondered if the odd little endeavor would ever get off the ground. At the end of the meeting when all the thirty teams had been chosen, a group cell phone huddle had been arranged. They each had to program a cell phone number into their phones with a specific ring tone. When the time came, they would get a text from that number.

His second thoughts had begun intruding the next day. What had he been thinking? If there were legal issues, even if his car won, how could he admit to designing the car? Then there was the time commitment. Would he have to leave his teaching position to fulfil his obligation? Despite his longing to see his designs emulated in fully working detail he had no idea how this kind of group could actually succeed. And that had been long before he had found out that the race team had to include a mechanic to ride shot gun who would also have to be trained as a weapon specialist.

Right now his cell phone did ring in that old fashioned science fiction movie siren that heralded aliens attacking, monsters rising from the black lagoon, or some other B rated tragedy where some other species was on the precipice of taking over the world. And his reaction to the tone was true to its origins, it made his heart sink with dread, tinged with a slight thrill of fear.

Jenkins pulled from his pocket his phone and looked at it. A text with two words stared at him. "It's time."

~~~

    Katrina Meservier sat in a large auditorium at a local high school with hundreds of other students who attended MIT. There was a low rumble throughout the attendees about why they hadn't assembled at their own school. Not to mention that is was very early on a Saturday morning for college students to congregate.

    Today they were picking interns for a special team. It was an unusual internship. The most critical part was that they would actually get paid. Therefore, just about every mechanical engineering, electrical engineering, mathematics major, and materials engineering student on campus had applied for one of the precious fifty available slots. There hadn't been any interviews. All that they needed to do was sign up and let their school work determine who would get the positions.

    Katrina was one of only five girls in the auditorium. She sat uneasily among the crush of boys. Many of them hadn't taken the time to shower before they came. She, on the other hand, had gotten up early and dressed for the occasion, including investing an hour plus on her long curly brown hair. She had a tall thin body, though it was hard to tell at the moment. She was so slouched back in her seat that an imaginary beer belly had blossomed.

    Even though Katrina was uncomfortable among the stinky boys she was excited to be there. Katrina, like the majority of the others in the room, was working towards a mechanical engineering degree. It had been a difficult decision to major in this field. She had originally thought that she would choose a more artistic field. She had inherited several traits from her father, artistic talent being one of them. But she had felt a calling to build and fix machines.

Before she had been accepted at MIT her goal had been to go to a school that taught automotive mechanics. Her father had suggested that she push herself further and try for mechanical engineering first. He thought that if it ended up being too hard anything else would seem easy. So she ended up getting accepted to this prestigious school and she was doing well. It still surprised her although she did look back at her art occasionally and sometimes wondered what she would miss by being here. Then again, the reverse could also be true.

Doctor Jenkins walked into the auditorium and approached the old rickety podium. Today he wore jeans and a blue button-down shirt. The serious students sat up straighter with excitement despite the early hour. Katrina was one of those students. She had to squeeze her shoulders through the boys on either side of her who remained slouched.

Towards the front of the auditorium she noticed the curly golden hair of a boy she knew only as Frodes. He was the most focused person she had ever met. He was in several of her classes but they had never spoken. Today he sat taller than the rest on purpose. He desperately wanted a position on the team. As if sitting up straight would be enough to be chosen.

Professor Jenkins paused and took in his audience before he spoke. "Today I arranged this intern selection off-campus because of several institution rules. I won't go into a detailed explanation because it's not important. What is important though is that today we are going to choose fifty young men and women to participate in a unique project that will not only affect your future careers, but will significantly advance automotive technology.

"Congratulations in advance to the selected few, however, to those who do not make the cut, there is still some good news. The pool of candidates for all of the other internship programs will be slashed by fifty so the programs will offer a higher percentage over last year because fewer students will be applying. I encourage you to do the math.

"Now it's time announce the team. Of the many categories being called out, there will obviously be a higher concentration of mechanical engineering students because we are going to actually build a car. The other fields will participate as part of the support team. Therefore only one mathematician will be chosen, and so on and so forth. The criteria by which you were chosen are: Grades, attendance, and participation in your respective classes. To those not chosen, it wasn't because you were not smart enough but rather, how you presented yourself as a whole to this school and to yourself because we are also looking for professionalism.

"The interns will be required to participate in a forum after the job is done to show how they achieved the results of the finished product. So intelligence and professionalism are each important qualities in our team members. To those not who are not chosen, I believe each and every one of you are capable of filling this role. Look at the people around you. Do they present themselves in a professional manner?"

Most everyone looked around to view the students near them. Katrina looked like a model compared to those sitting around her. The boys on either side appeared unkempt, their hair wasn't combed, much less clean, and their clothes smelled like they were several days old and had been stored on a floor somewhere. Many of the boys knew right then that they didn't live up to the professional standards that Dr. Jenkins had described. They sat up straighter and straightened their hair as best as they could with their hands.

Dr. Jenkins began to announce names over his microphone. Despite Katrina's feelings being bolstered by the time she had invested in her looks compared to many in the auditorium, she was still not confident about her chances of being chosen. She knew that mechanical engineering was mostly a man's field. Looking pretty wouldn't get her on the team. She prayed that her work in class was good enough to be recognized. Luckily, Dr. Jenkins was her advisor so he at least he knew that she existed. And in truth, that was the only reason she had bothered to sign up. Otherwise she would still be in bed right now.

She had allowed herself to hope but now boy after boy was being called to the stage. Some of them she knew, others she had never heard of. William something or another, Jake, blah, blah, blah. The only thing Katrina heard was number so and so, then another name, and another number closer to the cut off at fifty. Her mood soured in a direct proportion to the odds of her being chosen dropping the closer he got to fifty.

Finally a girl's name was called. "Silvia Thruwell." Her heart soared. Almost immediately another girl's name was called out. "Kristin Dramicus." She felt better knowing that at least two women had made the team. When there were only five names left the boy on her right stood and prepared to leave. He was sure that his name was not on the list.

As an afterthought he stopped when he was in front of an annoyed boy who was still trying to see if he might be next. The boy with tousled hair had turned back towards Katrina. In his mind he was in the process of asking her out when Dr. Jenkins called out "Katrina Meservier." Katrina jumped up excitedly. No words ever left his lips. Feeling defeated in more than one way he turned back towards the exit and began to push through.

Katrina started toward the group of chosen interns in a rush of excitement. She threw her arms in the air and screamed like she had been chosen to be on stage with the Beatles. She ran up to the boy who was trying to leave, and who was now blocking the way out of the row of seats. She threw her arms around the boy's neck and kissed him. Quickly she turned with him on the spot, like they were dancing and then proceeded quickly towards the end of the row leaving the boy flush and wondering what had just happened.

When Katrina finally made to the end of the row, she ran towards the stage. Dr. Jenkins wasted no time and continued on to the next name on the list. Katrina took her place with the other interns on the stage, beaming. She took a moment to look down the row see if she knew any of the other students among her.

Sadly she only knew one student other than Frodes, who had been among the first to be chosen, and it was the know-it-all from her English class. She didn't like him very much, although to be fair she really didn't know him well. She just didn't like his pompous attitude. Katrina caught the eyes of the two other girls who had been called up. They beamed at each other, proud of their good fortune. For now they were all smiling as though they just won a million dollars. Little did they know that a tremendous amount of work lay ahead of them, paid or not.

Chapter 2

Katrina woke up suddenly at her clock's alarming screech. It reflected the unwanted time of five-thirty in the morning. There was a meeting for the students that had been chosen to be part of the new project at seven, in a lecture hall across campus. Even after a shower she was still groggy from the party that she had attended the night before.

The party had been held at the Phi Kappa Theta fraternity house, of which several of the new interns were members. The four story brownstone had been rocking from the party that had been thrown in celebration of the project, as no less than three of its members had been chosen for this prestigious team, more than from any other fraternity.

Everyone had drank too much, partied too much, and were probably now afflicted in the same way that she was. Thank god coffee would fix some of her problems.

~~~

Dr. Jenkins showed up at his office at the same time every morning. Today he was supposed to have the first of many meetings with his newly picked team in a class room down the hall. After today they would be meeting off-campus in a building that had been provided by the investor, who had turned out to be much more 'hands on' than he had expected.

He sat at his desk with his coffee as he waited for the appointed time. He forced calm into his nervous body while waiting for the investor's representative to arrive and discuss the guidelines for the project.

At exactly six o'clock there had been a knock at his door.

"Come in."

A pudgy man walked in. He was balding and had a bad comb-over that in no way covered the large bald spot. He had also reeked of cigarette smoke. The man wore an expensive light gray suit and carried a briefcase. It too looked expensive; its faded light brown leather could only have been intentionally 'distressed'. The man had waddled around the chair in front of Dr. Jenkins' chair and had seated himself without being asked. Dr. Jenkins had raised an eyebrow at his lack of consideration.

If the man noticed his lack of consideration, he ignored it completely and instead began to speak. "I'm here at the request of my client."

The man wheezed when he inhaled.

"I am Silvio Brenant, one of his many lawyers. All of your communications with him or from him will occur through me." Wheeze. "My client is very confident in your ability to produce a car that can win this contest. He has done much research into your career." Wheeze.

"The first thing that my client requires is with respect to the mechanic. As you know, in the contest rules, a driver is allowed to have one mechanic to accompany them for the race to help maintain the vehicle, among other things. He wants that mechanic to be a woman. Apparently the driver that he has chosen has some 'social issues' and in an enclosed environment would prefer to have a female teammate." Wheeze.

"I wanted to begin with the driver's preference in order to allow you time to find a worthy candidate so they can be part of the team early enough to know how fix any problems that may arise when the time comes.

It's very important. To win this race, this girl must be up on every aspect of the device."

Dr. Jenkins put his hands together to mull over what he just heard. "I have already chosen three girls to be part of the team based on the applications that I received. They were chosen because of their skills in mechanical engineering. If all three of them stay on the project throughout its entirety I will choose one of them to be the race team mechanic."

Dr. Jenkins sat a little straighter. "So... you arranged this meeting to say that the investor is comfortable with my ability to design a winning racecar but that I need to find a female weapons specialist to sit next to the driver so that he can try to win the race without being distracted by his 'social issues'? Seems like a lot of money spent to deliver a message in person when an email could have done just as well."

The lawyer smiled before he wheezed. It was a long wheeze this time. "Because of the sensitivity of the information, all communication will be handled in person. There will be no documentation left behind as evidence nor will there be any possible electronic 'monitoring' by rival teams. All communication and all designs must be on paper that will be hand delivered. I will pick them up at the end of every day and return them the next morning. The chain of information begins and ends with me on a daily basis.

"Your workspace will be inspected every day and any computers that you use (off-line) will be kept under lock and key. I will have the only key. All documents will be backed up on thumb drives that I will keep under lock and key as well." Wheeze.

"Therefore I will arrive every day at six and be here until you call it quits at the end of each day." Wheeze.

Dr. Jenkins listened to Brenant's wheezing. The sound of it grated on him as if it were fingernails on a blackboard. He couldn't focus and instead wanted to be out of the confined space of his office so the wheezing wouldn't sound so terrible.

Finally, Jenkin's said "I have to caution you though; you cannot approach any of the students to ask questions about what they are doing or bring up even the possibility of a mechanic who will ride along for the race. It would only sidetrack the enormous amount work that needs to be done. Is that clear?"

"My only purpose is to show up at the beginning of the day to deliver materials and unlock the work area then lock it all back up at the end of the day. What you do in between is not my concern. While you are in the process of finalizing your project team I will find a suitable location for the actual work to be done. I understand the need for proximity to the campus for logistical purposes. New computers with the most advanced engineering software on the planet will be provided, along with drafting tables and whatever else you may require." Wheeze.

At the end of the meeting Dr. Jenkins had stood, walked toward his office door and opened it to allow his visitor's exit. "If you are in need of an office while we are working please feel free to..." he began.

Brenant had stood as well. "Your offer is kind but I will also have work to do. You will see me again soon." He picked up his expensive briefcase and left through the open door.

Jenkins shook his head as he passed. He had known that there would be some oversight on the project but this guy rubbed him the wrong way in more ways than one. He sighed at the thought that he may have to walk on eggshells going forward.

~~~

Katrina dragged herself into the lecture hall ten minutes before the meeting was scheduled to begin. Those who had already arrived exhibited symptoms similar to those of her current affliction. Katrina at least felt that she was on equal terms with everyone. They were all very quiet, their wide eyes blinking as if fighting to stay awake. A couple of the guys in the back looked like they had lost that battle. But at least they had all gotten the message about professionalism with respect to clothing choices and showering schedules.

Slowly others filtered in. Dr. Jenkins came in a few minutes late but was excited and full of pep. He strode into the hall and took his place at the podium. When he first took in the faces that looked down at him, or in some cases at the floor, his attitude changed quickly to that of disappointment.

"I thought that everyone would be excited to be here this morning. Judging by what I'm seeing I may have to call another roster to fill the positions I thought you wanted."

The entire hall of students sat up slowly and pretended that their eyes didn't hurt to have them open so wide. Jenkins laughed.

"Can I assume that the party to which I was invited last night is the cause of everyone's pain this morning?"

Almost everyone nodded.

"Let me assure you that this day will not get any better. I know it's the end of the year and finals are upon you. But you have to make time for this project. After classes, we will meet back here until our new meeting location becomes available. Luckily for me, most of you will have recovered from the party by then and I can fill you in on the specifics of what we are going to create. Take this time now to get know each other, without any stimulants. All of you will be working closely together through the summer. Be back here at three thirty."

Dr. Jenkins smiled before exiting. He stopped short of the threshold and turned. "Those of you who are in my classes have finals tomorrow. I expect high marks if you made this team."

Katrina watched him speak but her head had a hard time processing his words. She watched him leave before she realized she had her final with him tomorrow and that she had already known that it would be her hardest this semester without the newly added pressure. She sighed and slouched back in her seat.

As Katrina stewed in her dismay, one of the other female students that had made the team walked up and introduced herself. "Hi. I'm Silvia Thruwell."

Katrina sat up and extended her hand, "Hi, Katrina Meservier, what's your major?"

"Mechanical engineering. You?"

"The same." Katrina said. "Glad to see there's a few of us in this all male field, well almost all male."

They both chuckled at the remark. Katrina observed Silvia a little more closely. She was pretty with blond hair, somewhat lanky, but somehow shorter than a lanky person should be. Of course Katrina was seated but she could tell that she was much taller than Silvia. For a moment she considered that Silvia was perhaps a tall midget. Something about the proportion of her body was off but she couldn't put her finger on it.

"...I think we can show up some of these boys." Silvia finished.

Katrina realized that she had missed the first part of the conversation as she had been scrutinizing her teammate's looks, an unfortunate habit of hers.

Katrina just said, "Yes, I think so," trying to cover for her inattention. Afterwards Silvia trundled off to meet others in the room. Katrina got up and did the same.

What was difficult about the meet and greet was the fact that all of the boys considered her more of a mascot than a teammate. Katrina was getting more disheartened after she met the fifth boy. They had all asked her major, as Silvia had, but with the boys her response was met with either disbelief or humor, as though she were not worthy to claim the title of engineer of mechanical studies.

She was a junior and graduation was only one year away. The only way she wouldn't achieve her goal was if she were to die in a car accident or something equally ridiculous. So why was it so hard for them to believe that she was an engineer? She gave up and headed to her class with plenty of time to stop for more coffee in between.

Katrina attended her classes as normal but her heart wasn't in it. All that she could think about were her own possible inadequacies. What was it about her that made all the men think that the only way that she could contribute to the project was by making them coffee?

By the time she returned to the lecture hall to meet with the same team that met earlier in the day she had hit a low that she hadn't seen in many years. For one thing she was very sure that she had just flunked a final and for another she had perhaps alienated her roommate completely.

The explosive nature of their argument had been based on something so trivial that she couldn't believe it had escalated to the level it had. She felt very certain that she now needed to find another roommate for her senior year. To think, it was all about what type of pizza she had ordered and how she should have known better. Obviously something had been building up over the entire year, and pepperoni and pineapple had been the straw that had broken the camel's back.

In the same seat that she occupied that very morning, Katrina threw herself down and slouched as far back as possible crossing her arms. It was uncomfortable but was a testament to her mood on such a bad day. She was brooding about the possibility of having to take one of her classes over again next year. Would they kick off this team if her GPA dropped?

A nerd from the team sat next to her. Admittedly almost all engineering students were nerds at heart or in body. The one that sat next to her was both. He had scruffy brown hair, matching eyes, a short pudgy stature and was wearing a black t-shirt with jean shorts and unlaced Nike sneakers.

Katrina recognized him. He lived in her dorm. He said "Hi" every day when he saw her. Katrina hadn't responded early in the year but as the winter had faded she had tried to be nice to an occupant of the same dorm. He wasn't exactly her type. In fact none of these nerds were her type. She was still working on that. But Dillon Trackson was never going to be her type. She smiled, trying to play nice one more time despite her sour attitude.

"Hey Dillon, how are your finals going?"

"Pretty good, you?"

"I think I failed one. Jenkins will probably kick me off the team once grades are in and I haven't even taken his final yet." Katrina said ending the sentence in a higher than normal pitch. Her lower lip began to tremble and suddenly she couldn't stop the tears. She threw herself on Dillon's shoulder and sobbed.

Dillon eyes opened wide. He appeared as stunned as he would have been if he had been hit with a taser. A girl that had never given him the time of day was now crying on his shoulder, her arms around his neck. He put his arms around her and held her close. Comfort was required at times like this but he desperately liked this beautiful girl. Holding her close felt differently to him than what his actions were supposed to be providing for her. It was terrible that Katrina felt so bad, but was it horrible that this moment gave him such joy? He became conflicted and had no idea what to do next.

His nerves were beginning to get the better of him. He had never had a girlfriend before. Did this moment mean they were going to be a couple? His breathing became erratic. Can your body forget how to breathe? This was too much feeling all at once. His long forgotten episodes of childhood asthma came back to him and panic took over. He had no inhaler with him. He tried to speak but couldn't get enough air. Finally he stood; tearing himself away from the comforting embrace and running out of the lecture hall.

Katrina, with her tear-stained face, sat blinking, confused at what had just happened. She realized that she shouldn't have cried on his shoulder, she barely knew Dillon. Great! Someone else she just alienated. She wiped her face and went back to sitting with her arms folded. At least no one else had noticed her outburst. Once Jenkins showed up and gave them their instructions she could go back to her empty room and really let the tears go.

Dr. Jenkins came in late and was accompanied by Silvio Brenant. By then the lecture hall was full of students. Jenkins looked winded when he arrived at the podium. He pondered a moment to calm himself before speaking.

"Today I would like to introduce Mr. Brenant. He is our..." Jenkins paused, unsure of how he should be addressed. Finally he settled on, "Our professional connection to and security consultant for our investor's capital purchases. Today he has delivered the first of many pieces of equipment to aid us in our project. Soon we will be heading over to our off campus location to start getting set up and to make sure everything works. Be aware that we have equipment coming that will challenge the most computer savvy individuals out there." Jenkins smiled when he said this.

None of the students smiled. They knew it just meant more work.

"But before we head over I will be separating you into specific groups for the project. There are many aspects of the project we need to work on concurrently in order to facilitate a smooth and timely finish. This is work, but work that you will be well paid for. This is the time for you to step up and show your skills."

Katrina slunk further in her chair at his last comment. Her thoughts went towards her final and how she might not even be on the team in a few days.

Jenkins began looking through his notes. He read them aloud.

"For the team of conceptual design, there will be...," Dr. Jenkins read off eleven names that Katrina did not recognize. She had probably met them at the party but she wasn't even going to put in the effort to try and remember their faces.

Next Dr. Jenkins called out the mathematics team that consisted of a single student. Next to be called was the powertrain team, then the frame team, the body team, interior team, software team, suspension team (to which Katrina was assigned) and last but not least the wiring and logistics team. Kristin was on the frame team, Silvia on wiring. Katrina felt bad that they were all on separate teams. Having all of the girls working together could have been a powerful collaboration.

To Katrina it was hard to believe that they only had four months to go from drawing board to full scale car. As she pondered the complexity of the problem, Dr. Jenkins answered her questions without having them voiced aloud.

"Just so everyone is on the same page, we are building a racecar. But that doesn't mean that we are building every aspect from scratch. Only one team has the job of designing a product from the ground up and that's the conceptual design team. All the other departments will be using off the shelf technology. We already know that we need wheels to make a racecar roll. Lucky for us there are companies out there that already do that. We already know that racing suspension is required and there are companies who already build racecars, so on and so on. We will provide parameters from which you will design and build.

"And on that note, I will add that the body has already been designed and built. It will show up in three weeks. We will be building from the top down. That's all I have today. Go and unpack your new equipment and see if it all works."

Several moans came from the seats. "We can't design how cool this is going to look?" Another student immediately followed with, "We can choose what color to paint it right?"

Dr. Jenkins chuckled. "I'm afraid not. The body is the only thing we can do absolutely nothing about. The skin has photovoltaic properties so we can't paint it or put stickers on it. Every car must look the same with the same coloring and style. We cannot add to it or take parts away. We are to build everything else then bolt the shell on before we drive to the race on race day."

More moans followed.

"Chop, chop." Jenkins said to the team at large. "We have work to do. Katrina, Kristin and Silvia, please stay behind. I'd like a word with you."

If Katrina could have melted into her seat and disappeared she would have. She was afraid of what was coming. Silvia obviously didn't feel the same way at all and bounded down the steps towards the podium, full of excitement. Kristin walked down with a bit more reserve. Katrina sighed heavily and got up slowly to follow.

As Katrina approached the podium she could see that Silvia almost jumping up and down while standing next to Dr. Jenkins with his calm demeanor. Mr. Brenant waited patiently off to one side, wheezing as he did so, and holding a briefcase.

Jenkins used his hand to indicate that the other girls move a little closer for a more private conversation. "I will be assigning each of you additional responsibilities on top of your assigned team's workload. The first is a position mostly of oversight where you will learn what is going on within all of the other teams."

Katrina frowned. "You want us to find out if the other students are doing things wrong?"

"No I want you learn every aspect of this project. In the event that a critical person drops out of any one of the teams, you will be able to jump in to take their place." Jenkins said plainly.

Instantly Katrina's eyes grew at what was being asked. The implication equated to learning every word in a long play in case any person quit, so that you could take over in an instant. Silvia was obviously excited at the prospect. Kristin remained silent, unreadable.

Jenkins continued, "Your roles in the original groups I had put you in will be minimal. Your real goal is to completely understand all aspects of each group while participating in your primary team. But I will also be pulling you to work on a secret side project involving a more... aggressive racing strategy."

This was when Silvia's face changed. She wasn't as excited now. "Secret? Like, we have to keep it secret from the rest of our team?"

Dr. Jenkins frowned at Silvia. "This whole project is secret; we will be working with serious security measures in place. If you can't do this job I'll find someone else. Decide now."

Silvia looked to Katrina for help. Katrina made no expression of sympathy at her plight. Katrina knew what secrets could mean in her chosen trade and she was okay with it. She kept a straight face hoping that this might be just what she needed to keep her position on the team. She had no affinity towards Silvia so she maintained her silence in this matter out of self-preservation.

Silvia had the jitters suddenly. She didn't want to be part of a secret cabal within the project but on the other hand she knew it must be an honor to be chosen. At odds with better judgement, she decided to stay and be part of it all. "Alright, I'll do it. I mean, this racing strategy... we're not talking about murdering anyone right?" Silvia said sternly.

At this statement Dr. Jenkins turned his gaze towards the attorney and laughed. Katrina followed his gaze, unsure of why he was laughing. Was he agreeing with Silvia that the secret was exactly what she said or was he laughing at the outrageousness of her statement?

"Nothing quite so cloak and dagger. I'm merely pointing out that many aspects of this project are a secret to all other team members involved. And it is within that layer of secrecy that you three will be working.

You will be designing and building a device that will help ensure that we win this race. Every race team has the same secret project running in the background. That is the secret to be held by you. I'll go into more detail later but I need to know that you are willing to take on the additional responsibility."

Silvia and Katrina both felt better about the assignment now, even Kristin appeared to be slightly relieved and they all nodded in agreement.

"Good." Jenkins said. "In the equipment that is being unpacked as we speak, there is a laptop that is labeled with my name. That is the one you will focus on. That device has the programs you will need to do your job. Find it, make sure it works, and place a label on it that says "Project overview only. For Dr. Jenkins.""

They nodded, understanding the task.

"Go on. Everyone is already unpacking the equipment." Jenkins said. "They'll wonder were you've been."

The girls left the lecture room almost at a run. Once in the hall they slowed to a walk again, each lost in their own thoughts about what their project leader had said. They moved quietly towards their destination until Silvia couldn't take the silence anymore. She used her arm and held the other girls back to talk. Her short stature left her looking up at the taller girls.

"Listen, I know I said I would be okay with this side project but..."

"No you listen" Katrina shot back. "I don't have a lot of opportunities like this just fall into my lap. There was a reason we were chosen, three girls on this team, no boys. I don't know all the reasons but I know it makes us more important on some level than the boys. You better not screw this up. We have to design something and build it. That's good enough for me. That's what we came to school for.

"If we're part of a larger group working on some insignificant part of the car, how much acclaim would we get even if the car won the race? Only that we were on the team. That's like being the janitor. I think our resumés would look so much better if it said we had built one of the most important parts of the car.

How do you think that would look as opposed to being just a participant on a team? Do you want to be looked at as the janitor, or worse, as the girl who did nothing more important than show up every day and bring coffee? An hour ago I was happy to be selected as a participant. That in itself was great but now that I have been chosen to be on special team, I want that acclaim, that step up… badly. I need it considering the nose dive my GPA is going to take after today." Katrina quickly placed her hand over her mouth. She had said too much.

Kristin and Silvia stared after Katrina as she ran down the hall. Silvia looked fearful.

"No cloak and dagger, my ass! Something else is going on." Silvia whispered, almost to herself as she and Kristin ran to catch up.

Chapter 3

The next day Katrina sat with Kristin and Silvia in Dr. Jenkins' office. They were meeting to go over some preliminary sketches so that they would have a rough idea of what their special team project entailed. Katrina picked up one of the drawings to see the detail without the distraction of the markings that were showing through from the sketch on the piece of paper that had been beneath it on the desk. The paper was so thin that light could pass through it if you held it up to a lamp. It was like tissue paper, only slightly thicker.

Katrina had a hooded sweatshirt on. Silvia wore an over large coat with a hat that covered her short hair. Both had decided on jeans that day which irked Silvia. They were each using their hat and hood as a way to avoid superfluous eye contact and they were both happy about it.

Since their last encounter Katrina had kept Silvia at arm's length and had chosen not to communicate. Silvia was unsure if Katrina was just embarrassed about having blurted out that she might have to retake a class or if there was another issue that she wasn't aware of yet. She had tried to maintain the distance Katrina wanted, hoping that Katrina would eventually open up. But it hadn't happened yet. Kristin seemed oblivious to any potential conflict between them. She sat in her MIT t-shirt and khakis engrossed in the material she had been given to study.

Dr. Jenkins had specifically scheduled this meeting for a time when the girls could arrive unnoticed in the deserted hallways. Jenkins had locked his office door after they entered and had asked them to turn off their cell phones as he showed them to the seats he had arranged around his desk. Brenant, the Lawyer, was already seated off to the side.

"This meeting is to get your side project started. Of course I must insist that you not discuss this project with anyone, even those who are part of the larger team. This is the one and only meeting I will have with you about this project. Illustrated in pen is a set of instruments that are being provided by the race committee as an offensive means to advance in the race.

"Obviously when cars are disabled with this device, they will be disqualified and removed. Your job is to make a device that will work under extreme race conditions. The electrical will be provided. All controls must be through bluetooth. No wiring will be set up in advance. You have to create the best possible device to make the laser work effectively."

The girls studied the design. "The design in pencil, is that what we are supposed to build?" Silvia asked.

"No." Jenkins said. "This is just a starting point, a very basic design. I'm sure that with the talent sitting before me, you can come up with some much more creative ways to make it work for our team."

Katrina had set the drawing down and put both her hands in her sweat shirt's pockets as she studied the other drawings on the desk in front of her. "Wait, so we are going to build a weapon that will disable another car in the race? And the race committee will supply the laser. How can such a small laser disable another car?"

Dr. Jenkins nodded and smiled. "Ahh, now we get to the most important part. The bodies are already built. They were designed to have two conductive layers separated by epoxy. No one else on the team knows why the bodies were prebuilt. This aspect of the race is supposed to be the secret weapon built into an already secret race. Your job is to create the delivery system that will utilize the laser in a way that will allow our driver to win.

"The idea here is that this small laser," Jenkins pointed to the piece of paper on the desk that showed the image of the device, "will fire its beam into the surface of the body for at least three seconds. The exterior surface of the specially made body will be heated enough by the laser to melt the epoxy beneath it and cause the two layers to touch. When that happens the car will shut down and signal that the car is out if the race."

Katrina looked up at Silvia and saw a reflection of her own relief in the other girl's eyes. They initially had thoughts of missile launching systems, not this virtually harmless low power laser. Kristin actually looked vaguely disappointed.

Jenkins saw their reactions and quickly added, "Oh, you thought we going to destroy the cars? Watch them crash and burn?" He laughed. "No, we don't want to kill anyone. You are to design a device that will disable the car only. How the driver reacts is up to them but for the most part, the weapon that you will create will burn the fuselage of the car only. That's all. Of course, it is still a potentially dangerous device. It will have enough power to catch clothing on fire, melt skin or burn wood if it's focused on the same spot for any length of time. You will have to take safety measures when you are working on it, and during the testing phase of the project.

Now I'm going to leave you to start working on this." Jenkins said one last thing as he got up and collected his things to leave for the night. "Remember, how it is designed and applied is up to you. There is no budget ceiling for this part of the project and you must control all aspects of material acquisition including machine shop services. Any money to pay for this project must be paid for in cash through Mr. Brenant. Any questions?"

Jenkins turned to the attorney as if making sure that he shared all of the information that he was expected to, giving Katrina the impression that he was far more involved in the project than an attorney would be normally. When the lawyer didn't add anything to the conversation, he nodded that he had indeed conveyed all the information required.

The girls shook their heads in response, excited to get started.

"Good. Get to work. Since there are only three of you, you have your work cut out for you."

On that note Jenkins moved towards the door. The girls were already discussing an idea. Dr. Jenkins had to clear his throat loudly to interrupt them. "Katrina, a word please?"

Katrina followed him out into the hall.

"Listen," Jenkins began, "I know that you have been worrying about your test grades. Let me assure you that you passed all of your finals. I didn't want you to have that hanging over your head while trying to work on this project."

Katrina's eyes lit up followed by a huge smile. "How did I do?"

"Let's just say that you passed without flying colors."

Katrina's smile faltered.

Dr. Jenkins smiled more broadly. "No, no, they weren't bad. There are a couple that might be a tad lower than you're used to, that's all. It's all good."

"Oh, okay." Katrina let out a deep breath as though she had been holding it for days.

"Now go in there and bang out the best offensive weapon you can build." Jenkins put a hand on her shoulder when he said it.

Her eyes suddenly had too much water in them as her relief settled in. She wouldn't have to retake any classes after all. "Thanks!"

Dr. Jenkins took his hand off her shoulder and watched her run back into his office, her long brown hair bobbing back and forth. "Make sure you lock the door." he reminded them and waited until he heard the lock click before turning away.

Chapter 4

Days started to turn into weeks. Daily meetings churned out many great ideas and some that were less so. Over time the slew of ideas began to turn into something concrete. Parts began to arrive from the junk yards and machine shops.

The junk yard items were cleaned and repaired. They were the simplistic parts that didn't need to be redesigned: Wheels and strut systems, brake housings, a drive shaft, a Cadillac frame with a standard transmission that matched, a steering assembly and dashboard components.

Kristin got pulled out of the special team to fill in on the power train team. One of the interns had needed to fly home due to a death in the family and would not be returning in time to keep that part of the project on schedule. Dr. Jenkins had decided that Kristin would be the best fit for that team and that it would not leave her enough time to invest on the laser's design. Katrina and Silvia knew that it would increase their workload, but they were more worried that if anyone else dropped out then they would lose their chance to work on the weapon system.

Other team members quickly went to work on designing the sub-unibody that would accept the special body kit that was to be delivered. When that epoxy structured body arrived it had to mate with an aluminum underside which would allow all the other components to fit inside. A lot of welding was required to build the sub-unibody.

When all these components were done, two days before the scheduled delivery of the epoxy skin, the vehicle looked more like a shallow boat with wheels than anything else. It had no engine or any of the required computer components that would allow the driver to operate the vehicle. But that didn't stop each and every intern from siting inside and holding the steering wheel for a photo.

When Katrina and Silvia took their turns behind the wheel they were also taking the time to study how their offensive weapon could connect to the body.

For some reason Silvio Brenant insisted on standing near enough to the car to be seen in all of the students' souvenir photos. It gave Silvia the feeling that he was responsible for more than just security, but no other explanation came to mind.

One day when Katrina and Silvia were cloistered away working out the final designs for connecting the 'offensive device' to the racecar, Silvia stopped what she was doing to ask a question. "Have you noticed that there are two seats in the racecar? We always only talk about the driver and his job but why would they have designed it with a second seat if they didn't intend for there to be a passenger?"

"I don't know. It's not important to me." Katrina paused, giving the idea some thought, "Maybe the seat is for a technician to sit in while they perform diagnostics and they will take it out later when they finish the cage."

Silvia shook her head. "No I think there's going to be a passenger. Our interface may be Bluetooth connected but we had to design the weapon system to be installed on the passenger side of the car. I'm getting the impression that someone other than the driver will have to operate the weapon. Think about it, the driver can't drive and try to work the laser at the same time. There's too much going on at the all at once for him to handle both."

Katrina pondered for a moment. "Well I hope they are well trained on what we've designed or it would have been a tremendous waste of our time to build it in the first place."

Silvia pointed her finger at Katrina. "Exactly! What if one of us is supposed to be the rider?"

Katrina's mouth dropped open, suddenly understanding some of what Dr. Jenkins had said in the past. "You think so?" She was picturing the design for the control panel that had been on the schematic that they had been given as a template, a control panel that was supposed to be cut into the passenger side of the dashboard. How had she not realized that before now?

Silvia nodded her head. "What if it's just one more secret that they haven't let anyone in on yet? I don't think I would want to do it. I'm not into racing. It's too dangerous."

Katrina opened her eyes wide at the prospect. "I think it would be great. Think about it, go out and actually be part of the race team? It would be fun. And no one would die. The point of the race is to prove the technology of the car, not crash them. The worst that can happen is that our car would get disabled and we'd be out of the race."

Katrina thought back to when she had sat in the driver's seat checking out the car. It sat pretty low and so did the passenger seat. She would have no problem being able to use the laser but Silvia was so much shorter than she was. She would need a box to sit on just to have the viewing capability to operate the weapon. That was the most important part of their design. The operator had to be able to see where the extension arm would potentially reach out to another car and set off the laser. Suddenly Katrina was getting very excited about the prospect that she might be the one chosen.

They both went back to work without much more consideration as to who might be asked to operate the laser. There was so much still to be done. They were going to be hard pressed to finish on time as it was.

Thirteen days before the race, after the epoxy body was fitted down into the aluminum cradle to complete the fuselage, there was a meeting of all of the teams. Silvia and Katrina sat next to each other. When Dillon Trackson showed up he plopped himself next to Katrina. He looked exhausted but managed a smile for her, ignoring Silvia altogether. Silvia made a grunt at his rudeness. Katrina elbowed her.

Dr. Jenkins cleared his throat to get everyone's attention and began, "I have the pleasure of stating that our project is running not only slightly behind schedule but also way over budget. I have spoken with the investor and he assures us that he will maintain the project's funding until the end. But we still have a lot of work ahead of us. All of you need to plan on some all-nighters until we are back on track. The car must be finished when the truck arrives. The good news is, the pizza is on us."

Many groans floated over to him. Jenkins smiled. "This is the critical moment of this project. Every project that you will encounter in your future will have the same benchmarks that we have seen through our trials on this car, a beginning, a middle, and the crunch. We are beginning the crunch phase as of today. I want all of you to bring whatever you might pack for a camping trip when you come in tomorrow morning. After today, we will be living here until this car is loaded onto the truck. Do I make myself clear?"

Myriad side conversations began abruptly in response.

"Quiet!" Jenkins shouted.

The crowd fell silent.

"Now to work. Time is of the essence. The power plant is complete but we have to finish the computer interface and programing plus all of the wiring still needs to be installed. The teams that are finished with their original assignments will now be part of the engine team. And as of today a secret part of our project will come out into the open. Katrina and Silvia, please stand."

Both girls' eyes opened wide. They hadn't expected this kind of focus all of a sudden.

"Come on, stand up. We haven't got all day, there's work to do." Jenkins said again, somewhat short tempered.

Katrina and Silvia both stood slowly. "These two girls were chosen to design and build a device that will disable other racecars once it is positioned properly. Every car in the race will have one of these. We hope that these brilliant women designed the most effective version so that our driver will be able to bring our car through the finish line."

Clapping began to ring out among all the other interns. Jenkins continued on, not waiting the customary amount of time for them to finish.

The girls sat quickly, a little red faced. They hadn't had any warning that their 'secret team' would not be a secret anymore.

"I have decided that the members of the wheel team, who have now completed their project will be reallocated as well. Dillon Trackson and John Killbreth will join the defensive weapon design team. The remainder of the wheel team will join the wiring group. Any questions?"

Many heads turned to their fellow interns, still taking in all that had just transpired. Dillon focused only on Katrina. Katrina didn't know what to make of his attention but Silvia was instantly jealous. Katrina didn't notice Silvia's reaction because Kristin had caught her eye. The other girl looked more than a little disheartened that she hadn't been included in their team. Katrina's expression became instantly apologetic, she knew how she would have felt if she had been the one chosen as a replacement on the power train team.

Jenkins had one more announcement. "Alright, one last item to cover." He looked over to Brenant and waited for his nod of approval before continuing. "On the last day, before the truck is to arrive and take our car to the race, we are going to announce which member of the team will accompany the driver during the race."

The entire group of interns burst into discussions about the prospect of being chosen. Silvia turned back to Katrina and tapped her on the shoulder. "See, I told you that the second seat was for a rider."

"Yeah, but it won't be one of us. Vincent Frodes is the team leader, he'll get it. He's on the engine team and he worked the closest with Dr. Jenkins. You'll see. He's the one to watch for."

Silvia shook her head, "I don't think so. I think it has to be one of us."

Katrina perked up. "I would love to be on the road but I really doubt that either of us has a chance at it."

Silvia's eyes turned back to the podium where Dr. Jenkins stood answering questions. Katrina's denigration of their own capabilities grated on her despite the fact that she didn't really want to be chosen as the passenger. Anger was bubbling just under her skin. She turned back to Katrina to respond but once again Katrina was in the middle of an animated conversation with Dillon. They were completely ignoring her, again. Somehow she was always the one who was forgotten.

Dr. Jenkins clapped his hand to gain everyone's attention. "It's time to get to work. Remember, I will choose the lucky individual on the last day of the project, so work hard and maybe you'll do more than just build the car, maybe you'll be helping the driver win this race."

Chapter 5

It was the last day before the truck was to arrive
and pick up the finished racecar. Excitement was in the
air. Many of the interns were outside enjoying the sun
now that their parts of the project were complete. Some
of the team hung around watching the last minute
adjustments but a few still had work to do. Much of the
conversation revolved around how badly the other race
teams would lose because their car was so fantastic.

Vincent Frodes was heading up the finalization
team, which meant that he was trying to finish
uploading thirty-seven updates to the car's computer. As
the team leader he shouted out orders to several of his
team to facilitate their latest attempt to make the
necessary changes to the car's software. He stood proud
in his navy blue t-shirt that said 'Team Leader' in bold
letters across his chest.

Unfortunately the computer kept kicking out the
new version of the software and the whole process had to
be restarted. After the fifth attempt the action was
getting old. The decision had been made that if the
updates didn't take on the latest attempt, Vincent and a
few team members would have to follow the truck to
keep trying until they were successful. Several members
were hoping the computer would kick out the flash just
so they could go on a road trip. Getting to travel to the
race's starting location would be fun.

The only other team that was still trying to work
on the car was the weapons team. They had originally
been called the Offensive Disabling Weapon Team, which
of course had been abbreviated over time. They all wore
red t-shirts that each had a large missile with fiery
propellant being expelled printed on the front along with

the words 'Watch Your Back, I'm Gunning for You' and with 'Weapons Specialist' printed on the back.

Unfortunately both the finalization team and the weapons team needed to work inside the cockpit area of the car. Silvia, who currently sat in the passenger seat, was getting very agitated by a boy named Dennis who was trying to follow Frodes' instructions. To accomplish his task he had to keep leaning over almost completely on top of Silvia to play with the corded access that they thought might be causing the problem with their upload. He came very close to touching the fiery missile on her t-shirt several times.

She had her own job to do and it involved installing the last of the electrical interface for the mechanical arm that stuck out up off the roof of the car. She was the perfect person to do the work because she was so short that she barely had to bend over to reach beneath the dash.

The robot arm was a strange looking addition to the car's roof. Their design was comprised of a squared off human looking arm. Where the hand was supposed to be was a harness with an angled sleeve. Other small devices protruded from that central hub but the one item at the center caught everyone's attention. A silver bulb approximately ten inches long and fifteen inches around stuck out through the hub with three large suction cups surrounding the head.

A mass of thin wires ran from the hub up the robotic arm and were stretched towards a spool that was attached at the top of the wrist joint of the arm. It was clear that the silver bulb, presumably the laser, had the capability to leave the 'hand' and stretch as far as the spool would allow. The design of the arm allowed not only 360 degree access around the vehicle, it could also reach almost four feet when it was extended, allowing side access of the vehicle as well as over the roof of a nearby car.

Katrina and Dillon both stood on ladders plugging in stray wires. Their red t-shirts stood out in stark contrast to the bland eggshell color of the fuselage of the car. Silvia yelled something from inside the cockpit area telling Dennis to stop touching her. After a while it became a kind of game to him. He was enjoying the close confines of their workspace, unlike Silvia.

When Dillon connected the last wires he told Silvia that she could start the computer initialization process. She picked up a small case from the ground just outside the window on a cart and connected it to the cars computer interface via bluetooth. She typed furiously for a few seconds and put the case back down on the cart. After that she beat off the boy named Dennis again while she kept track of the wireless interaction on the cockpit screen that could only be viewed by the passenger.

Katrina and Dillon went over to the refreshment table off to the side and each took a bottle of water. Katrina noticed Silvio Brenant who was sitting off to the side holding his customary briefcase. They were all so used to the sound of his wheezing that they didn't notice him much anymore.

Dr. Jenkins had warned everyone when the car's body had been attached that from that point on there could be no pictures taken of the racecar. Brenant had confiscated one phone when one of the interns had tried to sneak a selfie with the finished car. She heard him tell the owner of the device that he could have the device back once the race was finished. Katrina made sure to keep her cell phone in her pocket.

She was pretty sure that the only secrecy revolved around the weapon. No one had complained about pictures when the tech for the engine was being built, and now that the body was on all of the cars should look pretty much the same.

Once the car's computer was allowing software updates to be uploaded Dr. Jenkins called everyone over to where Silvia and Dennis sat, still in the car.

"Well, I'd like to thank you all for participating on this project. I know everyone here put their hearts into their work and I trust all of the knowledge put forth. The trials will begin tomorrow in Kingston, which is also where the race will officially start. Now I want you all to understand that although we are calling this a race it is not a contest about speed. It's a race based on the endurance of the vehicle in everyday driving conditions.

"The driver will have to negotiate across country to an as yet undisclosed place in a desert on the west coast. Every night the racers have to stop at a designated place for the night, and the time that they arrive at each stop will determine the time that they leave the next morning. The idea is to test all of the new technology that each team is using. The cars will have to drive through the rain, heat, face terrible traffic conditions, and deal with cold damp mornings. Once the lead cars arrive at the desert they will have to negotiate the sand until they reach the finish loop in the desert.

"The finish loop is the same as a finish line but it's positioned up in the air on a dais. So every car must carry ramps to get through. The concrete hoop has electronics embedded that will identify the car that passes through first. If a car is eliminated before the end, the owner cannot truck it to the hoop and hope to win by tossing it through. Once disabled the team is out of the running. The winner must drive through the hoop. It is an obstacle that will make the driver, and passenger, think about how to accomplish their win. Remember, this is an engineer's race, not a speed race. According to contest rules, any way through the hoop will be allowed as long as the entire car passes through.

"Now for the most interesting part. Since the race is not based on speed and the investors want a little drama to make the whole affair exciting, every team was allowed to build a low powered laser weapon system to use to attempt to disable other cars. Each car's body can convert light into electricity as a way to supplement the car's power supply. It is made up of two layers that are separated by epoxy. If the epoxy between the conductive layers is heated enough to evaporate and the two layers touch, the car will shut down ejecting the car from the race."

Hands went into the air as though this were some class session. Frodes, the team leader, spoke instead of raising his hand, "What would happen if the car got into an accident?"

"The design allows pieces of the layer to crack and break off without making contact between layers or damaging its ability to supplement the car's power." Dr. Jenkins said. "So, in a less than ideal situation where one car is trying to avoid being attacked by another car and gets into an accident, they can fix their mechanical issues and continue the race.

"Which brings me to my final point. Each team entered into the race is allowed to have a passenger to operate the weapon. Part of this is for safety reasons. It would not be realistic to have the driver be also trying to operate the weapon. And the other reason is to allow more than one person to drive. If for any reason the driver is incapacitated, the passenger will take the driver's place, either intermittently or permanently."

Vincent Frodes, who knew of his status on the team as the uncontested leader, stood apart from the crowd of interns around him in preparation of being called. His smile stretched across his face as though he already knew the answer.

Katrina and Dillon watched his demeanor with smirks on their faces. Dr. Jenkins began to announce their choice as Katrina brought up her water bottle to her lips for another drink. Dillon was watching Katrina drink as he lifted his own bottle. In a small way, she thought she wouldn't be in the running with Frodes being the obvious choice. Silvia's conviction about one of the weapons team being chosen hung in the back of her mind. But she knew Katrina was mostly right, Frodes was the obvious choice.

When Dr. Jenkins announced, "We have chosen Katrina Meservier to be the alternate driver!" A dead silence fell onto the engineers. It seemed apparent that the others also thought of Frodes being the obvious choice. In an instant of held breath and watch flowing, Katrina began to choke on her water while Dillon's sprayed his out of his mouth in his surprise.

Dripping, coughing, and sputtering through it all as Dr. Jenkins called out to her again. Katrina was not in Jenkins' line of sight as she was seated towards the rear of the group and he had to call for a third time. "Katrina?"

Katrina put her hand in the air to register that she was indeed present as Dillon slapped her on the back to dislodge the remaining water from her lungs. Finally when she could take her first breath she arched her back so that she stood straight again and said "Here" in a squeaky voice.

"Ahh, at last." Jenkins said with a smile.

Frodes looked shocked that he hadn't been chosen and shrank back into the crowd. He looked very dejected and hurt.

Silvia, on the other hand, had watched the doctor speak and was horrified that her design partner had been chosen after all. Just then a beep sounded out from the car's dashboard. It stole Silvia's attention for a second. The software package initialization of the bluetooth handset had finalized. The weapon was ready to be used. That was the straw the broke camel's back. Everything was complete for Katrina to become famous and ride off into the sunset with equipment she had helped design and build. She stood out of the car and shouted, I can't believe you chose her over me!" before storming off. This got everyone's attention. They watched her stomp away angry.

Another silence fell on the group. "Here is an example of what can happen in this field," Dr. Jenkins said. "The education that you receive in a classroom never prepares you for the realities associated with working in your chosen field as an internship does. Here you have confronted how to handle stress, disappointment, rejection when your designs are not used, and dejection when the investor has different plans for the device you built. There are times where others around you will move forward on a set of plans that you felt were a waste of time. Being an intern is where real life is taught in your respective fields. I'm sorry that Silvia feels left out, but all of you are a team and we need every one of you on this team to win this race, no matter who gets to sit in the passenger seat."

Katrina walked up towards Dr. Jenkins with a smile, even though she was still dripping wet. Jenkins held out a baseball cap that had the words "Weapons Mission Specialist" written on it along with the same image of the missile that she had on her shirt.

"Most of you are probably wondering why the shirts and hats that we have had printed throughout the project don't say MIT anywhere on them. This race is an attempt to introduce new technology, but the race itself, using our designs on public roads, is not strictly legal. In fact, this race is called an invisible auto race for that reason. Therefore we cannot advertise any association that could negatively affect the school. And even though the car itself is done you still cannot discuss any part of this project with anyone.

"The racers will be followed by a crew of support staff to further ensure their invisibility. If any accidents happen along the route, these crews will clean up the sight and box up the car and take it away leaving nothing behind for any kind of law enforcement investigation. If any of you are uncomfortable with this, please speak to me before we leave here today.

"A lot of you will be exposed to this same kind of scenario in the future. As engineers, when you work for any kind of corporation, they rarely disclose what the object that you design and build will be used for, sometimes the uses for a particular design aren't fully appreciated until years after they are built and may or may not be used for their originally intended purpose. In truth, if you're hired and you get paid for the work, then you have to let it go. Today we are letting go of our baby. We can be proud of the work we've done and we can sit back to watch the race to see what other organizations have done in their racecars designs."

Katina had finished wiping off all the water on her face.

A student among the crowd of interns raised their hand. "We can watch the race?"

"Oh, I forgot to tell you." Jenkins said. "I mentioned the crews that follow the racecars; well there will also be a film crew for each car. The footage will be uploaded to a secret location that the investors have set up somewhere and it will be put into a kind of reality tv show format before being released over the internet. We'll be able to watch the entire race."

Katrina looked horrified while the rest of the students began to clap and cheer. She turned to Jenkins. "You mean to tell me that I'm going to be on tv? I don't think I can do that."

Jenkins turned to her and said. "You don't have to worry about anything. The show's focus is not on you but on the cars' journey across the country. You'll be in it from time to time but for the most part you'll just be someone in the car. You have nothing to worry about. Now Mr. Brenant has a uniform for you and you need to go pack before we head out. You're leaving with the car in an about an hour. Oh and since Miss Thruwell has stormed away, I believe you're going to have to have Dillon pack up everything to maintain the weapon while you're on the road. He'll be going with you. I'll let you tell him the good news."

Chapter 6

   At the appointed meeting place twenty-seven
almost identical looking cars had congregated, gleaming
under the bright morning sun. Their unusual
construction materials lent a specific reflective value to
the fuselage that made them blinding to look at if the
angle was wrong. Their positions in the small parking lot
were haphazard. There seemed to be no order to their
arrangement. To anyone who drove by the small church's
parking lot on a Saturday morning, it would appear to be
an assemblage of the oddest cars ever built.
   It was getting close to 9 a.m. but many of the folks
that were here had been up since way before dawn to
prepare. Their support staff and their vehicles were not
far away in a mall parking lot, waiting for the race to
begin. They would fall in behind the racecars after all of
the racers had passed their location.
   The town was so small that there hadn't been a
single place where they could fit all of the vehicles in the
race and the vehicles that supported the racecars. The
camera crews' vehicles were lined along the road
stretching from the church in the direction opposite of
the racers' course. One cameraman from each car's team
wandered between the cars, filming the events, ready to
return to their crews when it was time for the race to
begin.
   Katrina stood with Dillon, waiting for Dr. Jenkins
to arrive with the investor of their project and their
driver. Her uniform was a typical racing coverall with
flame retardant fibers and was light enough to be
somewhat airy so that she wouldn't sweat to death. Her
long and slender body showed off the grey and brilliant
orange as though she was ready to walk the runway in a

fashion show. Her long brown hair flowed with curls that suggested that she had also stepped out of a salon moments earlier. None of which was true, of course, and her hair was always that way.

She paced wondering why the driver was still missing; worried that he wouldn't arrive in time for the race to begin and that she would be the only participant for her team. They were to depart at nine-thirty, would she have to drive across the country alone? Katrina searched the lot to see if Dr. Jenkins had stopped at some other car by accident.

Frodes had the car up and running. It hummed flawlessly. Pride radiated from his entire body. The car had an electric propulsion system so humming was the proper term here. Most traditional racecars emitted such high decibel levels that they could be heard from many blocks away. Their car hummed so quietly that if you didn't know it was on it would be hard to tell one way or the other.

Frodes had his blue team leader shirt on as a testament to his position with the project. He tinkered with the car's software. Katrina couldn't tell if he was tinkering just to make everyone at the race aware that he was an important team member on the project or if the car still needed work. She sincerely hoped it was the former. She would have to do some work on the road if there were still bugs that hadn't been corrected before race time. But that's what she was here for, that and to manage the weapon. Nervous butterflies grew by multiples of ten in her stomach over the lack of a driver.

The weapon... a thought occurred to Katrina. She should be checking out other cars to see their designs. That would help when she came up on one or was being attacked. Being prepared could mean the difference between winning and losing.

Dillon was wearing his 'weapons specialist' t-shirt. Many of the people from other project teams had commented on his shirt's graphics. Most of their uniforms had only the name of their sponsors. Dillon was beaming from the attention. He wished he had been on the weapons team from the beginning and could say that he had helped design and build it, instead of only being there at the end to help install the hardware. But the others only knew that he was on the weapons team and that made him happy.

Katrina stormed over with a nervous intensity in her stride. People got out of her way when they saw her moving through the crowd. She butted into the small crowd of t-shirt admirers, took Dillon's arm, and dragged him bodily away so they could converse privately.

"What are you doing?" Dillon asked in an upset tone.

"I just thought of something. We need to be looking closely at all the other cars' weapons to get a handle on what we are up against."

A look of understanding dawned on Dillon's face.

Katrina followed with, "Yeah, you see what I'm talking about? I'm going to need some background on all of these weapons."

"How am I going to do that? I'm not going to be sitting in the car with you."

"We have radios." Katrina said. "Check with Frodes about what kind of communications we have set up between him and the car's headsets. If we can get a handle on what we're up against, we will have a better chance."

Dillon nodded and ran off. Katrina began a two-fold intensive search of the parking lot to take in the vehicles' weapons and to find her driver.

To Katrina's surprise there were many different car designs. Even though all the cars had the same bodies, some of the teams' ideas for how they had built the substructures baffled her.

One team had obviously centered their design needs on the end run through the sand in the desert. The car looked more like a dune buggy with over large knobby tires in the rear and much smaller ones in the front. The cockpit had a downward slope which created a blind spot in the rear. Apparently no one had realized that because their weapon traveled on a rail system around the leading edge of the body and did not encompass the rear. They had even put their engine in the rear. Katrina thought this was a bad idea for many reasons.

Another team had taken a wildly different approach. The car was completely split down the center lengthwise. Each half sat slightly off center. It reminded Katrina of two motor cycles that had been stuck together. Their weapon system hung off an open window edge, another bad idea. They would have to be right next to the other car to engage it and their speed would have to exactly match their opponent in order for the laser to burn a proper hole in the body.

As far as the weapons went, most of them had employed the same simple tactics. Either it was on a rail system or it was connected to the end of a long tube hanging out of a window. There was one that had a window mounted weapon that almost sat on the wheels. It was so low to the ground that any bump in the pavement would cause damage. She wondered how that would hold up in the desert.

Harvard Bertrand put his hand on Katrina's shoulder. It scared her and she jumped. She had been inspecting racecars and hadn't seen anyone approaching her. She didn't know who he was at first and thought that her wandering eyes had gotten her in trouble.

"You are Katrina Meservier I believe? I'm sorry if I didn't pronounce your last name correctly," he said.

Bertrand's voice carried with it a stench of alcohol that made Katrina wave her hand in front of her nose involuntarily. She stepped back to ask who the hell he was. "I'm sorry I don't know…"

Dr. Jenkins appeared at Bertrand's side. "Oh good, you found each other. Mr. Bertrand, this is Katrina Meservier. Katrina say hello to Harvard Bertrand, our investor."

Katrina's exuberant smile returned as her excitement for the project bubbled to the surface. The man was the reason that she had the opportunity to be here, after all. Katrina retook Bertrand's hand and shook again.

"Katrina is also half of the team responsible for designing the weapon." Jenkins added. Bertrand put his arm around Katrina as though they were close friends.

"I gotta tell ya, having the weapon on a multi-directional arm was genius. I think we are the only team with that design. I'm not an expert like you guys but it might be the single item that will win us the race. Do you know that some of the teams have professional drivers on them? Yes, they do" he nodded in affirmation and continued without waiting for her to respond. "Other teams have only students driving, winners of a lottery, or something like that." Bertrand slurred the last word but continued on. "We have something even better."

As if on cue, a tall handsome man approached. He wore a racing uniform that matched Katrina's. He had dark wavy brown hair that hung over his face. He had just used his hand to brush the hair away from his eyes revealing them to be a deep brown with hazel overtones.

Katrina gaped at him, then her mind switched gears and she hoped that he had been chosen for a better reason than his looks.

"Let me introduce you to my son, Richard Bertrand. He's an up and coming racecar driver on the NASCAR circuit."

Katrina was instantly glad that her thoughts had not spilled from her mouth a moment ago.

"Father, you really have to stop hanging on the pretty girls that way. What will mother think?" Richard rescued Katrina from his father's arm and led him away. "Let me find you a good seat to watch from."

"And get us another round my boy," Harvard added.

Richard looked apologetically at Katrina before taking his father to a makeshift set of stands by the church parking lot's exit.

Jenkins approached Katrina. "You know, sometimes people with money are..." Frodes ran up with Dillon on his heels. Jenkins never finished his thought. They both tried to talk over each other.

"Stop. I can only understand one of you at a time," Jenkins said. He pointed to Frodes first.

Frodes started. "I did a final diagnostic on the transmission. There are still three codes."

Jenkins grimaced and said "Call back the team. Tell them to begin transport of the backup transmission to the first overnight location and we need everyone on the install team to meet us there. Plan on a long night. Dillon your turn."

Dillon fidgeted. "I have photos of all the other weapons. I think we have the best design! I just need to send them to Katrina's phone."

Jenkins looked at Katrina. "Your idea?"

Katrina nodded sheepishly.

Jenkins' laughed jovially. "Now I know I picked the right person to sit in that seat!"

At three minutes before the green light none of the cars had lined up into any kind of order. They still occupied their haphazard positions in the parking lot. Richard sat with both hands on the wheel studying all of the controls and electronic displays, trying to understand what they all meant.

Katrina was struggling with the headset for the weapon. It was live, and every time she changed its position on her head the arm on the roof changed its position. She was trying to find the override to keep it still so that the other teams wouldn't see all of their design's functions.

The movement of the weapon got Richard's attention and he finally turned away from the dashboard. "What are you doing? I'm trying to concentrate here."

"Don't worry, I fixed the problem." Katrina said.

They heard the announcer shout through the bullhorn. It was Grant Phyindress. "One minute."

Richard pounded his hand on the dashboard. "There's a transmission warning light on. There must be something wrong with the way you guys built this thing." He banged his hand on the dash again. One of the screens flickered.

Katrina put her hand over the dash to thwart his next attempt. "Stop it. We have another transmission coming so it can be replaced tonight. Just baby it today and..."

"Ten..."

"This is an automatic, why would you build a racecar that's an automatic?" Richard asked, disgusted.

"Nine..."

"You know how to drive it, right?" Katrina asked, mystified at his irritation over a transmission that should be easier to drive.

"Eight…"

"Of course I know how to drive an automatic but a racecar is supposed to have a standard transmission."

"Seven…"

"Suck it up and we'll deal with it tonight when the team takes this one out." Katrina began to shout.

"Six…"

"What if this one doesn't make it that far?" Richard blurted out.

"Five…"

"Don't worry about it, just drive like you're supposed to!" Katrina shouted.

"Four…"

"And what are you supposed to do? I don't need a backup driver."

"Three…"

"I'm supposed to burn a hole in your head if you don't shut up and drive!" Katrina said angrily getting very upset.

"Two…"

They both stared at each other full of hate.

"One…"

Richard turned away. "If you want to get out now, it won't hurt my feelings one bit."

Katrina turned her head towards her new driver and tried to burn a hole in his head with just her eyes. She furled her brow and pursed her lips. This was not going to be a good trip.

The bullhorn sounded as Phyindress shouted "Go!" and a girl in very little clothing waved a green flag at the exit to the church.

Richard put his foot to the floor then pulled it back immediately. No one in front of them had moved more than an inch. The beginning of the race was having the entire lot of cars negotiate out of the lot from their positions. There was no lead position or line, they had to figure it out and jockey their positions, like leaving a drive-in after the movie was over. It was another challenge designed for the engineers, another puzzle for them to solve.

Quickly the lot became very congested. No one wanted to let the other cars out ahead of them, but neither did they have enough space to allow for their own passage. That's when the weapons came out.

Since everyone was so close to each other, this was the perfect opportunity to try out the technology. Those who had window mounted devices worked feverishly to get their systems mounted in place and functional.

The crowd of investors in the stands stood and began shouting instructions to the respective drivers. Camera crews that were still on foot had no problem keeping up with the drama as it unfolded.

One of the cars that had angled themselves to be next to leave the parking lot had a window mounted laser. The passenger was hanging half out of his window making the final connections when the device caught on fire. All of the camera people were running between the cars to get in closer.

Unfortunately positions of the cameramen wouldn't allow any cars to move unless they chose to run them over. The whole event was becoming a catastrophe and would soon be a tragic accident scene unless someone helped the drivers of the burning car.

Smoke began to billow from the window of the burning vehicle. Conscientious individuals had run in to extricate their team members. Investors were still shouting from the bleachers and in some cases were running toward their cars to give orders to their teams.

Bertrand's team sat transfixed. They didn't know what to do. The exit was hopelessly blocked. Even if the fire was put out, it would be a while before they could leave. Suddenly a red light came to life on the dash and a terrible alarm echoed through the cabin. Richard put his hands over his ears to block the noise.

"What the hell is that?" He shouted.

"The alarm is telling us that another car has a weapon lock on our car!" Katrina shouted.

Another alarm went off.

"That makes two weapons locks! We have to get out of here."

Richard Bertrand was in trouble. He had never actually driven this car before. His head turned this way and that trying to find which button would turn off the alarm. It looked like the race was over and he had never even left the parking lot. He knew nothing about the configuration of all the instruments on the dashboard or what the LED screens showed for information.

He only knew how to do was drive. This car had a gas pedal, a steering wheel and a break if he needed it. He had no idea what all the dials and numbers changing before him meant, or why the engineers had chosen to put an automatic transmission in a racecar. An automatic transmission that had already tripped the warning light... Any racer would tell you that you couldn't trust an automatic tranny. What did these pencil pushers know about racecars?

Bertrand gave up trying to shut off the alarm and put the gear shift into reverse. He shouted at Katrina, "Racecars are not supposed to have an automatic transmission."

Katrina knew what was going to happen next. She shouted over the alarm. "Don't stomp on the gas! If we crack our body we can do the same thing as the weapon would do, disable our car and disqualify us. Coast over to the bumper of the car behind us and push him back." Another alarm came on indicating a third weapon was now trained on them. "We really need to leave."

Bertrand rolled back and hit the car behind him softly as he was told, then he pushed the accelerator more firmly. One of the alarms immediately ceased. "How much power does this engine have?"

"Why?" Katrina asked as she was trying to set up a weapon strike of her own.

"Because I'm going to push two cars out of our way."

"You have almost 400 horsepower on demand. Just be careful, don't move off the push bar, and move straight back. I need three seconds minimum. Don't go too fast. I'm going to shut one of these bastards down." "400 hundred horsepower?" Richard shouted with surprised excitement.

"Just go, damn it!" Katrina shouted over the alarms.

Team MIT's car started to move further than the initial strike against the bumper. The car behind was losing ground against the more powerful engine of the MIT car. All of the alarms had shut down now. Cars on either side of them were changing positions to realign their weapons.

The car behind them was most ordinary in the way that it looked. The rail system for their weapon was pointed to the rear of the MIT car. Lucky for the MIT team, the extra horsepower that they had allowed for features that the other cars didn't have, and one for the push bar on both the front and the rear of the vehicle. Today this was a godsend. They moved backwards crushing the other car's laser assembly, bending the rail track under the pressure and ending their attempt to disabling Harvard Bertrand's car.

Richard eased down on the accelerator until the rear tires began to smoke. Slowly the car being pushed began to move backwards. The 400 horsepower showed its teeth until the car they were pushing struck the car behind it with a sickening crunch.

Katrina turned her visor towards the vehicle on her side of the car. The arm of their weapon spun above them to align itself with where her sight was focused. She used her controller to set up her shot. When she thought she was ready she shouted, "Burn baby, burn!"

The arm that sat on top of the MIT car extended its head towards the approaching car and fired a projectile with suction cups at its tip from the arm's wrist. The silver bulb with suction cups stuck to the body of the intended car at an odd angle on its roof.

Katrina was so happy that it worked she shouted, "Yes!"

A light came on over the arm and smoke began to pour out of the fuselage where the laser was burning into it. Their drivers were all shouting now, trying to figure out how to get it off their car. They struggled to move their car away but the laser stayed put stuck to them. Katrina's design had taken movement into account. The passenger of the car next to her was now trying to use his hands to reach the position on the roof where the laser was burning, but he was still unable to touch it. The driver gave up trying to move away and climbed out of his window with a wrench in one hand to try to knock the laser free before their engine died but they were too late. A red light filled their cockpit indicating that they were now a disabled car.

Richard shouted his excitement as he continued to push the two cars backwards until they hit a third car. Now the MIT car came to a stop and only the tires continued to move, spewing copious amounts of acrid smoke. Bertrand turned his wheel and started the whole process over again except this time moving forward towards the vehicle to the right that had been disabled. Katrina worked several buttons on her controller and retracted the laser head.

Camera men were running away from the fire to capture the new developments. Investors were running to get out of the way of the MIT car. Clearly Bertrand was not going to slow down if they got in his way.

Bertrand moved the car that they were pushing until it began to slide away off the push bar. Because it had no power to its engine it was sliding ominously toward the side of the MIT car. The occupants of that car were shouting for their lives thinking that their car would roll and that they would be crushed. Bertrand continued on his mission without thinking about the dangers involved.

Katrina screamed for him stop knowing that he would crack their fuselage if the car they were pushing spun and hit them. Bertrand pulled a maneuver using the break and the gas together to spin their car to match the sideways turn of the vehicle that they were moving.

Through the lenses of the cameramen it appeared that the MIT car was computer controlled with four wheel steering and unlimited maneuverability. Their car was on course to move the dead car back to its original position except with its nose pointing in the opposite direction.

Without notification Bertrand slammed on the brakes and hit the gear shift so that it landed on reverse. Bertrand threw his head back to see where he needed to go and slammed on the accelerator again. The MIT car traversed the entire parking lot in reverse at high speed until they reached the end.

Each parking space in the lot had a concrete abutment at the end closest to the street. Bertrand stopped and decided that if he wanted to leave he had to go forward. He turned the car around and drove until he was right up to one of them aiming so that the passenger wheel could go through the gap.

"How much clearance do we have?"

"Not enough to clear the concrete." Katrina said.

Bertrand grunted in response. He rolled slowly until the driver front tire bumped into the abutment. He goosed the accelerator and the engine pushed the car over the top easily.

"This is going to sound bad but at least we'll be out of this fucking mess." He accelerated again so the car was going fast enough to allow the back wheel to pop over the concrete and not get stuck. A loud grinding noise issued from the rocker panel on the driver side as it slid over the parking abutment.

Katrina screamed until the back wheel popped over the abutment into the air and they landed hard against the grass. The weapon arm bounced around as the car landed, striking the roof of the car. It sounded bad.

Katrina's eyes went to the roof in concern.

Bertrand didn't stop to see what had happened to the car. He drove over the grass until he reached the pavement. Precious time had been lost while they had been hung up in the parking lot. He had no idea how many other cars had made it out.

Katrina turned to see what was happening behind them. To her amazement she saw the car that looked like a dune buggy do the same thing that Bertrand had done, but their higher ground clearance had allowed them to go over the abutment without any trouble. And to her surprise, the car that was split down the middle was in the process of separating into its two halves. When it was done it resembled the two motorcycles she imagined and reconnected end to end. It easily drove between the concrete barriers and followed the dune buggy out to the road to finally begin the race.

Katrina realized then and there that they had some real competition. The other teams had some formidable designs. She was both very impressed and very worried about their chances.

Chapter 7

Mr. Bertrand, the investor, stood next to Dr. Jenkins and Frodes who both had shocked expressions on their faces at what they just witnessed. Bertrand whooped with excitement as Dillon Trackson ran up to them. "There are parts on the ground where the car went over the concrete abutment."

Bertrand completely ignored the statement. "I can't believe it! My son actually has a skill, and it's something other than bitching. We may have a chance yet. This is fantastic! I have a lot of money riding on this."

"But, your son just ruined several components of the car." Jenkins said in disbelief. "They'll be lucky to even make it to the desert in California."

Bertrand turned to Jenkins with a huge smile. "That's why you will travel with your team to make the necessary repairs at their stop in Ohio. Get going old man, you're already behind. I want to win and your car is going to do it, come hell or high water."

Bertrand walked away leaving Jenkins lost in thought about the car's possible problems and how to fix them with a traveling work team. He turned to Frodes and made a snap decision. "Call the team and order everything we need to fix the car, not just the transmission. I will arrange transportation for us. Make sure that we have a new set of tires for every day of travel and…"

In the MIT car, the second Bertrand was very pleased with himself. He repositioned himself in his seat as he drove and thought about winning the race, standing in front of a whole crowd of people all cheering for him. He'd show his father that there was more to racing than just going around in a circle. He had just gotten their car out of a very tight mess back at that parking lot. Katrina wasn't present in his day dream but he could feel her tapping him on the arm bringing him slowly back to reality.

What was really happening was that Katrina had been beating on him with all her might. She was so full of anger at his stupidity. When Richard came out of his reverie he was confused by why his racing partner was beating on him.

"Whoa! Stop! What are you going on about? I just got us of that mess back there."

"You idiot! For starters, 'We' got us out of that mess back there, and because you obviously didn't bother to read the manual we sent you, you…"

"I didn't need to read some dumb manual about how to drive. There's a gas pedal and a steering wheel. That's all I need to know. And," Richard raised his voice to forestall Katrina's continuing objections. "Racecars don't have automatic transmissions."

"You fucking idiot!" she raged. "This isn't a traditional race. It's not all about speed. It's about testing the endurance of the technology. It's about conducting the race in as much of an invisible manner as possible." Katrina shouted.

"You said we have 400 hundred horsepower. What's all that horsepower for? We have it and we should floor it and get to California as soon as possible."

"You ass! The top speed of this car is seventy two miles per hour. We are supposed to drive within the speed limit. That power is there when we need to use it, but we have to recharge afterwards. That stunt back there…"

"That stunt got us out!" Richard shouted.

"That stunt did more than that. See this gauge? That tells us that we are almost at minimum power right now. Another stunt like that and the battery will overheat from a brown out. Then we'll be out of the race permanently."

"Brown out? We'll just get a new battery when we get gas." Richard said, like he knew all about cars.

Katrina started hitting Richard again, over and over again. She was so frustrated. He had his right arm up to block her blows as he continued to try to drive. He noticed movement in his rear view mirror. Many other racecars now had caught up, there was a line not far behind him.

"Cut it out, we have to go. Everyone is catching up."

"You can't. We have to recharge." Katrina jabbed her finger to the active video link of all the operations of the vehicle. "If you gun it and this set of numbers hits twelve, the engine will shut down."

The linear gauge showed their recent usage history with very high spikes across an overlay line that showed where the usage should be. Now they were way too low, down to twenty-two and it fell to twenty-one as they watched.

"Great, now we're going to lose the race because we're out of battery power?" Richard asked.

Katrina hit him again. "We're not going to lose. Let them pass us and we'll be recharged fully in twenty minutes. We have five days to finish this race. It's all about balance and endurance."

"So we'll catch them when they stop for gas?" Richard asked, hopeful.

Katrina looked like she was about to blow a gasket. She got all red in the face. "Yeah, stop for gas, right." She hit Richard again. "Read the manual!"

"Fine, tell me about the manual then." Richard shouted back as racecars started passing them. He was clearly upset that they were losing their position in the lineup.

"Tell you about the manual? It's over 700 pages long! You ass! I can't believe the most talented engineer on the planet designed this car only to have it be driven by the greatest screw up in the world." Katrina slouched in her seat, disgusted.

The rest of the MIT team sat in a cramped room staring at a large television screen. An uplink from the internet fed the images they were all seeing. Displayed was the church parking lot with twenty-seven racecars of all different designs parked without any order and pointed in different directions. The exit out was at the opposite end and it was narrow. Girls in skimpy clothing, with green flags, were waiting at the exit for their signal to wave them wildly indicating the beginning of the race.

The room was full of chatter about the other cars in the lot. Images of their designs were up close and personal. It was easy to see why. In each image camera men could be seen in the background checking out other vehicles. Moments after one image showed a particular car for three seconds, the scene switched to another car. When the MIT car came into view the room erupted into applause. Katrina could be seen anxiously waiting for her driver.

The scene switched over and over. Many comments were made either about the weapons systems or the cars' designs. When the race was about to begin the cameramen finally started to move toward the edges of the lot. One of the angles showed the make-shift seating platform where the investors and guests were seated. Many held drinks in their hands; some were busy on their cell phones.

A voice through a bullhorn shouted the word "Go!" and all of the cars began to move. It didn't take very long for everyone in the room shouting for their car to "Go, go, go"! They watched the cluster of cars make a mess of trying to get through the narrow exit. Many interns shouted angrily at the screen in disbelief. When the weapons came out they shouted even louder.

After six cars had exited, two more fought to be the next one out causing a terrible log jam behind them, ensuring that no one could move. Four of the cars that were bunched up while trying to get out all had the same idea. Their window mounted weapons powered up. It was clear that they thought that once the car next to them was disabled, they would have a commanding lead over the many stuck behind the disqualified car. No one counted on poor wiring in one of them shorting out and catching on fire.

The room of spectators got to their feet with looks of incredulity. The MIT car was positioned too many vehicles back to be able to leave. A ripple of disappointment crossed the room as they realized that their chances of even starting the race were decreasing by the minute. Suddenly they could see weapons on all sides of their car being deployed. They knew that it only took three seconds for a laser to disable a car and their car was trapped.

Then the MIT car was moving backwards. The weapon deployed on the car behind them had been crushed by their push bar. Shouts of hope filled the room. When smoke began to billow from the dead laser more shouting erupted. The design team engineer who had suggested placing a push bar back there got several pats on the back.

Smoke appeared from the MIT car's tires. The car behind them was being pushed back until it struck the next car back. When both cars were actively being pushed out of the way the room began to go crazy. Full of hope, they shouted at the screen as though Katrina could hear them. They had no idea who the driver was so she was getting all the credit.

Then the weapon on the roof of the MIT car came to life and shot its head at the vehicle beside them. When it made contact the room fell to a hush, waiting expectantly. When smoke started to rise renewed shouts of exhilaration filled the room. The team watched the driver and the passenger of the car that was under attack struggle to find something to detach the MIT laser but nothing that they had could reach it. Three seconds later their car died. The energy of its occupants deflated, they knew that the race was over for them.

The MIT laser head retracted into the roof mounted arm. Cameramen were running around the cars trying to get better angles of the action. They watched their car maneuver around the lot. In disbelief everyone in the room viewed the car as it scraped its way over the concrete abutment. All of them knew what just happened. One of the cameramen chased after the car on foot. By the time he arrived at the abutment the MIT car had accelerated away so quickly that he knew he couldn't catch them. He stopped to focus on the abutment the MIT car had just gone over and there on the screen was something that had been left behind. A wet spot started as a series of drops on the concrete where a deep scratch could be seen ending with a small puddle on the pavement. The room became quiet. A puddle meant something bad. No one was excited anymore.

Katrina hit Richard again. "Will you just shut up and listen. For starters, the reason most of the drivers are the actual students that built the cars is because it's about more than just driving. You have to understand the technology to be able to use it most effectively. It's not just about speed. In fact if you get a speeding ticket we are automatically disqualified. You can't get into an accident or break any of the other rules for the race. We just need to get from point A to point B every day and try to be one of the first five cars.

"Being one of the first to arrive at the stop for the day guarantees us an earlier start time for the next day. Even if we crossed the finish line tomorrow we wouldn't win because we have to hit all our stops at the end of each day. Letting those cars go ahead of us doesn't matter yet. We will catch them again when we hit the highway. We have the power to make that happen if you just give it a few minutes to charge."

Richard let out a long breath. "This isn't what I signed up for. I was supposed to be driving in a race not a slow motion technology test. Yeah, we'll catch them at seventy two miles per hour. What fun is that? A race is about being fast, finishing first, and using your skill to beat your opponent. It's not supposed to be taking your time and hoping that your car lasts that long."

"Most of these engine designs can't go that fast on the highway. They're efficient at slower speeds but we're going to crush them at over fifty." Katrina said. "You'll still be using your skills as a driver but you have to drive smarter."

"All right then, explain to me why we have so much power, but only if we slow down to charge?" Richard asked as though this was an anomaly that couldn't possibly exist in the real world.

Katrina sighed. "It would take way too long to explain it to you. Just know that we only have to stop to pee and get food. We aren't using any gas. If we didn't have to stop at all we would just keep going."

Richard pointed to the battery indicator. "Looks like you have plenty of time to explain. We are only up to twenty-four percent and we have to be at eighty according to this monitor."

Katrina sighed again. "It took Dr. Jenkins thirty years to figure it out and he's a genius. How am I supposed to explain it to an idiot in fifteen minutes?"

"Use small words." Richard said.

Katrina hit him again, her anger flaring. "Okay, here goes but I'm only going to do it once. If you can't figure it out, you're out of luck."

"None of the girls I meet need it more than once so I should be fine."

There was a deafening silence for a whole minute before Katrina slapped him across the face. He never saw it coming. The car swerved wildly until Richard got it back under control. Luckily all the other racecars had passed and the both lanes were clear.

"What was that for?" Richard asked confused.

"If you don't know then I can't explain it." Katrina said as she turned to face forward as she crossed her arms.

"What! I was just saying that most girls only need me to explain what I do for a living once, so why wouldn't I be able to figure this car out on the first try? I'm not stupid you know. I graduated..."

"You're an ass. I know what you meant and it had nothing to do with your driving skills."

Richard smiled, knowing that she was already on to him. "Alright, you got me. Tell me about this engine and I promise not to hit on you."

Katrina thought a moment before starting in on her explanation of the electric engine based on the one tree. "What we have is call the One Tree design."

Richard began to ask her for a little more information but Katrina said, "Shut up and listen."

"The idea of the One Tree comes from a fundamental concept that states there are energy sources that are natural in the world. We simple humans are of the understanding that if we need power, we must burn something to get it. Animals do the same thing. If you need energy you eat. Our bodies burn the food chemically to make energy. In many instances, if you need a power source outside of our bodies, something must be burned to make a form of energy there as well.

"The One Tree idea is based on the fact that there are not armies of gremlins running around a forest that start little generators to power every tree."

Richard chuckled. "The idea of little gremlins running around is funny." Katrina hit him again. He stopped talking.

"As I was saying, each tree doesn't have the autonomy to grab whatever it wants to feed itself and since gremlins don't go around giving them power, they must use all of the natural forces around it to survive. We know that a tree uses a form of hydraulics called capillary action. This allows water to rise up the little straws inside the tree called capillaries. This natural action brings up the nutrients from the soil to feed the tree. Every time the wind blows the tree around capillary action becomes stronger drawing water higher in the tree. But at some point the water will not go any higher because the weight of volume inside each little straw is too great.

"That's where sunlight comes in. Each and every leaf uses the process of photosynthesis to give the tree life; however, they serve a dual purpose by causing the water present in the leaves to evaporate. This evaporation draws more water up the tree. Therefore the tree can continue to grow and find more sunlight. Higher and higher into the sky the tree can reach up to compete with those around it. The whole process relies on the environment around it. And there is a kind of momentum to this process. Stop any part of it and the tree will die because it cannot actively change or fix what stopped the process.

"Dr. Jenkins realized that if he could take several energy sources and put them together so that a type of natural momentum can occur, then it could run practically forever, provided that nothing stopped any one part of the process. It takes a minimum of three different types of energy sources to keep the momentum going.

"The battery I talked about earlier is a critical component. There are two in this device. One is electrical and the other is pneumatic. Each balances the process to which it accompanies. If one or the other is damaged the engine will stop working. The engine makes mechanical power. We use that power to run a generator. Electricity has the greatest potential of work on the planet. Humans have invented many devices that can turn electricity into work. We use that electricity to power all the electronics on the dashboard, our communication system and most importantly the motor that moves the car. So to put it in plain English, if you don't overuse the electrical battery, we will have enough power to last as long as the bearings inside the device don't break down or overheat. Or in other words, the car doesn't ever have to pull over to get energy. The devices inside it keep the momentum going and we always make our own electricity, thus, our power."

Richard remained quiet for a few seconds to digest all that was said. He looked at the dashboard computer again to see where the battery life was at that moment. There he noticed the check transmission light again. "So we have an automatic transmission in case the team got an inexperienced driver?"

Katrina raised both hands in the air in a kind of hallelujah moment. "Yes. Holy shit I can't believe you got that, as stupid as you appear to be. The act of shifting can be detrimental to power usage if the driver isn't accustomed to driving a standard in the first place. Since we had no idea of the capacity of the driver we were to get, had to assume that it might be someone without experience driving a standard. Since our engine makes so much power we could afford to lose some to the automatic transmission rather than take the chance of interrupting the momentum."

Richard gave a look of incredulity. But he had a question just the same.

"So, what does this other light mean with the brake picture on it?"

Katrina's mouth hung open in shock. "That means we have no brakes."

Chapter 8

"We don't need brakes, we just need to drive, right?" Richard said, in an attempt to lighten the moment. Katrina went back to hitting him.

Richard raised his arm to fend off the blows from his passenger when he noticed a box truck following them. In fact there was a whole line of box trucks behind them. Soon the trucks were passing them like they were on their way to a fire.

"What's up with all of these trucks?" he asked. "None of them have any markings."

"They're the support vehicles that will make our race invisible if a car is disabled or gets into an accident. What we're doing is illegal. So the investors have to clean up after themselves as the race proceeds."

An idea struck Bertrand. "That means we have a truck that will follow us too?" he asked hopefully.

Katrina nodded. She was tired from using so much of her energy to hit her driver and she slumped back in her seat. She was tired of answering questions that wouldn't need to be asked if Richard had bothered to read the manual.

"Yes, a truck and a camera crew are following each car. But they can't help us or interact with us in any way until we are out of the race."

"I'm sure we can convince them to get us some oil," he suggested.

"You really are some special kind of idiot aren't you? We need brake line repair and brake fluid. Oil won't help us at all. We need to pull over so I can get a good look at the problem and fill the burn holes in the car's skin. Since we need to charge some more we should do it now where there's very little traffic."

"But we're already in last place. If we stop now we'll never catch up."

"Listen carefully." Katrina said through gritted teeth. "This is a slow motion race. We are not supposed to break the speed limit. Everyone has to stop to pee and get food, or recharge their car in some way before the end of the day. Optimally, everyone will only stop twice each day. We will just choose to stop early. At the next store you see, pull over and we'll get food, I'll fill the holes, and we can check how bad the leak is."

"Why fill the holes? Who cares?" Richard said irritably.

Katrina sighed, it was as if she was traveling with a child and she had to explain herself every time she opened her mouth. "Like I mentioned before, there are two layers of material that make up the skin. If the weapon burns through the first layer and the inner epoxy is burned away the two layers will touch and short out the car. What do you think will happen when we drive through rain?"

Richard pondered on that thought for a whole minute before the light bulb came on over his head. "Water conducts electricity and the car will short out."

"Oh my God, he does have at least two brain cells." Katrina shouted. Richard smacked Katina in the arm at the insult.

Frodes had a phone to his ear. All he could hear was ringing. For some reason no one was picking up. The students were all supposed to be watching the race back at the shop where the car had been built. The call finally reached the number of rings allowed before the recorded voice of a woman came on to inform him that the person on the other end was not responding.

Frodes hung up the phone and tried again. Finally someone answered.

Frodes had to pull the phone away from his ear. The noise blaring though the receiver was so great that he thought he would go deaf. He switched ears but held the phone a bit further away in self-defense. He could hear a voice but it was fragmented as if the line had a bad connection. Moments later the voice became clear and asked "Hello?" again.

"This is Frodes," he said. He assumed that his name alone would command the attention of whoever had answered the phone but the shouting in the background had resumed. Frodes realized that they had just watched what had happened in the parking lot. Then it occurred to him that everything that was being streamed on the internet was not actually live, it was being edited and would be many minutes behind the real events. When the shouting subsided Frodes finally began.

"I know that what you just watched made for good entertainment but we have real problems. We know that our car needs some serious work that will have to be done when they arrive in Circleville, Ohio. I need a team, as many people as you can get to come out here. We need manpower and tools. Bring the second transmission and all the specs to replace anything that needs work. Also I need twenty more tires, the same kind that we already put on the car. We need another team that is staying at the warehouse that can track down parts so we will have everything we need when you get there. Dr. Jenkins is getting transportation set up and I'll call again as soon as I know more about what we need."

The screaming started anew and Frodes had to pull the receiver further from his ear again. He hoped that the person he had spoken to had gotten everything written down. He sighed. He would have to call again in fifteen minutes to make sure that the situation was under control.

      The intern who had managed to pick up the call walked back into the room where the television was located. He shouted and shouted for everyone to shut up. Finally when the energy level had shrunk enough for him to be heard, Christopher Franq took a deep breath and began to speak to the now attentive crowd before him. "That was Frodes. He said that the car was damaged from the exit out of the parking lot. He needs a team of as many members that want to go out and make repairs. Who wants to go?"

      The entire room went crazy. They had just witnessed now much better designed their car was compared to most of the other cars in attendance. It had displayed better design work in both the operation of the car and in the weapon. Now they were being asked if they wanted to be the mechanics for the best car in the race? Not one person said no.

      The entire group in the television room threw their arms in the air in excitement at the opportunity that had just been offered. It was like being asked to go to the moon to fix the landing craft so that their team could come home safely. Who could say no? Pride, in combination with lots of energy drinks, fueled everyone's desire to be part of history, got everyone to their feet. The whole room cleared out not knowing what they had to do or where they were supposed to go. The energy was too great to contain. When the last intern left the room and Franq was about to leave, the phone rang again.

The MIT car was slowing down though they were still a long distance away from the Shell station that they were approaching.

"Why do we have to slow down from such a distance? I feel like we are an old couple who doesn't know how to drive anymore." Richard asked.

"Because if our brakes cut out all of the way we'll be able to stay in traffic, hopefully without causing an accident." Katrina said. She had been looking over her shoulder the whole time. She didn't want anyone to crash into them.

Richard came to a stop in a parking spot easily, as though nothing was wrong with the car. "See, I told you, you were worrying too much."

"Just go in and buy enough food to last us the entire day and I'll do the hard stuff."

"Right, because you're so smart." Richard quipped. "I'm the one who got us here."

Katrina made a rude gesture with her finger in his direction but he had turned away before he could see it. She opened what would have been considered a trunk for most cars. In this case it was used mostly to store tools. She took out a container with two tubes in it. Similar to epoxy, she squeezed equal amounts and mixed them together. As she prepared the mixture the truck that was assigned to follow them pulled up behind the car.

A black man popped out of the cab of the truck and asked, "Are you guys broken down?"

"No, just making a few minor repairs," she said quickly, afraid that they were going to try to take the car.

He was a large man, handsome to a fault with big brown eyes, a shaved head, and large muscles. He introduced himself and the cameraman who was still sitting in the truck playing with his camera.

"Hey, I'm Jersey and that's Lucky. We're the ones who'll be following you throughout the race. You're sure you're all set?"

Katrina had every intention of telling them the truth until Lucky jumped out with his camera already rolling. He was a creepy looking guy. She froze, wondering how much she should say if she was 'on camera'. If the race was being shown over the internet then every investor would know if they were having problems. That wouldn't look good. It wouldn't look good at all. She needed to maintain some secrecy. She definitely didn't want any of the other teams learning about their current weaknesses.

"Nope everything is fine," she said. "Just doing an inspection and filling some holes." Katrina raised the epoxy compound in the air so that they could see it properly. She looked at Jersey when she spoke but knew it was the camera that was really watching. "We don't want rain to be a problem."

Richard popped his head out of the Shell station's door. "So what do you want to pee in? A Gatorade bottle or a Pringles can? Or should I just get toilet paper and you'll just do it out the window as I drive?"

Time slowed to a trickle as embarrassment engulfed Katrina. Her face flooded. The weight of what he had just said in front of the camera made her feel very insignificant. All her friends and perhaps future employers were watching this race. Emotions raced through her with thoughts of his stupidity and carelessness and false bravado. Something inside of her snapped. She wanted to beat Richard to within an inch of his life.

Katrina carefully set the epoxy on the roof of the car. In an instant her anger overcame her composure. She turned with fury on her face and ran full tilt at Bertrand.

Richard didn't move a muscle. He waited for Katrina to approach him as though she were going to tell him off in a whisper so that the camera wouldn't hear her. He even smiled, thinking of his coming retort. He was very witty, he thought to himself, and Katrina was just another woman who would bend to his will in the end.

When she didn't slow down, even at four feet away, his smile faltered, then faded completely as Katrina dove the last few feet. She tackled him in the chest. Both of them flew backwards into the store through the open door Richard had been holding open. The items he held in his hand flew away into the air. Loud angry epithets spewed from Katrina's mouth and could be heard outside despite the fact that the door had swung closed behind them. Lucky ran in followed by Jersey. They pulled Katrina off her driver as she punched every bit of Richard as she could.

Richard drove silently down the interstate. One eye was in the process of blossoming with color. Katrina was resting the knuckles of one of her hands against an ice cream sandwich in a plastic bag that was melting as it molded around her fist.

"The next time I talk to my father, I'm going to tell him what you did." Richard said.

"That sounds about right, cry to daddy. You can't even be a man about your own stupidity. You go and tell him a girl beat on you. I'll tell you what, you drive to Ohio and I'll let you off the hook for the rest of the race. I'll drive the rest of the way and win this race for my team, you sad excuse of a man." Katrina barked.

Richard brooded, knowing that if he did call his father he would become the laughing stock of his family, more so than he already was.

Lost in their problems neither was paying attention to what existed in the rearview mirror. For the most part they considered themselves in last place at the moment and were trying to make up time. No racecars were behind them anymore. More than the customary amount of time had been used back at the Shell station between the fight and the triage of the car.

Lucky had watched the whole thing through his camera lens, sniggering. Katrina was so embarrassed. She had barely had enough time to fill the holes in the car's shell before they had left. They hadn't taken any time to buy food, and now they had to drive straight through to their scheduled stop in Ohio.

Katrina's phone rang. She dug it out of her uniform's pocket and answered it. "Hello?"

"Are you alright?" Dillon asked. "We just watched you attack Bertrand's son. He's furious. He wants to pull out of the race now because he thinks you're unstable."

Katrina looked over to Richard, who was still trying to avoid her gaze, before answering. "Yeah I did beat up this idiot. But you can tell his father that it's his son who has a problem not me."

"What can you tell me about the car?" Dillon asked. "We have a team coming to meet you in Circleville."

Katrina brightened instantly. "Really? That's great! Alright, I need new brake lines for the rear wheels. The transmission light is still on but it's doing okay for now. If it's replaced it should be a standard, he's an idiot but he can drive. We need new rubber all around and a couple new tubes of epoxy. Pretty boy here screwed it up..."

Something slammed in the rear of the MIT car hard. The entire car surged forward and Katrina dropped her phone, cutting off the conversation. Richard rushed his free hand to the wheel to help with stability but the force was too great and the car began to cut out from the rear.

Richard's skill as a driver took over. Although an hour ago she would have gladly wished to exchange some of his skill as a driver for integrity as a human being, at this moment she was glad he had the ability to stay in control. An older model maroon Ford Explorer had rear-ended their car. Luckily it had struck the push bar and not anywhere else.

Richard kept them from crashing after they had begun to spin from the strong hit but when he was done both cars were driving next to each other with the racecar in the wrong lane. Katrina's head was still spinning, waiting for her stomach to catch up. Then she felt sick.

"Hang on!" Richard yelled. "We're going to see what 400 horsepower feels like." The MIT car shot off like a bullet, leaving the Ford explorer behind like it had been standing still.

After a few hundred feet separated them from the Explorer, they were both able to breathe again. They found their turn and got onto 495 hoping that the Explorer was far enough behind to miss seeing which direction they had gone. They were both fairly sure that that guy had been gunning for them. No one would crash into the rear of another vehicle that hard unless it was intentional.

It wasn't long before Richard looked in the mirror and saw the Explorer coming up on them again. "I know there are a lot of rules for this race, but I'm pretty sure that what they're doing isn't allowed. I wish I had some real speed to lose them for good. Can you disable the speed control module? If it comes up we can say the strike from that Ford knocked it out of whack and we had to drive faster to defend ourselves." He pulled into the passing lane and went by an old Ford Escort that was in the slower middle lane.

Then the MIT car passed another racecar that was in the middle lane. "See, I told you we would make up lots of time on the interstate." Katrina said and she watched it until it was behind them.

Katrina turned to look out the back window. The Ford was catching up quickly and it looked like it was going to try to hit them again. "I don't think we're going to outrun this guy and there's not enough traffic to lose him."

The Explorer had caught up to the other racecar. Suddenly it cut its wheels hard and ran through the driver's corner of the fuselage shattering the body of the other car into thousands of pieces. The driver of the other race car lost control and crashed into a pickup truck that had been next to it. The resulting mess of vehicles running into them and others that were trying to avoid the accident made Katrina's eyes grow wide in shock.

Pushing a button on the dash, Katrina quickly activated another type of screen that rose out of the dashboard along with a removable keyboard. The screen came to life instantly. All kinds of information began to stream in a linear fashion from left to right. There was no time to check things out. She hit the key for the letter M and F1 key together. A menu popped up overlaying all of the other information. Quickly she went through the drop down menus that followed until she came to the speed governor override. At that point the Explorer had caught up again. Richard had begun to dart and weave through traffic to try to avoid what had happened to the other racecar.

Being tossed around the interstate, Katrina was having a difficult time typing in the override code to disable the seventy two mile-per-hour limit.

"Keep still or I'll never get the password entered."

"I need speed and brakes to get out of this mess! I can't magically avoid getting hit forever, unless they run out of gas!"

Richard pulled hard to the right to switch lanes, tossing Katrina around in her seat. The computer screen blinked and went out for a second then came back up. Katrina had to start over again to get deep enough into the software. She was thrown again as Richard made another maneuver to try to keep them alive. Richard was getting very stressed. "I need speed and brakes or we're dead! If I step onto the brake pedal now we will lose control because we only have front brakes."

"For God's sake, use the emergency brake. It's on the rear wheels. It's that handle there." Katrina pointed and shouted as she made yet another attempt to log into the system.

The Maroon Explorer made another attempt to hit them but crashed into the side of a light blue Honda Civic just as the MIT car had vacated the spot next to it.

Richard was using an interesting maneuver based on the car's current capabilities. He would slow down until the Explorer came in for a hit then he would floor it and dart ahead. But he could only keep it up as long as there was a way out.

The Civic had lost control and had hit the guardrail before rolling onto its roof. Running along the rail had caused a fire to break out. Richard craned his neck to watch the crash.

Katrina screamed at the near miss and as she watched the Civic catch on fire.

"I need speed!" Richard demanded.

"You keep moving too much for me to type in the code." Katrina apologized.

Richard yanked on the steering wheel again, avoiding the Explorer once more. Katrina lost her position on the keyboard and the power flickered on her screen. She screamed again but this time out of frustration. She hammered both of her fists on the dashboard. The computer took that as a command to close up and withdrew back into its unused position.

Katrina felt like a waste of space, she had no idea how to help. Richard pulled the emergency brake and the car spun in a circle. Katrina screamed as she braced herself against the ceiling.

The car spun a whole three hundred and sixty degrees and ended up behind the Explorer. The weapon's control module fell out and landed on Katrina's lap. An idea struck her and she took the controls and touched the bluetooth link on her headset. "I need you to position the Ford on the passenger's side for one second on my mark."

"What! It's not like I have a lot of control here without more speed."

"Just do what you need to do and I'll take care of the rest." Katrina shouted.

"What can you do?" Richard asked suddenly becoming interested.

"Get ready to reposition the car." She shouted.

Katrina was worried that this was too much of a radical step to get the Ford to back off. People could get seriously hurt and that bothered her. She wasn't a soldier; she didn't kill people; and most of all she didn't think she could live with herself if she did. But she had to do something.

The weapon on the roof came to life. Katrina turned her head towards where the car was supposed to be any second and shouted. "I'm ready!" The arm stretched out before lowering to eye level. The wrist repositioned upwards slightly so the laser was pointing just higher than level. Richard pulled the emergency brake and spun the car around. They were suddenly going backwards in the other lane but keeping pace with the Explorer. The driver looked over at Katrina and pointed a pistol at her. It appeared that their last ditch contingency to get the racecar off the road involved more than just the destruction of their car. Katrina was scared to see the gun but she now knew that this was the only way to survive.

She moved the joystick and the weapon's "On" LED flashed as the laser leveled on the Explorer's window. The red light of the laser appeared on the Ford driver's face. The smallest amount of time passed when nothing happened. It was clear that the laser worried the driver but he didn't understand what it was for. When smoke appeared from his melting skin, an absolute loss of control of the Ford occurred. The gun dropped out of his hand as he used both of his hands to block the laser. The Explorer fell back and drifted toward the side of the road before running into a bridge abutment.

Richard yanked on the emergency brake again and straightened out. He sped up to put as much distance between them and the Explorer as he could. Katrina got a good look at the Explorer in her mirror just before it caught on fire.

Her heart felt conflicted. Part of her wanted to celebrate, after all she had just saved them from a terrible crash, but in the process she had also maimed someone and caused a crash that had surely killed both the driver and the passenger of the Explorer. She felt terrible.

Richard cheered as Katrina cried.

Chapter 9

Internet television is a fairly new phenomenon in the world of entertainment. While it is a less than mainstream version of entertainment, it is a convenient way to stream very real events to the world uncut and uncensored.

While most of the MIT team had been packing to fly to Circleville, Ohio to set up shop, one team member had not been not actively packing. He had been watching the television in his office in complete shock.

The screen that he was watching showed every cameraman's video feed, each in its own section of a large grid, in order to keep track of all the cars at the same time. At the moment his eyes were riveted to a small rectangle two-thirds of the way down on the right side of his crowded screen. Dr. Jenkins' shock had come from witnessing their car having barely survived an accident, although what had happened had clearly not been accidental at all. He had just watched as Katrina had resorted to using the weapon that had been designed only to disable another racecar, to instead fend off assailants. His heart sank. The weapon should never have needed to be used on a person. He imagined the tremendous pain that could be caused by the burning and melting of human skin.

Jenkins had also watched as one of the other racecars had been destroyed by the maroon Explorer. He hoped that the passengers had survived and wondered who had sent in mercenaries to destroy the racecars. He had no love for Bertrand and he didn't know Bertrand's son, but he knew Katrina and he had never expected her to be in any real danger. In a low speed race, any possible danger caused by their car being disabled should have been easily minimized by any decent driver. Now there were other vehicles trying to take out the racecars? His heart leapt for her when they managed to use their weapon to fight off the bastard in the Ford. But he knew that she would be regretting her decision to use the weapon, even if it had been the only way to save themselves.

Dr. Jenkins considered who would have dispatched a hunter to get rid of entrants. Obviously they were trying to increase the odds of their own car being the winner. The one person who might be able to help him figure it out was the person who had a family member driving his investment. Bertrand would understand the motives better than other people. Had he known that his son would be in danger of being killed? Had he known that there would be a hunter out there trying to destroy racecars? Jenkins considered these questions and more.

Jenkins went back and forth with his desire to call his investor. Surely he had also been watching and had witnessed what happened with the MIT car, so calling to tell him what happened would be a waste of time. Asking him why however... Jenkins wondered what would happen if he asked too many questions. That might be a mistake as well. He put his brilliant mind to the task.

It could only be someone who had inside information about the race, but that meant that it could be anyone from the investors to any of the individual team members. Although the range must be more limited than that, it could only be someone who had more at stake than would the average team member. He remembered his first meeting when the head of the race, Grant Phyindress, had spoken about people wanting change in the auto manufacturing industry.

Could someone in the auto industry have enough information about the race to want all of the cars to fail? Or could someone with a weak entrant want to win above all else be trying to fix the race? That, he could see as a more likely possibility. He wondered how much money was at stake. If an investor was desperate enough, and their entrant was weak, that could provoke someone with connections to attempt to stack the deck.

An idea struck Jenkins and he turned off his television. He spun his chair around so that he faced his desk. He went into his file of information for the race. The one thing engineers did better than anything else was keep good records. To give the lead engineers a method to gage their position among all the other entrants they had been given access to an internet site that showed statistics that could be used to measure their position against the group. There, they could log in and see if they had been falling behind in comparison to other teams.

He typed in the website's address and followed the links. When the lists came up Jenkins saw that thirty fuselage skins had been made, but only twenty seven teams had been at the starting gate. If thirty teams were supposed to start, what had happened to the other three? Had they not finished in time? Or had they not passed the initial inspections before the race? He looked for the three teams that didn't make it, George Platz, Lin Hong, and Marcus Appleton. He didn't recognize the first two names but he knew Marcus from way back. In fact, he was pretty sure that he still had his phone number.

After Dr. Jenkins pulled his phone out of his pocket he searched for the number. Sure enough, it was there, just as he had remembered and pressed send.

"Hello?" Appleton answered. His voice had a level of excitement to it that could not have been inspired by the call.

"Marcus, is that you?" Jenkins asked, not completely sure that the voice matched his friend's.

"Yeah, but I'm kind of in the middle something. Can I call you back?"

"This is Dr. Jenkins from the MIT team. Can I ask you a quick question?"

"Jenkins? Really... Oh my God. Did you see what happened?" Appleton's voice turned quickly to worry.

"Yeah, I just watched it happen. Listen I have a question about the car you were building."

Appleton laughed derisively. "What a waste of effort."

"What do you mean?"

"We got the whole car finished and the day before the truck shows up to take it to the starting line, a fire destroyed it overnight."

"A fire? Did they find out what caused it?" Jenkins asked.

"No. The guards didn't see anything. We're thinking it may have been electrical. The amps for the laser unit were pretty high and if someone wasn't careful, you know... We just don't know."

There was a silence between the men. Finally Appleton said. "Listen I should go."

"Wait. I was thinking. You have video security of your work area like we do, right?" Jenkins asked.

"Yeah."

"Do me a favor and check where your interns parked. I'm looking for a late model maroon Ford Explorer."

Appleton caught on pretty quickly. "Wait a minute. Do you think that the nut that tried to kill your team is the one that destroyed my..."

"I think it's possible." Jenkins said more confidently now that his friend and he were thinking the same terrible thing.

"Oh my God. Yeah... I'll call you back." Appleton said and he hung up without another word.

Chapter 10

"There. It's done." Katrina said as she typed in the final key strokes to disable the speed governor.

Richard didn't need permission from Katrina to test out the car's speed. They needed to put some miles on now, before any other vehicles showed up to do them in. In a few short seconds the powerful electric engine propelled them forward with enough energy to bury them in their seats. The video screen showed their speed increasing so fast that the car hit a hundred and twenty in a mere few seconds. They flew passed the other cars as if they had been standing still.

"Okay, okay, okay." Karina said with rising fear. "You can slow down. We can't get a ticket, remember?"

Richard slowed to eighty and held that speed for a long time. He studied traffic conditions, slowing only to traverse the known speed traps that had been outlined for them on a map that the team had made. They traveled for hours without any problems. Along the way they also passed many of the other contestants of the race. As Katrina had explained, their engine system was very powerful and could out strip anyone on the highway plus make up for all of the time they had lost at the beginning.

Katrina was fearful that the other contestants would notice the speed of their car and might complain to the race officials about their car not following the rules that had been set regarding speed. Certainly they would at least get docked points.

The ride felt long without any discussion. Richard seemed lost in thought, about what Katrina couldn't imagine. He seemed like a very shallow person. Maybe he just had nothing to talk about. She on the other hand had many doubts about how the day had passed thus far. There was a large pit in her gut about how she had used their weapon.

There could be little doubt that the two people in the Explorer had been killed. She struggled with the idea that it had been what they deserved. If she had not done it she knew that it would have been the two of them that had been killed instead, but somehow that didn't make her feel much better about what had happened.

Time marched on. Of the many racecars they passed, Katrina hadn't seen the weird one that possessed the ability to split itself in half. She considered the mechanics involved and knew that the designer had to be very brilliant to come up with that idea in the short time they had been allotted to build the car. She wished that she could get a better look at it. At least she would be able to see it in Ohio.

Dr. Jenkins had been working on his One Tree engine design for over thirty years. So it made sense that their team had been able to pull off this miracle in such a short time frame.

A light came on the video screen. It was a warning light to tell them that the fan for their battery was dead. Not good she thought. Luckily it had been positioned just behind her seat and they had brought a spare, the only contingency that had happened according to plan so far.

Katrina unfastened her safety belt and turned so that she was on her knees facing backwards.

"What are you doing?" Richard asked.

"The fan for the battery died. I have to replace it."

"It's our first day and it died?" Richard questioned.

"The team couldn't find a good heavy duty model that ran on low power. It's a motor thing. The stronger the required speed, the more power you need to run it. So they decided on a small one but packed some replacements for us to swap out when they die."

Richard watched Katrina's butt wiggle as she worked. Katrina noticed his head turning from the road to her butt and back again and figured out what he was doing. "Are you staring at my butt for some reason?"

"Well honestly, it's kinda cute, and you can't hit me when you're in that position."

Katrina used her hand to slap the backside of his head. "I can still reach you. And if you touch me, the next time I hit you it will be with a screw driver in my hand. We'll see how far it penetrates your skull."

Richard turned to face the road again. "You're no fun."

"You'll be less fun with a screwdriver sticking out of the back of your head," Katrina returned. She quickly changed the subject. "I don't know about you but I'm starving and I have to pee. It's after two-thirty now and I'm thinking that we should break our GPS route to pull over for a few minutes. We have a significant lead and we still have no brakes. If we follow our route we will end up going through the middle of a city."

Katrina pulled herself back from the uncomfortable position and sat properly in her seat. She put her seatbelt back on and continued. "And we can't risk getting into an accident." She was still holding a screwdriver in one hand and it waved around dangerously as she spoke.

Richard took the tool carefully from his passenger before engaging in the conversation. He tossed into the backseat. "That's a little safer. What about Circleville Ohio?"

"We can stop before that. Look how far behind everyone is. And I'll need to go to the bathroom again after I suck down a thirty-two ounce Gatorade. I'm so thirsty."

"I'm game. My stomach is growling pretty badly at the moment too." Richard said.

Katrina's fingers started typing on the dashboard computer. The status feed was replaced with a map which highlighted their route towards Circleville.

"If we get off in Milford, we can head down 11 for a while before jumping back on the highway. There will be some places where we will have to stop at red lights and stuff but we'll be avoiding any major cities."

Richard nodded in agreement. "With the emergency break I'll be fine."

"Alright, the exit is in the next few miles." Katrina said.

~~~

The phone rang on Jenkins' desk. He had been waiting on the edge of his seat for Appleton's call, hoping that the maroon Explorer hadn't shown up on his video.

When it finally did ring, the pit in his stomach sank further into his gut. His first impression had been that the Ford would be seen in the video, and when Appleton spoke he confirmed it.

"It showed up twice." Appleton said. "Once when we were all here working and once before we closed up shop. The second time they never got out. The guys just sat in the truck and watched the interns walk around. They did leave before the lot was empty. Not sure what that means though."

"It means," Jenkins said "that they were confident that everyone was going to leave before they needed to do whatever it was that they had planned to do. Did you get a good look at the guys' faces on the video?"

"No. The angle wasn't very good. I can call the FBI and have them look..."

Jenkins interrupted his friend. "No. We still have to protect our people. Remember that this is still an unsanctioned race. The FBI will arrest everyone involved, including you for your participation."

Silence followed.

Jenkins broke the uncomfortable moment. "Listen, I made some investments early on to protect our team but I need someone to jump in and take my place to spearhead the effort. I need to go out and follow my car around the country to make sure it runs properly. It's the least I can do. I got my passenger into this and I have to try to keep her safe. But I can't manage both at the same time. I need someone who has been on the inside to take care of my... contingency plan."

Appleton considered the invitation. "I'll do it for you, but I have to know what it is first. I'm not going in blind."

Jenkins smiled. He felt a little better about Katrina's future now. "Listen I can't tell you over the phone or in an e-mail. We need to speak in person. Can you come out to Circleville, Ohio tonight? I know it's far for a meeting but I'll spring for dinner at the very least."

"Isn't that where all the racecars are supposed to meet up for the night?" Appleton asked.

"Yeah. Our car needs quite a bit of work before tomorrow's start time. I have to be on hand to make sure everything is perfect."

Appleton sighed audibly. "You know we go way back, back far enough to remember our college days, and I wouldn't take this on if it wasn't you asking, because I really trust you. If you need my help this badly I'll be there. Where am I supposed to go?"

"The Harper Motor Court, and thanks." Jenkins said with a smile.

"You'll owe me after this."

"No problem. I'll see you there at eight." Jenkins said with finality and hung up.

~~~

A phone rang on a ratty wooden desk. There were several pieces of paper littering the top. Some of them had water stains, or perhaps it was coffee. The person who picked up the receiver pulled one of the papers close to him and listened as he searched a drawer for a pen. The man at the desk had a plump look and a large nose that appeared to have been broken several times in the past. He had short hair that had been cut recently and not well. His eyes were beady and as dark as spots of black ink. His shirt was not quite big enough, causing it to bulge in places as he sat. There were others in the room but his back was to them. He wrote several notes across the printed information that had already filled the piece of paper he had chosen at random.

As he hung up the phone he turned to face the rest of the room where four men and one woman sat waiting. When he spoke his voice squeaked like a young girl's.

"That was our contact. It would seem that our hammer has failed. We now have to consider a more high-tech option to fix our little problem."

Silvia Thruwell sat nervously in the corner. She had no idea what the hammer part meant but she was confident about what the high-tech part was.

"Our employer has given us the green light to move forward on this. Tell me what you need Miss

Thruwell so we can set you up to work. Are you sure you can do this to your former classmate?"

Silvia smiled. "I would love to get Katrina back for getting one up on me. I'm the one who came up with most of the ideas for our project and she got all the credit. It's time for me to teach her a lesson."

"Good, as long as you're up for the job." The plump man turned to the group of men. "You two, get a list of what she needs and you two set up a space for her to work." He turned to Silvia and added. "You need to be up and running by tomorrow morning."

"But boss," one of the men asked. "How are we going to set up internet overnight? We can't get the cable company here that fast."

"I set up this facility weeks ahead of our arrival. Miss Thruwell here will make sure that the final connections are established once all the equipment is here."

Silvia fidgeted in her seat She had something to say and wondered when the time would be right. She imagined that now would be her only chance and wondered if she could pluck up the courage to actually do it.

When the boss finished speaking she raised her hand.

He laughed at her. "You are not in school any longer young lady. Speak your mind."

Silvia was really nervous now. She began to speak but stammered instead. "I just wanted to know... when I will get paid?"

"You get paid when the job is done, not a minute sooner. That's how our business is done. You want your money? Finish what you promised as fast as possible. Now get to work."

Silvia walked out of the office while the boss turned back to his desk and began making a barrage of phone calls. Her heart was pounding.

She crossed an enormous, empty, work space and walked towards the back wall. The whole wall was full of close set windows. The view outside was of an alley across from which there was another large building. From the furthest window she could make out Lake Michigan if she looked at an extreme angle. If she hadn't been scared half to death she might have appreciated the view more.

Silvia thought that the building must have been a factory of some kind in the past. Not that it mattered at the moment, of course. She had a job to do and she had to survive the process so she could get paid. She had a lot of student loans and the money from this project could go a long way. She took another moment to look at the view before she started making out her list of supplies.

Chapter 11

The MIT car pulled out of a Sunoco station. The entire cab of the car had been filled with junk food and Gatorade. "Can you drive and eat pizza at the same time?" Katrina asked through a mouth full of her own slice.

"Sure, it's an automatic." Richard said. Preparing to be hit, he moved his shoulder in towards the steering wheel. Katrina tried to hit him but missed.

"Smartening up I see." Katrina said. "It's like intentionally doing something wrong and then putting yourself in a time-out afterwards. I did that a few times when I was a kid."

They both smiled for the first time since they met. Katrina noticed but was sure that Richard did not.

The stop at the Willow Hill Sunoco had been refreshing. The race felt like a race again in their minds and the part where Katrina had used her weapon to kill someone had slipped away for a moment.

After Willow Hill, they both felt better. The race stayed true to what the race was designed to be, a test for the technology.

Too much junk food may have ruined their appetite for dinner later. But that didn't matter. The ride had been safe since... well... since, she had killed two people. And there it was, Katrina's emotions suddenly fell into a spiraling crash course of dismay and self-loathing. Tears started to flow down her cheeks.

"What's wrong?" Richard asked, when he finally noticed that she had begun to cry.

"You wouldn't understand."

"What wouldn't I understand? I'm guessing that saving our lives is the problem? Honestly, I think you did the right thing. If I had known how to run that thing, I would have used it. And I wouldn't have felt bad about it either."

Katrina frowned. "You wouldn't feel bad about killing someone?"

"You don't know that you killed anyone. You turned its power to people who were trying to kill us. You showed them that we have the power to defend ourselves. When they didn't back down they forced you to use that power. They lost control of their car during the process. You don't know if they died in the crash. I've seen horrific crashes before where the driver got out and walked away without a scratch." Richard said.

"But I saw the driver's face burn." Katrina returned. "It kind of melted."

Richard put a hand on Katrina's knee to strengthen his message and show his softer side. "Listen, you can feel bad for a year about what we had to do. But what if we find out that they were arrested and put in jail for running that other car off the road? You might have hurt that driver but mourning their deaths without knowing what really happened seems like a waste of time."

Katrina nodded. She understood what he was trying to say but she still felt bad about what she had been forced to do. At least Richard's view made a little sense. She should get all the facts before she spent too much time grieving. She wiped away her tears. Maybe Richard wasn't so shallow after all.

Katrina decided to do some work to try to distract the pit in her stomach. She changed the computer screen on the dashboard to show a map for a few minutes before changing back to watching the vehicle statistics. She could see that they only had a little less than four hours left until they arrived in Circleville, Ohio and she needed to make sure that they had enough power to get there. Many minutes went by as she investigated the health of their systems.

She also needed to call in soon and preorder the work that would need to be performed on the car overnight. In the back of her mind she thought that the decision to not make the car internet capable had been a mistake. Having to call in the work she needed seemed like a waste of time. Their car was so advanced that, with an internet connection, one of the team members could have watched not only what the car was doing performance-wise, they would also have been able to diagnose any problems and makes changes remotely that would have been beneficial to its operation.

For that matter, the team could have disabled the speed governor when she had not been able to during that crazy few moments when they thought that they were going to die at the hands of the Explorer. Although, having internet capability brought with it a whole other type of vulnerability as well.

While Katrina considered benefits and liabilities of internet connections, a new light came on. It was the image of a heat gage on an old steam pipe was now lit, next to the check transmission's light that had been on all day. This image brought Katrina back to the real world quickly.

"We have a new problem." Katrina said as she typed madly trying to get more information. "The transmission is beginning to overheat."

"We have a CVT. It can't overheat." Richard stated plainly.

"Yes it can. The reason it can is that our power plant is oversized compared to what the transmission is actually rated for. This whole car was designed on a Cadillac CTS frame. The reason you were able to pull off all the fancy driving when the Explorer was trying to kill us was because this chassis is really a kind of racecar. We took all the steering components along with the suspension to make this vehicle as close to a racecar as possible without going out and buying one. All of the components are designed to go a hundred and sixty MPH and more. Our engine is crazy powerful, but because we knew about the speed limitations for the race the CVT made sense at the time."

"So what you're saying is that everything is race ready except for the tranny?" Richards asked with confusion. "Great. We're going to overheat before we get to the end of this crazy day?"

Katrina pondered a moment. "The last leg takes us through a small town but if I plot us a different route through back roads, we can come up to the hotel we're staying at with minimal stress to the transmission. Try to keep the transmission in the same range as much as possible."

"But we'll lose all of the time we made up on the highway."

"If we don't arrive at all we're out. For today I don't think it will matter if we finish first or last. We just need to finish."

Richard made a "Hmmp" kind of sound and slunk into his seat mumbling, "Racecar without a manual transmission, what a stupid idea."

Katrina pointed to the video monitor which now showed a new set of directions across a map of the area. "Follow this. I need to make a phone call."

~~~

Frodes stood at the entrance to the Harper Motor Court. Many vehicles from the race had already arrived.

He didn't count how many had driven in but he was certain that it was far fewer than what had been gathered at the church parking area that morning. He had no idea how long it was going to take for their car to show up, but he knew that the longer it took his car to arrive the less time he would have to do their repairs. He was starting to worry.

The rest of the team all stood around the parking area. There were many high powered lights to illuminate their work place. Boxes of all sizes were stacked neatly, waiting to be ripped open and their contents removed and installed. Everyone on the team had planned to pull an all-nighter and several cases of Monster energy drinks were stacked next to their boxes of supplies.

At the center of the team stood a portable lift that was painted blue and yellow and was ready to be used. Clearly this team was dedicated to getting their car ready for the next race day.

There were other teams working in other areas of the parking lot. The other racecars had small groups of people trying to perform more work than they had been prepared for. There was a lot of shouting amongst the other groups who were obviously worried about the amount of time in which they could make their repairs.

Camera crews buzzed around like black flies. A red Toyota Corolla drove in and parked in a space far not far from where the MIT team had positioned themselves. Frodes looked at it briefly before resuming his impatient search for their car.

Marcus Appleton got out and gazed in amazement at the MIT team's preparations. He was impressed. Dr. Jenkins had also noticed his arrival and walked up and tapped him on the shoulder.

"Goofy!" Appleton said and he shook Jenkins' hand.

"Daffy. Welcome to the pit stop." Jenkins said with less enthusiasm. "Uh, by the way we probably shouldn't use our old college nicknames in front of the team. All business tonight, okay?"

"Where's the restaurant? I'm starving. I used the company jet to get here but I'm not important enough to get food served." Appleton turned, looking around to see what restaurants were nearby.

"If you don't mind, I'd like to wait for our car to come in before we head over. It's my baby you know. I have a stash of granola bars if you want one to hold you over. The whole team is high on Monster drinks and granola bars to get through the night."

Appleton hesitated before he said "Okay."

As Jenkins handed one over the MIT car finally drove in. Frodes was running back to the worksite behind the racecar. Richard and Katrina both stepped out. The team cheered their arrival and swarmed around Katrina to pat her on the back, disregarding Richard completely.

Richard walked up to Jenkins and took his hand and shook it. "Sir, this is the most fantastic car I've ever seen. But a racecar needs a manual tranny."

Katrina hit him from behind. It was so common an event that he barely winced over it. Richard didn't wait for Dr. Jenkins response he instead mingled with the team that had converged on the car as it was rolled onto the lift. He wanted to talk to them about things he wanted to have fixed.

Jenkins put a hand on Katrina's shoulder. "How are you? I'm so sorry I put you in that seat. I had no idea how rough the race would get and I'm still trying to find out who was in that Explorer."

"You saw that?" Katrina asked looking horrified, afraid of what would happen to her for using the weapon on someone's face.

Jenkins pulled Katrina in for a hug like a father. "I'm so sorry."

Katrina started to cry. "I didn't want to use the weapon on them but they were trying to kill us and, and..."

"It's alright. You did what you thought was right. It was the only way for you to survive. No one will think any less of you."

"What happened to the Explorer? Did those guys... are they dead?" Katrina asked.

"We don't know. I checked with the local police and there was no accident reported. I have a feeling the race's cleanup crew took care of that too." Jenkins said as he eyed Appleton. "Go and get something to eat and take a shower. We have your street clothes ready for you in your room."

"My street clothes? How?" Katrina asked mystified.

"It was Dillon's idea. He wanted you to be more comfortable." Jenkins said.

A dawning came over Katrina. She stood still silently pondering on the very idea of Dillon. Jenkins pushed her towards the hotel. "Go on, the night is short and you need to get some rest. Someone will wake you at five-thirty."

Appleton watched Katrina walk off. "You have a pretty big soft spot for that one."

"Of course I do. Look at what I did to her. I forced her to be on the weapons team, then I made sure she was the one chosen to be with Bertrand's son. Right now I feel quite like a bastard. After what I saw them go through earlier, and what they had to do today, I feel just as bad as Katrina does. I need to find a way to keep her safe." He raised a finger in the air. "A word with my project manager and then we'll talk about my protection protocols over dinner."

Marcus Appleton sat at a '99' restaurant eating popcorn while he waited for their food. He was hungry. His friend was still explaining what he wanted him to do.

"Tomorrow morning I have a young genius arriving in Detroit. He will set up an internet monitoring platform. I want you two to dig and find out everything you can about the people on the list I'm going to hand you after dinner. I want to figure out where all the video goes from the cameras and who profits from all of this. I want you to become an information collector." Jenkins said.

"I need to figure out where the money goes. Someone is paying out big money to ensure a certain car wins. You saw what these people are capable of. In the video link I watched the explorer also ran another racecar into the guardrail. I have no idea what happened to that team. It looked pretty bad." Jenkins put a hand through his thinning hair.

"I know of your work in internet protocol design. If you and Kalby can work together maybe we can root out some of the insanity and keep my team safe. The list is the names of all of the people and companies that we know are involved with this race. Grant Phyindress, owner of the company Driven Motor Innovators, is at the top of the list. He set up and organized the entire race."

Dinner finally arrived and was served by a different waitress than the one who had taken their order. Appleton got the turkey tips he had ordered and Jenkins his burger and fries. Appleton wasted no time in cutting his meat.

When the meat touched Appleton's lips Jenkins asked his question. "Here's what I really want to know. How did an internet protocol designer end up designing a car for this race?"

"We all have our pet projects. I've been following your One Tree project for as long as you've been publishing. Mine is a special software package that operates electric motors. I know it sounds weird but my software makes motors run so efficiently that they can run on a battery for more than four times longer than a standard electrical set up. So I got roped into making this car on the pretext that my software..." Appleton paused to take another bite. "Can make an electric car run longer than anyone else's. Everyone associated with this project knows that the electric motor is the wave of the future in automobiles. It made sense to throw my hat into the ring since everyone that entered will go that route..."

Jenkins had a big mouth full of french fries when he asked, "How did you generate power? I mean... a battery wouldn't be able to last all day powering a racecar would it?"

"We went with the multi-generation route. All the fuselage skins made power, so that was a no brainer, we used a braking regenerative power, and we separated water to produce hydrogen and filled a power cell. We used the first two to power the water separator and collect the hydrogen. The hydrogen part made the bulk of our power. Our biggest obstacle would have been the desert stretch of the race. But we figured if we collected enough power and made the best use of my software there would be no problem to cross the desert to the finish line. Honestly, if I had any idea how your One Tree thing worked I would have asked if I could use it. Do you realize that with your machine and my software, we could have scaled down your half and made the car lighter, and still produced all the power the racecar required?"

Jenkins nodded. His mouth was full of burger but he managed another question. "Does anyone else know about your software? Other than you and me?"

"Yeah, NASA wants it." Appleton said.

Jenkins made a weird face. "Why NASA? You can't fly a plane or a spaceship with an electric motor."

"No, but it would be really useful to power servos for satellites, and a moon buggy."

Jenkins nodded approvingly.

~~~

Katrina was changing out of her racing uniform. When she had only underwear on there was a quick rap at her door. Before she could even say "I'll be there in a minute" the door flew open with Richard rushing in. He closed the door right behind him.

She screamed. "What are you doing here? Get out, I'm not dressed." Quickly she pulled her dirty uniform back up to cover herself.

Richard laughed. "Well I'm not dressed either."

Katrina looked him over and saw that he only had a towel on. There was no denying it; Richard was a very good looking man. His wavy black hair and dark eyes drew her in just as it had when she had first met him that morning. But now she knew better. He was a shallow, uneducated, pain in the ass that used women and tossed them aside when he was done.

"Get out." She said again.

"Oh, you're no fun."

"Get out or I will damage what you have under that towel and finish the race alone." Katrina scowled.

Richard pulled off his towel and tossed it on the bed. "There, no more towel to worry about."

Katrina stood in place, shocked by what he had just done. He was better looking than all of her other boyfriends put together. But he was such an idiot. She snapped out of her shocked reverie and ran at him. She started beating him hard. A moment later he was standing outside her motel room door, naked.

The commotion caused many interns to turn to and see what was going on only to find Richard standing there naked. He waved before turning towards his room mumbling under his breath. All the interns who could see Richard laughed at him, the women especially. The camera men ran in to get a better view as he hurried three rooms down and disappeared into his room.

Katrina stepped out minutes later in her street clothes and went over to her team to hand her uniform in to be cleaned. She took a Monster energy drink and a granola bar.

Dillon approached. "What happened in your room?"

Katrina laughed. "That ass. He actually thought we were going to hook up."

Dillon looked shocked. "Are you okay?" Dillon's face was so full of concern that Katrina could see him building up his courage enough to knock on Richard's door to have words.

"Of course." Katrina laughed again. "I pushed him out my door. Did you see him naked outside my room?"

Dillon nodded and smiled weakly.

"Does anyone know if there is a Subway nearby or someplace else I can grab a sandwich?" Katrina asked the crowd around the car. Frodes told her she only had to go a block down on the left. Katrina turned on her heel and went for a walk. Frodes turned back towards the new transmission install.

Chapter 12

At five-thirty in the morning a knock came on Katrina's door. She screamed out "If that's you Richard, I'm going to beat you to within an inch of your life!"

"It's Frodes. I have your uniform. It's time to get up."

A moment later Katrina opened the door a crack and stuck her head out cautiously. The sunlight made her raise a hand to cover her face. Her hair stuck out at odd angles and was full of static. "Are you kidding? It can't be time yet."

"Here's your uniform. You should get ready as soon as possible so I can go over the changes we made before you have to go." Frodes said. His eyes were at half-mast. He looked very tired and had a grease stain over his right eyebrow.

A few minutes later Katrina emerged, dressed in her uniform and with her hair in a damp ponytail. Dillon met her with an energy drink in hand. They walked over to the racecar where it sat off the lift, all clean and shiny. The burn holes had been filled with exacting precision. Katrina couldn't even tell where they had been anymore.

Richard walked up a second later and ran his right hand down the hood as if he were 007. "Did you install that ejection seat I ordered for the passenger side in case she gets too unruly?"

Frodes smiled but said, "No, I installed it under the driver's seat in case your hands get too close to Katrina."

A lot of laughter emanated from the rest of the team, deflating Richard's ego a bit.

Dr. Jenkins arrived followed by Appleton, who stayed at the back of the crowd to listen. Jenkins walked to the center of the group to get everyone's attention.

"Listen up," he started. He was speaking to the team but made eye contact with Katrina. "I only have a few minutes before the racecars will start to line up. Frodes and the team went the extra mile last night not only to fix all the items that had been broken, but have also to make adjustments to other components that will aid you in the race. I'll let Frodes fill you in on that in a moment. This race covers five days and four nights. Last night was night number one. The team is only allowed to make repairs to the car on the first two nights, so it's important that we make good notes about what needs to be repaired tonight and what feels like it may require future repairs. We want to make sure that you have all the parts you need while on the road. Do you understand?"

Richard and Katrina both nodded.

Jenkins continued, "Now I mentioned that tonight is the last night repairs can be made, the next night, you have a required overnight stay at a motel that is already loaded in the mapping system but the team will not be there to make any repairs. On the last night of the race, things are different. There is no requirement that you stop to sleep. You can drive straight through to the finish loop in the desert."

Richard raised a hand into the air. "How exactly do we get the car in the air to get through the loop?"

Jenkins brought up his right hand and moved it towards his team leader, nodding to indicate that Frodes should reveal that information.

Frodes stepped forward and cleared his throat. "Last night we inserted the method of raising the car high enough to get up on the platform where the finish loop is located. There are ramps hidden in the frame members. You remove them through an opening at the rear of the frame and slide them out. There is a lip on one end that sits on the platform. You drive up the ramps and through the ring, simple basic technology. But don't lose them or you'll never get the car high enough to finish. A lot of the other cars now have their ramps as well. If you look around, you'll find them on the roof of their respective cars."

Richard and Katrina both turned to look at the other cars on the lot. Some indeed had their ramps strapped on top of the cars. To Katrina it only meant fewer target areas where her weapon could be utilized. But it probably also meant that other's weapons would be restricted and she was once again impressed with her team's planning. Then Katrina noticed how few cars had made it to this point. There had been a lot more racecars in the parking lot yesterday when they had started in Massachusetts.

Richard raised his hand again. "Why did you put in the ramps last night instead of waiting another day, won't they just add weight?

Dillon answered the question this time "We wanted you to get a full day of driving in with the ramps off the car, in case there were any issues that we need to be fixed last tonight. It looks like most of the other teams had the same idea."

Jenkins spoke up to draw everyone's attention back to him. "I want Frodes to talk about the changes that have been made to the car, and then I need a word with Katrina." Jenkins pointed his finger at Frodes.

"Okay. There is a new transmission, and all of the code issues are gone. We put in new brake lines and a shield so we won't have brake problems again. We refilled all the burn holes with a special compound that's more similar to the composition of the original shell, and we upgraded your processor so you can do more things at once."

Katrina said "Ooooh."

Richard looked at her like she was crazy. "The only thing you're interested in is the new processor?"

Frodes answered for her. "The processor enabled us put in a voice command option in case you can't use your hands to change computer options. After what we saw yesterday we thought that voice activated commands might help you. But that's not all. We also used a beefier transmission so it won't overheat, and we put on a better set of heavy duty tires.

Richard heard only 'transmission'. "Talk to me about that tranny." He said excitedly.

Frodes wiped a sweat bead off his forehead before answering. "We took out the CVT and put in the OEM for this car."

"Another automatic?" Richard grumbled, downtrodden.

"No, actually in this model the manual transmission was OEM." Frodes corrected him.

Richard jumped for joy, throwing his fist in the air. He turned to Katrina. "Now you'll see some real driving."

Jenkins cut off his celebration. "Okay, that's enough bragging. Our day is all about having this equipment shipped to your next location and letting the team get some sleep. I know they've earned it. I hope you appreciate all the work they did for you last night."

Katrina wasted no time and gave Frodes a hug. Dillon was next in line and he got his. Quickly a line was beginning to form but Jenkins pulled her away.

"We have no time for this, Katrina, I need to talk to you."

Katrina hugged him too. Jenkins blushed. He didn't usually get attached to the students that came and went, but considering the circumstances, and his role in placing her in the middle of them, he couldn't help but have become a little emotionally involved.

"Listen," he began, as they walked away from the group, "I saw the video of everything that happened yesterday. You need to understand that there are people out there that don't want you to see the finish loop. I need you to be on your guard."

Katrina nodded. "I'll try my best."

Jenkins shook his head. "I have the rest of the team trying their best. I want you to succeed, I need you to succeed."

"I have Richard. He's a great driver..."

"I'm worried that he may be part of the problem. He's the investor's son. There may be other agendas coming in to play here that we know nothing about. Richard may not even know it himself but he still may be part of the problem. Rich people play games, and we regular people are only pawns in those schemes. I'm trying to get the upper hand here but it will take some time. Stay focused." Jenkins said.

Katrina nodded in understanding. A bullhorn keying up brought everyone back towards a central point in the parking lot. Grant Phyindress stood tall in his thousand dollar suit and wing tip shoes. His black hair was slicked back and he had a smile that suggested that it was going to be a good day whether anyone else liked or not.

"First, I'd like to congratulate all of the racers that are here this morning. Your cars have passed the most vigorous of all tests, surviving the first day. Look at all of the work that the teams put in overnight to prepare for today. That is a testament to the commitment we each have in our investments." All eyes went towards the MIT group who clearly had the largest team in the parking lot.

"So… to give a tally of where everyone is, let's start with the numbers. I know all the engineers out there will like that. Initially we had thirty teams. Three cars never made it to completion, leaving twenty seven cars at the starting gate. Yesterday morning, after the starting flag was dropped, an unfortunate event occurred. A jam up at the exit created the perfect opportunity to draw weapons. It felt like the shoot-out at the OK Corral." Grant chuckled. "One car caught fire, three received burnout, and one more was too damaged to race before they ever saw the street, bringing down our number to twenty-one. Throughout the course of the day, two more were excluded from our ranks, one from burnout and one from a traffic accident."

The MIT team members all looked around at each other realizing that the car in the accident that had just been mentioned was one that they had witnessed being run down by the maroon Ford Explorer. Katrina noticed that that the speaker didn't mention if there were any injuries to the driver or passenger involved in the 'accident'. His cavalier attitude showcased his lack of empathy towards the victims. Katrina and Professor Jenkins looked hard at each other.

Phyindress continued. "This morning we count among us nineteen participants. Take a good look around drivers. Some of you will not be with us tomorrow morning."

All the drivers looked around. Most of them were easy to pick out among the teams. Some were obviously students that had been chosen to drive. When Katrina's eyes found the driver for the split car team they widened is surprise. He looked like gang member even in his racing uniform. Tattoos littered his neck, his face was scarred, and his long black hair had been covered in a red and black bandana while his ponytail stuck out of the back. How had she not noticed him yesterday? His passenger, or second driver in their case, exhibited many similar attributes although he had a crew cut, was blond, and stood a head shorter.

The racecar team that drove the vehicle that looked like a dune buggy had positioned itself right next to the split car's team. Their driver appeared to be more clean-cut, with sun bleached dirty blond hair like that of a surfer. When he turned his head Katrina could see a heavily pockmarked visage.

The car beyond the dune buggy was built very low to the ground, more like a real racecar, and their driver was a woman. Katrina was impressed, wondering why she hadn't at least noticed the female driver at the starting line yesterday. But at the time she had been more interested in the weapon systems designs than the drivers.

Grant Phyindress began speaking again but a thought struck Katrina. He had said 'Some of you will not be here tomorrow'. Had Phyindress just said that some of the racers would be dead? No, no. He meant that other racecars will have been disqualified, right? That must be what he meant. Katrina's heart was hammering.

Katrina shook off her ominous feeling as Grant Phyindress pressed on. "Remember what's ahead. Two more required night's stays, only one of which where more work is allowed to be done to your vehicle. The night after that, however, there are no requirements. It's straight to the finish loop and to victory. Any team that survives that long will go down in history."

Survives that long? Katrina thought. Clearly the incident yesterday had left an indelible mark on her psyche. She was starting to think the worst of every word Phyindress said. Richard's cell phone rang, interrupting her thoughts. Grant Phyindress was still speaking but Katrina focused all of her listening skills on Richard's call.

"Father, what a surprise. You never call me." Richard's face screwed up in concentration, trying to listen to his father over the loud bullhorn speech.

"Yes, the incident could have been horrible."

Phyindress' voice boomed out. "And think of what history will remember you as..."

"You... you really mean that? You want me to look after myself? That's a first." Richard's voice went from surprise to anger in flash. "Since when do you care what happens to me? Are you drunk this early in the morning? Where's mother?"

Jenkins and Appleton both looked at each other with concern and shared comprehension. Appleton turned on his heel and left, there was work to be done.

Katrina watched Dr. Jenkins' friend turn and leave. She wondered what that was all about.

At the same moment Richard shouted into his phone, "You don't care about me, you're just worried about the stupid car!" He pulled the phone away from his ear and threw it across the parking lot away from the crowd as hard as he could.

~~~

In a mostly dark room Silvia Thruwell sat in front of a long table filled with many computer screens and three keyboards. It seemed odd that there were more screens than keyboards but the maniacal look on her face resembled that of the scientist who had brought Frankenstein to life.

Several men stood behind her, each breathing hard, as though they had carried each piece of this conglomeration of hardware ten miles uphill. One of them managed to say a few words before he had to pull in more breath. "The Boss will be here in ten minutes or so. You better get to work. He doesn't like broken promises."

"He certainly doesn't." Mac Killington stepped out of the shadows of the large room. The man filled the room with his ego. The old mill that they had chosen to set up shop in had massive rooms with light that only stretched so far and had created a large shadowy area from which he had been observing them unseen. He had an unlit cigarette in his hand. He placed in his lips and withdrew a lighter. In a well-practiced move, he tilted his head as he lit the lighter and took a drag all at the same time. It took perhaps less than a second before he was blowing the putrid smoke out into the room through his crooked nose. "How long do you think it will take to see some results?"

Silvia used her hand to move the air around, swirling it under the bright lights, hoping to clear the smoke away before she took a breath. Killington waited patiently for his answer as he took another drag and refilled the space between them.

Silvia ended up giving a small cough before she answered. "I have to wait about eight hours to start up all the equipment. It was transferred here in the cars upside down."

Killington laughed. "Is this from the same book of fallacies that states that you must wait an hour to swim after you eat? Start up the equipment. I expect to start to see results in an hour."

"Uh." Silvia said interrupting Killington's attempted retreat. "Even if I do a cold start now, it will take me hours to write enough code to break in..."

Killington put on a smile. "Then you have two hours. You wanted to know when you would get paid? We only pay out after a lot of hard work. Do some, and stop whining about not having enough time. Do some, and I'll let you live long enough to do this again tomorrow. Do some, and I'll pay you what you're worth."

Killington dropped his cigarette butt onto the wooden floor and left without bothering to crush it. Silvia wondered for a moment about what she had gotten herself into, all out of her desire for revenge.

Silvia turned on the power strip and began to power up her creation, hoping that she could type fast enough to satisfy her new boss.

~~~

The bullhorn blared. "Drivers! Take your positions!"

Katrina and Richard climbed into their car through its open windows. None of the cars actually had doors. It helped maintain the electrical continuity throughout the entire fuselage. The cars began to line up as they were instructed.

Katrina remembered the mess at the parking lot entrance the previous day. When the jam had occurred all of the racecars had pulled out their weapons. This morning she would be ready and have her weapon already active. Unfortunately every other team had the same thought. All of the weapons were powering up as the clock counted down to the starting time.

At the starting line Grant Phyindress stood next to a pretty girl in tight clothes that was easily three decades his junior. She was blond with skin tight spandex that allowed her to show lots of cleavage, belly, and leg. He handed her the green flag with a big smile before checking his stop-watch. When the moment finally presented itself, he waved his hand up and down. The young girl next to him used the green flag to further accentuate his hand motions. The race had officially begun. Cameramen from all of the teams were positioned to catch the fight or flight of all the cars as they maneuvered themselves to the hotel parking lot's exit.

Richard revved the engine a couple of times before engaging the clutch. The car moved so seamlessly it felt like an automatic. Katrina noticed Richard's skill but said nothing as she kept watch over all of the cars. Her fear of weapons being drawn was first and foremost on her mind.

Clearly the expectation of another log jam, as the racecars all jockeyed to find their way out, filled everyone's mind. After the flag was waved, the pretty girl followed Phyindress as he hurried to a safer vantage point. Camera lenses panned the parking lot to catch any unusually aggressive maneuvers.

The laser platform on top of the MIT car moved around as Katrina moved her head. Its arm rotated exactly in sync with the headset that she was wearing. The other cars gave their car plenty of room, clearly intimidated by their weapon's range. It didn't hurt that by now all of the other drivers had seen the internet broadcast that had shown in great detail how that weapon had been used.

As the contingent of racecars moved towards the parking lot exit the closest ones were able to squeak out fairly quickly including the split car and the dune buggy looking car.

The MIT car had come in last the night before but because of the other drivers' fear of its formidable weapon they had easily moved up in the line more than twelve places and exited the hotel parking lot unchallenged. After the MIT car had left the lot, to many dropped jaw expressions, the remaining cars had lined up and left without incident. Those who had come for the show left feeling cheated.

Jenkins shouted to his group. "Okay! Let's pack this up! Our transportation will be here in less than a half an hour."

Not three minutes later a tractor trailer and a tour bus drove into the lot. "Once the truck is packed we'll have breakfast on the bus. I expect you all to sleep until we get to our next destination. Time is ticking people. Let's go!"

Chapter 13

"Wow! Did you see that? Almost everyone moved aside to let us go by." Katrina marveled as she took off her head set.

"Yeah, but I think it was for all the wrong reasons." Richard stated as he stared at the head set, glad that he was on this team and not one of the others. "Can you pull up the GPS of our route? I think we need a back-up plan."

Katrina touched the button on the dashboard so that the screen and keyboard would be available. She typed in the command for the map and seconds later it was on the screen.

"What's up?" Katrina asked.

"This is what's up." Richard used his finger to point to the town coming up next. "We are going to enter rush hour traffic here. We're all going to be stuck in traffic together."

Katrina got Richard's meaning quickly. "You think we should cut around and try to miss the downtown area?" she asked.

"Absolutely," he replied. "Anything that keeps us away from the other drivers as much as possible."

She stared at him for a moment before turning back to the screen. The memory of his phone call from his dad came back into her mind and she decided to ask about it. "So what happened with your father?"

"It's nothing." Richard said curtly. His tone showed his displeasure.

"I heard you say you were in bad accident in your first race?" Katrina prodded.

"Yeah, I learned a lot of lessons that day, hard ones. You really never know your family until..."

A sleek looking racecar passed them as if they had been standing still. The speed limit was forty-five and the car that had passed them must have been going eighty. Richard downshifted to give pursuit but Katrina placed a hand on his arm.

"We don't want a ticket, plus they're going to get stuck in traffic, remember? We'll catch up another way."

Richard made a "hump" sound and sped up a little just the same.

Katrina breathed a sigh of relief. She had a feeling that his anger could make him do something stupid. Then something else caught her eye. The split car had pulled over on the side of the road. Both drivers were out of the car, leaning against it. They looked completely at ease about the race and life itself, as if their cigarette break was much more important.

It seemed odd to Katrina, and to Richard too after she nudged him show him what she had seen. Shouldn't they have been racing toward their goal like all the other cars? Katrina and Richard both stared as they passed them.

"What was that all about?" Richard asked. He checked his rearview mirror to see if any other racecars were near them.

Sure enough there were three other cars coming up quick. They were all driving erratically, each trying to avoid the other's weapons. Hot on their heels were the chase trucks with cameramen hanging out of their windows to get a better angle.

Richard swore softly and accelerated.

"What are you doing? We can't get caught speeding." Katrina stated again.

"Check your six." Richard said.

Katrina looked over her shoulder. Shock and surprise filled her face. "Already?" Katrina shouted in disbelief, "And at this speed?"

Her stress level skyrocketed. She put on her head set once more and the arm segment of the weapon twisted towards the coming cars.

Richard glanced at the speedometer, they were already doing eighty. "You want me to lose them?" he asked.

Katrina checked the gage then looked toward the trio of cars coming up on them. "Wait until they are almost on us, then accelerate just enough to match the lead car as they approach. Make sure they end up on my side. It's time to use this weapon for what it was designed to do. Be prepared to launch us forward when I tell you."

Richard nodded.

Katrina turned her head to point the arm towards the coming cars. She had no fear of Richard's driving ability. After yesterday with the speed governor on, and half the breaks disabled, his ability to control the situation had gained her respect as a driver. As a person, that was another story, but as a driver she knew he could trust him to handle it.

~~~

Silvia typed furiously on one of her keyboards. She had sweat running down her forehead, onto her brow and into her eyes. She used the back of her hand to wipe it away. On the screens before her were images of many different kinds. One showed the code she was actually typing, long strings of code that ran past the top and bottom of the screen. The one next to that had two open internet windows, showing different websites dedicated to code writing. On the two screens to the extreme right, the broadcast of the race had already begun. The first screen showed nineteen picture-in-picture squares, one for each racecar, and the other had a single, full screen image of the MIT car's feed.

Silvia stopped for a moment to watch the MIT car have unfettered access to the parking lot exit on the large screen. All of the other cars had moved aside to allow them to pass. She stood and screamed at what she had just witnessed. "Mother fucker!" She knew they had come in last the previous night and now they were moving up the line all because of the weapon she had helped to design. It infuriated her that Katrina was once again reaping the rewards of her efforts.

The armed men who sat nearby on guard duty were startled by her outburst. They stopped the card game they were playing to see what had caused her anger. When nothing looked out of place they turned back to their game.

Silvia threw herself back in her seat, more determined than ever to extract some form of revenge. She began to type again with renewed resolve.

~~~

The three racecars were weaving in and out of the building traffic. Each seemed hell bent to use their weapon to disable the other. Of the three cars, one sat much higher than the other two. It appeared that they had chosen a four wheel drive chassis from a truck to get them through the desert sands at the end of the race. The other two were on normal two wheel drive systems that gave them a more normal clearance from the road and better aerodynamics.

The taller car had the advantage of looking down on the other two cars, each busy in the process of attempting to eliminate the other. One of the lower cars had two ramps strapped to its roof and a track system that ran around the entire car. It was comprised of two narrow gage tubes of galvanized steel. A small trolley of sorts that contained a laser bulb ran on the track system. It moved back and forth trying to match up with the other car but had been so far unable to stay in one position for the three seconds required to burn a deep enough hole to shut them down.

The other low racecar was also in the process of using their laser on their opponent but with a much cruder design that hung from their window precariously. Their weapon design may not have been great but they had obviously put a lot more focus on the car's steering capabilities. If the weapon required driver's side access, the entire steering mechanism slid over to the passenger side and the passenger became the driver. At that moment the original driver had become the passenger and he was using the portable weapon from the driver's window.

The taller vehicle was trying to use their weapon and had changed their speed to match the other two vehicles after coming up quickly behind them. The driver had relinquished the steering to his passenger so he could attempt to use their weapon by hanging out of his window. The passenger had to lean over and control the wheel from his side, unlike the elaborate mechanics of the other car.

The weapon of the taller vehicle was attached to a long tube with wires hanging out that powered the device, a very primitive design. Once their higher vehicle matched the speed of one of the lower racecars, it forced them to be in the center of a racecar sandwich.

The tall vehicle, which had their weapon hanging on the end of a PVC tube, pushed their laser head onto the skin of the other low slung entrant between the ramps. It came off the tube when the middle car slowed again to try to break contact. The tall car's driver fell back to allow room for the center car to maneuver, while the wires hanging between them and the tube were still sticking out of their open window.

Brilliant light flashed from the laser head, similar to the arcing from a welder's torch, as the weapon did its work. Immediately the occupants stopped their attack on the car to their left and attempted to reach the laser head to knock it off. The men in the higher car laughed at them. As promised, after three seconds, the center racecar's power died. It slowed dramatically. The taller racecar slowed to match their victim's speed until they were both stopped in the middle of the road.

Traffic was starting to back up in the lanes behind them as three lanes of traffic vied for the remaining open lane and a chorus of horns was evidence of their aggravation.

The driver of the still viable racecar leaned out of his window to pull his laser head back onto the tube and began to drive away. He smiled and waved at the two guys slumped back in the seats of the disabled car. Their expressions of utter humiliation spoke volumes.

The driver turned back out his window and shouted "See you losers!" He and his passenger laughed in jubilation of their success as they picked up speed. The weapons specialist turned around in time to witness the arrival of a box truck. In less than two minutes the dead racecar had been dragged into the back, occupants and all.

The third racecar had increased their speed as soon as they had realized that the car who had been their opponent was now too busy to bother them. Richard had allowed it to pass them as he had slowed enough to allow the taller racecar catch up. Its four wheel drive system was causing it to bounce slightly as it approached. Katrina turned her body around to watch the tall car catch up. The ominous arm on their roof rotated in equal measure.

The two men in the tall racecar were still celebrating their mastery of their weapon and their victory over the other car. In their celebratory mood they didn't notice the MIT car waiting for them where it had been partially hidden in front of a beige Buick Century.

Katrina didn't turn to face Richard when she said, "Get ready, remember, I need them on my side."

"No problem." Richard said. "We have plenty of power and brakes."

It was game on and they both looked completely focused. This was perhaps the most dangerous part of the race, interacting with another vehicle to disable it without crashing into it or into anybody else. Hearts hammered in their chests and their breathing was short and measured.

As the four-wheel drive racecar approached, Richard's fingers twitched on the steering wheel in anticipation. Katrina, however, remained as still as steel. She knew her head's movements would be reflected in the weapon above her in plain sight.

When the moment came to take action Richard closed his grip on the steering wheel. He cut into the far lane and accelerated away from the Buick then stomped on the breaks.

This got the other racecar's attention. The driver moved into the middle lane, the only unoccupied lane open to him. He didn't understand the brake lights but knew that the car could be trouble because they shared the same skin.

The driver pursed his lips and accelerated to try to get ahead of it quickly. His passenger noticed the weapon on the roof and pointed excitedly, swearing loudly enough to be heard by the traffic around them and slapping the driver's arm to make sure he knew of their predicament.

Katrina used her side mirror to watch the car's progression. When she felt that the other racecar had reached the point where the weapon could become active, she turned her head to face out the rear window and said. "Get ready to launch us forward!"

The driver knew they were in trouble when the arm turned towards them. In his mind the only way out was to speed past the most formidable weapon in the race. Speed would be their saving grace, or so they thought.

Katrina called as she aimed the weapon to an imaginary point behind them. "Almost there!"

Richard kept checking the rearview mirror. "If you wait too long you'll miss."

"Shut up! I know what I'm doing."

The other racecar was poised to overtake the still slowing MIT car. With sheer speed bolstering their confidence the driver smiled before he began to say to his passenger, "I think we're going to make it.."

Katrina shouted to Richard. "Now!"

Richard questioned the timing in his mind but stomped on the accelerator just the same. When the car shot forward Katrina fired the weapon. Its head traveled into the empty space before the other car.

Richard was sure that the laser head would pass in front of its windshield. To other driver, the image couldn't have been more horrifying. He could see the laser head traveling right at him and was afraid it might sail into his open window. He had no time to react, all that he could do was watch, horrified. Milliseconds passed as he watched the laser head pass by his open window. Relief washed over him. Then the laser stuck itself against the skin twelve inches behind the side window's frame.

The driver never even noticed that the MIT car had begun to pace their vehicle, its powerful engine had easily rocketed them to an equal speed. The driver tried to reach out his window and pull the laser head off but he couldn't turn his body that far. The driver shouted to his passenger to have him take the wheel.

Richard had to do some crazy maneuvering to avoid getting hit by the swerving car during their change of hands on the steering wheel. He decided to fall back a bit and give them a little more room. Other cars who were watching this unfold attempted to get by them, a few driving in the breakdown lane temporarily to try to avoid any possible crash.

"How far back can I go without running out of room on the spool of wire?" Richard shouted.

Katrina shouted back over the wind buffeting through her window without turning to face him. "You're almost at your limit now!"

A white unmarked box truck pulled up behind the MIT car, a cameraman hung out of the window. Their driver kept pace far enough away to stay out of the fray but still close enough to get good video.

Three seconds seemed to last forever as the racecar driver stretched to grab the laser head. He had pulled himself out of his window far enough to almost fall out as smoke poured profusely from the hole the laser was creating. Once the driver had actually touched the laser but the laser head was so hot that it had burned his hand. Pulling his hand away suddenly had made him lose his balance but the car had already begun to power down.

Richard had to veer wildly to not get side swiped by the slowing racecar and managed to pull away. Katrina activated the release. The spool of wire had suddenly became taut and the laser head popped off the disabled car. In an action similar to that of a fishing pole reeling in its line, the mechanical arm retracted the line very quickly until the laser head approached. When it sensed it was near the arm the line's pull slowed, and the laser head sagged from the lack of pressure against it. A much slower retraction rate reattached the head into its cradle. Katrina turned off the head-set but left it on her head. The arm rotated into its holding position and became still.

Katrina jumped up and down in her seat happier than she had been since the race had begun.

Richard patted her on the shoulder rapidly shouting, "You did it! That freaking thing is awesome!"

He checked his rearview mirror. A white box truck had stopped directly in front of the disabled car and was preparing to swallow it up.

~~~

The interns began boarding the bus with tired, overworked expressions. They had just finished packing up the tractor trailer and were showing signs of extreme fatigue after being up for thirty-six hours straight. They threw themselves into seats hoping that they would soon be deeply asleep.

After they had all boarded Jenkins stepped on. "The food is here. Make sure you eat something before you drift off."

Jenkins stepped back off the bus while a crew of twelve, dressed in the black uniforms of the local McDonald's, stepped on carrying bags of food and mini cartons of orange juice.

One of the interns shouted out. "I need coffee."

Jenkins voice filtered in through the open bus door. "No coffee, only juice. You all need to sleep!"

His cell phone rang. He dug in his pocket and turned away to answer it after he had looked at the screen to see that it was Appleton.

"What's up?" he asked.

"Calling with good news," Appleton said. "I'm watching the race broadcast and I just witnessed your team pull off a stunning disabling maneuver. Stunning I'm telling you. That girl of yours could work for the military and show them a thing or two about ballistic arcs and distances. Never seen anything like it. And that Richard can drive. Are you sure you still want me to check…"

"Yes, absolutely, no question."

"Alright. I should be with your guy by this afternoon. I hope they do as well for the rest of the morning as what I just saw." Appleton said.

Jenkins sighed and said, "Yeah, me too." He closed the connection and stepped back onto the bus after the last of the McDonald's crew stepped off.

"Alright, lights out." Jenkins announced. He turned to the squat old looking driver. His driver's cap sat askew and his expression had a permanent off-center scowl. "You need to get us to the Super 8 in Fort Dodge, Iowa while we get some rest. Pick a place somewhere in the middle for a rest stop and food. Can you do that or do I need to arrange for a second driver?"

The driver smiled. He spoke with a drawl that was southern accent laced with retired Army lingo.

"Buddy, I drive because I can't sleep. I can drive for a week straight if I have to. Keep the coffee coming, the bathroom stops regular and I can drive you to Hawaii. And we don't have to make any stops over the ocean, I'll piss right out the window."

Jenkins chuckled. Driving to Hawaii, that would be something to see, he thought.

~~~

Richard drove silently after their small celebration.

Katrina couldn't help but ponder on the events of the morning and the bad phone call he had received before they had left. Even though they had only been together for a day and a half, and for the most part she had wanted to kill him for every second of it, his silence bothered her.

It bothered her that his father would call before the race to mention… something. And had he actually been drunk at the time? What could he have said that would have caused Richard to destroy his phone?

It also bothered her that she cared enough to want to help him. Based on their fights the day before she should have been ready push him out of the car and finish the race alone.

She knew that it was a weakness of hers. She desired to help those around her that needed help, whether they deserved it or not. She took a cleansing breath and asked, "I can see that the call from your father is still bothering you, did he accuse you of doing something wrong this morning?"

Richard turned to Katrina. "It's not what he said so much as what he implied."

Katrina shook her head. She had no way to appreciate the difference without more information.

"You wouldn't understand," he said, sullenly.

Katrina turned toward the screen in front of her to retract it back into the dashboard. "I get the feeling that your father disapproves of something, your lifestyle, your career choice, or maybe your sexual..."

Richard slammed on the brakes and pulled into the breakdown lane sparking another chorus of horns.

He pointed his finger in Katrina's face. "You know nothing about me."

Katrina took a piece of gum and stuck it into her mouth. "I know that your father doesn't like something about you. You're closer to your mother but she's not happy with your racing career. That's why she didn't show up for the starting line yesterday. You intentionally strut around like you're big man on campus, probably because you're hiding something. That's usually how it works. Every once in a while when someone walks around with a stick up their ass it really is what it looks like, but I don't get that feeling with you. Not to mention that I saw your ass strutting around last night, didn't see a stick there."

Richard blushed. He actually seemed embarrassed by his behavior.

Katrina chewed loudly for a second before going on. "I think you're an only child and your father expected more from you."

"Stop." Richard said. He didn't want to talk about his problems to a girl he barely knew. "You don't know anything about me. We're here to run a race, not to psychoanalyze each other."

Just then another two racecars passed by in the building traffic. Richard had to accelerate hard to cut back into traffic.

"Where are we anyway?" he asked.

Katrina pushed the button to bring up the computer screen and typed the commands to initiate the GPS. "We're on Route 3 heading into Cincinnati. We are supposed to get on 71 which goes through the heart of the city. But if we stay on that route we'll be up close and personal in rush hour traffic."

Richard raised a finger. "Do you think that was intentional? I mean, letting us get stuck in traffic to put us all in close proximity to each other again?"

"I don't know." Katrina said grumpily. "It will be longer to go around, there aren't really any shortcuts, but if we're stuck in traffic and someone comes in close enough to use their laser there won't be enough room to run away."

"Okay," Richard agreed. "Tell me where to turn and I'll make sure we get there."

"Take the next exit. It doesn't matter which one. I'll plot us a route from there."

~~~

Silvia Thruwell was smiling. She took a deep breath, it had worked. She had written the code required to hack into the internet device. Of course she still had to test it. She lifted her head to face her many computer screens to lay eyes on the one that had the least important items. She turned her head back to her keyboard to make some changes.

When she gazed back, up Mac Killington's face was staring at her from between the screens. She screamed. The men at the table, who were supposed to be her protection, more like prison guards, laughed at her over their card game. They had seen him approach and had kept quiet. Killington's face looked like the Cheshire

Cat's floating head. The smile that greeted her made her skin crawl.

The look of malicious intent curled the corners of his mouth as though he were about to eat her. His eyes showed absolute cruelty and the knowledge that he had the power to do whatever he wanted made Silvia scared by what she saw.

Killington meandered around to where Silvia sat. He hung over her shoulder to look at all of the screens above her keyboards. Images from the race broadcast took more than one screen and there was still one with code streaming down. Each had continual activity. Only the internet screen, oddly enough, had no activity at this point. The flickering of the monitors lit the dark space behind Killington and Silvia and was reflected by the glass panes of the windows on the other side of the room. He placed a hand on the chair's backrest. She shivered at the idea of being so close to the powerful man behind her.

Killington broke the silence. "What's interesting to me is how one person can learn all this and not go crazy. All of this internet and computer stuff is so complex. I can't even imagine sitting still long enough to do half of what you have accomplished today. So what have I paid for? I have people in high places expecting results."

Silvia leaned forward away from the reach of Killington's fingers before answering his question. "I wrote a program to hack into the internet software employed by many of the projects' managers to have access to their engineering projects. This will allow me to take some portion of control over their racecars. The idea is to get into the software that controls the skin. If I can find the command in the code that exists in their computer, I can send a message to disable their car without having a laser burn through it. Even if they go and fix the problem I already know for a fact that once the disable code is given the car cannot be registered as a winner even if it does pass through the finish ring. I should be able to thin the race by quite a few cars before the fifth day of the race."

Killington nodded, impressed. "You know, these skills you have sound very impressive. If this works I might be able to use someone with your skills in my organization."

Silvia shook her head. "I signed up to extract revenge on Katrina. After the paycheck I was promised, I'm done."

Killington laughed maliciously. The men at the card table joined in, though it wasn't clear that they even knew what he was laughing at.

"Here's a little secret about our business, once you're in, you're in. You'll get paid, but if this works you like you say, I may have a business proposition for you that you can't refuse. And if you really want out there's only one way. You seem like a pretty smart girl, I think you get my drift. But for today let's get on with the job. Pick out a car and do your magic."

Silvia turned to the divided screen over her work station. Her heart was hammering in her chest. She thought about her goal now. Getting revenge with these thugs now seemed like a very stupid idea. They may have had the money she needed to build this work station in order to exact her revenge but now she wasn't sure that it would be worth it, especially if she was going to get dragged into this organization indefinitely. She was so stupid. Why hadn't she just let it go? She had no interest in hurting innocent people or using her technology to benefit the mob. In her heart she couldn't do that. She sat stock still, afraid to move.

"Well, are you going to do something?" Killington asked.

Silvia began to breathe very hard, like a panic attack had begun to build. Killington snapped his fingers and his men got up from the table and withdrew their pistols. Killington took one of their pistols and cocked it before pointing it to Silvia's temple. She began to whimper between her gasping breaths. She didn't want to die.

There was a long pause where the barrel of the gun held its position at Silvia's head while she continued to whimper. Then suddenly the gun dropped.

Killington laughed. "I need to know if this will work. Pick out a car and do something." He snapped his fingers again and said 'Chair'. One of his men quickly ran to the little table and retrieved a chair for him. When he sat down he took out a cigar from his suitcoat's inner pocket and lit it. Smoke drifted through the light streaming in through the high window over the work station. The equipment's cooling fans pushed it around. Silvia wiped her hand across her nose as she began to calm down a little.

"Let's start small." Killington said as he laid the business end of the pistol on her shoulder indicating a pressure to proceed. Silvia leaned in towards her keyboard. She typed in a command and a list of organizations that had built the racecars populated the screen directly in front of her.

"I... I hacked into the database of the secret organization that is running the race. They keep track of all the cars that have already been eliminated and the ones that are still active. The names on the screen before me are all of the cars that are still in the race." Silvia turned to a different keyboard and prepared to type. "Pick a car on that list and I'll go to their server."

Killington said mockingly, "Oooh, I get to pick?" He took his gun off Silvia's shoulder and used it to point at the fifth car on the list. Silvia began to type.

"All of these organizations use one of three servers as their connection to their projects. It will only take me a second to find the right one." Silvia said.

Sure enough, on the second entry the search bar activated to pull up the active link to the company's project list. "This car was built by a mid-western group called Build Pro. They make all kinds of products that get sold to the big box stores in the country." A list popped up all of the projects in their R&D department. Silvia scrolled down and found one that was called 'The Car'.

"Not a very original name. But if your company name is Build Pro then I wouldn't expect too much," Silvia said as she opened the file. It took only a second to find the right PDF. That's when she turned to the third keyboard. "This keyboard goes to a special server that pings this connection all around the world so no one can trace it back to you." She pointed to the screen all the way to the top, on the right. It showed the signal traveling around the world until it came back to the state of Montana. When the connection was completed a string of code began scrolling slowly from bottom to top on the screen just below the one that showed the global arc of the signal.

Silvia chuckled. "No serious firewalls here. This will be child's play." She pointed the internet broadcast of the race on the large screen on the upper left. "I'm going to depress the brakes on one of these racecars. I need you to find it on this screen. This is a live feed."

Killington and his men followed Silvia's finger towards the screen that had multiple picture-in-picture views of the race in real time. They stretched their eyes trying to see all of the images at once.

"Give me a second. I have to find the right port." Silvia said.

"What does the car look like?" Killington asked, trying to discern how to best narrow his search.

"I don't know. I can only see code. That's why I need you to watch for which car is affected."

Killington pointed to the screen. "I'll watch the top cars, you two take a bottom half each so we don't miss it."

The henchmen nodded in agreement, one of them pointing to which side of the screen they would take.

"Alright, I found the brake ports." Silvia stated. "There should be some lag time between me activating the brakes and it actually happening on the screen. I've got this signal running around the world before it hits the car. Think of it as me communicating almost half way to the moon."

Killington gazed over to Silvia, seriously impressed. He handed the pistol he had been holding back to the man he had taken it from, who quickly holstered it.

Silvia typed like mad then stopped abruptly. "There, you'll see something in a second."

The men all sharpened their gaze. The smallest measurable amount of time crawled by, millisecond after millisecond. Finally one of the henchman said 'I found it'. The rest of the eyes turned to watch the unlucky recipient of their attentions as their car's break system activated. It skidded sideways for a tenth of a second before the break released and they recovered normal driving.

~~~

On a highway outside of Cincinnati an accident had brought traffic to a crawl. The MIT car was getting closer to the gridlock without knowing that their unhindered run was almost at an end. They could see one other racecar ahead of them but neither sought to use their weapons, finishing the day was paramount in their minds.

As the racecars approached the accident scene another racecar started to pass them on the passenger side. They could see that it already had two bad looking burn holes in its skin, each the size of a baseball. Richard let it go by. He had finally understood that it wasn't the end of the world every time someone tried to pass them. He was confident about the car's remarkable abilities and with Katrina's skill with the weapon. He and Katrina just watched them drive on by. The other car didn't try to engage them. It probably didn't hurt that the weapon on the roof was in active mode and it had mimicked Katrina's head movements by following them as it passed.

Moments later the car with the damaged skin's brake lights suddenly lit up. The wheels had locked up completely and smoke filled the air as the car slowed rapidly and started to twist in its lane. Richard had to make a few sudden moves to avoid traffic that had tried to go around the problem car. The section of road that they were on had only two lanes and didn't offer the luxury of space to maneuver. He had to swerve into the break down lane once avoid a small red Cobalt that had children in the back seat.

Suddenly the brakes on the car released and the racecar could accelerate once more. After some loud horns from angry drivers the traffic pattern began to go back to normal.

The Build Pro car was now behind the other racecars as the driver tried to re-establish their pace while the passenger ran diagnostics to try to find out what had caused the problem.

They accelerated, trying to catch up to their peers, weaving through traffic. As soon as they had passed the MIT car for a second time their car went dead. They lost all power. They struggled to use their momentum to get into the breakdown lane. When they realized that they had already slowed too much to clear the driving lane completely, the passenger slid out of the window and began to push the car the remaining distance to safety. Another chorus of horns echoed off the guardrail around them.

~~~

Silvia punched the air when the software displayed the message 'Command delivered' on the screen to the right. All eyes turned to the screen where the racecars were displayed in their little boxes and waited. They watched the Build Pro car trying to regain their position as the leader on that stretch of highway. It passed the MIT car then the disable code shut them down.

Killington stood and shouted at the multi-screened work station. "Yes!" He turned to Silvia and smiled his evil smile. "Keep going, do them all that way except for these two. We want them to have an unhindered avenue towards the finish line. I will check in often, and please, be careful you don't accidentally turn off the wrong car. I'm getting paid a lot of money to ensure that they succeed. Of course the little lady you want to exact revenge upon is not on the list of winners. Feel free to hack them down at your leisure."

Killington turned on his heel and started to leave but stopped as something else occurred to him. Without turning to convey his message he said. "The guys will help you in your duties."

~~~

Katrina and Richard's heads both followed the slowing car as they passed it again.

"What the hell happened to them? No one else was close enough to use a weapon on them." Richard stated.

"I know, right?" Katrina said. She wondered what could have happened to the car that would have triggered the disable code. "You know, I bet they have a window mounted weapon and they accidently turned it on when it was in the back seat and burned a hole bad enough on the inside to shut them down."

"That can happen?" Richard asked.

"Well, if it's not mounted in place it might have been turned on accidentally when they were swerving around before. Or if they threw something in the backseat and it hit the power switch. Or the capacitor inside the weapon could have failed and caught on fire."

"Well I'm glad this one is on the roof," Richard said as he depressed the brakes. Brake lights all around them were coming on. Traffic had quickly come to a stop.

"I wonder what's going on?" Katrina asked.

"It's rush hour. Maybe there's an accident up ahead somewhere." Richard added.

Over the next half of an hour they waited in slow motion, through stop and go traffic without ever seeing the source of the problem. People changed lanes frequently, hoping to stay moving but neither lane moved far. Over time people began to look around in the lanes for something different to do than watching the guy in front of them not move. Katrina had leaned toward her window a while ago and Richard thought she might have fallen asleep.

The eyes of a lot of the other cars' occupants watched their unusual looking vehicle. He had known that the design of their racecar would stand out but the arm on the roof was the biggest point of interest. Luckily, no one around them knew what the arm did. He imagined what would happen if Katrina turned in on. He chuckled. People would probably jump out their cars and run away, keeping him from ever getting off this highway.

As Richard had been lost in his imagination, another racecar had come up on them from behind. It had taken many minutes to position themselves perfectly. Slowly, methodically, they had attempted to sneak up on them, moving only when Richard had been looking in the other direction.

This racecar had a track mounted weapon that was housed in a small box in the rear of the vehicle above the back window. Its track trailed from its home on top of the rear window, down along the side of the vehicle below the door window, circled the entire front end, then followed the exact route back along the opposite side to its parked position.

When the car was close enough to the MIT car to deploy its weapon the weapons specialist checked once more on Richard's attentiveness and then nodded with confidence to the driver, and pressed a button on a hand-held controller. A little trolley wheeled itself out of its home and made its way to the front of their car.

Next to the two racecars, which were now end to end, sat a pale blue Nissan Quest minivan with four children inside, all under the age of six. Occasionally the children fought as the movie they were watching failed to keep their attention. The woman at the wheel looked ragged. This traffic jam had messed not only with her schedule but with her mind. She felt lucky that she had loaded their favorite movie in the player when they had left that morning, otherwise she might have completely lost her mind.

One of the children noticed the trolley and pointed it out to the others. The movie suddenly seemed blasé compared to what looked to them to be a train attached to a car. Many eager faces stretched to gain a better view. The operator looked at them and smiled.

The child closest to the door opened his window. When the racecar driver could see that they were going shout out the window, the trolley had already arrived under the operator's window. The operator looked down to his rolling device then back up to the children. He placed a finger over his lips and pointed the MIT car to indicate that it was a surprise. The children nodded their heads. The driver and passenger of the racecar both smiled at their young audience.

All of the cars rolled forward, taking up space, tightening up the line. The racecar very slowly inched its way closer to the MIT car. The trolley was almost at its furthest point so that the laser could be switched on. The operator turned to the children again and reinforced his desire for quiet by placing his forefinger back to his lips. They all nodded, watching with excited faces. Of course, none of them knew what was going to happen so it appeared to be innocent and fun.

The operator positioned the trolley between the push rack supports that were attached to the back of the MIT car and adjusted the angle of attack. He looked back to the children and put up his thumb indicating it was time. All the children nodded. He depressed the red button on his controller and the laser came to life.

Richard was very relaxed, his arm rested on the doorframe partially outside of the open window. The line of cars had barely inched forward twenty feet in twenty minutes. He was so bored. Katrina hadn't moved in a while and he was sure she had fallen asleep. He looked at the clouds, grateful that there wasn't full sun or he might have gotten a sunburn hanging out of the window for so long. But it still felt hot out, his racing uniform felt sticky against his skin. Suddenly an alarm sounded in the car. He could hear children laughing loudly and pointing at the back of his car. Richard was very confused at the combination of sounds.

Katrina jumped so violently that she hit her right arm against the metal brace of her window. Between moaning in pain and trying to think over the alarms she shouted, "Move, you must move."

Richard looked in his rear view mirror to figure out how much room he had to navigate. That's when saw the other racecar up so close that he could only see a small portion of its hood. "Shit!" Richard spat out. He knew that he had missed the car sneaking up on him.

"Shit!" Richard called again. He grabbed the shifter and dropped it into reverse. "They're on our ass." He said as he popped the clutch. The MIT car lurched in reverse and they hit the offending racecar with their push rack. The racecar behind them barely moved, as if it were anchored to the ground somehow.

The children's continued laughter taunted Richard. He turned back again to see what was going on. The driver and passenger of the other car were smiling him. He could see deep black smoke beginning to rise from the back of his car and he could smell the burning shell.

The two guys in the racecar with the trolley-styled weapon laughed. They were confident that another car would soon be disqualified.

The children in the minivan were laughing with them. Their mother looked horrified at what these men were doing to the car ahead of them and tried to shush her children. What kind of people had a laser on their hood to attack innocent other cars? From her position she could see that the car with the laser also had a stabilizing system similar to that of a backhoe. When the car with the arm on the hood had rammed their car back the laser had fit right into the space between the push rack, and the stabilizing feet had taken most of the force of the ramming. Essentially the MIT car was in no better position than when they started, the movement had only changed the contact point of the laser slightly.

"Move a little more. Try to keep the laser from hitting the same spot. I need a little more time." Katrina said.

Richard moved as far forward as he could go. He could hear hydraulics operating behind him. In his side view mirror he noticed the feet rising off the ground from the racecar behind them. The attacker was trying to inch up and trap them more completely. Richard had an idea. He angled their car as though he was planning to change lanes.

Occupants of other cars had also started to watch what was happening. When the line Richard had pointed himself at started to move, a red F150 allow him to enter so that he could try to get away just as the racecar with the trolley mounted laser bore down on him.

It was ridiculous to think that they could actually get away, they were not even registering five miles per hour, and then the line of cars stopped again. The MIT car was barely ahead of the other car but in the next lane. The driver continued to laugh as the trolley moved to a new position where it could aim at their rear quarter panel. It took a few seconds for the alignment plus the burn time. Richard knew that they had only gained maybe thirty more seconds of life.

Richard had moved up as far as possible in his seat to see if they were far enough away from the laser. He couldn't move any further in his lane without hitting the driver in front of him. Trying to push another vehicle in a street that looked more like a parking lot wasn't wise. Richard moved his head up until it reached the ceiling. He looked out the window on Katrina's side towards the aggressor car. It was difficult to see but he was confident that he had managed to get far enough away.

A klaxon still blared inside the MIT car. It seemed that the laser of the enemy car was still focused on their skin. Katrina finally got their weapon powered up. When she had fallen asleep the weapon had automatically shut down and she had needed to restart cold. She struggled, the computer wasn't moving fast enough, and she swore loudly. She was waiting for the bluetooth connection to be made so she that could control the weapon.

When the trolley had lined itself up to reach the only part of the car close enough to them it became clear that they were in fact too far away to do much damage. For the weapon to be effective they had to be within six inches of the intended victim. However the weapon's operator looked Richard in the eye confidently and mouthed to him, "You're not far enough away to be safe. Say goodbye to winning."

Richard could read every syllable his lips had formed. "Are we close with the weapon?" He asked of Katrina.

The trolley stopped at the closest point to the MIT car. It was still easily twelve inches away, and its angle of attack was very oblique due to the rest of the cars in line. But it didn't matter, having the laser on a trolley allowed such interactions. The weapons specialist didn't fret over the fact that they couldn't get any closer. He just pushed another button on his controller. The laser head began to extend. A tube pushed the laser head out towards the MIT car like the lense of a camera.

"Katrina?" Richard said using her name as a question rising in tone from beginning to end.

"On line!" Katrina shouted as she turned her head to face the threat.

The robotic arm came to life and turned in the exact position, mimicking Katrina's head. She extended it out towards the other car. The aggressor's weapon lit before it reached the optimal distance to their fuselage knowing that if they started their three second laser barrage of energy then they would have enough time.

But a lot can happen in three seconds. Children, who had been rooting for the aggressors only moments earlier, were now impressed by the moving arm on the roof of the MIT car. It silenced their laughter as they watched in awe. A camera man ran up through the traffic on foot since the truck he had been assigned to had been stuck too far back to get good video footage.

A memory floated to the top of Katrina's brain as she struggled to maneuver the weapon into place to come out on top.

She and Silvia had still been
working on the final designs of the weapon

that had not yet been built. Design sketches had been littered around the large table where they had been having an animated conversation between them about what components would be necessary. They both were over tired.

"Numbers don't lie." Silvia had said. "We can't add anything else to the head or it will be too heavy to launch."

Katrina had pleaded "But we can make it really light and it won't take much space."

"Give me an example of when this will be necessary." Silvia said with her arms crossed.

"Alright." Katrina had started. "Imagine someone already has their weapon bearing down on you and their laser is lit. What choices do you have?

Only one, launch the weapon on their car. But what's the point? You can't take away the time that their laser has already been on. It's a race you can't win. Even if you launch the laser head at their weapon hoping to knock it off it would be a fifty-fifty shot, not to mention that it would probably break our laser and then it wouldn't be available to use again. Plus the Capacitor could rupture. If our arm could reach their laser and spin it hard enough to knock it free the hit would probably disable our weapon permanently."

"Alright already, I see your point." Silvia said as she picked up her cup of coffee. "You can have your little device. You just better hope it's not too heavy."

Katrina's mind snapped back as the robotic arm was almost in the right position. Effortlessly she maneuvered the buttons on the controller. When she was about eight inches away she depressed the button that would deploy the item that she had fought so hard to keep in the final design. A small mirror flipped out of the laser head's housing.

Katrina thrust the arm's head forward until the mirror was under the laser beam. She breathed a sigh of relief before she articulated the head up, changing the beam's direction. Now they were safe from any additional burning at least. They would have to stop when they were off the highway so that she could see the damage and make some repairs. At least they still had power.

The aggressors were too busy to notice that three seconds had already passed or to see that a mirror had been inserted under their laser's beam. When an alarm had started to wail on their dashboard they were stunned, trying to find out what was going on. The weapon's operator started to push buttons when smoke started to rise again.

It was the MIT team's turn to smile. They had averted a devastating setback. The little mirror being inserted in the path of the beam had changed everything. When the MIT car had almost been out for the count they had fought on, making all of the difference in the world.

Richard and Katrina watched the reflected laser burn into the trolley housing until it caught on fire. Smiles turned to giddy laughter. Soon the fire spread. The laser finally died but the fire grew. The extreme expressions on the faces of the driver and the weapons specialist corresponded directly to the size of the fire. Both scrambled to get out of their windows to try to put out the fire before their own car was disabled.

The lines of cars started to move. Richard turned to the front to get going. It looked like they wouldn't be bothered by that car again.

"Can you believe they were so cocky about their weapon design?" Katrina said.

"I would just be happy to have it work properly, not be cocky about it." Richard returned.

A shocked look spread over Katrina's face. "Do you hear yourself? You're cocky about your... yourself just like they were. You're no different."

Richard's happy face turned sour at her judgment.

They could hear horns from a distance behind them. Richard turned his gaze towards his side mirror and Katrina poked her head out of her window to get a better look. What had begun as a small fire in the trolley had spread to the whole car. Apparently setting a car's weapon on fire could lead to the entire car's destruction.

Katrina turned back to Richard. "Let's talk about your cocky attitude."

"Shut up," was all he said.

Chapter 14

        Marcus Appleton had met up with Kalby Mitchell,
the much younger associate of Dr. Jenkins, in Detroit.
The sky had a gray, overcast look about it, not
threatening rain but not letting the sun through either.
After a hearty hand shake Mitchell had led Appleton to
his office. Appleton couldn't help but be impressed by the
space in Cadillac Tower.
        The whole building was empty except for
Mitchell's office, its affordability was a side effect of the
hard times that had befallen Detroit over the last decade.
        As Appleton walked next to Mitchell across the
lobby and towards the elevator, he took notice of their
opposing characteristics. Mitchell was younger by many
years while he himself had rounded the corner into his
fifties. Mitchell had filled out from too much time behind
the computer screen and easily hovered around the three
hundred pound mark. He, on the other hand, could still
fit in his high school jeans if he wanted too. He had blond
hair while Mitchell's was very dark brown and framed a
very round face. Appleton didn't consider his face to be
long or thin but he had to admit that it didn't carry the
same roundness that Mitchell's had. Mitchell was
obviously affected by his sedentary lifestyle.
        As the two rose in the elevator Mitchell talked
about the Cadillac Tower. Appleton's mind wandered
back to their opposing differences and wondered why he
seemed exempt from the obesity bug when he and
Mitchell did the exact same thing for a living. He too
lived behind a computer most days. This had led him
towards carpal-tunnel syndrome and the surgery to
correct it, but had not prevented him from the amount of
exercise necessary for the sake of his health. Mitchell

was still young and perhaps had not been confronted by such things as potential health issues just yet.

When the elevator door opened Mitchell ushered Appleton onto the third floor. What surprised Appleton was that it was completely devoid of anything. Empty space stared back at him. In the far corner a few eight foot tables had been set up as workspace with many computers spread out, three on each table. The only other space that was furnished contained a fully set-up breakroom with a full-size refrigerator, a stove, microwave, and stacked boxes of Lay's Potato Chips. It looked like the average college student's idea of the perfect workspace. Although, Appleton considered, judging by Mitchell's appearance that may not have been too far off the mark.

"What do you think? It's perfect, right?" Mitchell asked.

Appleton looked at Mitchell with a wry smile. "Yeah, it's perfect. All you're missing is a little art to bring it all together." He said with a satirical tone.

"I thought of that to." Mitchell pointed to place off to the left.

Here, Mitchell's finger pointed to his collection of full-sized cardboard cutouts of each cast member of the movie *Star Wars, A New Hope*. Each individual character seemed alive with their character's demeanor. Chewbacca's expression was lost on Appleton because he had no idea what Wookies looked like when they smiled.

Appleton raised an eyebrow. "Yes, I see you have the art all taken care of too."

Mitchell put his arm around Appleton's shoulder and dragged him in. "Come in and see what I've already dug up."

Once at the table closest to the outside wall, Appleton took his indicated seat. Mitchell pulled his chair closer and sat next to him. He pointed and spoke of what he had done, where his research had taken him thus far, and how much further he needed to go. His hands pointed to the other computers as he explained their purpose.

"I've isolated each of these computers to work independently of each other and to pull all of their information from servers outside of the United States. That way no one will figure out where any of these workstations are if they try to trace them back. Dr. Jenkins wanted us to find the source of the money trail and consequently who is behind the attacks on the other racers. He's very afraid that his driver and weapons specialist may be in trouble as the number of participants start to dwindle. The purse is large enough to create headaches for..."

Appleton stopped Mitchell. "Have you figured out who sent the explorer after them? The MIT team, I mean."

"I put an information gathering worm in the Bureau of Motor Vehicles in every state right after that incident happened. What I got back might surprise you," Mitchell said, as he leaned back in his chair. He paused for dramatic effect.

"Well?" Appleton asked.

"The Explorer belonged to a thug that is a known associate with the mob here in Detroit named Kelly Durrin."

"Belonged?"

"Yeah, I'm pretty sure Durrin's dead, along with his passenger." Mitchell said. "I'm not sure who the passenger was just yet. There are no records from the hospitals, of course, but I got a hit from a search in the police database for mob activity here in Detroit. They posted chatter from a guy named Killington. He's the guy in charge. Anyway, two guys got promoted within their ranks, the same number of ones we assume are dead."

"How do we know this is accurate?" Appleton asked as began to type in a string of commands on the computer in front of him.

"The police have undercover cops in the mob. The chatter they report is stored in the police database. I'm pretty sure it's accurate. But that's not really the concern. The fact that the mob is involved gives us a unique problem when trying to track down the money source behind the attack."

"How so?" Appleton asked.

"Because the mob doesn't use traceable currency like checks or credit cards or even electronic transfers. Since they usually deal in cash it will be very difficult to track who it came from." Mitchell stated.

"Not really." Appleton corrected. "In the United States, every bank is required to report large sums of money being withdrawn. If I can hack into the bank information conduit at the National Reserve, I might be able to start searching for large sums of money that are moving around and match them up with all of the investors of the race."

Mitchell shook his head. "Two problems with that, first is that the mob doesn't use banks, and your idea would only work from the time you began. It's way too late for that now since the mob doesn't do the work until they get paid. The trail would already be cold."

"Okay," Appleton said. "Think of it this way. Someone paid the mob to do this job, right... so we can assume that someone took the money out of the bank to pay Killington. We can still look at banking transactions."

"But we can't go that far back. Like I said that trail would be cold." Mitchell restated.

Appleton smiled confidently. "What you might not know is that there is a master copy that is held for only one month and then retransmitted every time the information is dumped to the National Reserve in case there is a transmittal problem. Call it an insurance policy that delivers the same information thirty times over, then repeats over the next month. We can hope that Killington wasn't paid in the month before the race began. If so we would really be out of luck and would have to try another idea. If not, we can have a working list in two minutes." Appleton began typing away on the keyboard in front of him.

After much typing and several minutes of waiting, the computer was ready. Appleton turned the screen towards Mitchell. On it there was a long list of names of people who were probably guilty of nothing more than spending their money. "Want to bet that one of these names is on our list?" Appleton asked.

"Cool. You want a Monster or some Mountain Dew?" Mitchell asked in return.

~~~

Katrina moaned about being hungry again. They had finally gotten past the traffic jam. "Please can we stop somewhere? I have to go to the bathroom too."

Richard had a sour look about him. Katrina had wanted to talk about his father and why he had been so angry after receiving the phone call that morning but he didn't divulge anything. Of course five hours of listening to Katrina have a one-sided conversation about her views had only infuriated him more.

Her pleas to stop for food and now a bathroom had been ignored and he had passed every possible stop along the way. Katrina knew that his stoic disregard of her needs was her punishment for pestering him about his private life, but it didn't stop her from needing to go.

"I'm telling you, if you don't pull over soon you'll be cleaning up a mess in this car." Katrina finally spat out as she did some finger pointing to an exit that had a sign which advertised many restaurants and gas stations.

Richard put his blinker on and took the off ramp. In two minutes time he was pulling into a parking space at a Subway restaurant. Katrina squeezed herself out of her window and bolted for the entrance. He on the other hand leaned on his window lost in thought. It didn't take long before he had to admit that his hunger was getting the best of him and he followed Katrina inside.

Being in a race didn't allow them the luxury of time to enjoy a quiet meal. Not ten minutes later both were heading back out with enough sandwiches, chips and drinks to last them through the last leg of the day. Unfortunately it had not occurred to either of them that they had needed to keep watch on their car.

While they had been inside, the racecar that looked like a dune buggy had pulled up next to the MIT car where it had been parked. The passenger had slipped out and was in the process puncturing their tires through the side walls when they came back out of the store.

Richard immediately dropped everything that he had been carrying, yelled at the guy, and ran at him to take care of business. The passenger dropped the ice pick that he had been holding and ran back to his car. The driver had already started moving away and the passenger had to dive into his open window. They kicked up small rocks and dust from the asphalt as they sped off.

"Bastards!" Richard shouted with his fist in the air. He picked up a rock by his feet and threw it at them even though they had traveled too far for the rock to do anything other than help Richard blow off some steam.

Katrina sat on the curb by their car and stared at the only tire that had been spared the thrust of the ice pick.

Richard walked back, slightly less angry than he had been a second ago. "So... what did they get? Two tires?"

"Three." Katrina said. "You know it never occurred to me that we couldn't ever leave the car unattended. The chance that another racecar would see us here should have been infinitesimal since we are way off course."

"I'm willing to bet that as more cars become disabled, a lot of different tactics will be taken to undermine our car, especially if they don't think they can overpower our weapon." Richard said, before he sat on the sidewalk next to Katrina. "Please tell me that we have three spares in the car?"

"We don't even have one. It was a weight saving thing. We have enough goop to put into the tires to fix flats, but we can't use it." Katrina said.

"Why not?"

"The goop is designed to fill a hole where centrifugal force pushes it, to the tread area. These holes are in the side wall. The goop won't work here. We need new rubber," Katrina said as she unwrapped her sandwich.

"How can you eat at a time like this? We need to find something that will work or we'll be the last car in again." Richard's voice climbed as stood to pace.

Katrina patted the curb next to her. "Sit down and relax. We can be last by one minute or by twelve hours and it won't make any difference. Since we are going to be last one way or another, eat your sandwich. I have phone numbers for companies that can fix our problem. After I eat I'll call one of them and have them come out and bring us new tires."

~~~

Frodes paced back and forth in the Fort Dodge, Iowa Super 8 Motel parking lot. It was after nine-thirty. Moths had begun to collect around the parking lot lights. His team of interns, all hyped up on energy drinks, joked and goofed off loudly around the equipment. All of them were waiting for their car to come in. Other teams were already working on their cars.

Compared to last night, Frodes could see far fewer cars than normal in the lot. There were only nine teams working, eight really, since their car had not come in yet. He didn't know just yet how many cars were still in the race. He was certain, however, that the number had dropped drastically.

He looked at his watch and thought that it might have started to go backwards since it had barely moved since the last time he checked it. He sighed loudly as Dillon walked up and stood next to him to wait. He had a worried look about him.

"I feel the same way." Dillon said.

Frodes voiced his exasperation. "Why are they this late again? I mean, Katrina said that they had to contact a company to come out and replace their rubber, but that was hours ago."

"Well, after tonight that won't be a problem anymore." Dillon said. "I secured a set of tires that can't go flat."

"How much did that cost us?" Frodes asked indignantly as though it was his money that was being spent.

"Dr. Jenkins said that I needed to find the best possible tires so that they wouldn't have this problem again, because, you know, we can't help them after tonight." Dillon said sheepishly.

"So how much?"

Dillon cleared his throat before he answered. "$1600 each."

"Oh my God!" Frodes said. His hands rose in the air in disgust as though they were connected to balloons.

As if on cue Richard and Katrina drove into the parking area. Dillon's laughter brought other teams members' eyes to the car. Bertrand stopped in the center of the lot as their team approached, laughing and pointing fingers. Katrina placed a hand over her face out of embarrassment.

When the crowd grew there was more finger pointing and a lot more laughter. Katrina plucked up the courage and slipped out of her window.

Frodes walked up with his jaw hanging open and said, "What the hell are those?"

Richard answered the question. "The only company that could help us didn't carry the right tires to replace what we had. So, we had to go to a different size tire and different rims because ours were too wide. The only rims they could get on short notice were for a minivan."

Dr. Jenkins walked up as Richard was explaining their new look. When he indicated to have everyone move out of the way so he could get close enough to see the car he understood why everyone was laughing. The sleek racecar before him had rolled in on a narrow set of tires mounted on minivan rims. The thin white walls on the tires shone brilliantly under the bright parking lot lights. It truly was an abomination, an insult to their car's design, and deserved to be laughed at. Jenkins laughed too, in spite of his consternation.

"Hey, it got you here didn't it?" Jenkins said before he turned to Frodes. "You know what to do."

Jenkins turned towards Richard and Katrina. "First a meeting, then you guys can get cleaned up before dinner. Follow me."

Richard began to exhibit his anger over the tire puncture incident but Jenkins waved a hand to indicate that he keep quiet. Richard hadn't noticed but they had been walking past the dune buggy car as its technicians worked on it. Jenkins led them to his hotel room and closed the door behind them. After opening up the mini fridge, he took a couple of bottles of beer and offered them to Bertrand and Katrina. They each took one and sat at a small table set by the window.

"I have information to share with each of you." Jenkins started.
"First, I've learned that someone inside the race hierarchy has hired people to disable cars in the race to give their car an edge. The incident with the red Explorer was not against you personally. But, unfortunately they don't care who gets hurt as long as they win."

Katrina pulled on her Budweiser as though the news didn't surprise her. Richard, on the other hand, didn't take a drink. His eyes were wide as thoughts ran wildly through his head.

"I need to ask you a question Richard. I don't want to sound insensitive but I think I need to know what you and your father were talking about before you launched your phone across the parking lot this morning."

Richard got up and left the table. He was startled by the question and it took him a moment before his automatic reaction of anger faded. His eyes welled up and he kept his back to both of them. Katrina wanted to get up to go and comfort him but Jenkins placed a hand on her arm to silently tell her that she should stay put.

When Richard composed himself he started to speak. "My father only became an investor in this race because I wanted him to. I wanted to compete in a race that would help launch my career. I convinced my mother to talk him into it. Eventually he caved and committed to the race.

"He has done a lot of things right in his career and even in this venture he decided that he wanted to win even though he would not have had any part of this if it wasn't for me. Honestly I was pretty sure this was going to be his biggest flop because I was the one driving, like he would set me up to fail. But he jumped into the project with both feet. He went out of his way to hire you Dr. Jenkins. He researched all that you had accomplished and fell in love with your engine design."

One day, toward the end of the building stage, I walked into his office to ask him for something and found a pile of applications. All kinds of people wanted to be the driver for this car. When he came in I fought with him about how I was supposed to be the one driving, that I had been the reason that he had gotten into the race to begin with. He just laughed. He said I didn't have what it took to drive in a race that pulled in a purse so huge, that..."

Richard paused again.

"You see, he is very disappointed with me. I'm not quite what he wanted in a son. But he loves my mother enough to do anything she asks."

Richard paused for a long moment. Katrina and Jenkins looked at each other. The fact that he was the driver made them realize that Richard's mother had most likely forced his father to allow him to be the driver.

Richard started again but on a different tack. "We fought the day before I was to show up to the starting gate, or in this instance, the parking lot. My father said he didn't want me to drive anymore, that the race wasn't safe. I thought that it was just his way of trying to talk me out driving, that he wanted to win and he felt that I couldn't do it. So I used my mother's influence again and here I am... getting exactly what I wanted.

"That morning, at the start of the race, he was drunk and I thought it was because he thought that we were going to lose if I was driving. When the Explorer came into the picture things changed. I started to wonder if there wasn't more going on, if he might have been telling me the truth about why he didn't want me to drive. I thought that my father might have feared for my life because he loved me.

"Then this morning when he called, he was really afraid. I could tell because he was all choked up when he said he was happy that I had pulled out of the close encounter with that Explorer, that the gun had really scared him. But he still wanted me to drop out of the race. He said that he had another driver in the wings to take over for me. He explained that the race was about the cars not the driver, and walking out wouldn't change anything. He begged me to come home. Then it hit me, no one knew about the gun except Katrina and myself. It didn't show up in the video. I watched it after the first day. The only person we told was Dr. Jenkins. The only way he could have known was if Dr. Jenkins said something to him. But I knew Dr. Jenkins would never give up that kind of information. My father had to know more about what was happening than the rest of us."

Richard paused on that thought but pressed on. "But I couldn't walk away after spending even one day with Katrina. How could I leave her to whatever was going to happen with another driver who was only being sent in to fail or maybe die. I had to see this through. I have..."

Finally Richard's feelings overcame him and he dropped his face into his hands.

Katrina's mouth hung open in shock at what Richard just said. Not only was he confessing to what his father may be mixed up in, he had confessed that he didn't want her to be hurt in any way either.

Jenkins sucked down the rest of his beer before he turned back to Katrina. "I think you have a pretty good handle on what we're facing. Not only do you have to finish a race, but you must confront whatever his father might have done to hijack his investment. He doesn't want to see you finish, but, on the other hand, he doesn't want to see you hurt either. I had a feeling last night when he said that he wanted me to spend whatever it took to ensure that you have all of the tools that you needed to stay safe that something was up."

Jenkins turned back to Richard. "Not to excuse your father's actions, but I believe that he had no control over how you might have been disqualified. I think someone else is pulling the strings. I believe the leader of the group is hedging their bets to make their own car win. I wonder how much money your father was going to make just for agreeing to partner up with whoever is running this game? I'm sure he regrets it now."

Jenkins felt bad for Richard, who now knew that his father had known the danger involved with the race all along. He turned to Katrina in a downtrodden way. She still looked shocked. He realized that this information was destroying the morale of his team. He wouldn't be surprised if Richard or Katrina decided not to leave the parking lot in the racecar the next morning. And could he ask them to? He sighed.

Jenkins turned back to Richard sitting on one of the beds. "Listen, I'm sure your father tried to talk you out of driving specifically because he knew it would be too dangerous. He probably only agreed to let you drive in the end thinking the car would be disqualified. If your car got disabled quickly then it would break your racecar driving addiction. I'm also sure that no matter how the race ends he still wins in some way, we just haven't figured it all out yet.

"What he didn't count on was that whoever was set up to do the disqualifying would go to the extremes of hurting the team members. I'm sure he never wanted to see you hurt. He may not like you sometimes, but you're still his son and your mother's son.

Imagine if you died because of his actions? What would happen if your mother found out that he had caused your death? I think he knows that and is worried about your safety, and his wife's opinion of him."

Richard raised his head, hope in his heart.

Jenkins continued. "I have a couple of guys I can trust looking into who might be running the game and who might be in charge of taking cars out of the race. I don't want to say what my thoughts are just yet, you know... in case I'm wrong. But tonight is the last night we can perform service to the car.

Now my job is not only to have you survive but also to give you the tools to stay safe and to win. So we are going to put on tires that can't go flat for starters. Frodes has another update to the car's computer and we are going to give you another set of tools that you might need to help you along the way.

Remember that you have ramps in the back that are the only way to get the car high enough to get into the winners loop. The finish line is in the middle of the desert. Anything else that you need to finish the race you need to acquire before you reach the last town.

"Richard, I have seen your driving skills. If anyone can win this race it's you, despite all of the problems the team is facing. You need to understand that. You also need to keep Katrina safe, but let her do her job. I'm sure she'll surprise you if you let her. The two of you are a good team."

Richard chuckled from behind his fingers. Jenkins turned to Katrina. "Try to keep his head on straight. He really is a good driver," Jenkins reiterated.

Katrina kicked back the last of her beer before answering. "Yeah, he really is, as long as he doesn't get too full of himself."

Jenkins walked toward the hotel room door thinking about all of the damage he had just inflicted. When he opened the door to leave he found Dillon waiting at the threshold.

"Yes?" Jenkins asked.

"Uh... I came to ask a few questions... from Katrina." Dillon said sheepishly.

Jenkins turned to Katrina with raised eyebrows but left the room so that she could come to the door to talk to him.

Katrina stepped outside of the room to give Richard some privacy pulling the door partially closed behind her.

"What's up?" she asked.

"I was wondering if you weren't too tired if you wanted to go out for dinner?" Dillon asked.

"Dinner?" Katrina asked, as though she had never considered needing to eat. Her confusion seemed deep.

"Uh... yeah, you know, with me." Dillon's confidence strengthened as Katrina didn't outright say no. "I'm supposed to set up your meals tonight and I thought maybe I could sit with you and... and stuff."

Dillon's self-confidence began to evaporate again as she just looked at him without answering.

Katrina looked back to the room's door thinking about Richard's fragile state.

Dillon took that look to mean that she wouldn't consider him as a dinner companion when a famous racecar driver was waiting for her. He was just a nerd.

"Um, it's no problem. I understand." Dillon said changing gears. "I only asked in case you were dining alone, that's all."

Katrina's stomach was in knots. She knew that she needed to spend some time with Richard to help him get through this mess but she didn't want to hurt Dillon.

She put her hand on his arm. "Listen, I would love to have dinner with you but tonight isn't good. Can I ask for a rain check until after the race? I need to talk to Jenkins again," she lied, "and I wouldn't want to cut short a wonderful dinner. We have to be at the starting line pretty early."

Dillon brightened instantly.

Katrina pressed on so she could go back inside. "If you're in charge of getting us dinner, can you get us a six pack of beer and some Chinese food? You know, fried rice, chicken fingers, teriyaki sticks, crab rangoons, sesame chicken, the usual stuff?"

Dillon nodded and his expression gave her the impression that he was storing the information away somewhere in his head. He smiled and said, "I'll be back in thirty minutes."

Chapter 15

Silvia Thruwell was having a wonderful dream. It showed on her face as she slept in a sleeping bag under her table full of computer equipment. The humming of the computers' fans had lulled her into a sound sleep after such a late night of pressured work from Killington.

He had wanted her to be able to shut down another racecar when they were getting ready to start the race for the day. But of the remaining nine racecars, all of the teams had strong firewalls in place to protect their cars' technology. By the time she had conceded defeat, her neck and back had been sore and her fingers had actually hurt. It hadn't taken long for her to fall asleep but in that short amount of time she had come up with a new plan for how to break into the remaining firewalls.

Killington came in early. He was fully dressed in another expensive Italian suit, his eyes bright with energy and anticipation.

Of the men that had been assigned to watch Silvia during the night as she slept, one had dozed off and the other was blinking heavily. Several cups of takeout coffee littered the floor around their chairs.

Killington approached the dozing guard and pushed him out of his chair. He woke angry shouting something incomprehensible and he went for his pistol. When he stood and saw Killington nearby, he quickly retreated. The other guard just laughed.

The noise brought Silvia around. She remained somber despite the laughter. When she sat up the sleeping bag fell away exposing her pink Hello Kitty pajamas. She crawled out from under the table and stretched long and hard. She still could feel the vestiges of cramps in her fingers and a lingering soreness in her neck. She didn't want to think about how much worse they would be after spending another long day at a computer keyboard.

"Good morning." Killington said. "We need to get an early start. What can my men get you for breakfast?"

Silvia wrinkled her nose as her gaze turned towards the guards. One of them already had a cigarette in his mouth. "Less smoke, a place to wash up, and a cup of coffee."

An hour later Silvia walked back into the room that was now considered her workspace. She had guards that didn't smoke, a tall cup of Dunkin Donuts' coffee in her hands, and clean clothes on. Oddly this felt to her like going to work. Except that she had slept under her computer array the night before and she was sure that the guards were not just for her protection, they were also to keep her there until the job was done. What had she gotten herself into?

Killington followed her into the room a few minutes later. Silvia was already in the process of starting up all her equipment. She noticed that the air in the room changed when he came in close to stand by her. Even though he wore expensive suits, he still smelled like a mobster, a mixture of cologne, cigar smoke and alcohol. Another smell, stale sweat and blood, filled her nostrils. Silvia assured herself that it was psychosomatic. One could not actually smell like the blood of the men and women he had killed as he had risen within the ranks of the organization. Maybe it was her subconscious' way of reminding her to be afraid of him despite his polished outward appearance.

"How long until you can shut down another car?" Killington asked, like it should be something that could be done without much effort.

"Of the nine cars that are still in the race, each has proven firewalls that I could not force myself into easily. So, unfortunately it will take as long as it takes. I have a lot of work ahead of me today." Silvia said with a strong attitude.

"So if I threatened your life, would the work go any faster?" Killington asked with a smile.

"No," Silvia said. "And you would be hard pressed to find anyone else who can do it better. This is the best equipment out there. If you want me to focus on a specific car first, instead of working them all at once, I'll get more work done. I might get 2 done today. If you want better results, you may want to send out some more of your goons to burn a fuselage or two to disqualify them. It might be easier in the end. You have to understand that there will probably be some cars that have systems that I won't be able to break into at all."

"You have seven cars to work on, not nine, two of them are off limits, remember?" Killington began.

Silvia rounded on him. "You don't get it do you? Breaking code is not like breaking into a bank by knocking down a wall or two. I have to learn a new language every time I hack into a competent engineer's code. Once I get inside it's easy. But to get seven codes broken, I have to relearn the language seven times. All I have to say is that you better have a contingency plan because I may not be able to learn all seven languages in two and a half days. I came into this to shut down Katrina and the MIT car, everything else is a bonus for you."

Killington's eyes moved almost spastically as he considered this new information.

"Just get to work," he said as he stormed out of the room.

~~~

Appleton and Mitchell were hard at work at their computer stations but neither looked better than half dead. The list that Appleton had pulled from the National Reserve conduit had turned out to be so large that they had ended up printing the massive document, all 843 pages, so that they could search independently. They had to search for each name on their list on the one printed from the National Reserve. Then each company listed on the Reserve's list needed to be researched as a precautionary measure, to ensure that each name was a real person or company, each with a real presence in the world.

Of the many tasks with which they had been entrusted, finding the money trail stood tall on their list. They had to search accounts in countries where the United States had zero control, and shell companies where transactions could be hidden in plain sight.

Most corporate money moved through wire transfers, rarely as cash. For the mob, usually it was cash. Not that mob businesses didn't use modern electronic transfers at all, but for many services rendered, cold hard cash still made the world move. Appleton was certain that if Killington had been hired to shut down race teams, then paper money would have changed hands.

When Appleton finished researching the names on each sheet of paper he crumpled it up and tossed toward a trash bin. Many other balls of paper littered the floor around the bin. Based on the amount of paper on the floor, it was evident that neither he nor Mitchell would be trying out for the company basketball team anytime soon. He had searched for names that cross-referenced to the list of names that Jenkins had provided, searched every bank in the country for other wire transfers, and cross checked them all to companies that operated in Cayman Islands or Moldova, countries known to do business with billionaires who wanted to hide something.

Unfortunately both he and Mitchell had barely made a dent on the list. He picked up the next page, number twenty six.

"I think we need to write a program to do the searching while we get some rest. The first phase will take the longest, so we might as well sleep through it." Appleton's words startled Mitchell, who had been deep in concentration on his own page of names.

"I know the brain power, between the two of us, is probably equivalent to a whole office at the NSA," Mitchell started, "But we do not have their computer hardware."

Appleton got up and found the bag that he had brought with him. He unzipped it and pulled out a tall CD stack. "That may be true, but we can use this instead. It's my software to make server farms do the compiling."

Mitchell raised a tired eyebrow. "You're going to hack into the NSA?"

"It's funny that you mentioned the NSA." Appleton said as he took the CD stack to the terminal he was working at. "I was hired by them to write this software so they could use it to spy on internet companies. When they got caught spying, policies changed in a hurry. Money used to pay for this software came out of their mainstream budget and I was nothing more than a subcontractor. So I got fired and they made me take all the code I wrote so they wouldn't get caught for another indiscretion against 'innocent' corporations."

Mitchell's second eyebrow rose to match the other. "So, exactly what does this software do?"

"Once I install it we can log into Yahoo, for instance, and upload a small program, kind of like a worm, then a subroutine will establish itself to create a work order. That will partition off a certain amount of space in the server farm to do a job for us. I'll upload a couple more of these CD's of information that will essentially tell their computers to do a detailed search for whatever I want. I will tell their computers to pull this list again and write specifics in the search parameters to do what we spent all night doing. We'll go to sleep and in a couple of hours we'll find the information already completed and waiting for us to use."

Mitchell became excited. "Brilliant! They won't know what we did?"
"No, because it'll look like someone in their own company asked for the job ticket. And there's no constant connection to us so it can't be traced back. All the information will be emailed back to us as a zip file when the job is done. We'll set up an email address to muddy our trail and we can pick it up at the internet café down the street in the morning. I can even give a command to erase all record of what we did once the email is sent."

Mitchell, full of renewed excitement, went and grabbed another energy drink. "You want one?"

Appleton looked back to him, "Thank you, but no. You should really consider a different way to get caffeine and start drinking something a little healthier."

~~~

The next morning the parking lot of the Fort Dodge, Iowa Super 8 Motel was even more like a circus. Last night there had been nine teams of mechanics working on their racecars, preparing them for the next leg of the race. Now there were three times as many people in the parking lot. Cameramen walked around capturing all of the activity, filming the last vestiges of work being performed by mechanics, orders being given by foremen with varying degrees of grease-stained faces, investors poking around to get inside information from their drivers and foremen, and reporters from obscure internet companies recording soundbites for their shows, not all of them in English.

Agents from automotive and tech companies circulated the lot handing out their business cards, stickers, and other promotional items that advertised their brands. Off in a wooded corner of the lot an array of television screens had been positioned so that everyone could see what was being shown on the private internet broadcast. Representatives from the group that was running the internet show were also mingling in the crowd attempting to grow their viewership by handing out a free day's membership if they signed up to view the race in its entirety.

Grant Phyindress walked around the site with an entourage of other investors showing off how important he was.

Richard stepped out of his motel room. Not only was the bright light of the day blinding him, all of the activity on the lot accosted the rest of his senses. He walked through the mêlée of overactive, caffeine fueled sharks towards the MIT car.

Many people tried to stop him to ask questions or to offer their brand by pressing things into his hands. He raised his arms over his head and pushed through the crowd, the slippery nature of his racing uniform lubricating his path. When he arrived at their car, he squeezed himself through the driver's side window and turned away to avoid speaking to anyone.

The race was set to start in about thirty minutes. Before he put on his seatbelt he noticed Katrina talking with Dillon discretely. Frodes stood not too far behind then, giving last minute instructions to members of the team. It occurred to Richard that Dr. Jenkins must be a really good professor to have garnered such support from these students. All of them were committed to the project as a whole. Their team was the largest by far of all of the teams who had traveled to work on the racecars. No one ever second guessed Jenkins' orders or voiced opinions against the path they had followed.

Richard looked at the car in which he sat in a slightly different light. He gazed at the dashboard as though it had been replaced the previous night. All of it looked new.

Katrina had constantly spoken about how special this car was, how it might save the environment, how technologically advanced it was compared to everything else out there. He had tried to ignore her boasts of the car's attributes and had never attempted to understand the science involved. Now, however, he had started to understand that some of what she had said was true.

The last leg of the race was all desert terrain, and not just for the last hour either. The heat could kill them, never mind all of the other sensitive equipment in the car. The greatest test of the race was not about having to drive in the desert, but driving in the heat of the desert. Would their car survive that kind of punishment? Would their special computer equipment melt? He knew that where they were going it would be at least 110 degrees outside. Any car would be punished to the extreme in that kind of environment.

Other aspects of the race filled Richard's head. Maybe he was focusing on the desert as a way to forget his father's traitorous behavior. Did his father really want him dead? Had he been that horrible of a son? They had never seen eye to eye, sure, but to kill him? It was a lot to absorb.

Part of him wanted to walk away, not out of fear at the prospect of death. No. He wanted to run and confront his father and make him explain why he would act this way. He wasn't going to change who he was at this point in his life just to gain his father's acceptance. But he still wanted to know why.

The race was about to begin. Katrina left Dillon and headed for the car. She felt relieved that Richard had made it to the driver's seat. Deep down she hadn't been sure that he would show up. The problems that he had to contend with could drive a person to do crazy things.

"Hey. I'm glad you're ready to race today." Katrina said after she slipped in through the passenger window.

A weak smile broke over his sad countenance. "I'm glad you stayed with me last night. It was a lot to ask for, I know, considering how I treated you at the beginning."

"I still haven't forgiven you for that yet." Katrina interjected with an intriguing smile. She placed a hand on his leg.

"This is probably the first time I was close to a girl without..." Richard caught himself before finishing the sentence. "Talking to you last night helped me a lot."

"You're a good man Richard Bertrand. If your father can't see that, then he doesn't know what he's missing."

Richard smiled again, accepting her kind comment.

Dillon came up from behind Katrina and stuck his head inside her window to say one last thing. He noticed Katrina's hand on Richard's leg. The smile he had arrived with evaporated. He blinked a few times as if trying to un-see what was in front of him. Katrina turned to see what he wanted but he had already turned to walk away. Katrina watched him go and shook her head in confusion.

"Okay, down to business." Katrina said. "Last night, the team made the final adjustments for the rest of the race. The biggest one is that we have new tires and rims. They can never go flat. They give a stiffer ride than the pneumatic version, so the suspension system was adjusted. Hopefully we won't have stiff backs by the end of the day. They did another computer update, but we probably won't really notice the differences in the operation. The ramps have a new clip so they can't fall out. Apparently one of the other cars lost a ramp on the highway so Frodes modified the design a bit just in case. I hope we can actually get it unlatched when we need to use it. Knowing him, he welded it in place. He has a tendency towards overkill sometimes. Other than that it's all us now. Oh, I almost forgot. We now have a large cache of tools. Any repairs from now on will be done by you and me."

Richard actually laughed despite his depression. "I won't be able to fix anything, I don't know how."

"But I do, and you have more muscle than I do, so we'll be fixing things together, buddy."

Jenkins didn't go to meet Richard and Katrina before beginning of the race day. Instead he spent his time on the phone with Marcus. He let Frodes perform all the functions of their entrants' preparations. It was the last time they would be able to be at the starting gate together and since he had done such a great job of running things, it was fitting that he should get the last word today.

Grant Phyindress was back at the starting line with his bullhorn. Frodes couldn't help but notice that he had a different scantily dressed girl with him than he had the previous day. Barely dressed beautiful women were somehow synonymous with racing. It didn't matter what kind of race was going on, there was always a line of women ready to be photographed in a bikini with the cars or their drivers. Since this race was supposed to be invisible to most of the public, Frodes wondered where these women came from.

Frodes stood next to Richard's door and gave the driving team some last minute suggestions about the coming day. He pushed away several cameramen who had been circling the racecars before he gave his final instructions. "Katrina, remember to start up the weapon now before the race begins, we want to see a nice corridor out of the parking lot, just like yesterday."

Katrina had already forgotten and immediately got to work on the procedure for power up.

"Now, since we can't help you after today, you'll have to rely on your wits and your own observations. We patched all the holes in the skin and tuned up the car, but if something bad happens and you need to some kind of service that the two of you can't handle," Frodes leaned in closer, "I have a list of companies that will help you out with everything except the computer related stuff. The list is on a pad of paper in the dash."

A cameraman had snuck his way closer and had positioned himself just behind Frodes as he had spoken. Richard cleared his throat. Frodes turned and chased the camera back twenty feet or so. He ran back quickly when he saw Phyindress prepare to speak into his bullhorn.

"Katrina, the wireless connection is shut off permanently. Jenkins says it's not wise to use it going forward."

"Wireless connection?" Katrina laughed. "It was only used for the GPS. I know because I helped set it up."

Frodes frowned. "Regardless, I was instructed to remove the connection, and I was told to tell you."

Richard spoke. "So how will we know where to go?"

Phyindress' bullhorn keyed up. "Welcome to day three. Only nine contestants are prepared to drive today. Numbers are dwindling people, numbers are dwindling."

Frodes timed his last statement to Phyindress' break in his speech. "You have a paper map in the dash."

Katrina took a second to express her view of this unexpected development by raising both of her hands in disgust midway through the weapon's boot up sequence. The arm came to life in that instant. Katrina's head gear, which had been fitted on moments earlier, caused the arm to point in the direction of her line of sight. Since she was facing Frodes, the arm rose into the air and rotated towards Frodes' head in a menacing fashion.

Frodes put his hands in the air and backed away from the vehicle. All eyes and cameras snapped to where he stood, hands raised, recording the weapon that had been turned on him.

The television screens quickly changed to a view of the arm snapping to attention and bearing the weapon's head towards the MIT's crew chief while he backed off with his arms in the air.

Katrina couldn't see the weapon coming to life and had turned away to finish her duties. They finished preparing as Phyindress directed his latest bimbo to drop the green flag.

Since they had come in last again the night before, their car sat at the end of the line of the cars waiting to start. Ahead, the dune buggy style car sat revving its engine. Apparently stopping to puncture tires had put them a little behind as well. A low, sleek, sporty car sat ahead of them and several that were more similarly styled to their own car filled the gaps towards the front. Some were angled in such a way that Richard couldn't make out who they were and honestly he didn't much care at this point.

The front of the line could only be seen on the big projection screen in the corner of the lot. Richard revved the almost silent electric motor. Assuredly, he was the only one to truly feel the power under his foot.

Katrina turned her head back and forth watching all of the other cars before them. The weapon's arm on the roof mimicked her moves. It made them look like a tank whose turret was ready to fire on any one who got in its way.

The green flag finally dropped. The blond bimbo waved it like it was the greatest moment of her life.

The first two cars bolted out of the lot, one of which was the split car. Every other car moved to the side and allowed the MIT car uninhibited access to the parking lot exit, clearly intimidated. No one wanted to be near that weapon.

Richard saw that the dune buggy style car was among those that had pulled over. His eyes met the other driver's eyes as they went by and many unsaid things about the intentional tire punctures of the previous day passed between them, disdain being the least offensive emotion that was expressed.

~~~

Silvia had watched the internet broadcast and the circus that had developed as the cars had prepared to begin the day. Her mood went from being afraid of Killington and his men to wanting to scream out in frustration at what she had witnessed at the green flag. Silvia got up from her seat in a surge of uncontrollable fury. She walked over to where the men sat drinking coffee and discussing their previous night's conquests. She grabbed one of the unoccupied chairs at the small table. The men stopped talking and watched her with questioning looks.

With both hands on the chair, her bitter resentment of Katrina flooded into her body. Silvia grabbed tightly and raised the chair over her head. With her long face filled with malicious anger, she turned and slammed it down over the table.

The men were startled and tried to rise out of their seats to get out of the way. It was the last thing they had expected from the small girl. It had been so unexpected that one of the men fell out of his seat backwards trying to escape. The other had managed his extraction well enough but then had landed on his knees after he had tripped over the table's leg. He quickly rebounded and fumbled to extract his pistol out of its holster. He pointed it at Silvia as he watched her slam the chair on the table over and over until it exploded into shards of wood. She picked up another chair and started anew.

Not a whole minute had passed before Silvia had destroyed two chairs and the small, cheaply made wooden table. They had been reduced to nothing more than firewood and only then had she collapsed to her knees. Both men had their pistols drawn, an automatic reaction more than anything else, but they also had fear etched in their faces. They had no idea what to do in this situation. Their instructions had not covered this type of scenario.

At that point Silvia had depleted her most of her energy and was breathing very hard. Outwardly, her anger appeared to have been diminished with the destruction of the furniture but inside it had barely made a dent.

When Killington ran in with several more of his men, he couldn't believe what he was seeing.

"What the hell is going on?" Killington shouted.

One of the men spoke. "Boss, she... she went crazy and destroyed the table and stuff. I thought we would have to shoot her to protect ourselves."

Killington thought a moment before he acted. He walked up to Silvia and placed a large hand on her shirt, bunching it together and using it to haul her to her feet. He dragged her back to the work station and threw her into her seat. Her small stature didn't present much challenge for Killington and she looked more like a rag doll than a human being as she flopped into her chair.

Killington walked back to the two men who still had their pistols drawn. He took a gun away from one of the men. "You were worried about that pint sized girl hurting you?"

The man looked worried and shook his head. He had been afraid of Silvia a moment ago but was now much more afraid of his boss.

Killington could see the fear and fired the gun. The man fell to his knees before tipping over onto his face. The sound of the shot echoed in the large expanse of the building, reverberating in everyone's ears.

Killington turned to the other men around him. "Are there any other men here afraid of a little girl with a temper tantrum? You know, because when I put you on guard duty, I don't want any of you feel the need to cower in a corner somewhere the next time she acts out."

All the men shook their heads to emphasize their answers as they stated vehemently "No."

"Good, now get back to work, all of you." All the men ran away except the one who had been in the room when the temper tantrum had occurred. He stared at his partner, now dead on the floor.

Killington walked back to Silvia who sat in her chair crying. He placed his arms on his hips as if he were the parent and Silvia the child. "Oh don't cry for that dumb ass, there are plenty more where he came from. You know," he said, "I've lost more men on this job because of you, and I was the one who shot each of them. I'm getting tired of making examples out of these losers. So, what's up with you, why the tantrum?"

Silvia pointed to the dedicated screen that showed the internet broadcast of the race. She pressed a few buttons to rerun the last twenty minutes. When she arrived at the starting point she scrolled through the images to show Killington why she had become so angry.

On the screen, the MIT car sat at the end of the line of racecars waiting to exit the parking lot. A scantily clad blond woman with big breasts began to wave a green flag. The first two cars in the line raced out immediately and disappeared. The remaining vehicles all pulled to the side and allowed the last vehicle, the MIT car, to move ahead of them. On its roof the mechanical arm of the weapon swung ominously, threatening everyone around them.

Silvia became enraged again. She hammered her fists on the workstation's surface. Like bubbling acid in her stomach, her fury came in waves. Each and every time it happened she pounded the table before her. The tall monitors all rocked back and forth under her abuse.

Killington watched warily, not afraid of what she would do, but a little worried about the time it would take to replace the equipment if it fell. Time wasn't on his side at the moment. "Alright, I think I know where you need to start this morning. I want you to hack into their car and shut it down."

Nodding, Silvia agreed.

~~~

In North Platte, Nebraska, under a blue sky, Richard sipped some of his orange Gatorade. Today had been the easiest day of the race so far. Many hours passed and it had been simple and enjoyable driving. It had rained several hours ago but it had been a fast moving storm and no one would have known that they had ever been under rain clouds judging by the color of the sky now.

Katrina was stuffing her face with French fries from the local McDonald's.

"I think that since there are so few of us now that there will be little contact until we get to the end," she said.

As though her words had been a summons the split racecar suddenly flew past them.

Katrina stopped chewing to comment, "We have nothing to worry about. There is one more required night's stay. Let them come in first today, it won't matter."

Suddenly the sounds of sirens filled their ears and three police cars flew past them. They wondered if it was the split racecar that the police were hurrying toward, but were not really concerned. That was his problem. The rest of the day felt quiet and easy.

~~~

Furious key tapping filled the room where Silvia sat in front of her computer array. The armed guards didn't play cards as their former compatriots had. They watched their prisoner intently, but they had no idea what she was actually up to. They owned computers at home and could check their email and do some banking, maybe search some explicit web sites when they were bored, but what this girl was doing was way over their heads.

Silvia was working off of two separate keyboards and three screens. Code streamed down the screen so fast that the men couldn't be sure if she was actually typing all of the code they were seeing or if she was just hitting the down arrow key hard enough to break it. She swore loudly every couple of seconds, threw anything that wasn't nailed down, and pounded the table under her equipment so erratically that the sound could have been mistaken for a woodpecker with a nail gun for a head.

When Silvia shouted out that she required more coffee, the two men just looked at each other. They were half exasperated but also afraid that she might attack whoever brought it to her. To them her crazed activities were evidence of a serious mental imbalance. From the guards' perspective they felt that at any minute she could turn over the table of equipment or just jump out of the window the thirty feet to the ground. And if anything happened, Killington would blame them and shoot them both in the end.

After her third shout for coffee the men grimaced and brought their hands up to play a game of rock, paper, scissors. The loser was to be the one to have to deal with the lunatic girl. The dark haired man moaned loudly when his choice of paper could be cut by the younger man who had his fingers displayed as scissors. He got up and forcibly kicked his chair before walking away.

~~~

Kalby Mitchell blinked awake, hearing someone clapping. Appleton was standing and applauding at something on his computer screen.

"What did I miss?" he asked blearily.

"The results just came in. I know who is paying off Killington to sabotage the race! And he is not even connected to the investors!

Mitchell rubbed his eyes. "How do you know he's not connected?"

"I checked the list three times and he didn't show up. We can report our findings to Jenkins and get some real sleep." Appleton said, as he too began to rub his eyes.

Mitchell got up and crossed the room to look at the information. Did you consider that this trail you found is just a setup to hide the real billionaire?"

Appleton's mouth fell open. "But..."

"That never happens?" Mitchell said. "Yeah, right. Why don't you get some shut-eye and I'll research this guy you found."

Appleton walked away, his eyes shifting back and forth considering the possible implications of what he may have missed.

~~~

Silvia had received her last cup of coffee more than an hour ago. Adding to her erratic behavior of angry outbursts and throwing things at the guards, she got up and kicked her chair around the floor until her foot hurt and she collapsed to the floor and began to cry.

Killington came in, disturbed that this girl was upsetting his plans for the day. The guards left the room, not taking any chances. He walked up to Silvia and knelt next to her. He ran the warm barrel of his pistol down her cheek.

"My job is to eliminate cars from this race. You are my tool to get that done. If you can't do the job, my next bullet will be for you. I'm tired of your temper tantrums. Now get to work."

Silvia held her breath as she looked into Killington's eyes. He smiled broadly. She dramatically turned away and Killington left the room. When the door closed on the far end of the room and she was sure she was alone, she got up quickly and ran to the computer station. She might only be alone for one minute. She had to hurry.

Silvia turned towards the door, listened for a second and then went to work. She took the video camera off the top of the computer and stuffed it under some old food wrappers then she turned towards the keyboard. After a few keystrokes, the video that she had been taking popped up on the screen. She dragged her cursor over the horizontal scroll bar. In doing so, stills from the video could be seen through the progression of the movie.

She stopped at the point when she began to destroy a chair and the guards got up and drew their weapons at her. She didn't want the segment where she antagonized them into some kind of action to show. She deleted the entire first half of the video to edit out her own irrational behavior. All she wanted to show was the guards pointing their weapons at her until Killington showed up, his actions, and the part where he had threatened her life.

Silvia worked as fast as she could. She saved it under the name of "Help me." and closed all the video software. As expected, the guards returned to their chairs. She turned her gaze upon them and noticed that their weapons were not in their holsters. They lay on the laps waiting to be used.

A large man chewing a cigar said, "I have a bullet with your name on it. If you twitch the wrong way, I'm going to shoot you where you're sitting." Then he laughed.

Tapping away, Silvia sent the video to the FBI in an email that included her location. This time she was the one laughing, quietly, but laughing none the less.

Chapter 16

"Wait!" Katrina yelled at the top of her lungs. "I need another second!"

"I have to turn in two." Richard shouted back. "Make the shot count!" Richard counted. "One, turning! How long is the cord?"

The MIT car changed lanes. The passengers of a black Nissan Sentra had just witnessed two racecars fly by them on the highway not realizing how closely they had come to being struck by the lead car.

The sound of the weapon firing its laser head resonated inside the cabin of the racecar. Katrina yelled at the top of her lungs. "Missed! Don't worry about me, just drive!"

Katrina immediately pushed the button to reel in the laser head so it wouldn't hit the ground and be destroyed. The cable that followed the laser head became taught and started to run in reverse at a high rate of speed.

Three racecars wove around traffic on the 76 westbound lanes outside of Wiggins, Colorado. The MIT car had too much going for it, plenty of power, a real racecar driver at its helm, and the formidable weapon on its roof. A couple of the other drivers had decided to team up and corner the MIT car in an attempt to get it out of the race for good. Now that there were fewer cars in the race the drivers knew that teaming up would be their best chance.

After starting out as such a quiet day on the road Katrina and Richard hadn't seen it coming. They had been lulled into a false sense of security. The trap had been set for a stretch of road where there would be just enough traffic to keep their quarry contained. Open highway was out of the question. The power behind Dr. Jenkins' One Tree Project had proved formidable enough that the other drivers knew that the MIT car could outstrip their cars' speed and be gone without the unwitting help of others.

What was unfortunate, however, was the fact that the weapon on the MIT car's roof was taking a beating. Between the buffeting winds hitting the arm due to their current speed, and the bouncing from hard lane changes, the accuracy of the laser head had become impossible to predict. Four attempts had yielded four misses and Katrina was seriously frustrated.

Richard, on the other hand, was in his element. This is what he had signed up for, racing in all its glory. And he was good at it. None of the other cars could corner him. In fact, one had been left behind and was now struggling to catch up. Apparently they were running out of power. The MIT car had power in spades. Unlike other teams, who would run out completely and have to pull over to recharge, their power plant still provided the car with enough energy as they drove.

Even if he ran the battery down, they could still drive at lower speeds to recharge the system. But he knew the battery might be an issue if he couldn't take care of business soon. Ninety mile per hour speed had that effect on batteries. Katrina had warned him that they only had five minutes left before they had to do something desperate. But Richard knew that if they had five minutes left then the other cars had less.

The MIT car drove on, always keeping the other two drivers confused and trying to keep up. One team had a weapon mounted on a PVC pipe. It stuck out of the passenger's window pointed at Richard's side of the vehicle. The other had a primitive trolley system that was poorly built and shook heavily at ninety miles per hour.

With all the weaving through traffic, the car with trolley system kept moving to be on the right side of their vehicle so that they would be in position to use their weapon. Richard kept a keen eye on it.

As if on cue, the third car, the one that looked like a dune buggy, ran out of power. It fell away quickly, smoking slightly. Katrina's and Richard watched the second victim fall away.

"There is an exit ramp coming up in three miles, we need to be on it." Katrina shouted.

She didn't need to shout, their car was well made and the cab was insulated enough to block most road noise. However her excitement couldn't be as easily tempered by the protection of the fuselage.

Richard nodded, before he shouted back. "Point the weapon forward and down. I have an idea how to get this bastard out of the race."

Katrina did as she was told as Richard cut off a box truck on the right and then dropped back next to the truck separating the MIT car from the other racecar. The weapon on their roof, in its energized position, wobbled badly in the wind.

"When I tell you to fire the weapon, do it and hang on." Richard yelled.

"We can't. We'll pass the exit. We can't run on low power on the highway. Leave the other car alone and take the exit." Katrina said.

Richard ignored her and followed through with his plan anyway. He floored the accelerator and their car launched forward past the box truck like a rocket. The bars on the battery gauge began to drop quickly.

Katrina began a low level scream as she sank in her seat. Richard checked his mirror to judge the amount of clearance from the truck then he pulled the emergency brake. The MIT car spun in its position at their high rate of speed. Katrina's scream went from low shriek to a wail so shrill that birds would have fallen out of the sky because they needed their wings to cover their ears.

The MIT car spun, Katrina screamed in horror a she hung on for dear life, and a determined Richard Bertrand popped the clutch as he rammed the gear shift in reverse. He let momentum turn him around in his seat and threw his right arm over the back, his accelerator pedal hammered to the floor with sure footed experience.

In a thousandth of a second they were racing backwards down the highway facing the truck. The driver's eyes grew large and his mouth fell open to see such action.

"Fire!" Richard hollered over the screaming of his passenger.

He calculated the amount of time it would take for Katrina to open her eyes and figure out what he was doing before she actually fired the weapon. He wove to the other lane in front of the other racecar and held still long enough for the weapon to discharge.

Katrina was finally out of breath and Richard took the opportunity to shout "Fire!" again. Katrina pushed the red button on her handheld controller. As soon as the head released Richard repeated his e-brake pulling, clutch popping, hard steering maneuver, forcing their car to move in directions the car wasn't designed for.

Katrina's arms flailed everywhere filling the cabin. Her body bounced around like a pinball. Her long hair spread out like a fan, as if not sure which direction to turn. The weapon's control device also flew around the cabin intensifying the perception of weightlessness.

A card carrying stunt driver in his own right, Richard controlled every aspect of their flight from hiding behind the box truck to attacking their unsuspecting assailant and using their weapon in all its glory.

As the MIT car spun around again the shocked driver of the attack team showed astonishment beyond words. The wide eyes and slack jaw were only some of the expressions on his young face, astonishment, defeat, fear, and disbelief at such impressive driving skills.

The MIT's weapon head struck the nose of their hood. Its trailing cable had curved around their car's roof as Richard had righted them on the highway beside their target. Black smoke rose from the hood where the laser began to burn into the fragile skin and the car suddenly lost power. Richard slowed rapidly as he took a few seconds to find the weapon's controller and pushed the retract button. The laser head popped off and retracted into the waiting arm. He turned the car toward the exit lane. Seamlessly they rolled into the traffic pattern like nothing out of the ordinary had just occurred.

Katrina sat up. Her long brown hair was everywhere. Her headset sat askew. Her eyes were wild, she had no idea what had happened and seemed surprised that everything seemed to be back to normal. Richard was leaning back in his seat, enjoying the ride, and smiling as if nothing had happened. They were no longer being chased. She looked around to see where they were. "What happened? Where are we?" She asked in disbelief.

"I took care of all of our problems and got another car out of the race. And we got off at the exit you wanted us to take." Richard said proudly. He handed over the weapon's controller.

Katrina took it and looked around again. She picked up her paper map from where it had landed near her feet and studied it to make sure they were where they were supposed to be. "So, just like that, you took care of everything?"

"Yeah." Richard said pleased with himself.

That's when Katrina exploded. "That's how you take care of everything? You almost got us killed. What the hell were you thinking spinning around in the middle of the highway?" She beat on his arm. "There were children in the cars around us..." Katrina shouted.

~~~

Dr. Jenkins sat in front of a laptop computer screen, he had been watching the race on and off during the day through the Denver International Airport's internet connection. He was in an airport terminal with Frodes, Dillon, Kristin and several other students from the team who were waiting for their luggage to be regurgitated out of the hole above the baggage carousel.

The investor, Richard's father, had instructed them to follow the team to their next location, but on the sly. No one was supposed to know about this part of their participation in the race. The ability to bring a crew to repair the vehicles was supposed to have ended the previous night. At this point only the driving team members were allowed to maintain the car.

But Jenkins knew that there was more going on than what the rules allowed. He knew that there were forces at work attempting to destroy some of the cars and to allow only one car to finish the race. And he was fairly certain that Bertrand was not supposed to be the winner. Today they were going to fly to their next stop and catch up on some sleep along the way. They would not be staying at any hotels from now on. They had to keep as low a profile as possible, and they couldn't do that using Harvard Bertrand's credit card.

He was making use of as many free and untraceable wifi hotspots as possible along the way. He needed the reassurance that his team was okay. When the other racecars could be seen converging on their car, all of the students who had been watching the screen over his shoulder began to shout. They all watched in horror. They knew that the other cars were going to try to use their weapons. People around them at the airport were both interested and wary of the strange group at the luggage collection center.

When Richard began to perform magic not seen anywhere but on a stunt track, the shouts of anger changed to those of exuberance at his skill. The students punched the air and made predictions of what he would do next. Almost every student ticked off odds for which car would run out of power first. Their confidence ran high. When Richard had maneuvered the box truck between him and the other cars they were all watching silently in suspense.

Other people had started to join the group to try to watch the small screen out of curiosity. When one of the cars ran out of power and fell away. Cheers of the students filled the luggage terminal once more. None of the people around them understood what they were cheering for. Then Richard sped up and pulled the emergency brake.

Surprise and shock filled the room. One woman screamed thinking that they were going to witness a horrific crash. The MIT car spun fantastically and changed lanes while in reverse. When the weapon launched itself from the roof's robotic base more gasps occurred. Dillon put his hands over his eyes. Frodes punched the air. He knew exactly what his driver had done. Jenkins smiled.

When the other car began to slow rapidly, the room exploded in applause. The cheering was so loud that security officers came over to see what the ruckus was all about. Jenkins suddenly realized how much attention that they had attracted and quickly closed the laptop and walked towards the door without waiting for his luggage.

Frodes followed behind with a jump in his step. "That was fantastic! Who knew Richard could do such stunts?"

Jenkins stopped. "Where do you think they were going?"

Frodes stopped serious thought in his mind. "That's a good question. They were supposed to stay on the highway to get to the next stop."

"I'm fairly certain that they need to generate some power, and that can only happen at lower speeds but..." Jenkins thought out loud.

Frodes piped up with an idea. "I can call them and ask where they're going?"

"Not a good plan if others in the race community are looking for them," Jenkins said as he stuffed his laptop in his bag. "We don't know who else might be listening."

The smile on Frodes' face fell away completely. The realization that other teams had found a way to gang up on Richard and Katrina was astounding. How had they found them on that stretch of highway?

Frodes was in master engineer mode. He spoke in a hushed tone. "Well, we can't call up the GPS unit any more. But I can ping their cell phones and triangulate where they are by which cell phone towers..."

Jenkins stopped his student mid-sentence. "Pinging... You want to bet that someone else is tracking them even though we shut off all communication to the car?"

Frodes gazed up, his eyes went out of focus. He looked into the space in his mind where the images came to life.

"I think Katrina and Richard's cell phones are..." Jenkins began as Frodes placed a hand on his arm.

"Richard threw his phone away after that bad phone call from his father, remember?" Frodes said.

Jenkins nodded.

"They're tracking Katrina's phone," Frodes continued.

Jenkins eyes went wide, his jaw went slack. "I was so stupid!" Jenkins said loudly. "I'm willing to bet that they're tracking her family's phones too."

"Why would they care about Katrina's family?" asked Frodes. "It's not like she's been calling them from the road."

Jenkins' eyes had a glazed look as he answered. "We're talking about the mob. If they want something from Katrina, wouldn't they use her family to put pressure on her?"

Frodes watched as his professor paced around the terminal, wondering how he could help. Every time Frodes began to speak Jenkins placed a hand into the air to forestall him.

After a few minutes Jenkins began to speak again. "First, we need to make sure that Katrina's family is safe. Do you know where they live?"

Frodes scratched his head. "Maine, I think."

"If they have passports, send them to Quebec. If they don't, find them a motel in some small town in Vermont somewhere. That'll have to do. Make sure that they leave all of their cell phones behind. Call some of the team back to get it taken care of as soon as possible. Second, we need to rent another car. Third, we need to get some cheap phones. Fourth, we're going to Walmart to buy a shotgun.

Shock spread over Frodes' face. They were engineers, not spies. He was not prepared for this kind of violence.

Jenkins continued. "I need to talk to Dillon. Get the bags and let's get out of here. We have a lot of work ahead of us, and we still need to arrange another set of tires for tomorrow."

Chapter 17

It was dark out. Night had quickly followed dusk and they were still on the road. Richard drove towards the Castle Rock Best Western on Genoa Way. They had found the right street and Katrina was now counting off numbers on buildings to find the hotel. It was located at 595, but in the dark it was difficult to see numbers on buildings that were not lit in some way. They had taken back roads for the remainder of the day and it had helped them recharge, but it had also taken them much longer to arrive.

Aside from needing to leave the highway to recharge, she also knew that the police could be looking for them. Stunt driving on a small highway may have saved them from the other cars but it could have also attracted unwanted attention. She wondered how many 911 calls had been made after their getaway. The only bonus was that their car's skin had not been burned, one less thing to worry about tonight.

Katrina felt so tired that she could easily fall asleep in the car, but she knew that Richard must be equally tired. She counted off another number, "487" before they stopped at another traffic light. There were no other cars at the intersection. Waiting at stop lights when there was no traffic infuriated Richard.

Then out of nowhere a young man ran up to the car and shouted at them. "Wait!"

Richard looked around cautiously.

Katrina recognized Frodes and said, "What the hell are you doing?"

Jenkins and Dillon approached the car and Frodes moved away from the window to allow Jenkins to speak to Katrina and Richard.

"Sorry to startle you but we needed to talk to you. We also need to take your phone. That's how they're tracking you." Jenkins said to Katrina.

Without question Katrina produced her phone and handed it to him. Jenkins stood and tossed it to Dillon. "You know what to do."

Dillon caught the phone and ran off.

The look on Katrina's face was that of extreme incredulity. "What is going on?" She asked.

Jenkins began explaining the plan. "We're trying to protect you. That's why we're stopping you before you get into the parking lot. When you get to the Best Western, park where you see a small white Toyota Corolla pulling out. Kristin is watching for you to enter. After you park, check in but don't go to your room. There will be a cab waiting for you, have them take you to Olive Garden, there is only one in town. When you arrive, I'll be waiting to fill you in. There is not enough time to explain more now, just go. And remember, do not go to your room."

"But I'm tired, I need a shower, and I need to rest." Richard whined.

Katrina added, "I really have to go to the bathroom."

"I'm telling you, there is probably someone waiting for you in that room." Jenkins said. "Just follow my instructions."

Frodes ran around to the other side of the car to be at Richard's window. He thrust his hand inside the cab in the customary handshake position. Richard took his hand apprehensively.

"Let me just say that your driving today was truly inspirational. I've never seen anything like it in my life."

Katrina's mouth fell open. "You thought that was good? I almost died."

"It was amazing." Frodes insisted.

Katrina hit Richard. "Men!"

"Ouch! What did you do that for?"

Jenkins interrupted them. "Just go, we'll see you at the restaurant."

Richard drove off with Katrina once again searching for the motel's entrance.

~~~

The last of the dedicated workers in the FBI office had shut down their computers and were preparing to call it a day. There were only three of them left, the others had gone home hours ago. There was no end to the work before any of them but at some point they had to admit defeat so that a hot meal and a night's sleep could attempt to rejuvenate them sufficiently to begin a new day. These three were young and filled with drive. Alcohol and cigarettes had not yet replaced the hot meal and sleep that they required.

Two men and one woman, all professionally dressed, approached the elevator at the same time while speaking very little, their backs still slightly hunched from their fourteen hour day. They were part of a much larger team that worked mob activity over many upper mid-western states. Their office was in Detroit, Michigan; the most central state of the five that they covered. The elevator took forever to climb the meager six stories to collect them, but the images in their minds kept them focused on work that had been left for tomorrow.

Their floor supervisor was still ensconced behind his desk trying to finish a report before the next day's scheduled meeting. He typed feverishly. His was very focused at that moment and he knew that if he could continue uninterrupted he could finish the report in fifteen minutes, tops.

Of course when all things in the universe are aligned and clarity is absolute, the phone will ring, and it did.

Finn Cosgrove took a deep breath, trying to get his sanity back. His report was long and detailed. Weeks of preparation had gone into its design and voice. This phone call was just one of many interruptions during his attempt to write. But it was after hours, did he have to answer? He grimaced and picked up the call just the same. "Cosgrove."

"You have three agents that are about to leave. Quick, grab them before they catch the elevator. I need to see all four of you, now. Your report is going to have a completely different ending after today."

Cosgrove looked out of his open office door and saw the three agents waiting for the elevator. "Yes, sir," he said with obvious surprise.

Finn thought about his almost 200 page report, wondering what could possibly need to be changed. Then, as he had been ordered, he stood and called out to the agents.

As their heads turned they could see their supervisor waving them back towards his office just as the sound of the elevator called to them. Deep measured breaths tried to cover up their tired demeanors but didn't cover their growling stomachs as they looked at each other and walked slowly back into the room away from the open elevator.

"Brockton, Weaver, Colliste, we just got called up." Finn said. "Let's go." He turned his head back to the phone receiver he was still holding and asked "We're all here, what do you need?"

"You need to pick up Mac Killington, tonight. We have video of him confessing to several murders. He's holding a woman hostage here in Detroit. And we know where they are."

~~~

In the Castle Rock, Colorado, Best Western, two men sat waiting in room 238. One of the men checked his watch. He was dressed nicely for a thug. His partner for this assignment was a short balding man in baggy jeans and a rumpled shirt who was currently lying on the bed staring at the ceiling.

"Can't we at least turn on the game?" he asked. "We've been waiting for hours. I have money on this one."

"No, I told you we can't, now shut up, we need to be quiet."

"You're talking." The balding man returned.

The better dressed man jumped from his chair and slapped the other man as he lay on the bed. They looked like brothers who had been forced to share a bedroom though they couldn't stand each other.

~~~

Richard drove the racecar into the Best Western parking lot. A white Corolla began to back out of a parking space that was partially hidden by shrubs on two sides. He waited for her to finish backing up then drove into the space. He and Katrina dragged themselves out of the windows. Wearily they made their way to the front desk.

Dillon watched Katrina and Richard walk across the lot from his hiding spot among the bushes. He picked up his two way radio and said, "Lock down in process."

Kristin walked across the parking lot and disappeared with Dillon into the shadows.

~~~

The portly gentleman at the front desk gave Richard and Katrina's racing uniforms a raised eyebrow. He would never have asked why they were wearing such outfits, but he had also just started his shift and had missed the other racecar drivers that had arrived earlier. The time was nine-thirty. When the check-in process was completed he handed them their room keys.

"Have a pleasant night's stay." he said automatically.

Richard turned towards the elevator but Katrina grabbed his arm and pulled him back.

"You can't," she reminded him.

"Listen, I'm tired and I have to pee so bad I'm going to pop." Richard said. "You go to the restaurant and listen to what Jenkins has to say. I need to lay down."

Katrina pulled him outside angrily.

The desk attendant looked at them quizzically.

"You can't go to the room."

Their cab pulled up and Frodes rolled down the front passenger window.

"Quick, get in," he said.

Katrina pushed Richard into the car and climbed in after him. The cab drove off in an instant.

Frodes turned to face them. "We're going to a different hotel room so you'll both be safe. And we have people guarding the car. We had to bring food to the motel though; Olive Garden was winding down for the night. I hope you don't mind Subway."

Richard sighed. "Subway again?"

Five minutes later the cab stopped at the Sunny Top Motel. Frodes led them into room ten and locked the door behind them. Richard wasted no time running for the bathroom. Katrina had to go too but she felt she could wait so she checked out the room as Jenkins began to speak.

"I'm sorry to say that you have to share a room tonight. All the other rooms are taken. Frodes and I will be working so we don't need one."

Richard walked out of the bathroom looking very relieved. Katrina jumped at the chance to take her turn.

He cast his eyes around the room to check out the accommodations "This place is a dump," he said.

Jenkins took a good long swallow of beer before he spoke. "It's a good thing you're going to be asleep for most of the time you're here, isn't it."

Richard threw himself on the bed and stretched out to rest his back. Katrina exited the bathroom and sat across from her mentor. "So what's going on?" she asked.

"We figured out how you were being tracked. We have your phone at the other hotel and we're watching the car," Jenkins said as he opened up one of wrapped sandwiches on the table. "Dillon is going to stay near the hotel and use your phone to make a few phone calls. It'll keep Killington at bay for a little while."

Richard sat up and said, "Who's Killington?"

"He's the guy that was hired to stop you from finishing the race. He's a mob boss based in Detroit. We also think he's the one who sent that maroon Ford Explorer out to shut you down the first day."

At once Katrina's expression changed at the mention of the accident that she had caused.

"I'm very sure he will try again, which is why you can't stay in your room at the Best Western, and why you can't keep your phone on you anymore," Jenkins said after another long pull from his beer. "Since there are so few racecars left it's a pretty safe bet that their efforts to hunt you guys down will only increase. The motel would have been one of the easiest ways to find you. They knew that all the drivers would be staying there tonight.

"Tomorrow is the beginning of the end. After you leave in the morning either you will be attacked by other drivers trying to disable you, or the mob will be trying to find you on the road. At least we'll have Dillon and Kristin running interference for you. Then there's your driving, Richard."

Katrina became concerned and interrupted Jenkins. "Wait, what are Dillon and Kristin going to be doing?"

"Don't worry about them. We have a lot of different plans running to help keep you guys safe."

Richard became indignant. "What about my driving?"

Jenkins smiled. "Your driving ability has proved to be just as effective as the weapon that Katrina designed. The combination makes you two the most hated driving team of the race, and the greatest threat against any other team. So my assumption is that after the green flag drops tomorrow morning, you will be very busy right up until the end. At last count, there are only six teams left."

No one spoke as Katrina and Richard tried to absorb what had been said. Jenkins ate his sandwich. For many minutes the silence hung. Frodes sucked on a beer. Finally Jenkins raised a hand towards Frodes as though he had forgotten to mention something.

Frodes stood to speak. "Oh yeah, after we watched your fantastic driving earlier..."

Richard smiled large. "It was good, wasn't it?"

Katrina threw a sandwich at Richard, hitting him in the head.

Richard put his hands in the air. "At least someone recognizes my efforts." He threw the sandwich back at Katrina and missed, but his dirty look didn't.

Frodes continued with a smile. "After we watched your stunt driving earlier, we came to several conclusions. First, your tires must be totaled so we've ordered another set of tires." Frodes said with an even larger smile. "I'll call you when they're ready. You'll have to go get them but it isn't too far out of the way and they will only take about five minutes to install. We chose a more aggressive tread to cover your driving through the desert, but they may be a little loud on the pavement.

"We also picked up burn phones to keep in touch with you. If we tell you dump the phone, it's because we found out you're being tracked again so throw them out the window, and we'll find a way to get you another one. Also we got you some paper maps. The best advice we can give you is to stay off the grid, take secondary roads and don't use any electronics that can be traced back to you. The remaining racecars are the best of the best but they still may not be able to keep up with your driving skills Richard."

Richard smiled and Katrina frowned.

"Their cars' technology is first rate though, and can probably almost keep up with your car in energy usage. You can't count on the fact that our car will always be able to out-pace them in speed for a longer period of time."

Jenkins finished eating and popped open another beer. "Vincent is right. In short stints our engine might be able to outrun everyone if we were on a track, but this isn't that kind of race. Your goal must still be to reserve power when you can, otherwise you may be in a position of low power under the wrong circumstances."

Chapter 18

FBI agent Finn Cosgrove and his three minions suited up and piled into a strike team van. Dawn had technically passed and there seemed no end to how fast the time flew them by. They were supposed to have picked up Killington half an hour ago but they hadn't been able to find a judge to sign a warrant in the middle of the night. Now they were behind the eight ball. Much of the chatter they had collected on Killington and his men over the last three years had suggested that there were collaborators within the local police department and perhaps even the FBI, since their office sat in Killington's home territory.

Cosgrove knew that if they were shopping for a judge to sign the warrant, someone may have already alerted Killington and minutes were slipping away far too quickly.

"Come on people! Time is ticking."

Brockton appeared wide awake and ready to run with the big dogs. The caffeine pills he had washed down with very hot black coffee had pushed him into a startled state of awareness. He looked jittery, on edge.

Weaver had pulled a new mask over her sleepy one. This new face looked sharp and mean. Her eyes said that someone was going down. She hoped the mask would stay in place during the raid, she didn't want to look or act sleep deprived at a bad moment. Unfortunately she had worn a skirt to work yesterday and now she had to go into a firefight wearing the same outfit. She resolved to bring an extra set of clothes to leave under her desk for similar events in the future. Thankfully she had found a pair of sneakers in her car to replace her heels.

Colliste appeared to have slept, though they knew that it would have been impossible. He seemed light-hearted about the operation and joked with the strike team as they prepared.

As Colliste made another joke that brought laughter among the team members, Cosgrove's phone rang.

He said "Shut it," before answering with "Tell me it's good news."

Everyone in the van listened intently. All attention was focused on him when he cut the connection.

"We have the warrant," he announced, "Two minutes to our positions, go."

~~~

Silvia Thruwell was thrown to the floor. The force of her landing had taken her breath away, her heart hammered against her ribs so fast that the second half of a full beat was drowned out by the echo of the first half. Tears streamed down her cheeks from extreme fear. Her top was ripped exposing her black bra. She turned to look for her assailant in the darkness.

A large man with a pudgy face was just visible in the light from the room's single fixture. He smiled as though he had just won the lottery. A second man stood in shadows with his gun drawn. He too expressed excitement.

Her guards had been pulled away late in the previous afternoon and had been replaced with these thugs. From the get go these two had seemed on edge. She hadn't understood then what guard duty might provide that would be so exciting to these guys. All they did was watch her work at her computer station.

At this moment, lying on the floor, she understood why the guards had been changed out. Killington was going to cut her down several notches so she would be more compliant to do his bidding. She knew that he wouldn't kill her, at least not until the job was done. But there were a lot of ways to torture a woman.

It occurred to her that she may have overdone it with her outbursts if this was his answer. These men had been sent to do whatever it took for her to become submissive. Everyone else was afraid of him and she had not shown enough fear, enough respect.

She knew that she possessed skills that Killington wanted. He wanted her to work for him for more than just this 'operation'. She knew that he would not just let her go after her job was complete. He needed her, but he also needed her to bend to his will. His plan was obviously to violate her badly enough that she would be willing to do anything. Silvia had no idea what she could possibly do to prevent whatever the two 'guards' had in mind.

The man walked over next to her as she lay on the floor. He grabbed her arm and dragged her under him. She cried out kicking and screaming. He leered at her and licked his lips. Silvia's punched and kicked at every part of him that she could reach but it didn't slow him down. He was so big and strong, her strikes had no effect at all.

Silvia knew her time was short and with renewed vigor attacked the giant. The other guard had put away his gun and had begun to salivate over the show before him. He knew that soon it would be his turn.

The hand that had been trying to constrain her arm went instead to her neck. Her body slackened. She no longer kicked at his body; instead she struggled against the hand around her neck, trying desperately to get air.

A door on the far side of the room exploded off its hinges. Smoke canisters came flying through. The canisters disgorged their chemicals. Agents rushed in as the chemicals began to dissipate, some of them were holding rifles and some had handguns. The guard who had been watching Silvia's struggle quickly drew his gun. A second later a shot rang out and he was down.

Weaver stormed into the room and saw the man who was only seconds away from destroying the girl beneath him. She never shouted to announce their presence or to tell him to stop what he was doing. She fired three shots into the man. He fell over sideways, releasing Silvia as he fell.

Weaver ran up and made sure that there was no other danger to the shaking, coughing girl. She reached down to touch Silvia and ask if she was alright but Silvia flinched under her touch. She gasped over and over again to catch her breath but all she wanted right then was for no one to ever touch her again.

Angry at their late arrival, knowing that they could have arrived before this had happened Weaver turned towards the dead man and used her foot to roll him on his back. She desperately wanted to shoot him in the groin for the action he was about to perpetrate against the small girl.

Inside the FBI trike team van Silvia sat engulfed in a coat that had belonged to Cosgrove and with a blanket around her legs. In her hands she held a hot cup of coffee. She shook almost uncontrollably, shock had set in. Cosgrove wanted Weaver to she sit with the victim to see if she would have any better luck getting information from the small woman. So far Silvia had been unable to speak. Her eyes were glazed over as though someone had painted scary images on them and she couldn't look away.

~~~

At the Best Western in Castle Rock, Colorado, Dillon and Kristin guarded the MIT racecar. They were completely camouflaged by the high hedges at the parking lot's edge. Darkness was complete for anyone looking in but not for those who were looking out into the lighted parking area.

A guy that looked like he belonged to a motorcycle gang, complete with skull cap and leather jacket, walked across the parking lot carrying something bulky covered with what looked like one of the motel's bath towels. When he approached the MIT car he slowly turned his head one way, then the other to see if anyone was watching him. He balanced his package on one arm and pulled the towel away, dropping it onto the ground. He pushed a button on the device and stepped closer to the car as if he were holding a bomb and the timer was ticking.

Dillon could tell immediately that it was a weapon from a racecar. Either a team had taken a weapon off their car to use or they had another handheld model for back up. Either way he had to confront the man. Dillon stepped out of the bushes.

"Don't even think it," he said "Get away from the car."

The other man's face turned into a menacing snarl as he said "What are you going to do about it?"

Kristin stepped out next to Dillon holding the shotgun. "We could shoot you," she said, and then in a reassuring voice she added, "I'm sure that the cleanup team can handle a bullet wound, we saw them clean up that accident. They might even be quick enough to save your life, depending on where the bullet hits."

The man in the leather jacket glared at Dillon and Kristin before turning away, wondering how the MIT team had managed to arrange for protection for their car so far from home.

~~~

Back at the FBI office, Silvia had been given some clothes to wear, some sweat pants and a sweat shirt that were meant for someone much larger, and she now sat in Cosgrove's office. Weaver sat in the chair next to her. Replenished cups of joe invigorated the sleepy agents and helped calm the small victim.

"Tell me," Cosgrove asked. "How did you end up in that warehouse? Did they offer you a job..."

Weaver slapped the desk angrily. "She's obviously the victim here!" She turned to Silvia. "But we need to know if he recruited you, hired you to do a job, or if he kidnapped you?"

Silvia shook her head. "It's not what you think. I offered to do some computer work for him because I knew about a job that he had been hired to do. I had my reasons, and he had the resources to get it done. I told him at the beginning that I was only going to do that one job. But once he saw how good I was with a computer he made other plans. If you hadn't found me when you did... I don't even want to think about what would have happened."

Cosgrove and Weaver looked at each other. Cosgrove repositioned the microphone on his desk. "What was the job that he was hired to do? And why would you want to help him do it?"

Silvia took a sip of her warm coffee. "There's this race. A race for cars, but about technology not speeds. They have all of these cars that are supposed to go from the east coast to the west coast to see which machine does it best. Killington was hired to get as many cars as he could disqualified, so that one of the cars would have a better chance of winning."

"How do you know this?" Cosgrove asked. Her words had whetted his appetite for details that could be used in his report.

"Because," Silvia said a little reluctantly, "I helped build one of the cars.

~~~

Katrina sat up suddenly when the alarm went off. Richard, right beside her, tried to use his arm to kill the clock making the racket. He swatted the air and hammered his hand on the empty bedside table.

When he couldn't find it, he shouted "Turn it off already, will ya!"

Katrina put her face in her hands so he wouldn't see her laughing soundlessly. Katrina got out of her bed and crossed the room to turn it off. She had been the one who had decided that it would be better to have the clock far enough away so that they couldn't reach the snooze button from the bed.

When she killed the irritating noise Richard turned over and immediately began to snore.

Katrina wondered how anyone could fall back to sleep that quickly. She walked over to his bed and grabbed the sheets. She pulled them away from him but he slept on. He continued to snore even as she dragged him to the bed's edge, until he fell off and hit the floor.

"Get up. We have to get ready. Last day!" Katrina said, trying to sound more energetic than she felt.

"What did you do that for?" he asked. "I'm awake."

Less than an hour later both Richard and Katrina sat in their racecar. They were both yawning as Richard pulled the car toward their lineup position. An individual in a bright green shirt was directing the order of the cars. The split car took its position as the leader, followed by the dune buggy car. Then two other cars fell into line. Katrina noted the similarities between the next two cars and assumed that they must have followed similar chassis ideas. The only telling difference between them was their weapon's design. The car closest to them had a weapon on a trolley system. The other car's weapon didn't attach to the exterior of the car at all. They had used a much cheaper and easier method that was a simple weapon head on a stick, more portable maybe, but a lot less stable in a moving vehicle. Katrina felt that it was an indication of their design team's lack of foresight. She wondered what else they cheaped out on.

Richard steered the MIT car to be the next in line. He didn't pay any attention to the last car as it was coming up behind him but Katrina was very interested in what was left of their competition. That car had the same fuselage as the rest but their design had an extra component jutting out from the rear. It looked like a wide housing of sorts with a single trolley track that ran the entire perimeter of the vehicle starting and ending at the rear. The additional housing made the rear of the vehicle longer than the rest of the cars by about two feet. It didn't take too much imagination to figure out that something ran around on the track, but the trolley system for a weapon should have required a tandem track design to keep it stable. One track didn't make any sense. She was intrigued by the possible design of the weapon that could successfully use a single track system.

Cameramen hovered around the cars filming, waiting for the green flag. One came in close to Richard. He waved his hand in front of the lens to show that he didn't want these pests so close by.

Grant Phyindress used his bullhorn to get everyone's attention. A different busty bimbo than the ones they had seen on previous days jumped up and down with excitement. This one was dressed in a yellow spandex outfit that had black and white squares checkered diagonally across the middle. Many of the men appeared to have lost interest in the race in favor of watching her jump.

Katrina shook her head in shame at both genders. She decided to take that moment to power up their weapon. That was something to get excited about. When the device on the MIT roof finished its powering up sequence, it had everyone's attention. The bouncing bimbo couldn't compete with that kind of power. Some of the cameramen moved back a little out of fear.

Katrina was proud of her and Silvia's design and was still sad that Silvia wasn't with the team watching the race. Silvia's anger at not being chosen to ride in the car as the weapon's specialist still bothered Katrina. They had both worked hard on this weapon and she had never intended to take any of the accolades away from her team member.

Katrina wondered if her absence meant that she didn't want any of the credit. Had she not wanted anyone to know that she had been involved with the race at all? If they did win the race Katrina wanted to include Silvia in any honors that they received. The awards wouldn't be handed out in the desert around the finish ring. The whole team would be invited to attend a special dinner to honor all those who had made the race a success. It was supposed to be held in Las Vegas a week after the winning car went through the ring. Katrina hoped that Silvia wouldn't still be too angry to show up for that.

Phyindress stopped shaking hands and walked to the parking lot's exit. The bouncing bimbo had finally stopped jumping but she still shook with excitement. Her busty figure did what it was supposed to do, as long as she moved, some would be distracted by her, and many were watching.

Phyindress raised the bullhorn and began, "Welcome to the last day of the invisible technology race of the century. As it stands, there are only six contestants left to race. I have to say that our online viewers are very happy with how the race has unfolded so far. I'm sure today, the last day, will not disappoint.

"Rules. There are no more scheduled stops. It's a straight shot to the finish ring now. The racers will keep going until the end. That means they will be driving around twenty hours, if my math is right." He paused to allow laughter at his little joke. "They will be driving through the intense heat of the desert. Will the technology survive the heat? Big stakes are on the line.

"There are two teams that will require an electrical recharge somewhere along the way, two that will need hydrogen refills, which I must say, is not a quick process. We have one car that will have to find a natural gas outlet, and then there's the MIT team, who claim that they have no need to stop for recharging.

"There are some who are laying their bets on the MIT team, but I know for a fact that their car has taken quite a beating. Will it go all the way? I think that the odds are pretty even across the board depending on what obstacles the day brings.

"Then there's the finish line. Since these teams are made up of engineers, we made the end as interesting as the race. The finish line is a ring raised up on a dais. The teams must have a way to get their car up on the dais and through the ring to win. The dais is approximately three feet off the ground so the driver and passenger can't just get together to lift their car onto it. Some of the cars have brought ramps with them throughout the race, others have plans that are as yet undisclosed. It'll be interesting to see how this race ends."

Much discussion broke out. Some pointed to two of the cars that had ramps strapped to their roofs. Phyindress smiled at the additional interest he had created.

Katrina turned to face her driver. "What does Phyindress mean by undisclosed? How else could you get the car through the hoop if you don't have ramps?"

Richard just shook his head. He still looked groggy.

"I don't know and I don't care. We have ramps, so what does it matter? I just need him to wave the damn flag so we can get going."

Katrina furrowed her brow at his surliness and sat back in her seat.

The weapon on the MIT roof followed her motion and arced from where Phyindress stood with his bullhorn towards the parking lot exit. People all around ducked, not sure of its intention. Everyone in attendance had some investment in the outcome of the race. They had all watched enough of the race to know what the weapon was capable of.

Phyindress handed the green flag to the busty bimbo. She began to jump up and down with excitement all over again. She waved it without waiting for the signal to do so and the first two cars sped off. The driver of the third car still had his attention focused on the woman holding the flag and didn't move until someone in the car behind them laid on their horn, then the rest of the line moved out of the lot.

Richard never even glanced at the bouncing sex object as he drove by. Katrina looked though, trying to understand the other men's reactions. Of course the weapon on the roof turned with Katrina's head and pointed right at the girl. She stopped bouncing and moved quickly out of the way.

None of the other cars had moved to the side to let them pass this time. Richard thought it meant that there would be no more niceties. Or maybe the other driver's had realized that their weapon had only been used defensively. Either way today was all about winning. He had waited four days for the intensity of the race to be about winning. Today was about hard driving. Today he was going to strut his stuff. He didn't want to have to worry about other cars trying to disable their opponents. In twenty hours they would win, that was his goal and nothing was going to stop him.

Katrina opened a note that she had found on the seat before she had climbed into the car. "We have to go Denver to get our new tires. I'll check the map, we need to go there first."

Richard nodded, grinding his teeth in frustration. "We don't really have a choice, do we? We don't need any complications on the rest of the way to the finish line... er, ring."

"We need those tires so we have to go to Denver."
Katrina started. "The Cadillac dealer we're supposed to
see is on Broadway."

"How far out of the way is it?"

"Not bad. As long as it doesn't take them long to
swap them we should be fine." Katrina added. She picked
up the note again and read the rest of it. "Dr. Jenkins
wants us to lose the box truck that's following us so we'll
be completely off the grid. That won't disqualify us will
it?"

"He wouldn't have told you to do it if it would cost
us the race."

They watched the rest of the drivers head towards
Interstate 70 while they drove into the city instead. The
only race related vehicle that followed them was their
assigned box truck.

Richard could see that rush hour traffic was
building all around them. They were heading into the
heart of Denver at the moment. All he needed was an
exit off the freeway soon and he could easily lose them.

"It shows that there is an exit not far ahead but it
won't take us into the city where we want to go, and it
doesn't really make sense to try to lose the truck until
after we've swapped the tires." Katrina said as she
studied her map.

"Shouldn't matter when we lose them, they don't
know where we're stopping." Richard countered.

Without waiting for a response, or an argument,
he stomped on the accelerator. The car lurched forward
throwing Katrina back into her seat. The racecar zoomed
ahead causing each of them to sink deep in their seats.
Richard's gaze went to his mirror. Their entourage fell
back quickly. The box truck was trying to navigate
around the cars to catch up but the clunky suspension of
the truck was not built for racing.

"What the hell are you doing?" she exclaimed while she hit him the arm over and over again.

"If you will stop hitting me, I'll show you." Richard exclaimed.

He switched lanes to be on the extreme left side of the highway. Richard looked over to the approaching exit Katrina had mentioned and counted down in his mind until the right moment. The white box truck was almost ten car lengths behind them now but it was getting closer.

Katrina only had a mystified expression on her face.

Richard finished his count down replacing zero with "Now." He slammed on the breaks.

The MIT racecar slowed incredibly fast and the box truck flew past them. Richard stomped on the accelerator again and changed lanes towards the right, dodging several pickup trucks and two cars to make it into the exit lane. He slowed to keep their speed in tune with the other traffic and watched the box truck continue on the highway. He was sure that they had not seen the racecar move toward the exit. All it would take was a few more seconds and they would be out of sight.

Katrina cleared the hair away from her face. "Are you trying to get me killed?" She hit him again.

Richard raised his hand and gesticulated towards the now missing box truck. "I got us off the grid, isn't that you wanted?"

Katrina hit him again and again. "You're not getting it! You have to tell me what you're doing so I can..."

"So you can tell me what to do? This was an easy maneuver. I didn't spin the car in the middle of the road this time." Richard defended his actions as he raised his voice.

Katrina hit him again and again as they continued down the exit.

~~~

In a small interrogation room Brockton had his turn at Killington. Amazingly, even at this hour of the morning he was still wearing a suit. During such early morning raids it was customary to find the person being arrested still in bed or in some form of bed clothes as they tried to avoid capture, but not Mac Killington.

Killington was also stubborn, and his calm demeanor infuriated Brockton, whose caffeine high was wearing off. His sleep deprived stupor was easily supplanted by anger.

Brockton slammed his hand on the table in front of Killington. "I want a name. Who's paying you?"

Killington didn't say a word. His smile spoke volumes about his security within the justice system. He knew that all he had to do was wait for his lawyer to arrive and he would be released. A soft knock came from the two-way mirror. Brockton knew what it meant and rose immediately.

"Time to send in the next round, or is my lawyer here?" Killington asked. His smug smile did nothing to fix Brockton's mood.

Brockton stormed out of the room.

Killington sat in smug confidence. He wore it on his face like an award, a reliable outcome based on years of bribes and payoffs.

Many minutes passed. Killington sat with the same expression knowing that someone on the other side of the glass was watching him.

Cosgrove opened the door and entered alone holding a file folder. Killington stood to greet him like an old friend. "Cosgrove, I wondered if you had a hand in this… misunderstanding."

Cosgrove smiled but didn't respond.

Killington added, "We could have met in a much less stressful environment. I've said time and time again that my booth at Charlie's is always open to you."

Cosgrove shook his head. "This is different Mac. I have you on some pretty serious stuff now."

"Ah… What could you possibly have? My Lawyer will be here soon and I'll be out of here within in an hour. You and I both know the drill. Why must we play these games?"

Cosgrove smiled. He leaned back in his chair as though he had all the time in the world. "An hour? Not this time. I have enough to hold you for a very long time."

Killington followed Cosgrove's move and cocked his head to the right before he said his next statement. "I guess it'll be up to the judge, then."

The file folder opened before the FBI agent spoke again. "Tell me about this race that you're involved in."

Killington just looked at him.

"We know that you were hired to disable as many cars as possible to hedge the bet for someone. And we know that as part of that process you murdered several people. What I want to know is where the race contestants are, and where they are headed. It might go better for you if talk to me before your Lawyer gets here." Cosgrove leaned forward to emphasize his final point. "Because you will not be out of here anytime soon."

Killington sat back in his chair to consider his situation then hitched up his smile again. "I've never killed anyone."

"Okay, how about attempted rape?" Cosgrove said.

"Nope."

"Kidnapping?"

"Nope."

"Conspiracy to commit murder?"

"Nope."

"How about racketeering?"

Killington's smile broadened. "You have nothing."

Both men chuckled. Cosgrove flipped another page in is file. "I believe I have enough evidence for all of those charges, and maybe a few more. In fact, the young girl we rescued from your men has given us plenty. Since we came in as your men were attempting to rape her, on your orders, I think our case is pretty solid.

"Silvia Thruwell says that you were keeping her against her will so that she would hack into the racecars and shut them down. Considering her background at MIT and the fact that she admitted to working on their racecar lends credence to her story. And I know for a fact that the thug who was trying to rape her works for you. So this jigsaw puzzle we're working on is coming together nicely. Then there's the murders you admitted to..."

This got Killington's attention at once. He sat straighter. "I didn't kill anyone. That little bitch can say whatever she wants but you can't prove anything."

"Silvia didn't tell me anything about the murders." Cosgrove said with a delicious smile on his face as Killington's faltered. "You did. You admitted it on video."

Killington's mind went into overdrive searching his memories as to when he may have admitted to killing anyone, ever.

Cosgrove stood and closed his file. "When your lawyer gets here, you might want to tell him to do some research on preparing for a murder case as well as the civil racketeering charges. You're not going anywhere."

Weaver leaned in a hunched manner on the edge of a desk trying to keep sleep at bay. Colliste appeared to be in a drunken stupor, leaning partially to one side of the chair he sat in, and Brockton pressed on with more caffeine pills and black coffee. He looked to be one most awake at the moment but the dark circles under his eyes suggested that he could fall asleep with his eyes open.

Cosgrove entered the viewing room with the two way mirror holding the file. Before he could utter an order, hopefully the one that would allow them some serious sleep, Brockton spoke in rapid fire, caffeine boosted words. "Boss, we have the location of the racecars. The state police in Colorado have reported picking up a very unusual car, a car that meets no factory specs. In itself that is not big news. But there were at least four other cars just like it on the same stretch of highway, heading towards interstate 70."

Cosgrove looked at the floor, thinking. When he lifted his head, he too spoke in rapidly fired words. "Tell the pilot to be ready to go in thirty minutes. We need to get to the airport. Have a plane ready to fly when we get there. Call the bureau in Colorado, tell them were coming and to find those racecars. We're stopping that race before anyone else gets killed. Get the rest of the team back in the office, we need logistics up and running before we leave. You guys can sleep on the plane."

~~~

A car lift started to ascend in a busy bay of a Cadillac dealership. The sounds of impact wrenches filled the cavernous garage that held forty lifts. Most of the bays were already full, with the flat rate technicians tearing through their work. Echoes of ratchet clicks and hammers mingled among the sounds of the pneumatic tools. The one thing that seemed very absent were the voices.

Katrina and Richard stood off to one side. Their race uniforms made them stand out against the drab uniforms of the technicians. The dealership's owner and general manager both stood nearby overseeing the work. The owner was a burly man with thinning hair, wearing a worn grey suit. His big smile could have been a genuine reaction to the amount of money he was making on this job but his years as a salesman were obvious in the frozen expression.

The general manager had fewer years on him and sported a light blue oxford shirt with a pair of tan Khakis. His round face matched his round stomach. His hair appeared exceptionally thick for his age, but instead of making him look younger it made him look a little creepy somehow.

The dealership was getting paid well to strap on rims that were already mounted with rubber. It would be the easiest money they made all month but it was the custom-made car that the top guys were interested in. While Richard explained about the website where they could watch the race, and the need for discretion, Katrina inspected the underside of the car. She could see signs of where they had been and what had happened over the last few days. Dried grass stuck out at odd angles from where they had needed to drive over the lawn on the first day out of the gate. Then there was the damage to the undercarriage because Richard had driven over the cement abutment, which had caused them to lose a brake line.

Katrina could see burned rubber flecks all over the inner wheel wells from, from... She considered for a moment what had occurred to inflict such damage. She thought of so many possibilities that she couldn't put her finger on any one particular moment. Hell they were here because of one of those moments yesterday! She ran her finger across the flecked rubber and it fell away at her touch.

"One more day of insanity," she thought. "One more day."

The tech who had been installing the tires cleared his throat. "I'm done, if you're ready I can bring the lift down."

Katrina nodded, suddenly feeling very tired. She began to walk out from beneath their racecar. The lever was moved, the pressure inside the hydraulics began to release, and the car slowly descended. That's when Katrina noticed something she hadn't thought of checking earlier.

"Stop, stop." Katrina said loudly enough to rise above the cacophony of the shop. The lift stopped descending. Katrina didn't wait for the technician to relock the lift for safety. She bolted under the car, her eyes focusing on one particular spot. Her finger went to the latch that held one of the ramps in place. Behind it an aluminum ramp wobbled under the touch of her finger.

She turned towards the other frame member where the second ramp was supposed to be stored. Katrina put her finger on the latch and pulled it back to free that ramp, but all she could see was air. The ramp was missing. She turned to the tech that operated the lift and asked for his flashlight, hoping beyond all hope that the ramp had just slid more deeply into the frame so that she couldn't see it. He gave up his light and she bore it down the tube. A crisp light beam lit the entire space. No ramp could be seen in the chamber.

Katrina turned away and threw the flashlight as hard as she could across the bay. She shouted at the top of her lungs, "Holy Fried Peanuts!"

Quickly and intensely her anger roared into being. All activity ceased just to see what had happened. Katrina felt like the Hulk roaring his displeasure, but from the outside she looked more like a skinny girl having a hissy fit. She ran to the pile of discarded tires that had just came off their car and kicked at them over and over again.

In the dealership's service area waiting room pleasant music played over the intercom, music that was supposed to be soothing. Many of the customers were female, some were reading, others were trying to keep their children entertained.

One old man stood by the bay window watching his vehicle. The last time he had brought his car in they had charged him for an oil change but he had never seen his vehicle come into the shop. This time he was going to be sure his oil change was done. Suddenly a flashlight struck the wall next to the window. The loud noise startled everyone in the room.

Several other people in the waiting area stood to see what was going on. The service manager watched, dumbstruck, as the girl in the strange uniform began to kick at some tires as hard as she could. The manager and owner both hurried over to see what they could do to help. The service manager just turned away from the window and headed back to his office with a sigh. His expression said that he had seen it all, and that he needed a new career.

Richard took hold of Katrina's shoulders and shook her before she could do any damage to the garage or to herself. Katrina suddenly realized that everyone had stopped working and was staring at her. Silence permeated the large room.

"What the hell is going on?" Richard shouted.

Katrina grabbed his arm and dragged him to the underside of the car. She pointed to the empty ramp slot.

Richard looked at the slot and shrugged his shoulders. "What?" he asked, not understand what he was looking at.

Katrina pushed him away and shouted, "Someone stole one of our ramps!"

Without stopping to think he asked, "What ramps?"

Katrina placed her hands on her ears and bowed her head. She might have to kill someone. She felt as if steam was radiating from her head.

"At the end of the race we need ramps to get on top of the dais to go through the finish ring. Do you understand what I'm saying? Is it getting through your thick head?! To get up high enough to drive through the finish loop we need those ramps!" She glared at Richard waiting for his thick head to catch up with what she had said.

Everyone watched Richard, waiting for his response, hoping that he would say something that made sense.

Richard's mind filtered through the many things he had learned about the race. Somewhere the idea of ramps came back to him. Frodes had mentioned them. He had secured them under the car so that they couldn't fall away. A light went on in his mind and he pictured the ramps being used to drive up onto a platform so they drive through the ring. Yes, he remembered, now.

Richard threw his arms out towards her and shouted. "Of course, the ramps! Why didn't you just tell me one was missing?"

The expression on Katrina's face fell. Infuriated beyond any ability to measure Richard's stupidity, frustrated at the human race as a whole, exhaustion wearing her down to a point where the blackness of rage could take over her senses, she launched herself on him and took him to the floor. She had both her hands bunched up in his uniform pulling him up from the floor then forcing him back down again.

Richard's head banged against the concrete. Exhibiting the completely opposite reaction to Katrina's rage, he laughed uncontrollably, punctuated by a few words.

"You said, 'Holy Fried Peanuts!' How was I supposed to know what you were talking about?" He laughed all the harder.

The owner and general manager both ran forward and pulled Katrina off Richard. Richard hoisted himself up on his elbows, his laughter almost infectious in that out-of-control way. He pointed his forefinger at Katrina and said, "I'm so glad that I was made part of your team. I've never laughed so hard in my life."

Katrina screamed at the top of her lungs and pulled free from the owner's arms before jumping on Richard again.

The patrons of the dealership's service area were congregated around the viewing port into the bay. They couldn't believe what they were seeing. Even the ones who had been eyeball deep into their iPads reading the news had now joined the mass of flesh around the single window. Children asked what they were all looking at but were hushed so their parents could try to hear through the double-paned glass.

They watched as Katrina was being restrained and as she broke free for another round. This time she didn't try to smash his head on the floor, instead she pummeled him anywhere she could. The owner shouted to the other techs for help keeping the couple separated.

Many of the customers turned away now that the moment of excitement had passed. They had certainly not expected anything half so interesting to happen in the garage.

~~~

Weaver sat on the far side of the interrogation room while Killington and his lawyer whispered at the table. They were supposed to be in the air by now but the helicopter that was supposed to take them to the airport had a fuel issue and they were still waiting for it to be cleared. She yawned and it didn't go unnoticed.

Killington's lawyer turned to her, exasperated. "If you're so tired why are you still here?"

She quickly brought her arm to her side where her pistol was located and had to resist the urge to pull it out and shoot him. She got up to leave the room, but Killington's voice stopped her.

"That bitch that said I killed those men, she came to me and asked for my help."

The lawyer turned back to his client. "Don't say another word."

Killington used his hand as if to wave the words away. "She didn't like how I treated her and now she wants retribution. That bitch can say anything she wants but I killed no one and without bodies you have nothing."

Weaver turned around to face Killington. "Silvia never said a word about you killing anyone. We have you on video." She paused for dramatic effect and repeated the words, "You confessed. The fact that you keep bringing it up only strengthens our case. Every word in this room is recorded.

"What is most interesting to us right now is the race. Who hired you and what did you do to all of the drivers that you eliminated? The other charges are for the courts to work out now."

Killington turned away. His lawyer was right. He should have shut up.

Weaver smiled and continued toward the door. She paused at the door on her way through. "That guy that you sent to rape Silvia? That was a mistake. You just ensured that she will testify against you."

Weaver closed the door behind her and entered the observation room, where her yawning wouldn't bother anyone.

~~~

Katrina sat on the floor, breathing hard. Richard sat up, remnants of his laughter still evident on his face. Katrina was close enough to kick him so she did.

"You know if we need another ramp, we're right here, in a shop. Richard said. "Why can't they make one?" He splayed one hand out towards all the techs standing around them.

She brightened as her eyes glazed over. She no longer saw anyone standing around her. Her eyes were searching the images in her mind. She stood up suddenly and reached over to help her driver up as though nothing had happened.

"That's a brilliant idea." Katrina said as she turned to the techs standing around her. "How much metal do you have here?"

The techs moved their shoulders up and down in a universal shrug. One of the techs, a big barrel of a man, stepped forward to answer. "We have very little metal unfortunately, not enough to make a ramp of any length."

Katrina let her head drop, disappointed. She thought for a few seconds then said, "That's it, were done. There's no point going any further."

Richard looked disappointed, not at the race being over, but because Katrina was giving up. "What are you talking about? You're an engineer, you can make anything. Maybe we don't need a ramp anyway. Maybe we need to put legs on the car or something. We only need to get, what, two feet in the air?"

Katrina corrected him. "Thirty-six inches."

"Okay, three feet. There has to be another way to do it. We're going to be driving fast, so maybe we only need a little ramp and speed will..." Richard stopped talking.

He was cut off by a single hand in the air from his partner. Her mouth fell open considering what her driver had just said. "Speed and a little ramp," she said softly.

Turning towards the big bear of a man she said, "Go get someone from the parts department, quick."

Almost three seconds later a parts associate came running in. Katrina didn't wait for him to catch his breath before she asked her question. "Do you have any airbag deployment packs in inventory? To any car, it doesn't matter."

Without pretense or ambiguity, absolute in the truthfulness of his answer, he said "No airbag pack can be kept here in storage. They're too volatile."

Katrina turned away to think.

Richard stepped up. "What do you need an airbag pack for? Is one of ours bad?"

An epiphany struck Katrina. She looked at the racecar still on the lift.

All the techs in the bay all stood around watching Katrina. They stared at the girl wondering how any of her questions made sense.

The best looking tech tried to interrupt her thought process. "If you tell us what the problem is we might be able to help."

Richard stepped up to explain before she could attack anyone else. "Our race is made for engineers. At the finish line the actual line to cross and finish the race is three feet off the ground on a platform."

Katrina corrected him. "Dais."

Richard ignored her. The techs all started to squeeze in to better hear his explanation.

"Anyway, there were two ramps beneath the car that we were supposed to use to get on the..." Richard turned to his weapons specialist and said "Dais" with emphasis before he continued. "Somewhere along the way someone stole one.

"Since it's impossible to get up on the dais with four wheels and one ramp and you don't have enough metal to make one we need to come up with something else. We were supposed to be on the road five minutes ago and today's the last day."

Katrina interrupted Richard. "I figured it all out. I just need to do a few more calculations." She took a black sharpie out of the closest tech's pocket and began to write on the floor. The owner began to protest but Katrina stated loudly that she needed to do the math and he backed away quietly, hands raised in surrender.

Figures poured out of Katrina's brain through her hand. At a speed not ever seen in a classroom she sped through the complex calculations. The floor was the largest writing space she had ever used. It resembled the blank white canvas of a painter, images already etched in the artist's mind just waiting for paint to fill the void.

Katrina poured her heart and mind upon the concrete. Whole ideas came to life mathematically.

Everyone in the room was transfixed, waiting to see what happened next.

Without warning Katrina stood. She turned, looking around the bay for the components needed to build a substitute ramp. She found welding equipment, a ladder, and tool boxes in every bay.

Katrina pointed to the ladder and began to shout orders. "We only have thirty minutes to make this work." She pointed to a young tech. "You, get that ladder and disconnect the battery in our car." She swung wildly to another tech and shouted to him. "You, get the torches over here and the welding equipment." Katrina turned to the lead tech. "I need all the metal you have in-house right here." To another tech she assigned the task of removing the other ramp so that they could take off the special clips that held it in place.

"I need a whole roll of electrical wire!" She commanded of the room not sure which tech could address this problem. "And I need a soldering gun, alligator clips, rope, and electrical tape, lots of it. Let's go people we have less than thirty minutes!"

The owner came up behind her. "Now hold on one minute! My people are working on jobs for customers, some of whom are waiting in there watching, you can't just take over the shop!"

Katrina turned on him and waved her finger in his face. "I'm sure we paid far too much for those tires.

But if you want the time for your techs paid for, then put it on the same account. I'll be out of your hair in less than thirty minutes." She checked her watch. Twenty-nine minutes people!"

Dollar signs popped up in the owner's eyes and he turned to his techs and took over for Katrina, shouting "Where is that roll of wire?"

Katrina was already deep into an explanation to two men under the car. The first was the welder. He put his gloves and helmet on as she spoke. The second was the bear of a man, the lead tech. He paid rapt attention as Katrina used her finger to point out specific spots on the underside of the racecar to help illustrate her needs.

When finished she turned to another man who was holding the wire and four rolls of tape. "After the air pack is removed, connect it here exactly, and run wire and rope anyway you can to the passenger side dash where my knees would go. and tape the ends heavily. Make sure they are separated by at least two inches so static won't...What?"

Richard had interrupted her explanation. "What do you want me to do?"

"Go and collect food and drinks to take with us. We won't be stopping for anything for the rest of the race."

Exactly thirty-one minutes after Katrina's outburst they were driving out of the dealership.

~~~

Finn Cosgrove watched three of his staff members board a helicopter as he stood by the door. They looked terrible after having had no sleep for more than twenty-four hours. He felt just as tired as his people did, but he had to keep up the image of being the strongest of them all. Somehow he didn't feel that way but he had to try.

The ride by helicopter would take them twenty minutes as opposed to driving two hours through rush hour traffic. He stepped up, the last in the line climb aboard. Could he stay awake for thirty more minutes before crashing on the airplane? Cosgrove closed the door behind him. When he turned around to sit, he found Weaver and Brocton already sleeping.

Weaver sat slightly at an angle, her head tipped onto her associate's shoulder. Brocton appeared to have crashed the second he hit the seat. His head was kicked back and his mouth was hanging open. Cosgrove wondered if Brockton had taken the time to clip his seatbelt or if Weaver had done it for him before using him as a pillow. Colliste, the only one still awake, struggled with his seat belt, fatigue inhibiting his motor functions.

At least now he didn't have to worry about falling asleep in front of his men, as long as he woke up before them on arrival. The helicopter rose into the air. The pilots knew they were running behind. Cosgrove hoped that they would get to Colorado early enough to catch up to the racecars.

Chapter 19

Dr. Jenkins and his team leader, Frodes, watched the race on one of the laptops while traveling by bus. Well, Dr. Jenkins was watching. What was actually playing out on the screen could put anyone to sleep and Frodes had already drifted off.

Jenkins' eyes were heavy. He wanted to sleep like Frodes but he was waiting on a call from Appleton. The need for answers was pushing him to remain alert. He couldn't put the last part of his plan into action until the scum bag was too focused on the FBI closing in on him to be causing his team any more problems.

He prayed that everything was going to go according to plan today. As a man of science his catholic upbringing had fallen to the way side. Now, he considered the man upstairs as the only one who could oversee Katrina and Richard's safety.

The bus hit a particularly large bump in the road. Frodes awoke with a start. As he came to his senses, he sat up a little straighter.

"Did I miss anything?" Frodes asked.

"No, just endless riding on the bus watching others drive somewhere else. This has to be the most boring thing I have ever seen. Since there are so few cars left in the race there is no real action." Jenkins said. "But I suppose that's the best thing that could happen, no action."

"Did the camera crews find Katrina yet?"

Jenkins shook his head. "No, that's the only good news."

"Why don't you get some sleep? I'll watch for a while." Frodes returned with a yawn.

"I won't be able to sleep until I hear from Appleton, and when we are sure that Dillon and Kristin are not being followed. They have Katrina's cell phone. If it was being tracked we should know soon. Kristin will call if they see anything suspicious."

Frodes sat up straighter and turned the laptop towards Jenkins. "You don't need to wait for her phone call, they're on camera now."

On the highway, white cars were as common as moths under a street lamp on a warm night. They watched the computer screen as a white Toyota Corolla cut in front of the box truck's camera but they knew instantly that it was Dillon driving the car; he had his head out the driver's side window and was shouting as loud as he could. Kristin's arm waved out of her window.

The camera couldn't pick up what Dillon was shouting but he was obviously trying to get someone's attention.

Frodes and Jenkins shared a confused look before Frodes picked up his cell phone and dialed. On the screen they watched as Dillon pulled his head back in to his rental car and accelerated away, passing the racecar that the cameraman had originally been following. A second later six other vehicles came into view, two black SUV's, a red pickup truck, three older styled sedans, and a light blue Honda coupe.

"Brilliant!" Jenkins exclaimed and started slapping Frodes on the arm to get his attention. "Put down the phone. We need to get those license plate numbers and call them into the state police. He brought them in front of the camera crew to get our attention."

Frodes dropped the phone and pulled out a pen and started to write the numbers on his hand. Jenkins read them off the screen for him as they came into focus.

As they worked to get plate numbers and make notes about each vehicle, Kristin pulled herself out of the passenger window with the shotgun in her hands. The wind blew her long hair around her face, obstructing her vision as she prepared to fire the weapon at one of the cars behind her. She fired several rounds before their Corolla swerved to stay ahead of the racecar.

Both Jenkins and Frodes jaws dropped, too shocked to continue, hoping that Kristin could keep her balance as the car shifted.

"Oh my God!" Frodes shouted.

Eyes from a teenager in the seat behind them peered over Frodes' shoulder to see what was going on.

~~~

Cosgrove slept soundly on the flight to Colorado. He dreamt of sitting in a chair at a beach eating an apple that tasted absolutely wonderful. Its flavor so enticed him. He sat on his beach chair in nothing more than a bathing suit. It was the best tasting apple he ever had and he had no idea what kind it was. Waves crashed on the rocks nearby with spectacular spray, sailboats in distance made the scene so picturesque in his mind, and the sun... oh the sun, it felt so warm on his skin. He took another bite. All he wanted now was someone to share this moment with. He considered several women in his mind's eye but none of them seemed quite right. On reconsideration, maybe all that he needed were the waves and this apple.

Someone shook him and his body rejected the very idea of waking. The person shook him again.

"Let me finish my apple first," he mumbled.

The dream came back strongly, as though he were on a rubber band and he had stretched the dream but not snapped out of it. A loud wave exploded on the rocks. The spray flew so high that some landed on his face. He laughed. Then he choked on the water in his mouth. The ocean water crashed over his face again. He choked some more and then woke in an instant gasping for air.

"What the hell!" He shouted between gasps.

Weaver stood over him with a water bottle. Work beckoned. Brockton and Colliste were awake and were rubbing away the last vestiges of their dreams just as he was attempting to do through his gasps and coughs. The flight to Colorado was still in progress. He could see nothing but clear blue sky through the plane's small window.

"I'm sorry sir." Weaver said. "But there has been a development. The Colorado State Police are on the phone and they need to speak with you now." She handed him a corded phone.

~~~

Silvia Thruwell sat in an interview room at the FBI office in Detroit. She had a desk phone to her ear. She was being treated as a witness, not as a co-conspirator in any of Killington's business ventures, so she had some freedom, within the office at least, she just wasn't allowed to leave. Killington had far reaching fingers and the FBI had no intention of losing the evidence she could provide. She was still wearing sweats as her own clothing had also been confiscated as evidence.

"No, I was careful about mentioning Katrina and the race. I still have work to do and the race is almost over, but I'm stuck here for... I don't know how long."

Silvia listened for a moment before continuing.

"There are hundreds of computers here but I can't use one unless I can use someone else's id and password. I don't want to try hacking in and have everything get shut down. I might be able to get in after someone leaves for the day, especially if I can distract someone enough so they forget to log off. The race will still be going on so I can have another chance to finish what I started. Sure. I can do that. Good, I'll call you later."

Silvia hung up. She left the office to mingle with the staff once more, a fresh smile on her face.

~~~

Kalby Mitchell stood to pace across the office. He had been sitting way too long, even for him. Marcus Appleton was asleep on the couch. Morning had come but even without shades on the windows he still managed to sleep on. Admittedly, Mitchell was just as tired. He paced as he considered his current problem. He rubbed his belly and stopped for a moment to stand a little straighter, stretching his back.

The problem he now faced was that the corporation that they had singled out was very well constructed. They had received the results of their computer mole's search, checking every name on their list against all of the corporations that the mob was known to do business with. Many things had come back in the results, but not one clear standout as to who had funneled the money. Unfortunately that was the entire reason that they were here, to find out who stood to benefit from winning the race. No other scenario made sense. There had to be a money motive, someone had to benefit from this, and that person had to be connected to the race in some way, but how?

Mitchell's pacing eventually took him back closer to the couch where Appleton slept. The carpeting ensured that his foot falls wouldn't wake the man. Between the two of them, they needed a brain wave strong enough to inspire a different approach. Maybe sleep would re-energize Appleton enough to be helpful. Kalby usually relied on his energy drinks to turn on his inspiration mechanism, but he too needed sleep. The race was close to finishing and he would not allow himself to shut his eyes until Appleton woke to take over. They had agreed that each in their turn would remain awake and working until they had the solution. An idea occurred to Kalby. Each in their turn...

"Each in their turn," he whispered out loud.

Maybe they were looking at the whole problem from the wrong angle? He walked quickly to his computer and madly moved his fingers over the keyboard.

~~~

The phone rang again in the plane carrying the four intrepid FBI agents to the Denver International Airport. There seemed to be no end to the number of calls streaming in about the race. So much for getting enough shuteye to feel awake when they landed. When the investigation had been opened into an illegal cross-country race all of the bureau offices along the projected path of the race had been informed. Now, less than seven hours later, information was pouring in like a fire hose on a camp fire.

"No, I don't know where they are going yet. I only know that it's on the west coast." Cosgrove listened to the voice of the director of the FBI. "Yes, the west coast is very large. We are still compiling information about their route."

Cosgrove snapped his fingers to get Colliste's attention and whispered loudly as he dared. "Quick, I need the map of the race route you've been working on."

His attention turned back to the director. "Yes sir, right here." Cosgrove snapped his fingers again to hurry his agent. Colliste handed over a map of the country that had yellow highlighter marks over the roads known to have been taken by the participants.

"Current information suggests that they left Castle Rock, Colorado this morning and... no sir, we didn't have time to question the Miss Thruwell more thoroughly. Uh... yes sir, knowing where the race ends is very important at this point. Yes. We have been getting regular reports from the Colorado State police and..."

Cosgrove pulled the phone from his ear as the shouting voice grew louder.

"Yes sir, it makes sense that the Colorado State Police will not be part of the investigation for very long. I understand. Yes, we will get that information."

Weaver picked up a different phone and called their office back in Detroit. "We need someone to talk to Silvia Thruwell again, as soon as possible. What do you mean you don't know where she is? Find her! Now!"

~~~

Richard was careful to keep the car at eighty-two miles per hour. Too much faster and he would be using more power than the One Tree System could produce. Too little and he wouldn't be able to catch up with the other cars. The time they had lost getting new tires installed and fixing the ramp problem had added up to about an hour and ten minutes, all told. Their best hope was to be fast but steady, and hopefully they would catch up in four or five hours.

Katrina had explained more than once that their drive system would allow them to catch up because they didn't have to stop to recharge. As long as the drive system made marginally more power than they consumed, they would eventually find and surpass the rest of the racecars.

Now Richard had to explain the next hurdle that they would have to confront. "You were brilliant," he began, "Coming up with a way to get the ramp problem taken care of, I mean, but we have a new problem."

"What now." Katrina snipped back.

"Well, now that we collected enough food to last us twenty-four hours we are on track to catch up as long as we don't stop anywhere. But... we will have to stop to go to the bathroom eventually."

Katrina frowned but said nothing. How had that not occurred to her?

~~~

Dillon stuck his hand out of the driver's side window. He had a lot of harsh words for the mass of cars that had been following them. He shouted into the gale force winds rushing past him hoping his words would reach their target. He laughed madly between shouts. This was far too exciting to sit back and let Katrina and Richard have all of the fun. The next time an offer came up to drive anywhere he would be first in line to sign up.

Kristin shouted information to him that quick glances into the rearview mirror couldn't provide. The cell phone on the front seat rang again. Finally Kristin noticed it and picked it up to answer the call.

"Hello?" She shouted at the top of her lungs hoping the person on the other end could hear her. Her long hair whipped all around the cabin space. She wiped it away from her eyes and then closed her window to give herself a better chance of hearing what was coming from the tiny speaker.

"Hello?" she said again.

Frodes voice came through. "Are you guys alright?"

"Never better!" she said excitedly.

"Really? Well, Dr. Jenkins wants you to stop shooting that shotgun and have Dillon take the next exit. Try to lead the mob away from the other drivers. The police are trying to set up a roadblock for you so once you get a few miles from the exit toss Katrina's phone and the shotgun out the window and disappear. Remember to wipe everything down. Dump the car and pick up a different rental. You need to get out of Colorado."

"But we're having so much fun. Are you sure we shouldn't keep up with the racecars?" Kristin asked with laughter in her voice.

Suddenly the sound of gunshots filled the air around them. The Corolla's rear window exploded.

Frodes was shouting through the phone, "Hello? Hello? Can anyone hear me?"

The burner cellphone that Kristin had been holding had fallen from her hand. Dillon picked it up and tossed it out the back window. They were moving so fast that the phone never touched the ground. It shattered against the windshield of the pursuing black SUV. Dillon cut hard to the left and took the approaching exit. A line of cars followed them off the highway.

Kristin wiped down the shotgun and waited for the right time to toss it out the window. Dillon pointed toward the back window. Kristin nodded knowing what he wanted. If the cell phone had shattered against the SUV's windshield, than the gun might go through it and slow down at least one of their pursuers.

Dillon took a right turn at the green light off the exit. He was sure that there wouldn't be too many more traffic lights in this small town. Once they moved further from the highway it would be a while before there were any roadside attractions, fast food restaurants, or even gas stations.

At the first light they came to that was red, Dillon took a hard left turn through it without stopping. All of the cars following him did the same. There just wasn't enough traffic to stop the others from following him. He flew through a green light and sped up again to be at the next light that was sure to turn red.

As he had expected it changed to red and he banged a hard right barely missing being squashed against the bumper of a tractor trailer truck. Even though they had almost gotten killed by the turn, the action had finally separated them from the group of following cars. Now only one SUV and the small Honda were on their tail.

Dillon floored the accelerator and sped ahead as fast as possible. He shouted to his passenger to get ready to toss the gun and added, "Cock the gun and take off the safety!"

Kristin had looked down to see what she was doing when the passenger in the SUV shot his pistol at them through his window. The bullet went through Kristin's blowing hair and out the windshield. Their windshield cracked from one side to the other. She didn't wait to throw the shotgun. Kristin, out of extreme fear, threw the gun out the rear window with an upward trajectory. It flipped in the air end over end until it hit the SUV's windshield.

The driver of the SUV had been confident that the object the girl had thrown from the car would just bounce off, as the cell phone had, so he didn't even try to swerve. Instead he had hammered the accelerator to bear down all the weight of his vehicle to ram the tiny Toyota so his passenger could shoot the bastards. But he was wrong, the shotgun hit the windshield at a downward angle nose first and it fired on impact. The shot blew through the windshield and into the dash of the vehicle. The burly driver slammed on the breaks out of instinct. Everyone in his vehicle flew forward while the broken glass flew at them. Behind him, the Honda slammed into the rear of the vehicle. The downward tilting SUV opened a larger than normal gap under the rear bumper where the Honda squeezed in nicely.

The explosion of sound created by the two vehicles colliding sounded like another gunshot right behind the echoes of the shotgun blast. The SUV lost control, being propelled by the force of the Honda's impact and they turned sharply off the road into a Jack in the Box restaurant's parking lot. The SUV bounced over a small mound of dirt separating the parking lot and the street, causing it to flip over in the air. The devastation continued as it rolled end over end, destroying everything in its path.

Dillon turned their Corolla sharply on the next available road to get as far away from the scene as possible. Katrina's cell phone flew out the window as they took the corner. Kristin's ability to throw objects out of the window of a moving car seemed well honed. The phone flew into the bushes of a small motel, hidden from everyone.

~~~

Back in the plane Cosgrove was on the phone with the Colorado state police. They had just informed him of the incident with the white Corolla. After he hung up the phone he pointed to Brockton. "I want every helicopter available fueled and ready to fly the moment we touch down, I want sharpshooters on board, and where the hell is the information from my victim!"

Colliste held another phone in one hand while his other hand covered its mouthpiece. "Sir, it's the director again."

~~~

In a dimly lit room with a two-way mirror, a metal desk, and two semi-comfortable chairs, a small girl sat with her hands on her lap. She wore black FBI issued clothing. It hung off her small frame because she had been too small for normal adult clothing and too large for their children's sizes. She fidgeted in her seat. She thought that someone had caught her looking over the agent's shoulders to get their passwords. That was probably a federal offense too, now that she thought of it. Could they prove it if she hadn't actually been able to try to use them yet? She kept her hands on her lap so no one would see how nervous she was.

After waiting a long time, one of the agents that she had been watching earlier that day walked in. He didn't say a word to Silvia and made an obvious effort not to make eye contact.

She couldn't tell if he was angry with her or if he was just angry because he had been asked to do something else that he didn't have time for. He could have been averting his gaze because he was uncomfortable with what had happened to her. But that wouldn't have explained his anger.

The agent slammed a conference call device down on the metal table causing it to ring softly, as if there was an actual bell inside it.

Definitely angry, she thought. Perhaps this was his way of setting the tone for the interview. She was more nervous now than ever. The agent left and the door locked automatically upon striking the jam. She knew she was in trouble.

Not five minutes later the agent returned. He still looked angry but this time he turned his blue eyes toward her. He didn't say a word but his body language spoke volumes about his contempt. He was carrying a small coil of wire. He used one end to connect the conference call device and unwrapped the rest of the coil as he backed out of the room. A female agent came in as he left. She did not seem as angry as she sat down across from Silvia.

The woman did not look like all of the other young agents she had seen. Her skin was dark and she was not as young or as thin but she exuded an aura of professionalism and authority that they had all lacked.

Silvia was even more intimidated and began to sweat.

"My name is Sylvia too," the woman began in a pleasant tone. "I'm Sylvia Barton. In a moment we will be having a conference call with Finn Cosgrove. It was his team that rescued you from Killington's men. I will be here to oversee our side of the conversation. He has several important questions for you about the race."

Silvia let out her breath in relief. Her phone call and spying may have gone unnoticed after all.

The agent continued, "I have been advised to warn you that should wait for your lawyer to arrive before saying anything that could incriminate you outside what you have already disclosed. However, your ongoing cooperation in the case involving Mac Killington would go a long way to keeping us from adding more charges against you regarding your activities."

Silvia Thruwell's mouth opened and closed rapidly, trying to utter words that kept slipping away. "Charges, against me?" she managed to stammer.

"Why yes. You were working for Mac Killington, and admitted to such activity when you were picked up. True there were other circumstances in which you were also seen as a victim, but that doesn't exonerate you. As I said, charges are being considered. Our investigation will determine what those charges will be. But, those charges may still be waived with your continued cooperation."

Agent Barton stretched out her arm to reveal a very expensive looking wristwatch. She gazed into its depths for a long second for dramatic effect. "The call should come in momentarily. It is up to you if you insist on waiting for your attorney to be present, but I urge you to be as honest as possible. Remember, cooperation will only help you in the end."

Silvia rubbed her palms against her FBI sweat pants. It didn't dry them in the least. Nervously she tried to make conversation as they waited so she wouldn't appear at guilty as she felt. "I don't have a lawyer. I didn't know I needed one."

"One has been contacted for you and he is on his way."

Before Silvia could consider this information the conference call device beeped. Agent Barton pressed a button and a man's voice said, "I have Agent Cosgrove on the line."

Agent Barton pressed the button again and said, "I am here with Silvia Thruwell."

Cosgrove had to shout to be heard over the noise of the plane. "Can you hear me?" he asked.

"Yes."

"Ms. Thruwell, I apologize for the background noise but we are still on our way to Denver. I have a few important questions for you. You told me that you were part of a team of students from MIT that was hired to help build a racecar to compete in this cross country race."

Silvia rubbed her hands even harder on her sweats. "Yes."

"Where does this race end?"

"It ends in Death Valley, off of route 190. The finish line is in the sand not on the road." Silvia stated as honestly as possible.

"Death Valley is a huge place; can you be any more specific?" Cosgrove asked with a hint of impatience.

Silvia gave him all of the information that she had, desperate to prove how helpful she could be. "From 127, its thirty-eight miles on 190 then twelve miles on the right towards the mountains."

~~~

Richard was bored. Aside from Katrina's outburst at the dealership and the redesigning of the ramp system, this day had to have been the least interesting from a driver's point of view. They were behind, and had to catch up with the other racecars somewhere, but at the moment it felt like they were driving towards Death Valley on vacation. It was ten past noon and he was eating popcorn out of a snack-sized bag that he had bought from a vending machine.

Katrina, on the other hand, was fidgeting badly.

"Will you cut that out? You're making the car bounce on the road." Richard admonished.

"I can't help it. I have to pee."

Richard smiled before he spoke. "But you said we can't stop for anything. So if you're going to hold it, stop bouncing around."

"How come you don't have to go?"

"I went more than an hour ago." Richard said.

"No you didn't. We didn't stop anywhere." Katrina shot back.

"I didn't need to. When you were napping I peed in an empty Gatorade bottle."

Katrina's mouth fell open in utter shock. "That's disgusting!"

"I took care of business." Richard said. "You're going to have to go at some point. If you want to hold it in, can I interest you in some salty snacks to help soak it all up?" He offered the bag to her.

Katrina punched Richard in the arm and popcorn flew everywhere.

"Hey! I wasn't done eating that."

"How can you be so juvenile all the time!" Katrina shouted before she punched him again. Mid-strike Katrina froze. Her eyes got very large and she squeezed her legs together.

Richard smiled before looking at her lap.

Katrina punched him again. "Don't look there."

"So how bad do you have to pee?"

Katrina pulled her arm back to punch him again, causing Richard to flinch, preparing for the strike. Instead she grabbed the steering wheel and tugged it towards her, towards the breakdown lane. The car swerved to the side of the road. Richard braked, struggling to keep the car stable. Luckily traffic was light and Richard managed to finish the maneuver without rolling the car or getting hit from behind. Katrina snapped off her seat belt and turned around to the storage area to fish something out. When she turned back she held a roll of toilet paper in her hand.

Richard was so surprised that there was toilet paper in the car his eyes were wide and his mouth hung open. Katrina took the roll and bounced it off of his forehead, and then scrambled out of the window and ran into the scrub brush along the side of the road.

Very little grew here, it could almost be considered a type of desert but there were low bushes all over the place. Katrina had to move much farther than she expected so that she would be out of sight of the passing cars.

Richard watched her negotiate through the brush from his seat in the car. He wondered how she could pee in her racing outfit. He had a zipper and could manage it easily but he had no idea how she was supposed to manage without taking the suit off. Within seconds of those thoughts, he saw Katrina remove the entire top half of the outfit. She had her back to him but her black bra showed easily against the color of desert scrub and sand. He could see her wiggling to get the outfit down low enough. The brush covered everything below her waist but that didn't stop him from imagining what was beneath her slick racing outfit. Then she dropped down, disappearing from view.

Unbuckling his seatbelt, Richard leaned over into the passenger side of the car to see if he could get a better view.

Katrina shouted, "I can see you trying to watch! Turn around or I will poke both your eyes out."

Caught! His head lowered, averting his eyes, he looked like a guilty child as he slowly moved back into his seat and reconnected his belt.

When Katrina returned, she slid into the window and took her seat. She stared at him, daring him to comment. She tossed the toilet paper into the back.

Richard didn't say anything. He stomped on the accelerator and they flew back up to speed.

After several silent minutes Katrina finally said something. "So, if you had to go again you would wait until I fell asleep?"

"Hell no, I would just whip it out and go." Richard said half laughing.

Katrina punched him. "If you whip that thing out in front of me I will break it off and throw it out the window."

"What's the matter? Never saw one before? Here let me show you what it looks like." Richard began to unzip his suit as he slowed the car.

He didn't know how fierce his weapons specialist could be until she leaned over and punched him in the face.

The car swerved wildly on the highway. Katrina took the steering wheel and yanked, moving the car quickly to the side of the road.

Richard stomped on the breaks and their new rubber squealed leaving its new surface on the pavement.

Katrina threw the shifter in neutral and pulled the break. She pulled him closer as if she was going to hit him again. There was a click of the seatbelt and then suddenly she was gone.

Richard raised his head above his arms to see if it was over only to find her climbing in through the driver's side window, feet first, kicking at him to get him out of her way. He balled up against the door on the passenger side of the car.

Without finding her seat belt, Katrina bore down on the stick shift. She stomped on the clutch with the same precision Richard usually showed and within seconds they were up to eighty miles per hour.

"What the hell are you doing!" Richard yelled.

Katrina shouted back at him in punctuated spurts. "My left arm was tired from hitting you! Now I get to use my right and we can still make up time! And don't even think about unzipping that suit any further. If you do, I will finish the race myself!"

Richard moved closer to the passenger side door trying to avoid further blows.

~~~

On the bus to Death Valley California, Dr. Jenkins and Vincent Frodes sat dopey-eyed watching the race on the laptop. Neither had spoken for what seemed like forever.

Hours had passed and nothing was going on. They needed to watch the race but as minutes passed, then hours, boredom stabbed at their brains. Watching traffic on a computer screen, while riding on a bus in a completely different state, felt wrong.

On a positive note, Katrina and Richard were nowhere in sight. The other five cars were all showing on the screen but the MIT car was still missing. The panel that should have shown their car showed only normal traffic as their tag-along box truck searched for them on the highway.

When the phone in Frodes' pocket rang, they both jumped. Frodes fumbled with it to keep it from falling out of his hands as he extracted it from his pocket.

"Hello?"

"This is Dillon. We're going to find a cab and head to the airport. I just wanted you to know that the guys that were following us crashed and are probably on their way to the local hospitals."

Frodes sat up straighter and leaned over to his mentor to share the receiver between them to share the good news. "Can you repeat that?" Frodes asked. On the other end Dillon repeated his statement, verbatim.

Both men smiled. This was a major victory. That may have been the last attempt by mob to interfere with the racecars. Maybe the racers need only be worried about the other contestants for a change. Jenkins let out his held breath as though he had been holding it for the last four days.

"All right, head back and we'll meet at the finish line. Great work!"

Dillon thanked Dr. Jenkins and hung up the phone.

Frodes was excited. "Maybe now the race can be about the technology!"

Jenkins shook his head.

Frodes slowed his enthusiasm and asked "Are you still worried?"

"If we don't know who financed this mess, we may still find other surprises before the finish line. A lot of money has changed hands in this race, and I don't mean the money invested in the tech."

"I don't understand." Frodes said.

"You have to look at the big picture. There is a lot of money to be made when this race is over. Everyone who is watching this race, including all of the big automobile manufacturers, will want the winning cars' tech to supplant it into their mainstream manufacturing. Whoever is paying to have other cars disabled knows that they can have all of that opportunity. To them the payoffs are just another investment in their product.

"Our car has a good chance of winning and that makes Katrina and Richard huge targets. When we identify the head of this ring, we can find out which car they financed and take them out of the race to keep everyone safe."

~~~

FBI agent Finn Cosgrove stepped off of the plane that he and three of his agents had just arrived in. His cell phone was pressed to his ear. He struggled to hear anything at all between the sounds of the jet engines powering down and the two helicopters in waiting mode ready to take off the moment their seatbelts were snapped on. "I'll call you back!" He shouted in his phone twice more before he gave up and pocketed the useless thing.

He took the stairs to the tarmac two at a time. His minions followed at a brisk rate. He pointed Weaver and Brockton toward one of the helicopters while he and Colliste climbed into the other. Within minutes they were in the air again.

Now that they were in a different type of vehicle the noise was more of an issue. Cosgrove and Colliste both had noise cancelling headphones on to muffle the sound of the loud engine located directly above their heads, and he couldn't call the director back on his cell phone. He touched the copilot on the shoulder to ask if he could use an open line to make the call. When permission was given, he turned to Colliste to have him take out the maps and look at all of the possible routes to the finish line.

"We need at least an eighty percent certainty as to where we're going after we land."

~~~

Driving through Utah was like driving underwater. The flat landscape seemed endless. Katrina couldn't help but wonder why anyone ever wanted to drive through this part of the country. In her home state of Maine and in her adopted state of Massachusetts there were vast stretches of trees, wildlife and interesting things to look at when going on a long drive. Here in Utah the flat land wore her down, there was nothing to look at, no trees, no towns, no gas stations. The clouds were nice but she wanted a hill to drive over every once and a while, any hill would do, something to break up the endless flat land.

To make matters worse, Richard was asleep. Now she had no one to converse with or to fight with. The radio stations were mostly static, flickering in and out like Christmas tree bulbs that were on their last leg.

Every once and a while she pounded her head on the steering wheel to make sure she was still awake and not just dreaming of this endless landscape that seemed to be burned onto the inside of her eyelids.

After what seemed like hundreds of hours looking at nothing she made the decision to wake the actual driver of the racecar. Talking to the bastard in the seat next to her was better than the watching the ocean of sand pass by the windows. She reached over and slapped him. "How could you sleep for all these hours?"

Richard rolled toward her and asked, "What do you want now?"

He had a black eye on the left side of his face and Katrina's face went slack from shock. She didn't realize that she had hit him that hard. Now she felt terrible. She pulled the car over thinking that if she could get him to drive before he looked at himself in a mirror she might be able to break the news to him later, when he was in a better mood.

"I have to pee and you need to take over driving, K?"

Richard, still groggy, started to slip over the stick shift as Katrina turned off the car and pulled herself out of the window. He never noticed himself in the mirror. He did notice Katrina walking away with the roll of toilet paper. That was his cue to either pee or watch Katrina undress in the distance. Since he couldn't focus on doing both, he watched Katrina.

Katrina had to walk much further out to find a bush to hide behind. Not only did she have to walk farther than she had wanted, but the bush she hid behind covered far less than she would have liked.

Richard watched eagerly; hope filling his dirty little mind. Katrina's jumper was pulled over one shoulder then the other. Her black bra stood out against the barren desert. Suddenly he was distracted by the sound of a vehicle passing by their car at a high rate of speed. In his peripheral vision he noticed it to be one of the race cars that matched the one he was in. He refocused on Katrina.

Another set of cars passed him as he watched, waiting for Katrina to pop up again. When he heard brakes squealing, he couldn't ignore what was going on around him any longer. He turned his head. Three cars were burning rubber to stop their cars. The three cars were all fairly new models and hadn't had any problem stopping quickly. Red flags were being raised in his head. Something was very wrong.

A hand came out of one of the car windows holding a pistol. The red flags in Richard's head disappeared and were replaced by a klaxon that made so much noise that he couldn't yell over it. He flicked the key to start the engine and cut the wheel toward Katrina hard. He honked the horn over and over again. His scream couldn't seem to make it to his lips. Once over the edge of the road and into the sand he let the wheels spin to throw up as much dirt as possible to give Katrina time and cover up and get back to the car.

Katrina shouted back. "Stop honking you bastard!"

When she turned to look at the sounds of dirt flying away from spinning tires he had already pulled up to her in the flat area as near to the bushes as possible. The car had skidded to a stop. The haze of sand slowly tried to catch up. She stood quickly and slipped back into her uniform. Before she could zip it, however, he was there at her window. He tried to shout something but no words were coming out.

She stormed toward the car ready to tear his head off when gunfire split the air all around her.

Finally, Richard found his voice but all he could say was, "They found us!"

Katrina stomach sank. She didn't need to ask who, she ran the rest of the way to her side of the car and dove head first into the window.

Richard yelled, "Take my arm."

More gunshots filled the sand storm. Richard took Katrina's extended arm and stomped on the accelerator. He wanted to kick up as much dirt as he could.

Katrina thought he was going to help her into the car. Instead he took her arm and pounded the accelerator to the floor. The car spun in a circle throwing dirt as it went around. The longer he depressed the pedal the faster around they went. Katrina screamed as her legs rose in the air and the only thing holding her in the car was the arm that Richard held on to.

Men in the three other cars drove blind into the cyclone of spitting dirt. The three each ended up hitting each other trying to guess which way the racecar went. The hits were minor but it did slow them down.

After Richard had thrown enough dirt to choke on, he straightened out to get away from the dust cloud, hoping that they were driving toward the highway.

Katrina stopped screaming in order to cough out the dirt that had started to accumulate in her lungs even though her legs were still flying around outside the window. When Richard slowed and changed direction her legs fell to the ground in an instant, her toes began to drag in the sand. For a split second she thought she was going to fly out of the window but Richard used all his strength and heaved her in. She landed half on his lap. She coughed and choked up more dirt.

He shouted, "Get away from the stick shift!"

She wiggled around managing to sit up. Slowly the dirt and dust started to clear and she could see where they were. The road was a welcome sight after what she had just gone through.

Richard pounded through the gears. In an instant they were flying at over one hundred miles an hour.

"What is going on?" Katrina asked.

"They found us somehow. All I could do was make a dust storm so they couldn't see where you were."

Katrina thought for a moment about what he had just said. "You went through all that, while they were shooting at you, to make sure that I was safe?"

"Of course I did. I'm not the bastard you think I am. But you might want to finish zipping yourself up."

Katrina wondered what he meant.

Richard looked at her bra and said, "Your boobs are showing."

Katrina looked down and her jaw fell open. She was still unzipped all the way down to her underwear. She turned towards the window and zipped herself up.

When she turned back she wound up to hit Richard, and he flinched getting ready to take the hit, but she stopped before actually touching him. "Thank you for coming to get me. You could have left me behind and you didn't, even though I'm not always nice to you."

"Yeah, you could say that." He pointed to his black eye.

Katrina bowed her head. She knew that she went too far sometimes. In a sheepish tone she said. "You knew about that?"

"Yeah, but I still couldn't leave you out there for them to find. Admit it, you'd do the same for me."

Katrina thought back to the moment when he had begun to un-zipper his jumpsuit. In that moment it would have been easy to consider leaving him behind. Her stomach fell. Maybe she was not as noble as he was. That bothered her and tears welled in her eyes.

"What's wrong?"

Katrina sniffed and wiped her eyes on the back on her hand before uttering in a broken voice, "Just drive, please?" She turned to look out the window.

"Great. I try to be the nice guy and all I get is the silent treatment." Richard openly complained. "You'd think she would at least let me see her boobs again for my trouble."

In an instant Katrina smacked his arm.

Richard smiled. Everything was back to normal.

~~~

Grant Phyindress sat in his office watching the racecars on a split television screen hanging on the wall that was the size of a theater screen. His computer was hooked up to the massive viewer so that he didn't have to squint at his twenty-eight inch computer monitor split six times. This setup had been installed before the race had started but it was only now that he got a chance to actually enjoy it. The busty bimbo from the racing start line came swaggering in holding two glasses. She was showing so much skin that the only other person in the room with them blushed just from watching her walk to the couch where Phyindress sat.

It was clear why she was there, and it was also clear that she knew exactly why she was there. She handed over one of the drinks and made very sure that her boobs rubbed on Phyindress' arm in the process. When Phyindress turned to take the drink, he accepted it with a smile. His intention to look in her eyes and say thank was lost as he stared at where she had touched him.

Ian Practor, who had already made himself a drink, went to take a sip just to have a reason to avert his gaze but found his glass to be empty already. He turned his gaze back to the giant screen instead. The girl was clearly young enough to be his granddaughter, but that didn't seem to bother either one of them.

Practor cleared his throat nervously and asked, "Uh... Do you know why we haven't seen the MIT team in a while? Are they finally out do you think?"

The old man raised both his arms out and rested them on the top edges of the couch before he spoke. "Don't know, but if they are out that would be good news for us. Now, can you go and prepare for our flight to Death Valley? Give me a few minutes. I shouldn't be very long."

Ian Practor stood, trying not to let his face broadcast his disgust, and left the room.

After Ian made sure that the door was closed behind him when he pulled out his cell phone. He found speed dial number 27 and pushed the button to make the call. When the person on the other end picked up, he made sure not address the person by name. "I still cannot see the MIT car. What is going on, are they out?"

The voice that greeted Ian sounded gravelly. "My contacts tell me that the car was recently spotted, but the guys lost them again."

Ian turned towards the closest wall and produced a forced whisper. "Lost them? How do you lose a car on a single stretch of road that lasts a hundred miles? They are not faster than bullets. We're running out of time. We need to think about alternative measures. I want a bird in the air with a sharpshooter. Got it?"

There was silence on the other side of the conversation for a moment. "You do realize that it would be impossible to do that without bringing unwanted attention to what we are doing?"

"No one knows that we are the ones financing this." Ian said. "Just get it done. Everything we have is riding on this."

~~~

Marcus Appleton pulled away from his computer station, pushing his fingers through his hair. This marathon computing session had worn his nerves. Night and day, day and night... the passage of time was slipping away. His internal clock had been completely disrupted and he had no idea what time it was. He had gotten some rest and had been up now for only about an hour, but he had no idea where Mitchell had gone. He looked towards the window and saw the low position of the sun. He had no idea if it was early morning or late afternoon.

Mitchell walked into the office carrying coffee and donuts from a shop around the corner. The smell was heavenly. Appleton dove into it to get the coffee and a nice glazed blueberry cake donut, his favorite. They both knew that they needed to be awake for the last stretch. The race was almost over and they still hadn't found any answers.

When Mitchell sat he only took a sip from his coffee. He looked deep in thought and didn't reach for a donut.

Appleton noticed that difference immediately. "What's wrong?" he asked.

"I have an idea about how to find out who is behind this."

Appleton raised an eyebrow. "Well, out with it. We've hit too many brick walls up to this point. We need a new angle."

"What do you think about drop boxes?" Mitchell hung it out in the air like a carrot.

Appleton took another bite from his donut and pondered. He shook his head after a few moments, not being able to put his finger on it. "Remind me?"

Kalby raised a finger in the air to begin. "In the fifties and early sixties extremely large banks had a problem. When organizations wanted to build something, like a church, or a new park, anything you can think of that has no collateral value before it's built, they had no way to secure financing. Companies that wanted to build a new location, or refurbish offices or equipment, took out a loan with collateral against their own holdings. But if you wanted to build a church in a town that cost a thousand times the value of the land, the collateral simply didn't exist.

"That's where the drop box comes in. It's a combination of loan and savings account. The bank writes the note and it collects all the money from donors and fundraising activities. When it reaches the pre-set goal, the bank distributes the money to its intended recipient. The bank collects interest on the money it's holding, and its fee for providing the service at the end.

"The only catch is in the auditing. In order to make it legal in the accounting department, its structure had to resemble a loan because it's making interest on the money that it's holding. So whenever a person makes a deposit or payment, it doesn't matter who it is, a name and social security number must accompany the payment. That satisfies the national accounting structure that keeps banks in check. It doesn't matter who payee is.

"The problem with the structure of this bank vehicle is that it can also be used to finance illegal activities. The bank doesn't care what the money is for as long as it makes money in the process. Mobsters started to figure this out and used it as a way to hide their activities. They just used stolen social security numbers to put money into these accounts. The people whose identities were being used had no idea any of it was happening. The deposits were small and mimicked other normal financial activities.

"So, because of all the illegal activities, a lot of countries banned the use of drop boxes. The international banking authority has a set of rules that govern banks. It pretty much says that if you play with the wrong people, any government can freeze the assets during prosecution, and the money can be seized depending on the outcome of the trial."

Appleton finished his donut and took another. "Okay, but how does that matter to us? You just said that the major countries don't allow this banking practice anymore." Appleton splayed his hands to further display his confusion.

"Well..." Mitchell said with a smile. "The countries that use banking as the focus of their economy still allow them to exist."

"But wouldn't they still need a lot of names and their associated social security numbers?"

Mitchell leaned in and picked up a donut as he said. "Don't employers have names and social security numbers on file for everyone who works for them? And aren't the names we are actively searching for related to organizations who, coincidentally, employ a lot of people?"

Lots of lights came on behind Appleton's eyes. Mitchell could see the connections coming together. He added one last item to make Appleton's day. "All we need to do is to hack into the bank holding the information from the Drop Box and release the virus to search their files."

Another light came on in Appleton's mind. He stood and crossed towards the computers. "We should be able to get by their security pretty easily. And the search shouldn't take that long either. The banks in the Caymans are nowhere as big as the giants here in the States. I should be able to hack in and make an information deposit."

Mitchell sat back with his donut and reveled in the sugar rush that was coming. Everything was coming together. Confident that this was the answer, he took his first bite of his chocolate coconut pastry.

~~~

Colliste stared out the window on Interstate 15. Nothing could be more boring than to watch a stretch of highway looking for one special kind of car among the thousands that they had already flown over. He was tired and wanted to get some shut-eye. The little sleep he had gotten on the plane had been much too short to satisfy his needs. His boss looked like a one person press room. His phone never stopped ringing and sometimes he was on two calls at once. A couple of times Colliste thought the only reason he was there was to look out the window and hold the second phone until it rung. And as if on cue, it rang.

He pushed the blue tooth connection on his headset. "Colliste here."

"This is officer Rands. I was told to call this number to speak to Cosgrove."

"Officer Rands?" Colliste asked.

"Yes, from the Utah State Police," The voice added.

"Please hold."

Colliste pushed the mute button on his headset and poked his boss in the shoulder. "Sir," He yelled over the loud rotors running overhead. "I have a Utah State Police officer on the phone."

Cosgrove took the phone and completely ignored his other conversation without bothering to let them know that he wasn't listening anymore. "Yeah, this is Cosgrove."

"Sir, I have been ordered to pick you up when you're ready to land."

"We would appreciate a ride to the border to meet up with another set of cars from Las Vegas. Our office there will take over after that."

"No problem, sir."

As an afterthought he asked, "Have you heard of any reports of odd looking cars running through your state at high speeds?"

"No sir, but there is some gang activity on the main highways. Is there a correlation between the two?"

Cosgrove looked over to Colliste and pushed the end button on the phone he had been ignoring and handed it to him. "Get the director on the phone."

Chapter 20

  The MIT car drove well above the speed limit, not
only to escape the gang who had pulled over to attack
them, but to also catch up to the racecar that had gone
by them. Richard thought that they had been in last
place all that time. Now that the other car had passed
them, he was sure they were in last place and the race
itself had his full attention. Seeing the other car had
reminded him of everything that they were working
toward.

  Richard was in a heightened state of awareness.
Katrina had the weapon on the roof powered up. The
latest confrontation and the sighting of the other car had
reminded her that their weapon was truly their best
form of defense. An energy weapon could be better than a
bullet any day, it had less continuous fire power, but its
range could be fantastic if controlled properly. It may not
blow up cars, but it could easily blind or worse.

  Richard pushed their car down the road at one
hundred and twenty miles per hour. He had a good
handle on all of the gages now and knew how long he
could maintain this speed. His primary concern was to
catch up to the five cars ahead of him. Based on past
performances, all of the cars still in the race had speed
problems, and they couldn't maintain anything above
eighty for any length of time. Jenkins One Tree system
could out strip any of the other cars in the race at
sustained speeds above eighty. But he still needed to be
careful.

  Katrina checked the maps. "Las Vegas is probably
only an hour away at this point and the guy that you
said passed us when we were pulled over shouldn't be
that far ahead of us at this point. You have to remember

that in at least four or five hours everyone will have to shut down or pull over to power back up."

"Yeah, well... I'm a little worried about why we haven't caught up to that other car yet. I'm burning a lot of battery at this speed."

Katrina said quickly. "It's better to slow down a little so we can recharge. They can't keep up their speed. We'll find them soon enough."

Just as Richard began to slow up a helicopter flew overhead following the path of the road.

~~~

Brocton, Weaver, Colliste, and Cosgrove were now riding in a couple of state troopers' cars. They were flying down the road almost as fast as they had been when they had been flying above it. The troopers didn't say much at all. They probably didn't think much of their assignment, playing chauffer to FBI agents, but they followed orders through their chain of command and did as they were told.

But that didn't mean that they were going to chat with them or give up information without being asked. The only benefit to the lack of chatter was that the radio didn't conform to the officers' silent treatment. It spoke loudly about all things going on within the state of Utah. When they had split up into the troopers' cars Colliste had paired up with Brocton and had fallen asleep soon after the drive had begun. Brocton, on the other hand, listened intently to the chatter. In the car with Cosgrove, Weaver took notes while her leader maintained a constant stream of phone conversations.

When a call went over the radio for all officers to respond the troopers responded by giving their positions and their current assignments.

The FBI agents all listened with intent. Brockton woke Colliste. The time between the officers checking in and the dispatcher releasing information about the complaint felt like forever. Finally the dispatcher announced that there were complaints of an illegal roadblock on the highway at the state border. Their two cars were the closest officers and were needed to respond. They had received several calls regarding the issue.

The troopers turned on their sirens and pushed their speedometers closer to their limits. Weaver put up an arm to protest the officers' decision to investigate a complaint instead of driving toward their rendezvous point but Cosgrove stopped her.

"Call the office and find out more information about those roadblock reports. If it's on this road, it might have to do with the race. Remember, Killington may be out of commission but that doesn't mean that there aren't others involved. This impromptu roadblock may be an attempt to catch the drivers of the race as they head towards California."

Weaver nodded and pulled out her cell phone. Cosgrove hung up with his party and made another call.

~~~

Out in Nevada at the Federal Bureau of Investigation building a phone rang in an office. It rang until it exhausted itself then began again. Josephine McGregor ran in, trying not to spill her coffee. She had walked to the breakroom to get a fresh cup and as always, as soon as she had walked away, the phone had insisted upon her quick return. Her skirt and heels had not helped. She set the coffee down on the desk and grabbed for the phone.

"Hello."

"Finally!" Cosgrove said. "I've tried to call six times."

McGregor didn't say anything.

Cosgrove continued on. "I need you to send a helicopter to meet us at the border. There is some kind of illegal roadblock and we will be stuck here if we have to stay with the state police officers that were supposed to bring us to your team. They've been dispatched to respond to the call."

"Who is this?" she asked.

"Cosgrove. The director sent a memo about a street race, and you were supposed to send two cars to meet us? Any of this sound familiar?"

"Of course, I got that memo, the cars are already on their way."

Cosgrove ager was rising. "We can't meet up with the cars because the troopers that we're riding with got called to an incident on the highway. I need you to send a helicopter to pick us up at the Nevada border. And make sure there is at least one sharpshooter on board." His tone seethed with the intent of his revenge she didn't act on his requests immediately.

"I'm sorry agent Cosgrove, the only two helicopters I have are already out on another assignment. I can check in with the cars that are en route and see how long it will take to get to the border."

Steam came out of Agent Cosgrove's ears at the news. He had to concede that waiting was now his only option. He tried to calm his tone before he spoke again. "Thank you. But I will still require the use of the helicopters when they come back in."

Agent McGregor's voice perked up as if she were enjoying his defeated tone. "Very well then. I will send what you requested as soon as they return."

Cosgrove terminated the line. He turned to Weaver. "Get Las Vegas Swat out here. We'll use their birds and they'll have more than one sharpshooter in house."

Weaver nodded and began her next barrage of phone calls to reach the right person to secure what they needed.

~~~

Richard was getting nervous. The line was building behind them as they waited in traffic to reach some kind of blockade. He kept sticking his head out of the window to try to see why everyone was stopping.

Katrina still had her head gear on and her nervous maneuvering within the car caused the weapon on the roof to move in many different positions. "You think they're checking for alcohol?" she asked.

"I'm not even sure they're cops." Richard said. "That helicopter that went over us earlier, I didn't see any police markings on it. And the vehicles that are blocking the road look like trash trucks. Last I knew only the biggest cities use trash trucks for anything other than garbage collection. Hell, New York City uses theirs for plows, but this is a pretty small town we're passing through. I doubt they even have trash collection. I'm getting a really bad feeling about this."

Katrina became aware that the weapon on the roof was moving erratically and it made her self-conscious about her nervous agitation. "I'm going to take this off. I'm only scaring the people around us."

"No." Richard said. "Leave it on. We need to make a move before we get too close. Otherwise we may not have enough room to move around, and we might need it."

"What are you going to do?"

"Hold on to something." Richard commanded. "Were going to see how good these tires are."

Katrina grabbed the handle of her door. They looked at each other, silently agreeing that his idea was the best option. Wait, they were agreeing on a maneuver before it occurred?

Richard waited for the car ahead of him, an ugly brown, older model, Taurus to move ahead enough to open up some space for him to turn slightly and position himself to launch out into the sand. Then he waited.

"What are you waiting for?" Katrina started to ask.

Richard had no idea why he was waiting. Perhaps, in his mind he had reservations about this move. When the sound of sirens blared from the rear of the line, Richard knew he couldn't wait any longer. It was now or never. He punched the accelerator to the floor. The MIT car launched itself over the pavement and into the soft sand beside the highway.

~~~

Two state police cars came up the inside edge of the highway with lights on and sirens blaring. Off to the left a racecar broke the line and bolted towards the sand. Upon seeing the police cars, the guys from the roadblock raced back to their vehicles and drove back across the state line into Nevada. A second racecar broke from the line and followed the first one away from the road. Suddenly, the helicopter that had passed them earlier moved above the line of cars and chased after the racecars.

The police cars could not get any closer to where the original roadblock had been. The cars that were in their way had nowhere to go that would allow the troopers to pass. Cosgrove hopped out of the first police car angry. He had replaced his phone with his side arm. Weaver was hot on his heels. Brockton and Colliste ran behind the state trooper on the opposite side of the line of cars. They moved as fast as they could, in the manner of trained agents with fire arms raised, down the line of waiting cars. By the time they had arrived at what would have been considered the front of the line, all of the trucks that had been blocking the road had disappeared. Cars were beginning to move. Oblivious to the officers' presence, people waiting in their cars were just happy that the trucks had moved out of their way and accelerated to get back going.

Cosgrove was pissed. He swore loudly followed by, "Where is my helicopter!"

All of the FBI agents watched the unidentified helicopter fly away.

"Colliste, get someone at the FAA to tell you whose chopper that is, and where it's going. Weaver, find out where our ride is at. We need to find those trucks. And Brockton, get a camera and take some pictures of the tire tracks from those two racecars. We'll need those later."

Cosgrove took a deep breath and thought about his assignment. He was seriously considering if it was worth the bureaucratic nightmare that he would create if he commandeered one of the trooper's cars. It was either that or they were going to fall behind waiting for their ride to show up. He knew that their chauffeurs wouldn't cross state lines.

~~~

The MIT car and the other racecar had both pulled back onto the highway but both drivers knew they were in trouble. They were now ahead of the trucks that had most likely created the roadblock specifically to pen them in and the chopper was probably working with them. They couldn't get caught by the trucks or by the police if they were going to stay in the race. But they all knew that their lives were on the line. Their only choice was to drive fast, very fast.

The cars were one behind the other on the highway, Richard leading the way. The thought of disqualifying each other never crossed their minds. At least in Richard's mind they were together in this mess at the moment, compatriots for a single cause, living.

Behind them, eleven vehicles bore down on them. Ahead the helicopter began to make a wide arc to turn back towards them. Every time Katrina turned to look behind them the weapon on the car's roof turned in tandem with her head. The car behind them weaved back and forth, unsure of their intentions.

After a few seconds of this the driver sped up and pulled alongside so Richard and the other car's weapons specialist were next to each other. Richard looked out the window to their counterparts and waved.

The weapons specialist in the other car waved back. Through the fast blowing air between them he shouted, "What team are you from?"

"MIT," Richard shouted. "You?"

The driver spoke this time. He shouted over his passenger. "Caltech. That arm on your roof is amazing. Great idea."

Katrina leaned in over Richard and smiled. "Thanks!"

Suddenly the Caltech car's passenger side mirror exploded as a bullet passed through it. Both drivers waivered toward the opposite sides of their lanes. The gunshot that had caused the mirror to explode echoed off the distant hills. A sharpshooter poised in the helicopter had made the shot. When the two cars realigned all eyes fell on the chopper hanging in the air a half mile in front of them.

Richard turned his head slightly towards their new friends and shouted, "Good luck!"

"Good luck" came back at them but Richard didn't take the time to see which one of them had spoken. Another shot came at them and ricocheted off the weapon's steel support on the roof. Katrina could feel the reverberations from the hit through her calibrated headset. Richard took the car back into the sand at over a hundred miles per hour, hoping that the dust would give them a little cover.

Katrina bounced all over the cabin of the car. Her seatbelt did little to keep her in her seat. The headset bounced askew as she hung on for dear life.

Richard had a plan. He needed as much dust as possible. He knew that helicopters couldn't fly during sand storms. Too much dust would clog the engine's ability to operate properly and cause the power to be sporadic. He didn't need Katrina's engineering skills to know that.

He also knew that they were more of a target than the Caltech team and he expected their car to be the focus of the shooter's aim. Expecting the helicopter to follow them across the sand he drove deeper into the desert away from the road. Richard watched the helicopter and when he thought they were close enough for him to implement his plan he shouted for Katrina to hang on.

Unfortunately Katrina had already needed something to hang onto and it was much too late for his concern. He cut his wheel. The high speed of the tires threw dirt in the air. He continued to turn the car making a cyclone of dust and dirt. Katrina became glued to her door and window.

Finally he stopped and Katrina fell back into her seat.

Outside in the dust cloud the chopper pilot was screaming to the shooter. "We have to get out of here! If the engine stalls, we're dead!" On cue the engine began to cough. The pilot, trained in combat, knew that auto rotating might save them but they had to be closer to the ground. He pushed the stick forward. It was too late to save the engine from dying if it was already choking so he prayed that they were close enough to the ground that their fall might only be a hard bounce in the sand.

Katrina was so relieved that they weren't spinning anymore she had no energy to hit her driver. But then she could hear the sound of something large coming at them, like that of a bomb coming down on their heads. Richard shifted hard into third. He floored the accelerator and popped the clutch. The car lurched forward. Katrina grabbed for her door and screamed.

Richard knew that it was impossible to predict where the aircraft would fall. There was still too much dust to see. The only thing that he could do was move as fast as possible away from the sound of its engine. In hind sight, if he had stayed where they were, the chopper would have missed them by a thousand feet or more. Richard, not knowing, drove like a bat out of hell trying to avoid it and almost struck the landing strut as it crashed to the ground. The sound of it striking the sand was a massive thump to the passengers of the car. It shook the vehicle. Richard kept driving as fast as he could to escape the mire of his own dust, adrenaline pushing him.

Finally the dust began to dissipate and Katrina tried to right herself in her seat. Richard reached out to help her but she waved him off. Her deadly stare made him want to laugh.

"I'm too tired to hit you right now. Think of it as... I owe you a major pounding tomorrow." She said very out-of-breath.

"I look forward to it," Richard said, as he allowed his smile to surface.

The crunching of tires over sand could be heard beside them, then a loud click. Richard could see vehicles approaching with weapons sticking out of the windows.

The shots started coming and he slammed on the breaks, forced the shifter into reverse and popped the clutch. Richard headed back into the remaining dust cloud straight toward the downed helicopter.

The two men in the helicopter had survived the crash. They couldn't see anything because of all of the dust. The shooter hadn't been belted in but oddly he had sustained no injuries. The pilot, on the other hand, moaned heavily. The shooter knew he had to get the pilot out and get one of his associates to pick them up. He knew how lucky they had been to survive the crash.

The sound of gun shots was getting closer. Consecutive shots, close enough to sound like machine gun fire, took his mind back to the battlefield. A bullet blew through the cockpit window. The shooter snapped into his old training and he ducked as more bullets raked the cockpit. He crawled on all fours to the pilot and released the man's seat belt.

The firing had stopped. The sounds of car tires skidding in the sand and more engines revving filled the air. The shooter pulled at his pilot. The dead body slumped over the side of the seat and fell to the floor. The shooter swore loudly, his friend had survived the crash only to be shot. He raised his head barely above the broken cockpit windshield. A variety of vehicles were driving at high rates of speed in the dust cloud. The racecar did easy spins in the sand making sure to kick up as much dirt and rocks as possible. The sound of those rocks striking metal fenders and hoods sounded like machine gun fire again but this time in a higher, tinnier pitch. The pursers all changed direction to avoid the helicopter except for one.

A white Dodge Caravan, with streaks on the windshield from having attempted to use its windshield wipers in the heavy dust storm, drove forward. Not having seen the aircraft in its way, it was coming right towards the cockpit. The shooter turned and dove toward the rear of the chopper. The Caravan slammed into the bottom of the chopper so hard that that it moved the entire aircraft. The shooter was thrown and landed in the cockpit again where he had just been.

After some hard breathing and thanking his lucky stars the shooter managed to roll out of the chopper door. He landed in the sand, happy to be on solid ground once more. It took a few seconds to stand. In his indignation he wobbled over to the van's driver's side door. The airbag had deployed and the driver was leaned over to one side, unconscious. The shooter took in the scene before him. The van's windshield was blocked by mud. The idiot driver had used windshield washer fluid to attempt to clear away the dust. Now the windshield was cracked and broken in several places. The front end was smashed but no liquids dripped to the ground. He looked back towards the chopper thinking of his rifle. If it wasn't damaged he would hunt down the racecar driver who did this to him.

He stormed back to his former ride and searched for his rifle. After finding it he determined that it was still in working order. He ran over to the van and opened the door. With one hand he pulled out the driver to ground. "Idiot," the shooter muttered to himself, "I'm better off with guys that are as smart as the one we're trying to kill."

He climbed in to the van and raised his foot to kick out the remaining part of the windshield. He positioned his rifle so it stuck out through the windshield opening and restarted the van. Within seconds he was off to catch the bastard who he was supposed to have killed from the air.

Chapter 21

Richard was flying down the road. Back on pavement the MIT car's speedometer held steady at one hundred and ninety miles per hour. Fear of being caught pushed him to go that fast. He knew that there at least ten cars chasing them and that they had guns. But at least the chopper was down.

Katrina was holding her breath. He didn't know if it was because they were going so fast or if it was the fear of being shot at that had caused her to stop breathing. Either way he figured that he needed to slow down. His speed had allowed them some measure of space from their pursuers but he couldn't sustain that rate for too long. When the car slowed to eighty, Katrina poked her head out of the window and puked.

"Oh man, now it's going to stink in here." Richard exclaimed.

When Katrina sat back in her seat and wiped her mouth on her sleeve, she said in a low voice. "I can't believe you got us out of that mess. I thought we were going to die."

"Well... yeah... me too." Richard said. Now that the memories of what had happened began to filter in he began to shake. He wasn't a commando. He only knew how to drive. Apparently that had been enough this time.

The car shook in tandem with Richard's hands on the racecar's steering wheel. Either the steering was that sensitive or he was shaking that badly. Katrina didn't want to find out which it was. She reached over and put her hand on the wheel to hold it steady. Richard turned his head out his window and repeated Katrina's gesture. When he turned back he looked green.

Katrina whispered, "Push the clutch in and take a break."

Richard leaned back and stared at the ceiling. He pushed the clutch in and took his other foot off the accelerator. He slowly braked trusting his weapons specialist to handle the steering. Eventually they stopped on the side of the road. Katrina took her hands off the wheel and leaned back in her seat. They both just needed a minute to breath clean air and the car could use a few minutes to recharge.

Katrina reached into the back and got them both a soda. Richard waved it off knowing that they needed to get moving. He put the car back in first gear and once they were back to their normal pace he took the drink from her. He took a big swig to rinse his mouth, and then spit it out the window.

Silence hung between them as they drove down the almost empty road. A helicopter flew over headed in the opposite direction. The letters spelling SWAT advertised the presence of law enforcement in the area and they were both glad that they were now driving a more reasonable speed.

It traveled over them moving back towards the state line. As it passed over they could see a man in black who hung off the side holding on to a large rifle that was connected to the craft. It was an imposing sight.

"At least they're not going to try to kill us if they come back." Richard said.

~~~

Colliste lit his fifth cigarette as they waited for their ride. The state police had left them behind. The FBI agents had nothing with them to drink and the sun bore down on them. But the worst part was watching

Cosgrove go off every five seconds about how little help they were receiving to catch the gang or the racecars. At this rate the racers might get arrested weeks after the race was done, after a nice leisurely rest, assuming they survived until the finish line.

Finally the sound of a chopper could be heard in the distance. Brockton spotted it first. They watched it land from a safe distance and in short order they were all in the air. The gunner filled in the FBI passengers as they fitted their headsets.

"We passed four racecars on the way here. We assume they are the ones you're looking for. One had some kind of instrument on its roof. Not sure what it was. Anyway, flying all the way out here to get you will mean they will probably already be in the city before we can find them again."

Cosgrove didn't look happy. "How many agents do you have looking?"

"We're it from the air but we'll find them once we get into the city. All of our resources are readily available there."

Cosgrove sat back and took the phone provided by the gunner. He first placed a call to his director, then to the FBI office in Nevada.

~~~

Richard saw an abandoned building on the side of the road and pointed to it. "Think that will do?"

It was a shack really, less than a house, and it was old, probably built in the twenties. The roof had more than partially fallen in, the one window in the front was missing all of its glass except for one small piece that was stuck in the upper right corner. Whatever boards had been there to serve as a porch floor had crumbled away to dust years ago. The front door hung at an angle which suggested that animals could have used this place for shelter on cold nights.

Katrina nodded and shut down the weapons system. After she removed the head piece she turned to extricate a tool bag from behind her seat.

Richard pulled behind the house to make them less visible from the road. He shut down the car completely and popped the hood. Katrina pulled herself out of her window and sat on the solid ground for a minute. She was still shook up from the last encounter. Richard came around and pulled up some ground next to her. She leaned her head on his shoulder.

"I think I've been a little too hard on you. If your father had decided to get another driver, I'd probably be dead by now. Where did you learn to drive like you do?"

Without smiling he said, "It all stems from trying to piss off my father. He wanted me to take over his business but all I wanted to do was drive. So we came to a compromise. He would send me to school, but I would have to come back and learn the business afterward. My father laid out all the schools I could go to, and I got to choose which one.

"So I chose to go to a school that offered stunt driving. He didn't find out what I was taking for classes until I was close to finishing up."

Katrina chuckled. "Your attempt to piss off your father has saved my life a few times now, so let me just say that I'm glad you did it."

Richard looked one way then the other, wondering why they were just sitting around. "Are you sure it's okay to kill this much time?"

"Yes, something in the engine compartment is leaking and it needs to cool for a few minutes before I open it up." Katrina stated. "One of those bullets might have hit something important. I just hope it isn't too bad."

Richard looked Katrina in the eyes. "So, why did you decide to be an engineer? You don't strike me as the engineer type. You know... you're not geeky enough."

Katrina looked away considering her answer. "It's nothing as warped as your life story. I come from a family of pretty smart people. My dad is an artist, and writer but he also builds things with his hands and can fix just about any machine you can think of. He has two brothers that are engineers, and another that worked on airplanes in the Marine Corps. My aunt is a teacher with a master's degree. My brother is really good with computers and works for a company that does software for card readers.

My mom gave me the skills that made me good in school. I was an 'A' student most of the time without even trying. So... I get the artistic creativity from my dad, and I also work on cars like he can. I worked at a car dealership while going through automotive school, but it wasn't enough to keep my mind busy. I wanted to do all kinds of art and make a living at it, but as my dad says, "Starving Artist is a harsh reality". So I broke down and went back to school to learn mechanical engineering. My uncles are both electrical engineers my dad is more of a mechanical engineering kind of guy, and so I kind of fell into the mechanical aspect of things, and here I am. I have one more year of school left and this race was supposed to help me financially and set me up for a good job in the future."

Richard laughed a little. "I don't know any engineers, let alone girl ones. All the girls I know are..."

Katrina finished his sentence for him. "Sluts?"

Richard wasn't hurt by this. "Well, that might be a little harsh, I was thinking bimbo, but maybe it's the same thing. But then I'm the love 'em and leave 'em kind of guy," he said with his cockiness coming back to the surface.

"I figured that out." Katrina added. "So when are you going to admit to yourself that it isn't really who you are?"

"What are you talking about?" Richard asked with incredulity.

"I think you know, the abrasive nature of your relationship with your dad, treating women like they're disposable... I think you're trying to hide something from your father and from yourself."

Richard stood like he had been insulted badly enough to want to walk away. "How would you know?" Richard asked.

"I've known since the first hotel stay when you were locked out of your hotel room naked." Katrina admitted. "I figured out then that you were trying too hard to prove something. I think the only person you're fooling is yourself really. All these girls you're sleeping with are happy to do so. You're a good looking guy. These sluts you hang with don't care. They only want sex, just like you. You have the equipment and the looks, why would they say no? They're drunk most of the time anyway."

Richard was not happy with this attack masked as a personal analysis. "You don't know anything!" He spat.

Richard began to walk away when suddenly they could hear loud car engine sounds coming down the highway. He ducked back down behind the car quickly. "I think our pursuers are about to pass us."

Their predicament inserted a perspective that overrode their previous conversation and they went back to working toward a common goal, living.

"Do you think they can see us?" Katrina asked nervously.

Richard shook his head.

"Well that's good news. Now we won't have to worry about them until we get to Vegas."

Richard asked. "Why?"

"Because they're going to be chasing air if we're behind them. And the helicopter is down. We just need to stay far enough back and we'll be alright."

Katrina stood and peered around the corner of the building to watch the vehicles drive by. "I think we can open the hood now."

Richard popped the hood and waved at the steam rising into his face from the odd looking power plant. "I think this is where you take over."

Katrina stopped looking at the steam and turned towards her driver. "I can't even contemplate what you're going through right now. And I don't have any advice, but when you're ready to talk I'll be here." She bowed her head.

Richard ignored her comment and sat back down next to the car to think. He had struggled with this for so long, and yet a girl who barely knew him had known through simple observations. Did everyone else already know that he was gay? Was he only fooling himself?

He felt as bad as he had the night Katrina had stayed to talk with him when he had been upset about his father.

Katrina looked at Richard sitting next to the car. He was deep in thought. Katrina knew she couldn't help him at the moment. She turned back towards the engine compartment to get back to work. It was the one way she could help them both.

~~~

The white Caravan rolled down the road despite its missing windshield. The incoming air made the remnants of the airbag flap around. The driver had tried to tear the material of the bag off but he couldn't and he had lost his knife back at the chopper. The only way he could drive with the airbag loose was if he kept his speed down.

So, he was stuck following along with no real hope of catching up to the racecar or the rest of the guys he had been contracted with. He contemplated cutting his losses and leaving the job unfinished. It was a lot of money to throw away. As he played with the flapping airbag, He noticed a small building on the side of the road that looked abandoned. For some strange reason a thin stream of light colored smoke rose from the back of the building. Maybe the shack wasn't abandoned after all.

~~~

Richard continued to sit on the ground sulking. Katrina had opened the compartment and a pocket of steam still billowed into the air. Katrina waved her hand around to keep the stuff away from her face.

"How bad is it?" he asked.

Katrina sat back down next to Richard. "Amazingly, not bad at all considering how many bullets were fired at us. We have holes in the skin in several places. If we had a normal radiator, that would be toast, but that's one thing we don't have to worry about. There is a bullet hole in the windshield that went through my window on its way out. And there is one bullet that passed through the fake grill, the skin, and hit the critical fluid chamber. That's where our problem lies. An aluminum tube that's inside that chamber carries coolant to the bearing for high speed usage and it has a nick in it. I have more fluid to fill it with but I have to patch the hole first."

Richard brightened up. "Great what can we patch it with?"

"I'm not sure that we have anything that will work." Katrina said as she shook her head. "In truth, we should replace it, but it's a specially made part. We can't just go and buy one."

Richard raised his hands, "So we drive slower so we don't overheat the bearings?"

"Sorry, I should have been more clear. It's the bearings in the power plant that need the coolant. Driving slower will not help us."

Richard threw himself back against the car. "So we're done? Out of the race?"

Katrina said, "No, I have an idea but I need some aluminum, like a soda can maybe, and some time to remove the whole tube to slide on some O rings."

"What?" Richard said with complete disbelief.

"The tube isn't high pressure so we should be able to just patch it enough to keep the fluid in." Katrina tried to explain.

Richard shook his head. "I'm more worried about falling behind again. How much time will it take?"

~~~

The shooter left the white minivan out in the sand on the opposite side of the road from the small shack. He had left it far enough away that he had a bit of a walk ahead of him. With his rifle he worked his way back to the road. Slowly he made his way from one scrub bush to another. Truthfully there wasn't much cover and trying to not be seen took him longer than he would have liked. He was pretty sure that the car he was looking for lay behind the decrepit looking house. The thin stream of smoke he had noticed earlier had turned into a large cloud. As hot as it was, no one would be making a fire to cook on.

~~~

"Shoot! I'm leaking all the fluid on the ground. Do we have anything to collect it with?" Katrina asked.

"Are you kidding me?" Richard asked. "Of course we don't, that fluid's a little too hot to use a Gatorade bottle. Just keep working."

They both watched the fluid drain into the sand below.

"So, what's the plan here? How are you going to fix it?" Richard asked.

"I'm going to make a patch with the old beer can you found, some O-rings and lots of duct tape."

Richard stood. "Really? You, the preeminent engineer, using a beer can and duct tape?"

"Don't forget the O-rings." Katrina added. "Here hold this so I can put it all together."

Richard held out his hands and held the tube steady. After a few minutes it became clear that it was impossible to put it together.

"Stop." Katrina said. "I have a better idea so we can get rid of the O-rings." She left him holding the aluminum tube and came back a second later with a tube of rubber door sealant. "This will be perfect."

Just then Richard saw something in the distance move. In a forced whisper he said, "Freeze."

Katrina's eyes went wide. "What is it?" She whispered.

"I think we have company. Work faster. I'm going to lead him away from you to buy some time."

Katrina put her hand on his arm before he could walk away. "You better come back."

"I will. I'm just going to create some confusion so you have extra time to work."

Katrina repeated her words, "You better come back."

Richard left but was back in about three seconds. "Do we have something that could be considered a weapon? I might need something to make a statement."

Katrina, still holding the tube, looked at the weapon on the roof. "You can use that."

Richard's look said *'Yeah right'* without saying the words out loud. Instead he said, "Like I can carry that huge arm around."

She said quickly. "You can use the head without taking the whole arm. It's self-contained. You can just disconnect it. The wires charge a capacitor inside. It's like a battery. If you do need to use it, there's a small panel with a red test button under it. It's just like the trigger I have on the control panel in the car."

Richard climbed on the roof and carefully pulled the weapon head from where it was seated in the arm. He unplugged all of the wires until he held it in his hands like a basketball.

"Do not look into the lens." Katrina said just as a gunshot rang out. Both ducked instinctively as a bullet ricocheted off the aluminum weapon's frame.

Richard slid off the roof and shouted, "Hurry up!" before running towards the road.

Richard had not really run anywhere in a very long time and the sand was not making it any easier. He also had no idea where the shooter was but he knew that he had to give Katrina time to finish or they were both dead ducks.

He ran across the road looking for any sand hill that might block an incoming shot. He needed to find the shooter. He wondered where this guy had come from. He had thought that the gang had passed them and for the love of God hoped that there weren't more guys on the way now. He doubted he could fend off the entire gang with the small weapon he held in his hand. He had no idea how long it would have power without being attached to the car.

Richard found a small knoll and dove over it just as another shot rang out. It missed him by inches. He felt the hot breeze of the bullet pass his hand. He lay low shaking in his shoes. This was not him. He had never been the brave one. What had Katrina done to him? He was out here risking his life to keep Katrina safe so she could work.

He took a deep breath and put his head up over the little knoll of sand by his head. He searched quickly and brought it down. He didn't see anything.

The shooter watched the driver raise his head above the knoll of sand by his head. He didn't want to take the chance of firing too quick. He knew if he waited, and let the driver become confident, he would get a better chance for an accurate shot. He could wait him out, and then go back for the girl.

Richard took in sharp breaths wondering what he should do. He thought back to what he had seen on television. If he had a mirror he could use it to find the guy without exposing himself. But he didn't have a mirror. Then it occurred to him that there was a mirror inside the weapon head he was holding. He had seen Katrina use it to deflect another team's laser.

Richard dropped his head to look at the buttons but couldn't find anything helpful. He flipped the small door where the test button was hidden and found a mechanical slide next to the test button. He depressed it and the mirror flicked out as if it were on a spring. He smiled and then positioned himself to lay flat on the ground and use the mirror to scan the surrounding area. He saw the shooter changing positions.

Richard thought about his next move. He needed to position the laser so that it would go through the rifle's eyepiece. Richard left the mirror in place and turned his head enough to locate the test switch so he would be ready. When the shooter dived down over another small knoll Richard rolled over and got up on his knees immediately. He turned the laser on and pointed it at the shooter's new position. Smoke began to rise where it struck the sand giving away the laser's position.

As soon as the rifle barrel appeared over the small dune, Richard guided the laser next to the shooter's head until it was just below the barrel. As the barrel leveled off and the sight came into view Richard lifted the beam. As the shooter raised his head, his eye moved towards the scope and Richard corrected the laser's beam in that direction.

The shooter saw his target but had no idea what it was he was holding. As his eye moved closer to the scope pain shot through all of the nerves in his eye in an instant. He screamed and fell over backwards.

When the shooter fell Richard knew that he had aimed properly. He flicked the switch to the off position and ran like his life depended on it, and it did.

Katrina poked her head up from the engine compartment. She began to toss tools back in her tool bag. Richard came running up to the car. He tossed the weapon into the air for Katrina to catch and slid in his window. "I hope you're done because we're leaving!"

Katrina dropped what she had been holding and caught the weapon. "But..."

"We're leaving!" Richard shouted again.

Katrina dropped the weapon on her seat and ran to close the hood. She slid in through her window. Before she was even seated the power plant came on, a second later she found her seatbelt and the racecar shot off kicking sand everywhere. The weapon head bounced all around as the car moved roughly over the uneven sand. Richard didn't care about anything except leaving.

"But my tools are still back there!" Katrina shouted.

"I'll buy you new ones." Richard shouted back. The racecar accelerated to ninety and beyond in mere seconds. When he hit 150 mph, he calmed a bit. "I hope you did what you needed to, or we'll be walking soon."

"It's done. But I have no idea how long it will hold at this speed." Katrina held up the weapon head. "What happened?"

Richard was shaking. He explained what had happened. When he was done Katrina was quick to point out that "It's not a good feeling, knowing that you may have killed someone."

"Yeah, well... I just hope it was worth it." Richard added.

"What do you mean?"

Richard turned away from the road and looked at her sternly. "I mean, did you fix the leak?"

Katrina nodded. "Didn't I say I was done?"

"Yeah, but that could have meant that you were done because you couldn't fix it." Richard returned.

Katrina leaned over and did something she never thought she would do in her lifetime; she kissed Richard on the cheek. He had risked his life for her again. He at least deserved some recognition for his efforts.

~~~

Helicopters travel very fast, in part because they can fly a more direct route than any road can take you. In this case, though they were following the road, they still travelled much faster than the street level traffic. The air speed of a helicopter tops out at around 200 mph, but the comfortable cruising speed is around 150 to 165 mph. As Cosgrove and his team were now in Nevada, he felt that they would soon catch up to the racecars, as long as none of them were driving much faster than the posted speed limit. The others on the team searched from their windows, ready for anything to happen at a moment's notice.

Without any warning the chopper veered suddenly away from the road. It was apparent that the pilot intended to leave the road behind. Cosgrove watched as the road became smaller, eventually turning in to a thin ribbon.

The team members leaned back in their seats now that they had nothing to do but wait. Cosgrove got up and leaned over toward the pilot. He tapped him on the shoulder. The pilot flicked a switch to open communication between their headsets. Cosgrove didn't bother with any pleasantries. "Why aren't we following the road?" He asked. "We won't be able to watch for the racecars."

The pilot nodded at the question before he answered. "We didn't stop to refuel before we came out to pick you up. And flying with four passengers uses more fuel. We need a direct route back to the city."

Cosgrove was about to have a meltdown. But he knew walking back would be an even worse position to be in and bit back his anger. Childhood memories surfaced of his father threatening to drop him and his brothers off if they didn't stop fighting in the back seat. There was a time when he had followed through with his threat. It had been a four miles walk but it had felt like a million.

The pilot's reassurance brought Cosgrove back to reality. "We know the cars are going through the city. That's where all the roads go. We'll find them."

Cosgrove nodded and watched the last view of the highway fade from sight.

~~~

Kalby Mitchell waited patiently for Appleton to work his magic on the Cayman Island bank that might have the drop box that they were looking for. Appleton typed away oblivious to what was going on around him. All Mitchell could do was wait. It was easier for Appleton to navigate the program that they were using, since he had written the original code.

In the hours that passed he ingested a few more sugary snacks, and drank far more energy drinks than what would be considered safe by the FDA. His bones felt jittery and skin itched wildly from the chemicals in the drink leaching themselves out of his pores. Maybe Appleton was right about working on a healthier diet and perhaps exercising a little. He should have included a treadmill in his office design, because right now he felt like he could run ten miles.

Had he ever run ten miles before? Probably not, but today might have been a good day to start. He had decided to step out and take a walk when Appleton pushed himself back in his chair and stretched as he hoarsely shouted "Yes!"

Kalby turned to his new friend and asked tentatively, "You did it?"

Mitchell stood and stretched more. "Yes, I have the information we've been searching for. It was Grant Phyindress all along! His company employees have made multiple deposits to the account we hacked into. And you know none of them would even know how to access one of those accounts, not even online. There are hundreds of deposits over the past year."

Kalby was confused. He stuttered when he spoke "I… I don't get it…. He… he started this whole race. Why would, why would he hire the mob to hurt the racers?"

Appleton noticed the stuttering. "How many of those energy drinks have you had today?"

"I don't know, I was, I don't know."

"You're going to have a heart attack," Appleton said, as though he was Kalby's mother. "But you're right. I don't understand why he would do it either. He started the race, got the investors to pay an entry fee, and I'm sure he will make a cut of whatever tech ends up profiting from the exposure. Maybe he's collecting on the internet broadcast, and more drama on camera keeps more people watching."

Kalby nodded, "Maybe."

"I need to get the information to Jenkins' contact at the FBI." Appleton sat back down, but at a different computer, and began typing away.

~~~

Silvia Thruwell sat in the FBI breakroom, bored out of her mind. She wasn't feeling very well after hearing about the possibility of being charged for working with Killington. She may have shut down a car or two, but she hadn't killed anyone. Working with Killington to get back at Katrina had been a really bad idea. Now she was going to pay for it. Her stomach flipped again. She knew she couldn't survive jail. Thinking of the whole mess ate away at her stomach lining.

On top of her current worries she still had at least one more job to do before this was all over. She had to try to get into one of the computers.

She had been watching people sign in and out all day. She had to stay calm and not attract attention to herself so that she could find an empty office to use. It felt as though her stomach acid had eaten through another layer of lining just thinking about it.

Her last instructions had been to try for a computer after 6 p.m. unless she heard back before then. It was after six now and she felt terrified. She had hoped that by 6 o'clock some of the agents would have gone home for the day but the entire floor was still full. It didn't look like any of them had left for the evening, at least not yet.

Getting caught using a phone probably wouldn't get her in too much trouble, and she would need to use one of those first, but she had no idea how much time she would need on the computer. And that would be much harder to explain if she got caught.

She stood, took in a deep breath, and decided that waiting would only make things worse. She wanted to try to use the elevator. The floor above them was a different squad, and may be working a different case. If that was true, she could have her choice of empty offices to use. She walked calmly to the elevator trying to appear confident so that she would be less likely to be questioned. No one appeared to notice and she was soon stepping out into the hallway one floor up.

Unfortunately, though the floor was dark and the offices were empty, they were also locked and she had to settle for a cubicle in the center of the room. Her stomach lurched. She wished she had a stash of tums. She took a piece of paper and scrunched it into a ball, and then smoothed it flat again and used it to pick up the phone's receiver.

With her fingerprints safely protected by the paper she used her fingernail to depress the number buttons that would connect her call. In the few seconds it took for the call to go through she noticed a bottle of Tums on the desk behind the computer monitor. The phone rang once and was answered with three words, "It's a go," and the call was disconnected.

Silvia took a handful of Tums and ate them, not caring about finger prints anymore. Instead of continuing her search for an empty office she decided to take her chances where she was and booted up the computer in front of her. She used a sign-on from one of the younger agents who hadn't seemed to mind her hanging around his desk earlier.

All that she had to do was hack the firewall for one last thing. Katrina may still be in the race, but her efforts right now would hopefully fix everything. She wondered absently if the dust from the Tums would make her fingerprints easier to find on the keyboard.

~~~

Professor Jenkins closed the laptop's cover and then his eyes. The continued viewing of the video screen while on a moving bus had made him feel sick to his stomach. Frodes had already drifted off. He knew that he needed to get some sleep soon himself or he would risk missing something at a more critical juncture. He thought he could spare at least three hours before the race would approach its climactic ending. He made sure that he kept himself awake long enough to get the information that he desperately wanted from Marcus.

He still had no idea where Katrina and Richard were. Their camera crew hadn't found them. But he knew that his other two students, Dillon and Kristin, were safely on their way to the finish line.

He knew that the remaining racecars would have to recharge soon. He felt sure that nothing bad would happen in Las Vegas. The drivers would be looking for a safe place to charge, and maybe for a place to eat. The only thing left for him to do was to say a prayer before drifting off. His prayer was that because his engine design didn't need downtime to charge, that Katrina and Richard would not only be safe, but that they would also have the opportunity to catch up and maybe even have a chance to win. In his heart he knew that winning would end the madness, whether it was their team or not. Dr. Jenkins stowed his laptop away and leaned back in his seat. Sleep swooped down on him like an eagle catching its prey, and he was gone.

Chapter 22

Las Vegas was a spot on the map in the middle of the desert. That spot was so brilliant, even in the middle of the day, that it was impossible not to not look at it. There were lights everywhere, and fantastic architecture seemed to rise out of the sand itself. Katrina was reminded of the Egyptian Pharaohs who had built amazing structures in the sand.

Katrina ate popcorn out of a vending machine sized bag. Occasionally she tilted the bag towards Richard and he took some. She smiled at the thought of how much things had changed between them in such a short time.

Richard too gazed at the wonder of Las Vegas. He had been here before but it was constantly changing, becoming greater than its former self time and time again.

According to Katrina, this was the time when most of the racecars would be recharging. On a normal day they would have charged the cars overnight while the teams were sleeping. This night no one would be sleeping, so the recharging would probably happen during late afternoon so that everyone could start the last leg to the finish line.

Richard daydreamed about stopping at one of his favorite hotels to have a real dinner. All of the other teams would be stopping somewhere. In fact they had probably already eaten and the cars could already be charged at this point. Time in the desert to fix the leak put them behind yet again.

Richard changed his mind. He didn't wish for a nice dinner, rather, he longed for a shower. Sand had buried itself in his every crevasse while he had been trying to take out the shooter. He itched in places he couldn't scratch while in his racing outfit. Peeling it off was not an option while Katrina was in the car. He took another handful of popcorn out of the bag before shifting down as he approached a red light.

As they waited for the traffic light to change in their favor Katrina noticed another racecar several lanes over. It looked like the one from Caltech. She pointed it out to Richard before she turned in all directions to see if any of the others were nearby as well. She couldn't see any. The light casually changed to green and noise burst out from a bullhorn nearby, as though the color green had triggered some kind of alarm. None of the cars moved, everyone was stunned by the noise. The message of the bullhorn was similar to an emergency alert system, but instead of being heard through their radios it was coming from an emergency vehicle.

"All vehicles need to remain stopped. SWAT is coming in to..."

The rest of the words were drowned out as the sound of a helicopter grew louder. The wheels of the cars all around them began to spin. Smoke filled the air. Apparently there was more than one car here that did not intend to follow the instructions. Everyone shot forward.

Katrina placed her hand on Richard's arm and said, "Wait a second." She turned to look behind them. SWAT vehicles were fighting their way through the traffic. "Go right!"

Without thinking Richard turned right, burning rubber like everyone else. Katrina hung on for dear life and grabbed the map that had fallen between the seats. "We need to get off the main roads."

That was all Richard needed to hear. He turned into a warehouse entry way and flew into the large empty parking area. It was full of employees' cars, hundreds of them. He pulled into a parking spot as though he worked there and they waited. The seconds that passed were tense. Both of them searched the entrances of the lot to plan their escape in case they were followed.

They waited, but no one followed them into the lot. "Do you think the SWAT team was looking for us?" Richard asked. "I mean, there were a lot of other cars that left that corner at the same time, maybe they're chasing some drug dealer."

Katrina took that moment to extend the weapon's arm so that it hung over her window. She took the laser head and began to reattach it.

"All I know is that we stand out. If the police are searching for racecars, the shape of the car and this thing on the roof clearly don't belong, if you know what I mean."

Richard agreed with a nod. "But if the police are searching for someone else we can just get going right?"

"I don't know," Katrina said. "Give it five more minutes and..."

Richard instantly became more paranoid. "What, can you see something?"

"No, but I have an idea." Katrina went back to studying the map. "Any idea where there might be a Wal-Mart in this town?" she asked.

Richard looked over her shoulder at the map. "You want to go to Wal-Mart?" he asked, incredulous. "Now?"

"Yes," was all that Katrina said.

Thirty minutes later the MIT racecar was driving out of a Walmart parking lot with a luggage carrier strapped to their roof with ratchet straps that crossed through the cabin from the open windows.

"That thing looks ridiculous. How are you going to be able to use the weapon with this on?" Richard asked.

"If we need to use it I'll raise the arm to break the top of the shell off then I'll cut the straps and the rest will fly off the roof. It's perfect. Now we look like any other tourist and the arm is still fully functional." Katrina said proudly.

"Yeah, I guess that could work, but we're down more time now." Richard came back.

"Stop whining and start driving."

Richard sped out from the corner light of the Wal-Mart parking lot. He left behind a little rubber and some of his dignity. No racecar should have a luggage rack strapped to the roof. Who wanted to look like a tourist?

Richard got them through the streets of Las Vegas as quickly as he could. While waiting at a stop light they saw SWAT officers on the parallel block that had pulled over two cars. One was a familiar looking blue Honda and the other, a small truck. Guns had been drawn and the occupants of the vehicles were being pulled out and cuffed.

Richard checked his mirror and nudged Katrina to get her attention. One of the other racecars had pulled to a stop two cars behind them.

Katrina turned to see if she could figure out which team it was. She knew there had been six cars left in the race as of morning. Other than the one that resembled the dune buggy and the split car driven by the motorcycle gang members, the others looked similar. Only the weapons separated their appearance. Katrina craned her head out of the window to get a better look. She was hoping to see the guy from the Caltech team that had liked her weapon's robotic arm. If it was his car she wanted to catch his eye.

With the SWAT team in such close proximity, the time spent waiting for the light to change grated on Richard's nerves. In the corner of his eye he could see his weapons specialist practically crawling out the window to look at the other racecar. Then he saw the split racecar, in its open position, roll up behind the other racecar. The guys in the first car had their eyes on the light while trying to observe the Swat team covertly.

The passenger of the split car, who normally sat on the right side of the vehicle had climbed out and crouched low as he placed a laser head on the rear of their opponent's car very carefully and then slid back into his seat. The split car moved into the lane next to the other racecar and waved to get that team's attention.

They already had Richard's full attention. He had craned his head to try to see over Katrina, who had blocked almost the entire window with her body.

The SWAT officers hadn't noticed any of the racecars, their attention was fully absorbed by the dangerous men who had been cuffed and were now leaning over the hood of the blue Honda.

Richard could hear the other teams talking but it was hard to make any of the words out. He caught a few words here and there.

"Glad the cops are busy chasing that gang." and "Man this light is taking forever." were the only parts that he heard well enough to understand. Meanwhile smoke had started to appear from the laser weapon sitting on the back end of the racecar. When the warning noise came from the distressed racecar, the conversation changed to shouting. A couple of the SWAT officers turned their heads to see what was going on.

The split racecar went into reverse and rolled back, waiting for their weapon to finish its work. The passenger of the car that was being attacked slid out of his window to go and pull off the weapon's head, but it was too late, the car shut down.

The SWAT officers didn't know what to think of the smoke and in the confusion a couple of the guys in cuffs had decided to run.

The split racecar went around the stopped cars and went through the red light in the lane designated for oncoming traffic. The SWAT officers split up. Some got into their vehicles and some ran after their prisoners. Richard slammed the stick shift, prepared run, but Katrina held him back.

"Wait! We're tourists, remember. As long as we can blend in we'll be fine."

Richard revved the engine, trying to resist the urge to burn rubber and get out of there. He felt trouble on their heels. But Katrina was right, the roof rack was supposed to help hide them in plain sight and he needed to let it play out.

When the light finally changed he drove off slowly, with traffic. He was edgy and on the verge of panic as more police officers came toward the intersection. He hoped that they were looking for the fugitives and not them.

In the rearview mirror both Katrina and Richard saw the white box truck pull up in front of the disabled racecar. The cameraman was trying to distract an officer who had stayed at the scene while they connected their cable to the downed racecar to make it disappear. That was all they saw as they kept driving, putting as much distance between them and the disabled car as possible without attracting attention.

It occurred to Katrina that they might have been caught on camera. "I hope no one noticed us at the light," Katrina said, "We may have been in camera view."

Richard didn't say a word. He just frowned and nodded in agreement, glad to be headed away from the scene.

~~~

For Frodes and Jenkins it was almost time to depart the bus they had traveled on for so long. They were now on route 190 entering Death Valley. Jenkins got up and walked forward in the narrow aisle to speak to the driver. The place where they needed to get off was located about forty minutes into this leg of the trip. They needed the bus to drop them off at a specific place along the road. Jenkins made his request of the driver, a stout man with a penchant for gum chewing, but instead the driver droned on about how they were not supposed to make unscheduled stops. He had a strong southern drawl and used a silly analogy about airplanes not stopping on the whims of their passengers.

Jenkins rolled his eyes. Obviously airplanes couldn't stop like a bus could but he didn't see the point of explaining the flaw in logic to the gum chewing moron. Instead he decided to try a different approach. Jenkins withdrew some cash from his pocket and peeled off two one hundred dollar bills.

The gum chewing driver's eyes widened and he said, "Well, I can stop but I'm going to have to throw you off the bus as trouble makers and make a scene about it. Don't want it getting back to my superiors that I take requests."

To Jenkins that was close enough and he smiled as he walked back to his seat.

Frodes had his laptop open and was watching the race. Jenkins walked up and said, "The Driver will honor our request."

"Oh, good," Frodes replied without taking his eyes from the screen.

"You may not think so when it happens." Jenkins said with raised eyebrows. "Make sure all your stuff is packed and ready for when the screaming starts."

Frodes looked flummoxed. "What?" he asked.

"I'll tell you about it when we're off the bus."

Frodes shook his head. He tried to shake free of the confusing thoughts so that he could share some information of his own.

"I think I just saw our car. There were two racecars stopped at the same traffic light but there was some other kind of thing going on with a SWAT team on the next block and the split car team distracted the other team long enough to disable their car. Man they got balls, to do that so close to the police... anyway, when the camera turned back to the intersection I'm pretty sure I saw our Katrina and Richard in the same line of traffic."

"That's great!" Jenkins said as he sat in his seat. "How did the car look?"

"Well, I think they're trying to disguise the car."

"What does that mean?" Jenkins eyes slanted when he asked this troubling question.

"They hid the laser arm so no one could see it." Frodes said.

"That's a great idea."

"It's covered up with some kind of luggage carrier." Frodes elaborated.

Jenkins was all smiles when the shouting began from the front of the bus. The smiles faded as the bus slowed and pulled hard to the side of the road.

"Quick grab your stuff." Jenkins said.

Not five minutes later Jenkins and Frodes were standing on the side of the road while their luggage was being tossed to them from the storage compartment.

When the driver was done shouting, he turned to them, smirked, and in a low tone said "Good luck. It's hot out here."

He then climbed back into the bus and closed the doors. As the bus rode off huge plumes of smoke and dusk washed over the apparently stranded men. They waved their hands against the offending dust trying to clear the air to a breathable level.

Frodes couldn't help asking, "What the hell was that all about?"

Jenkins coughed before he responded. "The idiot driver said that he couldn't just let us off anywhere we wanted. If we wanted to get off he would have to make a scene and throw us off. I had to pay him two hundred bucks to get him to agree to that."

Frodes looked around before he asked, "Where are we?"

Jenkins took in the scene and checked the GPS on his phone. "Damn! He dropped us in the wrong place. Two hundred bucks and he let us off way too early. Now we have to walk even further."

~~~

A chopper landed at McCarran International Airport in a designated police area. The gunner unsnapped his safety harness and turned in towards the passengers. To his surprise they were awake and collecting their gear. Cosgrove shouted over the dying engine of the helicopter. "How far to headquarters?"

"Not long. We have a car for you."

All eyes followed his extended hand as it pointed toward the waiting vehicle. As the four FBI agents crossed the tarmac sweat poured down their faces and they each wished that they had a clean set of clothes to change into. Once they were inside the air-conditioned vehicle Cosgrove's cell phone came out. It was time to get to work, but he didn't make his first call yet. He wanted some information from the officer that had picked them up first.

The officer quickly brought them up to speed. "As you crossed the desert, we received several reports of racecars in the city. One of the cars was disabled right next to a gang arrest that was happening. It was right under the noses of one of our teams. There has also been an extraordinarily large number of gang related cases in the last twenty-four hours involving cars and guns. What is the connection?"

Cosgrove told the story, short, sweet, and to the point. "A bunch of people organized a race. It's supposed to be a test for new technology. But someone was hired to stop at least some of the cars from finishing the race. And there is a lot of money on the line.

"The closer they get to the end of the race, the more dangerous the methods have been for stopping the cars from reaching their goal. They may be recruiting local gangs. Where is the car that was disabled? I want to see it as soon as possible and I need to talk to the passengers."

The SWAT officer back peddled. "Ah, about that," he began, looking embarrassed, "We lost it. We have the passengers but the car is gone. Local police arrested the passengers but the car was stolen. We have a clip of what you can see from their dash cam, but the nose of the police car turned away from the car before the officers stopped to park."

Colliste shook his head at yet another setback. "How can a car just disappear?"

Cosgrove turned away and dialed a number on his phone, disgusted by the whole affair.

Brockton stared down the SWAT officer. "Take us to the men who were arrested so we can interrogate them."

Chapter 23

Katrina couldn't wear the headset for the car's weapon while it was shrouded by the luggage rack. In a way her head felt naked. She made sure to keep the arm powered up just in case, but for now they were tourists driving through sin city with a luggage rack on their roof. Their car was comprised of the same fuselage as all the other cars in the race, but the push rack in the front and rear of the vehicle along with the luggage rack made it look like some kind of abomination from a redneck convention.

Katrina hated that they no longer looked like the sleek racecar they had started the race with. She wondered if the guy from Caltech was still in the race. If his car had been taken out she might never see him again.

Richard snapped his finger in front of her face. "Hello? Are you listening to me?"

"What?" Katrina snapped back.

"I said, I think we're being followed," Richard said. "Look in your mirror. See that silver SUV behind us. I'm going to change lanes. Watch what he does."

Richard changed lanes before the next red light. The SUV changed lanes to follow but ensured that at least four cars were between them. Everyone came to a stop.

"I think he is following us." She consulted her map. "We still have a lot of city ahead of us; we can try to lose them. But we look like tourists. Maybe we should just drive normally for a bit and see what he does."

"I hate to tell you, but we still look like a racecar. The luggage rack hides the weapon but anyone who has been watching the race will recognize the push racks."

Richard added, "Maybe we should have taken at least one of them off."

"That would have taken too long, and who knows, we might still need it." Katrina said.

"Which way should I go?" Richard asked as they waited for the light to change.

"Play it cool. If something bad happens, follow your gut. It's done pretty well so far."

Richard looked at her with surprise that quickly changed to a smile as he realized that she actually trusted him. He liked the feeling it inspired in him and knew that he didn't want to let her down.

A car horn brought him quickly back to reality as the light had changed and neither Katrina nor Richard noticed. Richard depressed the accelerator and said "Thank you" at the same time. He pretended to remove something from his pocket and lay it on the dashboard.

"What's that supposed to be?" Katrina asked.

"I'm a card carrying stunt driver and I'm pulling it out." Richard said.

Katrina smiled even larger this time and put her hand on his arm. "Let's go win a race."

~~~

The driver of the silver Trailblazer pulled the SUV out of their lane and stomped on the gas. It passed all of the other cars behind the racecar. The windows began to roll down and young men with rifles at the ready began to point them at the racecar.

Richard continued to move slower than the rest of the traffic, allowing the SUV to catch up quickly. The fact that it was so easy to catch up didn't seem to warn them that it might be a trap.

As the silver Trailblazer pulled level with the racecar Richard smiled at them. The men in the SUV looked at each other in confusion. Richard shouted through the wind passing between the cars. "It's about time you caught up." He pointed up and the eyes were all immediately drawn up to the sounds above him. Katrina had activated the weapon's robotic arm. It blew off the top of the luggage rack and the air passing over the sleek racecar filled the cover and took it away as if it were a sail.

The arm of the weapon rose up and turned towards the SUV. Shouting filled the SUV. "Shoot the rocket launcher! Shoot the rocket launcher!" The men had no idea what kind of weapon the racecar had. The robotic arm pointed the beam down onto the arms of the closest man who was holding a weapon.

Both weapons fired but the bullets missed and the laser didn't. It ran across the arms of all of the guys who were holding weapons. Screams of pain echoed through the car.

Richard stomped on the accelerator and shot the car forward. He pulled the emergency brake and swung them around in front of the SUV.

Katrina maneuvered the arm so it pointed forward during this process, and the beam focused its power on their assailants the entire time. Richard's stunt maneuver allowed the laser to touch every person inside the SUV, even those behind the windshield.

When the Richard pushed the racecar around to the driver's side of the SUV, he could see the complete shock on the driver's face just before the laser ran across it. The driver instinctively turned his head away from the laser, taking the wheel with him. The SUV crossed the lanes of traffic, taking out several cars, before crashing through the storefront of a small hardware store.

As that vehicle fell away, two others moved up fast. One was a teal Ford Tempo with oversized rims, and the other, a red Ford cargo van that had flames painted on the sides.

Richard had turned the car to face forward again and was driving only slightly above the speed limit. The two vehicles bore down on them. These men didn't wait to get closer before they began to fire. Bullets flew at them from their safer, more distant positions.

Richard sized up his situation. "I don't have a lot of road ahead of me…"

The rear window exploded and glass flew everywhere inside their car.

Katrina screamed then asked, exasperated, "Why does everyone want to kill us?"

Richard started a weaving maneuver. "I don't know, but you need to do something with that weapon!"

The weapon had been facing forward after their last attack. Richard heard the robotics grinding above him and calculated that they would be at the next stop light before she had time to do anything productive. He made a last minute decision and stomped on the breaks.

The two vehicles behind them quickly separated as an automatic reaction, allowing a path for the racecar down the middle. The van could have done serious damage to the racecar if the driver had just rammed them.

Richard took that moment to break away. He poured on the torque and spun his tires until it turned the vehicle facing the wrong direction. The MIT car took off like a bullet. It dodged oncoming traffic until police cars, more than he could count, came at him. They all turned hard and slammed on their breaks blocking traffic around them. Officers hopped out of their cars pulling out their weapons shouting for them to stop. Hot on Richard's tail the Tempo and red Ford van bore down on them firing their guns. The officers turned their weapons to the coming threat and fired.

A barrage of bullets flew back and forth.

Richard turned hard on the wheel and jumped the curb. He steered the racecar down the sidewalk. The people on the sidewalk scrambled to get out of their way. Finally an intersection came and Katrina grabbed the wheel to force Richard to turn right, where they disappeared around the corner narrowly missing a fire hydrant.

~~~

Inside the interrogation room, Agent Brockton sat with the gang members who had been arrested where the racecar had been disabled. Three officers stood by the wall watching, none of the gang members were in handcuffs and the officers were a precautionary measure.

The three black gang members seemed unconcerned with their predicament and sat reclined in various degrees. Their desire to look cool seemed to override any sense of self-preservation.

Two of the men were heavy set with bling glittering around their necks. The third wore rings on four fingers on each hand, all in gold. The thin one nodded his head to the other two and spoke as though he were giving orders, a cue Brocton didn't miss.

"Yo! I want a lawyer."

Brocton didn't answer. He just watched the men, and now more predominantly, the thinner man who was working so hard to appear like he didn't care.

Very little time had passed after the request for a lawyer before Agents Colliste and Cosgrove walked in. In an instant the room felt much too small.

Cosgrove looked like he was in a bad mood. Brocton was sure it was for show. Colliste smiled.

The thin gang member stared at Brocton and no one else. As Cosgrove flipped open a folder, he reiterated his earlier statement. "Man... I told you before. I want a lawyer."

Cosgrove looked up. "Or what? How has that worked for you so far? Are you imagining better treatment if there's a lawyer in the room? Stop being an idiot and listen. I'm not here to question you about the guns you have, or the stolen car you were caught in, which was also used as a murder weapon."

The fat man at the end of the table laughed. "Murder?" he asked in mock disbelief. "That wasn't murder that was an accident."

Brocton slammed his fist down on the table in front of the gang member who had spoken and said, "Shut up!"

Cosgrove stood and threw his folder at the belligerent fat man. Papers flew around the room. "Shut up both of you. We don't have much time. I don't care what you did. We're not even going to charge you with anything. I just want to know why you are chasing those racecars."

The man on the end spoke up questioningly, "You're not going to charge us?"

"No. Just tell me about the racecars and we can all get out of here." Cosgrove shouted back.

The three men looked at each other. The thinnest of the three nodded and the man on the end spoke up. "There is a bounty on the car with two push guards and a special weapon on the roof. We wanted our million."

"Thank you," Colliste said as he bent over and collected the scattered papers on floor. Brocton immediately stood and left the room without saying a word followed by Colliste. Cosgrove on the other hand stared at the thin black man. "A million dollars?" he asked.

"Yeah, man. Now can we get out of here?" The thin man stood as he answered.

The local officer who had been standing against the wall said, "No, you can't. The FBI has nothing to do with our case and I have a whole list of charges that will keep you three busy for a very long time."

Cosgrove shrugged his shoulders and walked out of the room. He met up with his agents in a small office that sat adjacent to the interview room.

Weaver was the first to speak up after hearing the reason for the gang involvement. "If there is a million dollar bounty on this car then we have a huge problem on our hands."

Colliste smiled and said, "No more than usual."

Brocton nodded his agreement but their leader shook his head. He let Weaver explain why by raising a hand to her indicating that she now had the floor.

"Because we are in a state where gambling is rampant, there are a lot of people who would be willing to do worse for less money. Plus this city has a strong gang network, plus all the mob activity that goes on here. So, we have greedy gang members with guns, we have mobsters with guns, and we have desperate people who have guns. What do you think that equates to?"

Cosgrove finished her statement. "A lot of fucking guns. That's what it amounts to."

The door burst open and a uniformed officer popped in, out of breath. "There's another shootout occurring on the streets right now and the uniformed officers have reported seeing a racecar with some kind of robotic weapon on its roof."

The four agents looked at each other then ran out of the room.

~~~

The MIT car screamed down the street perpendicular to the one that they had just turned off. Gunfire could still be heard in the distance. Katrina was studying her map.

"Take your next left," she shouted.

Without question or complaint he took the turn, skidding sideways on their new tires and leaving smoke in their wake. It became immediately clear that this route was a mistake. Two police cars that had been heading towards the shootout noticed them escaping the scene. When the blue lights came on it became evident that the police now knew what their car looked like. Richard increased his speed and blew past them. The police cars both made a sudden stop in the middle of the street using their inertia to spin them partially around. Floored accelerators completed their arc and soon they were in pursuit.

Street traffic tried desperately to get out of their way. Cars and SUVs jumped sidewalks to avoid them. Some crashed into each other. One ran over a fire hydrant, creating a water geyser. A small Yaris jumped the curb stopping just before a large business' front window. The bumper touched the glass and a crack worked its way through the pane. A second later the window exploded, raining broken glass onto the car and sidewalk.

Richard wanted to fly out of this place and their racecar could do it. Its torque could leave everyone behind in a tenth of a second; however, the stretches of road were either too full of traffic or not long enough to put any space between them and their pursuers. Richard cut the wheel hard to the left to avoid a large, slower moving delivery truck. He quickly cut back in front of the truck and pulled over towards the parked cars on the right, and put his blinker on to pull over and touched his brakes. The truck driver, indignant at Richard's stupidity, yanked his wheel to the left and pounded his horn.

The chasing police cars had already begun to pass the delivery truck when it jerked to the left. The first police car in line was jammed between the box truck and a parked car. The second police car slowed enough to fall behind the delivery driver and watched for the lane to reopen.

Richard's plan was working perfectly. He heard the crunching noise of the police car and hoped that he could follow the box truck long enough for it to run the second police car off the road.

As the truck drove by Richard waited to position himself behind it. Katrina hit Richard like it was his fault that the second police car had survived the set up but he paid no attention to her. Inspiration had hit and he said, "Shoot the truck tires on our side. Quick!"

Katrina didn't question him. She quickly maneuvered the weapon head to point down and to the left. The beam couldn't be seen well in daylight but it was easy to track its destructive path as it swept across the pavement and caused smoke to rise in a straight line. As the tires crossed the laser's path profuse black smoke billowed away from the rubber. In seconds all four tires on that side of the truck had caught on fire as all of the air that they had contained quickly escaped. The delivery truck's blown tires dragged the box side towards the MIT car's lane. Richard shot the car into the rapidly closing space. They pulled ahead of the truck as it slowed at an angle that blocked both lanes.

~~~

FBI liaison Josephine McGregor walked into a large conference room where other agents worked on laptops. The room had been commandeered to be the new command post for Cosgrove and his agents from the Detroit office. The head of the FBI, personally, had called her and told that if she didn't step up, the day that Cosgrove and his agents caught whoever was responsible for financing the hit on the remaining racecars without her help would be her last day on the job.

Cosgrove was the lead agent on the investigation, and in the end that was what bothered her the most. She and her people had just been demoted to busy work.

Agents working the computers were shouting out information about the activity that they were monitoring.

A young man's voice announced "Racecar spotted with a luggage rack on the roof traveling down..."

A woman announced a new message over the closing report of the previous one. "Another racecar spotted on... Wait a minute. I'm not sure I'm reading this right. This says that the car can split itself in half and become two motorcycles?"

"There's a report of shots fired involving a blue Tempo, a cargo van, and the racecar with the weapon on its roof." He paused in disbelief. "A laser weapon..." The entire room went silent to listen. "Holy shit that's cool. This report says that it burst through a luggage carrier and lit up..."

McGregor announced to the room. "Keep the comments to yourself. Just the facts, please."

"Holy shit!" came yet another man's voice from the sea of laptops. "Officers have reported that the driver of the laser racecar might be some kind of professional driver. He's managed to elude all attempts to slow them down!"

A woman stood to get everyone's attention. "Nevada police sent a video. I'm putting it up on the board. This was shot with the iPhone of a bystander."

All eyes turned to the giant screen hanging from the ceiling that was usually used for meetings and presentations. The television powered on and images of the MIT car performing a full 360 degree arc around the moving silver Trailblazer, burning tires the entire time. The vehicles were moving well over thirty miles per hour while the laser head fired into the SUV.

Jaws dropped as complete disbelief stunned everyone. In slow motion they watched the clothing and hair of the men in the SUV catch on fire. After the laser struck the driver, the camera view became shaky as the driver of the car containing the phone tried to brake when the Trailblazer suddenly cut across their path. The view changed to that of the SUV crashing into a store front as the video clip ended.

One of the men, who had been sitting on the edge of his seat to see the screen, leaned too far and fell out of his chair.

McGregor stammered, "Ahh, someone get, ah... get Cosgrove on the phone, then I want to talk to Nevada SWAT. After that get California SWAT on the line and someone get me the National Guard. And hurry up before that laser burns the city to the ground!"

~~~

Katrina studied the GPS monitor in front of her. "If we can just drive, we'd be out of the city in less than an hour."

"Isn't there a better route out of the city?" Richard asked as he appeared to be twitching while he kept moving his gaze from the road to check all of the mirrors.

"There were construction signs on the straightest route that's why we turned off. We can't afford to get caught up in it. I'm still working on a route around it." Katrina said.

~~~

Brockton and Weaver were in a SWAT bus driving down the road to the last known sighting of the MIT car. They, and everyone else in the vehicle, wore flak jackets and special glasses that could reflect lasers. The bullet proof vests that the FBI agents wore were printed with the agency's initials, and the SWAT vests reflected theirs.

The armored SWAT bus rumbled along as fast as it could. It was big and heavily loaded with men and armor. Top speed could only be reached if they were going downhill with the winds at their back and Las Vegas was flat.

Weaver yelled to the driver, "Can't this thing go any faster?" No one responded aware of this common problem.

~~~

Cosgrove and Colliste had boarded a SWAT chopper that was still powering up. The gunner behind them struggled into his harness.

Cosgrove's phone rang. He only had seconds before liftoff. "What?"

"McGregor here. I just saw some incredible video. Why are gang members hunting down racecars in my city?"

Cosgrove spat out information as fast as he could. The engines were in high gear and the rotors were almost at the deafening range of normal sound. "Bottom line," he finished, "there is a million dollar bounty on those racecars and that's attracting a lot of attention."

McGregor could hear the rotors and knew she might only get one more question in before the call was cut short. "How are they getting paid, can I track it?"

Cosgrove looked at his phone in disbelief at her stupidity. He brought the phone close to his mouth and shouted. "How are you going to track a payment that hasn't been made yet?" The incredulity in his tone broadcast his lack of respect as he ended the call.

~~~

Ahead a light flicked to yellow and then changed to red but all of the cars looked normal and there were no police officers in sight so Richard came to a stop. The sun hung low in the sky. Evening was fast approaching. Katrina and Richard were both breathing hard, as though they had pushed the car to the red light instead of having ridden in it. Every time Katrina looked behind them, to see if any police officers had followed them, the weapon on the roof turned with her movement.

What she thought was a cool thing to have on their racecar scared the crap out of all the drivers around them. When the light finally turned green they all took off faster than the MIT car. In that moment they did not feel like they were winning any race, but Richard didn't care.

"Where to next?" he asked. "I think we need to get off the main roads, maybe skirt the city, and make up the time when we're on the last stretch to the finish line."

Katrina nodded. She studied the map for a moment. "Take a right at the next light. We'll try to get a little closer to the edge of the city."

Richard nodded in agreement as they approached his next turn. His eyes moved in advance of the turn, to scope out what was ahead of them. He felt better when he took it all in. No police were around. He went as fast as he could without looking like they were fugitives from the law, which he felt strongly that they were, now. Moving several intersections from the last 'accident', without any further police interaction, made him feel a little better.

"How far do I need to go on this street to get out of the city? Richard asked.

Katrina didn't have to say anything. The view outside the windows answered all of his questions.

The buildings were not just businesses anymore. More and more houses filled the spaces between pizza shops, hardware stores, and places to buy cigarettes and booze. Eventually all of the business faded away except for the occasional corner store. The traffic also began to disappear. This made Richard a little nervous. He would have liked a little traffic to blend in with, if that were possible without the luggage rack on their roof. He wondered if there were in gang controlled neighborhoods in Las Vegas. That could be very bad, but he didn't see anything out of the ordinary.

~~~

A white box truck sat at a stop sign and watched in astonishment as the MIT car crossed the intersection in front of them. The driver, Jersey, recognized the car immediately and punched the air.

"Finally!" he said. "Try and lose me now." He waited until the car had moved down the street far enough so that they wouldn't be spotted and stayed far enough back to remain discrete. The camera guy smiled and turned on their hood mounted video camera.

A couple of older cars pulled out into the street behind the MIT car and gave the truck better cover. They were all driving normally, following the speed limit. The racecar's occupants had not noticed them yet, everything was calm.

~~~

Katrina watched out of the window as the neighborhoods scrolled by. Las Vegas was very hot and most windows were open to let the breeze in. Curtains moved around even in windows that were not open, and those windows didn't even have screens. Katrina wondered about that. She had grown up in Maine and even though cold weather controlled the living conditions for six months out of the year, the remaining six months wouldn't be comfortable without screens on the windows. Bugs could be horrendous.

It clicked in her mind that if the windows were not open that meant that they had air conditioning. Suddenly she felt every degree of the heat. The car's windows were open, either intentionally because they were still operational, or unintentionally because the glass was missing as a result of gunfire. The car had been designed without air conditioning. A cooling system for the cabin would have robbed too much power from acceleration.

Sweat was beading along the edges of her face. She had a sudden urge to pull off the headset so that some of the heat could escape but thought better of it. Instead she wiped the sweat off of her brow with a napkin and did the same for Richard. He smiled but never took his eyes off the road.

The sound of a helicopter grew louder as it moved closer. Katrina leaned into the windshield and looked up. The weapon followed her actions.

The cars behind them fell back a bit after noticing the weapon's movement. Suddenly she realized that all kinds of people on bicycles and on the sidewalks were watching them. Some of them were looking up at the chopper.

Katrina leaned back in her seat, suddenly fearful, "Uh... I think we..."

Cosgrove's voice boomed out of a bullhorn from the sky above them. "Stop! This is the FBI. Pull over and..."

Suddenly the quiet neighborhood exploded around them. It seemed like everyone on the street had a gun and was suddenly shooting at something. Many of them fired at the police. Others shot at the MIT car.

Richard stomped on the accelerator and shouted, "Not Again!"

SWAT vehicles poured into the neighborhood, stopping at the fringes of the gunfire. Men poured out of the backs of the vehicles ready to fight a war. Their specialized training allowed them to set up while being fired at and then return fire. These men were professionals. One at a time, anyone within their range who was holding a gun fell to the ground, injured or dead.

~~~

Agents Brockton and Weaver jumped out of the armored SWAT vehicle and waited. Weaver nodded to the chopper overhead. Brockton understood and pulled out his cell phone to make a call. Weaver covered him. It didn't take long for her to empty her rifle, she pulled out her pistol and fired again as she backed her partner inside the vehicle. Brockton listened to Cosgrove's instructions over the sound of bullets hitting the armor on the side of the truck.

"Our job is to stop the race but first we need to protect the racecar. Let the locals deal with the gangs." Brockton nodded as though his boss could see him ended and the call.

He turned to Weaver. "We have to protect the racecar. Drive."

Weaver pocketed her pistol and got behind the wheel. She drove even deeper into the fire fight. Brockton picked up a rifle and shot out of the back door towards houses where some of the shooters had sought cover.

~~~

The whole scene felt so surreal. Katrina heard Richard shouting at her as he struggled to keep moving, swerving the vehicle hoping to avoid the bullets, but she couldn't hear what he was saying. The firefight all around them was like being in a war zone and she was frozen, shutting down, waiting to be shot. She couldn't handle this kind of pressure. She had signed up for this race to help pay off her student loans. Now look at her. She felt so sick.

Richard punched her in the arm and her surreal moment ended abruptly.

"Ouch!"

Richard shouted again. "Light up the laser! Shoot at everything."

Anger filled Katrina. "Fine! You want me light up this town? I'll light up this fucking town!"

Katrina turned on the unit and slowly moved her head in a long slow arc before them. The laser burned a line in the arc of her gaze.

What Katrina didn't realize was that any wood that had been used in the construction of these houses had turned to kindling after so many years of sitting in the sun. A cricket rubbing its legs together could probably create a spark that would turn the dry wood and thus the entire neighborhood into a burning inferno.

The weapon's slow arc moved further across the line of people who were standing in a shooting stance or running to avoid being hit. When the laser beam struck them they crumpled while trying to cover the skin that was burned. Some had clothing that had caught on fire and they writhed on the ground trying to extinguish the flames. When the beam struck anything wooden the running line of the laser created a burst of flames that spread quickly.

The officers watched the destruction in disbelief. They watched the weapon's arc and dove for cover when it approached. Within moments whole houses were engulfed and thick black smoke billowed into the sky. More people were in the street as they ran out of the houses to escape the quick burning fires. Finally the shooting began to subside as the fire became the bigger threat.

A guy on a bicycle rode towards the center of the street into Richard's path. He was carrying an RPG and when he skidded to a stop he wasted no time in taking aim on the racecar and quickly fired. He was so close that missing seemed impossible. The rocket launched less than a second after he depressed the trigger.

~~~

Weaver was still driving down the street hoping to catch up with the racecar. The laser on the roof was catching houses on fire and initially she didn't see the guy on the bicycle. Richard's weaving allowed her to see the guy but it wasn't until she saw the launching tube that she fully appreciated what she was driving into. Her eyes grew wide. They were close enough to the racecar now to be engulfed in the explosion if it was hit.

"Time to bail!" she shouted to her partner who was using his pistol out of his window. "Rocket launcher! Jump!"

Brockton, having spent time in the military on the front lines in Iraq needed no further information. Rocket launcher warnings meant run for your life. He wasted no time, bolted for the rear of the vehicle, and jumped.

Weaver left the truck rolling forward and ran after her partner. There was no time to avoid what was coming and park.

~~~

Richard screamed like a girl at the sight of the RPG being fired. They were so close that he knew that he couldn't get out of the way. In a split second decision he grabbed Katrina's head and dragged it towards his lap while he cut the steering wheel as hard as he could while stomping down on the brake.

~~~

Cosgrove stared down from his window at the scene below. He couldn't believe an RPG was being used by a civilian. His perch in the air gave him a full view of the close-quartered attack. The armored vehicle had almost caught up to the racecar and had no possibility of getting out of range in time. He knew that Brockton and Weaver were inside. Once the missile fired he knew in his gut that his people would be dead. He slapped the window and shouted at his people, though he knew it was impossible for anyone to hear him.

"Get out of there, get out!"

~~~

Richard cut the wheel hard. The racecar spun 360 degrees. Time seemed to slow down. He waited for the explosion that he knew was coming. As the car spun fires exploded around them as the matchbook houses were hit by their laser.

In the corner of his eye he watched the missile enter through his door's window. He turned his face away to allow more space for the missile's flight path. He held Katrina's head down and the projectile sailed through the open window on Katrina's side of the car. He could feel the hot the gases being ejected from the tail end of the missile.

The MIT car was still rotating as the missile followed its trajectory straight into the windshield of the armored vehicle. It exploded with spectacular grandeur, as if it were in a movie. The truck blew up and backwards, spinning in the air. It landed with sickening crunch of metal and glass on its roof many feet further from the racecar that was already moving forward after coming out of its spin, trying to put some distance between the two vehicles.

One of the wheels of the truck broke free and bounced back up into the air. The force driving it was so great that it bounced several times eventually rolling all the way back to the box truck that had been following from what the driver thought had been a safe distance. The rogue wheel bounced onto the hood of the truck exactly where the camera was mounted. The camera was crushed and the hood of the truck was dented badly.

Richard was driving blindly; his only thought was the distance between them and the exploding SWAT truck, when there was a loud thud. He had hit the front tire of the bicycle and the guy with the RPG flew off. He landed in a crumpled heap on the brown grass on the other side of the sidewalk. The bike bounced backwards a bit and fell over. Richard swerved around it and kept driving.

When he looked back he could see the SWAT team encircling their RPG assailant, weapons drawn.

~~~

Brockton and Weaver had ejected themselves out of the rear of their vehicle and had lain in the street with their hands over their heads in pure instinct, as if that could have protected them from a blast. Fire exploded all around them. When the truck had flipped over in the air with the force of the explosion it had passed over them in the air. They felt the force of the blast pushing them against the pavement. A cloud of fire passed over the cowering agents as they prayed.

It had happened in less than a second. It wasn't until LVMPD officers ran up and covered them with blankets that they knew that they were still alive.

~~~

Katrina's head popped back up as Richard moved his hand back to the wheel to avoid the fallen bicycle. He sped away to get them out of the inferno that had once been a quiet neighborhood. He moved his left hand to his face resting his elbow on the open window as he steered with the other hand, trying to seem casual. Behind them he could see flames licking the sky.

"What the hell happened?" Katrina asked, as Richard turned left, still trying to put space between them and the mess that they had left behind.

~~~

Cosgrove was plastered to the chopper's window watching his agents on the ground. All kinds of emergency personal surrounded them. He had never lost an agent before, never mind two of them. His stomach felt to be in his throat. Colliste took a call interrupting the stunned silence.

"It's for you," Colliste said over the sound of the engines.

Cosgrove looked like he was going to be sick. "Tell them I'll call back."

"It's the governor of Nevada," he said, urging him to take the call.

With apprehension Cosgrove took the phone.

"Yes sir," Cosgrove choked out.

A harsh angry voice greeted him. "Cosgrove, let me tell you what I see on television right now. A whole neighborhood is on fire. The flames are so high they can be seen by the NASA robots on Mars. I understand from the Nevada Highway Patrol that a single racecar caused all of the destruction. Is that true?"

"Sir, that would be yes and no."

The voice became even angrier across the connection. "Don't speak in riddles. I want that car out of my city."

"But sir..."

"I don't want to hear excuses I want them out of the city now."

"But sir..."

"Agent, Do you know what I have the most of in this state? Sand, lots and lots of fucking sand. If they burn down what little city I have left, then my constituency will be geologic waste. And you know what agent, last I checked, sand don't vote!"

"Sir, it wasn't the racecar or our team that caused this catastrophe, it was the gangs in that neighborhood." Cosgrove yelled back before he could get cut off.

There was a pause on the phone and Cosgrove knew he had made a mistake.

"I have the highest ranking Highway Patrolman standing next to me whispering in my ear that this racecar has a laser weapon on its roof. From what I understand, the gangs might have started a war against this racecar, but it was the laser that started the fires. Is he lying?"

"No sir. But they were only protecting themselves..." Cosgrove was cut off again.

"It almost sounds like you're trying to defend those idiots."

"Sir, we were trying to protect them only to get them out of the city faster. I didn't want any more civilian casualties. I may have lost two of my agents down there." Cosgrove spat out so he wouldn't be interrupted again.

"Look where that got us. I don't give a shit what you do out in the sand but you are not to engage them in my city again. Is that understood?"

"Yes sir."

"If you can't figure out how to apprehend these racecars outside my city, I will personally make sure that your career with the FBI is over."

"But sir," he began.

"No 'But', get these cars out of my city! Figure it out. Give them a police escort, I don't care. Just get them out of my city!" the voice boomed out the last word before the line went dead.

Cosgrove looked at his phone, then down to the street where his agents were still on the ground. He took the helicopter's phone and slammed it into the glass, then threw it out of the open door past the gunner's ear. The gunner turned his head in surprise, glanced at Cosgrove, and immediately faced forward after seeing the anger on his face. The burning neighborhood was a more pleasant sight at that moment.

~~~

Richard drove, trying to keep his attention focused on the road while still resting with one hand over the left side of his face.

Katrina kept prodding for information since he had pushed her down and she had been completely unable to see what happened.

Finally he said, "I saved your life, okay! Leave it at that."

Katrina thought for a moment but wouldn't leave it alone. "What was happening that I didn't see?"

Richard didn't want to answer the question. He asked one instead. "Where am I supposed to go?"

Katrina immediately looked for the map and noticed that it was singed around the edges. "Follow this street for a while. We're on the outskirts of the city."

But she immediately went back to her previous question. "What happened?" she asked again, but this time she sounded less insistent and more motherly. That's when she realized that he was still holding the side of his face and asked, "Why is your hand over your face?"

Richard looked down for a moment without moving his left hand. The hand on the steering wheel began to shake.

"I did a really stupid thing." He admitted as he took his right hand off the wheel and covered the right half of his face too.

Katrina immediately grabbed the wheel and steered them into the parking lot of an abandoned strip mall. She was glad that he had at least had the presence of mind to take his foot off the accelerator. When they coasted to a stop Katrina pulled the emergency brake and unsnapped her seat belt. She leaned over to unsnap his seat belt and pull him into a hug. As he moved toward her he dropped his hands to reach out to her and the left side of his face was exposed.

Katrina gasped and Richard quickly tried to cover the injury again. Katrina pulled his hand away and saw the burn that covered the entire side of his face and neck.

"Oh my God, oh my God, oh my God!" Katrina said in quick succession.

~~~

The white truck, its mounted camera now damaged beyond repair, pulled to the side of the street when the MIT had stopped. Through the racecar's shattered back window they could see Katrina bent over in her seat but could not tell if Richard was in the car. The cameraman was now holding a much smaller camera and he panned the area searching for Richard. Perhaps he was puking after what they had just witnessed.

Chapter 24

In the middle of Death Valley, newly constructed stadium seating glinted in the sun where it rose out of the sand. It had been created to hold the people who would be arriving to watch the final minutes of the invisible car race. There were boxes above the top row of seats where the ultra-rich could hang out in air-conditioned comfort. These 'Top Boxes' had the best view of the finish loop and commanded the most ridiculously prices.

Some were by invitation only. One thing was certain, if you could afford a ticket to one of these boxes, or were invited to attend a party in one of them, you had the best seats at the finish line, or the finish loop, as it was called in this race.

The dais rose from the sand exactly three feet above the ground. Inside the hoop there were electronics that would recognize which vehicle finished first. There was no way that two cars going through at the same time could be considered a tie. Every car had exactly the same fuselage and an embedded sensor placed at exactly the same place on each car that would communicate with the computer inside the loop. And a computer couldn't play favorites. Whichever sensor crossed first, even by a millimeter, would be deemed the winner. After the winner was determined, every other car would be shut down no matter where it was in the country. If they didn't make it to the hoop they would be scooped up by their chase trucks and brought back.

The Finish Loop stood in the center of a four hundred foot diameter, circular, fenced in area. The stands only occupied one side of the area and it looked like half of a modern football stadium. The stands hugged the fence and traversed one fifth of the perimeter. The rest of the view was open to the desert through the fence.

Grant Phyindress stepped into the most lavish box and walked over to the light switches to turn on the overhead lights. A bar became came into view in the far corner of the room as well as a seating area in front of huge window. The view from the window encompassed the entire fenced area surrounding the finish loop.

A whole entourage of people walked in after him. Some were the catering staff, the bartender, and folks that were to ensure that this party would be one to remember for the ages. The computer staff followed as well. They were the ones who were keeping the internet feed running that covered the race. Others included the starting line girls, his personal staff, and the investors of the remaining racecars.

Ian Practor walked in last with a scowl on his face. He didn't look like someone who wanted to be at a party.

Phyindress shouted across the room to Practor. "Ian, I forgot to turn on the finish loop lights, they're on the wall next to you."

Ian turned around and turned on the ten light switches. The darkening desert brightened as though the sun were rising instead of setting before them. A moment later four monster televisions came on. Each screen was showing one of the remaining contestants of the race. Cheers filled the room and a line soon formed at the bar. As those in line waited for their turn to order a drink, their eyes followed the travels of the racecars through the city of Las Vegas.

Fingers pointed toward the screen when a particular landmark appeared, followed by conversation about a memory for that individual who had either won or lost a lot of money at the gambling institution that had passed into view. The room was filled with conversation and laughter.

When the MIT car drove into the residential neighborhood and the street began to fill with people and police officers, all attention fell upon that screen and they watched in silence. Some watched in horror at the events unfolding before them, others cheered. When the laser came alive on the roof of the MIT car, and the houses began to burn more exuberant cheers filled the room.

No one really cared about the people who were injured or killed. They only cared about the car. When the young man rolled out in the center of the street with his RPG the room roared again. The technicians had to turn up the volume to keep it above the level of noise in the room. Silence fell immediately when the rocket launched itself towards its target. Everyone thought that the car would be hit.

When the car spun suddenly spun and the rocket slid through the open windows to hit the SWAT vehicle behind them instead, the whole room exploded with excitement. Less than a second later one of the wheels of the truck came toward the camera and the feed went black.

The bartender laid out a line of glasses on the counter and made a continuous pour filling each glass for a toast. Hands reached in and grabbed them eagerly. No one care about the death and destruction that had just occurred. The only thing on their minds was how much money they were going to bet on the MIT car to be the winner.

Ian Practor folded his arms over his chest. He was probably the only person in the room who was not celebrating. He couldn't believe what he had just seen.

He had paid good money to find an RPG and get it in the hands of someone who could finish the job and instead he had witnessed another person fail to eliminate the MIT racecar. He checked his pocket, looking for his phone. When his head rose he found his boss standing next to him and it surprised him.

"Sir?"

"Did you see that?" Phyindress asked. "All of that destruction of private property is going to cost us big. We need the lawyers on board now to plan a defense. We need to get a team together that can nip this in the bud. If we're lucky, we might be able to keep the money we're making on the internet broadcast of the race. We've made a million dollars just since noon time." Phyindress said as he patted Ian on the back. "You deserve a raise."

Phyindress' smile was huge. Ian barely showed his teeth in the thin smile he returned. He looked more like he was going to be sick.

When Phyindress left to get closer to the bar Ian stepped back outside into the hall that connected the top boxes and made a phone call, however it wasn't to their corporate lawyer team.

It took a few seconds before anyone picked up. As soon as a greeting spilled out from the other side Ian began to speak in a low whisper that still managed to convey his anger.

"Do you know what I just watched? I watched your man miss the MIT car and blow up a SWAT vehicle. HOW CAN YOU HIRE SUCH INCOMPETENT PEOPLE OVER AND OVER AGAIN?!"

There was silence in response and Ian began again. "Call the drivers and tell them to take matters in their own hands. That car is only about an hour and half away from the finish loop. Everything we are working for will go down the drain if they win, and that doesn't even count the backlash from the police or the FBI.

"If one of those feds was killed..." Ian stopped to catch his breath wondering how to overcome such a catastrophe. "Keep the choppers coming and tell the gangs where the car is. That should keep the pressure up. A million bucks should be enough for a competent person to finish the job."

The line went dead.

~~~

Harvard Bertrand smiled like everyone else in the room. He even drank at the toast. His gut, on the other hand, squirmed. He had just watched his son survive yet another attack on his life. He would be lucky if his son survived the next two hours. If he had a gun right now he would do the cowardly thing and blow his own brains out. He didn't know if his heart could survive watching his son die.

He knew that all of this was his own fault. If his son survived things between them would change. He knew that he had been an ass towards the boy his entire life. What an idiot he had been. So what if Richard didn't want to run the company... So what if acted like a playboy...The smile on his face felt so fake that he hoped that no one else could tell. He just wanted to save his son. He kicked back his drink and tried to smile more convincingly.

~~~

Richard's face lay in Katrina's lap. Katrina sobbed; she didn't know what to do. They didn't have any supplies that would help deal with this kind of injury.

"I'm so sorry, I don't know what to do to help you. I'm going to drive you to a hospital."

Richard shook his head. "No, it was my decision to let the rocket fly through the windows. We just need to finish the race. It can wait."

Katrina crawled over Richard to try to set herself up behind the wheel and move Richard to the passenger seat. "We're going to the hospital. The race is over for us."

Richard placed a shaking hand on Katrina's arm. "We can't. There are still people trying to kill us. If someone recognizes us at the ER they'll just kill us there instead. We need to keep driving."

The white box truck flew into the parking lot and skidded to a stop next to the MIT car. Katrina raised her hand to block the dust and rocks coming at her from the quick stop. When she put her arm down she recognized the truck and saw the crushed camera and knew immediately who these people were.

The driver popped out and ran around the truck to speak to Katrina.

"Are you guys alright?" He asked in his deep baritone voice. His expression changed the second he saw the burn on Richard's face. Lucky climbed out of the passenger side of the truck with his small camera. He pushed the camera in through the open window trying to get the Katrina's wet crying face and Richard's burned one on camera but Jersey pushed him out of the way.

Jersey took his fingers and pressed them to Richard's throat.

"He's going into shock. He needs help now."

Lucky never said a word or offered to help in any way. He maintained the due diligence of recording the scene before him.

Katrina looked shocked. Jersey wasn't acting like a tow truck driver.

He turned towards the camera man and said, "Go grab my bag out of the truck."

"No way man," Lucky said. "I'm doing my job. You should do yours."

Jersey was angry. He walked up to the cameraman and took the camera out of his hands, threw it to the ground and stomped on it until it was a pile of broken plastic.

"Hey, I can't believe you did that! That was my last camera." Lucky shouted. "Now the feed is dark."

"Good, now you have nothing else to do! Go grab my bag." Jersey said again menacingly, and Lucky scrambled into the truck to grab the large duffle bag which he dropped on the ground next to Jersey.

"A lot of the chasers are also EMT's. I can help him enough to get you by. You can't go to a hospital right now. There are too many people hunting you. The safest place is out in front of them all."

"He can't drive like this." Katrina said.

"After I give him a dose of what I have, he'll be able to outrun this racecar on foot. It won't heal the burn but it will get you by until the race is over. Then the million dollar bounty on your heads will go away."

Katrina's eyes widened. "What did you say?"

The reason that there are so many people shooting at you is because there's a bounty on your heads. Someone doesn't want this car to win the race." The EMT began to open packages he had pulled out of the duffel bag. He shook open some large gauze pads to their full size. When he placed the gauze on Richard's chest to open another round of items needed to dress his face, he handed Katrina a small sealed packet.

"Give him these," he said.

Katrina didn't have to ask why. She tore open the sealed package and removed four pills. She held her friend's head up. Richard wasn't responding and his eyes were rolling back. She shook him a little to get him to stir. He moaned.

"It's the shock. You need to get him to swallow those right away." Jersey reminded her.

Katrina grabbed Richard's shoulders and shook him for all she was worth. Richard flopped around like a rag doll but still didn't open his eyes. Katrina took a different approach and whispered to him softly.

"I want to have sex with you."

Jersey's jaw dropped as Richard's eyes popped open.

"Here, swallow these first." Katrina said quickly, before he could close his eyes again. Richard did as he was told before he lay back down and shut his eyes.

Jersey stared at her and Katrina finally noticed that he had stopped working on Richard's bandages. Katrina squinted and said. "What? Oh... the sex thing. Um... That's what he responds best to. If anything was going to rouse him, it would be that."

Jersey chuckled and went back to work.

Lucky opened the doors of the box end of the truck and brought the ramp down so that Jersey could drive the car into the back. They had agreed that the easiest way to get the car out of the city was to keep it hidden in the truck until they were out in the desert and were ready to finish the race.

Not long after the car had been moved inside twenty or so police cars screamed by with their lights on and a helicopter flew overhead. Katrina got back into the race car once it was inside the truck to stay with Richard, cradling his head as he rested. Jersey and

Lucky got back into the cab of the truck and they finally began to move further from the center of the city.

~~~

Mac Killington sat in the lock up at the Detroit FBI office. One of the benefits of being in lock up at the FBI was that there were few other inmates. For the most part he had been alone and it didn't bother him in the least.

A man shouted Killington's name through the hallway. "Mac Killington, your lawyer is here."

Killington smiled. He hadn't requested his lawyer this time, but he knew who would be walking down the hall. Sure enough the officer of the day escorted a tall thin man in a suit to the cell. The man carried a briefcase that looked new but his suit looked slept in and his beard looked scruffy and unkempt. The officer stepped out of earshot but not out of visual range. The thin man moved casually to block the officer's view as if by accident so that their conversation couldn't be overheard and lip movements couldn't be read.

"Irish, you clean up pretty well. Who knew?" Killington said. "You probably should have shaved though."

"I'm sorry boss. The racers are almost at the end and my guys couldn't get to them fast enough."

Killington nodded. "That's okay, it's one thing to take care of business around the neighborhood but trying to keep up across so many states thins our resources. I still have a trick left up my sleeve. We need to finish this job and I know who to call."

The scruffy man looked incredulous. "What do you want us to do?" he asked.

Killington cocked his head to peer around his associate to make sure that the officer had maintained his distance before he spoke. "Get in touch with Kipper. He will know how to contact the two man team in California I told you about. Tell them 'Mac needs it done' and add Cosgrove, his team, and Josephine McGregor in Nevada to the list. She's FBI too. They may want to outsource the last one because there is very little time."

Irish stood taller, feeling more confident. He spoke loudly enough for the officer to hear. "I will check out that lead Mr. Killington. Will there be anything else?"

"No, that will be all for now. Just make sure you talk to the other lawyers to keep them all in the loop."

Irish nodded his understanding. He turned to the officer and raised a hand, he had to swallow hard to make his next statement without the scorn that he normally showed officers of the law. "Sir, I'm ready to leave."

~~~

A white Toyota Corolla pulled up next to Frodes and Jenkins. They had been walking for a while. The sun had nearly set and the falling temperatures, though still well above freezing, felt very cold compared to the triple digit temps of an hour ago. Both men's teeth were chattering as they had slowly walked towards the finish loop dragging their luggage behind them.

Jenkins lifted his head and recognized Dillon and Kristin. "My God, are you guys a sight for sore eyes."

All Frodes could say was, "I was hoping you'd be by hours ago. This stupid bus driver dropped us too far away and..."

Jenkins raised a hand to stall his rambled complaint. "Can we hop in and warm up?"

Kristin hopped out after popping the trunk latch. She took their bags and put them in the truck as the guys climbed into the back seat of the rental. Dillon turned the car around and headed back towards Nevada. Frodes objected immediately.

Jenkins only asked "What happened?" knowing in his gut that Dillon wouldn't be going back without a reason.

Kristin pulled out a tablet and turned it on. "You need to watch this." She handed it over to their mentor.

Frodes asked for water and sipped as they watched in horror as the events unfolded in the Las Vegas neighborhood. The scene changed to a handheld camera looking inside the MIT racecar with Katrina crying while holding Richard's head on her lap showing the burn on his face. The view from the camera suddenly pulled away showing a black man's arm and as the camera's angle changed Jersey's face came into view, then it went blurry and the feed ended.

Frodes had taken on a gray, hollow look. Jenkins just looked tired. He handed the tablet back to Kristin.

Dillon asked, "Who's the black guy?"

Frodes answered. "That's Jersey. He's the chase truck driver."

"We're going back to find them." Kirstin said quickly. "They're in big trouble and that burn, I think it might be from the rocket fuel. If Richard is down then Katrina will be driving now. We're going to run interference. They need all the help they can get."

Kristin had a pained face and watery eyes instead of her usual cheerful smile. She reached down to her feet and pulled up two shotguns. "Who's with us?"

All complaints about walking in the desert disappeared. The only thing on Frodes' mind was to save their friends. The mild mannered engineer persona melted away. He reached for the weapon and said, "Step on it."

~~~

Outside of the Nevada Federal Bureau of Investigation's headquarters, on West Lake Mead Boulevard, a black van pulled over in a parking spot across the street. The sliding door opened on the side that faced the building, and a man in a black face mask leaned forward.

On the third floor of the building a whole block of windows in the corner were lighted. Night had fallen but there were still many agents working at gathering intel, trying to locate the remaining racecars.

Through binoculars the man in the mask watched men and women pass in front of the windows. Clearly most had congregated in the conference room and that's where he decided to target. He felt confident that he had found his quarry. He turned inside the van and replaced the binoculars with a Rocket Propelled Grenade tube. When he returned his view to the windows he placed the weapon's tube on his shoulder and knelt on one knee. The rocket felt heavy, causing the tube to lean forward slightly. He was accustomed to this weapon and adjusted it easily using the eyepiece to focus on the spot he was going to destroy. He signaled the driver.

After the van slipped out of park and into drive, the man holding the RPG fired. A long line of smoke followed the rocket as it flew toward its mark. The van didn't wait for the explosion. Confident that the weapon would reach its goal, they sped off.

The rocket did indeed find its mark. The entire conference room exploded into a ball of fire that lit up the Las Vegas night. Glass blew out into the air and fell to the street below.

~~~

Katrina sat behind the wheel of the MIT racecar in the dark. The only light in the small space came from the overhead dome light in the car. She had one hand stretched out to the steering wheel and she leaned on her open window looking bored. Richard, whose face was bandaged along its left side, sat in the passenger seat. He was bobbing up and down from his newfound energy, the result of whatever had been in the four pills Jersey had given him.

The car still sat inside the back of the box truck. Katrina had originally thought that Jersey's idea of getting them out of the city incognito had been a great one, but now with Richard bouncing off the walls she wondered if they should have just driven.

"When I'm driving and you're not shooting at any particular moment, what do you do? Do you just sit here?" Richard pushed all kinds of buttons on the dashboard. He had energy to burn. "Do you just sit here while I drive? That sounds so boring. Oh my God... I don't think I can just sit here, you know what I mean? If you drive, what am I going to *do*?"

Katrina sighed. And to think she had been crying over his injuries only minutes ago. She sighed again. In less than two hours all of this would be over. At that moment two hours still seemed way too far away.

~~~

Jersey drove the white box truck as fast as he dared. Lucky leaned against his door, still sour about the fact that he didn't have his camera.

No one bothered them as they drove. In fact, though there were cops of every kind on the streets no one seemed to take nay notice of them. The officers seemed to be setting up to block the side streets. When he approached a light, an officer stood in the intersection waving the traffic through. It almost felt like they were part of some kind of parade.

Eventually he noticed another white unmarked box truck in traffic ahead of them. When traffic in his lane allowed them to get closer he could tell that it was a chase truck that still had a camera mounted on the hood. Then he saw the racecar that the other box truck was following. He slowed down to stay behind them so that the other box truck's camera wouldn't see them. A small change in the elevation of the road gave him a view of the traffic further ahead and he could see two more box trucks and their racecars.

Jersey felt suddenly uneasy. It was almost as if they were being corralled.

~~~

Cosgrove rode in the helicopter from hell. At least it felt that way. He had arranged to have all of the police agencies in Nevada create a corridor out of the city to keep the citizens safe from the racecars and their pursuers. It was all because they were in a state where grains of sand outnumbered the inhabitants. Voting potential seemed to take precedence over common sense. Funny how the world worked, he thought.

Then he received the phone call about the rocket that had killed a whole room full of FBI agents, including

Josephine McGregor. He hadn't liked McGregor, but she shouldn't have died because of a stupid race. He wanted to tell the gunner to shoot everything that moved, kill everyone associated with the race, instead he watched helplessly as the cars moved through the city in the traffic below.

~~~

Jersey and Lucky were both nervous now. They could see that this had to be some kind of trap. Lucky was trying to watch behind them to see what the officers did after the racecars passed their intersections. It seemed like as soon as the cars passed by, the officers were moving on as well.

Lucky turned to Jersey. "I think we're all going to get pinched outside the city limits. They're herding us out of the city so they can finish us off some place out where no one else will see what's happening."

Jersey nodded. "I agree. Grab the walkie and tell Katrina they're going to have to stay in the box a little longer than we'd planned. If there is some kind of roadblock ahead we might still be able to get them through. I'm going to try to get ahead of the racers and maybe they won't realize we're part of the group."

Lucky nodded and picked up the two-way radio from the seat to convey the message.

Jersey added one more thing. "Just tell them to take a nap or something." Then he thought about Richard and the drugs he was on. "Never mind, Richard will never be able to sleep with what I gave him."

Lucky nodded again and spoke into the walkie.

~~~

Katrina nodded as she agreed with the new plan. "Got it, we'll sit tight."

She looked over to Richard. He was climbing out of the window. "What? What the hell are you doing?"

"I've got to do something. I'm going crazy sitting here. I need to run."

"Get back in here, they may tell us that we have to leave at any minute." Katrina pleaded. "Please come back."

"I need to run!" Richard exclaimed.

Katrina climbed out to drag him back into the car.

~~~

As the last of the city faded from view the line of traffic on South Highland Parkway was still moving at a pretty good pace. The three racecars and their box trucks were mixed in with a wide variety of other vehicles. They approached Interstate 15 where the vehicles began to spread out.

The Interstate was a much faster road. It felt easy to be driving eighty. The Parkway had felt congested and fifty-five had felt so slow but safe. There were no other cars on the interstate other than the line of traffic that had come off of the Parkway. For the three racecars this was the best ride they had found in the entire country. They could easily have driven 100 mph or more but the three racecars did as they had been instructed at the beginning of the race, they stayed just above the speed limit.

Jersey and Lucky were encouraged with the maneuverability that less traffic and more speed gave them. Jersey pulled into the left lane and everyone could hear the engine roar as he floored it. The diesel engine blew black smoke into the air from working so hard.

He passed one, two, then three of the white box trucks with cameras mounted to their hoods. Every time they passed one of the trucks the drivers stared at them. Jersey hoped that it was because of the dented hood, not because they recognized the truck and noticed the absence of its racecar.

He got worse looks from the racecar drivers but ignored them and was soon in the lead. Fortunately other traffic began to catch up as well, not everyone on the highway was content with driving the speed limit. Big rigs bore down on them as well as minivans with soccer moms drivers and small Hondas and Toyotas with fuels conscious commuters all in a hurry to be somewhere else.

Four helicopters flew over the interstate. Two were assigned to the FBI; the other two were on loan from the Air National Guard. These were not recognizance birds, they were armed Apache style choppers. On the horizon they could be seen settling down to the ground.

After watching the war birds land, all of the vehicles at the front of the line began to slow. This allowed even more of the regular traffic to catch up. Jersey pressed on to be as far ahead of the racecars as possible. He knew what was coming. There was a giant police roadblock just before the California state line.

As everyone pressed closer to where the helicopters had landed, the racecars slid farther and farther back in traffic. They were now realizing that they could be trapped here and were trying to figure out how they could get off the highway. Jersey didn't slow any more that the rest of the traffic. He knew that his best chance was to blend in and hope that they wouldn't be taking the time to inspect the trucks. He drove up to the roadblock confidently, as if he had nothing to hide.

There were a few cars in line ahead of him but no other trucks. He sat higher than the other vehicles and had a good view of the patrol cars that blocked the road in front of the helicopters. They had also commandeered some tractor trailer trucks to spread over the highway's sandy buffer zone like wings to prevent anyone from making a break for it. A couple of military Hummers, with machine gunning stations on the top, took positions beyond the extent of the tractor trailers with their guns pointed towards the coming traffic on each side of the highway. Towers of lights made the whole area brighter than it would have been in full sunlight.

The blockade funneled cars into a single lane that had to negotiate through a curved passage of lined with military vehicles ensuring no one could drive straight through if they had enough momentum to try to run through it.

The helicopters were on the ground ready to take flight on a moment's notice, their imposing weapons pointed at the line of traffic. The FBI chopper hovered fifty feet above the road, a gunner at the ready.

~~~

Katrina presented put both of her hands on the hood of the racecar, out of breath, facing Richard. "I told you to get in the car right now!"

Richard just laughed. He faced her from the other end of the vehicle. "I'm only getting in if I can drive."

How was she going to convince him? She couldn't catch him, he wasn't even out of breath.

"You can't drive like this. Hell, you shouldn't even be in the car. You should be in a hospital. But please just

get in. We have to be ready on a moment's notice."
Katrina pleaded.

The truck that they rode in slowed and then
stopped. Both of them stopped talking to listen. The
truck didn't move and the only sounds were that of the
truck dieseling.

Katrina pointed to the passenger seat and
whispered harshly. "Get in now or I will have to do
something desperate."

"Oooh, what are you going to do, make me?"

There was banging on the truck's side. Richard
turned to look but there was nothing that he could see in
the mostly dark truck box. When he turned back to taunt
Katrina some more, he found a pissed off Katrina flying
through the air over the hood, with her hands up aiming
for his neck.

~~~

Jersey had one arm extended over his wheel,
looking bored to be held up in the line. He was doing his
best to appear normal and slightly agitated at the delay.
Lucky looked nervous and Jersey threw him a quick
scowl as an officer walked up to his window. Jersey
turned his gaze to acknowledge the officer's presence.

"What are you carrying?" the officer asked.

"Produce." Jersey said pulling off his bored
attitude well.

"It doesn't say produce on the box."

"The regular truck broke down. This is a rental."

"What kind of produce?" The office asked.

"Watermelons."

The officer nodded and was about to wave them
on but then noticed how nervous Lucky seemed.

"Why are you looking so anxious?"

"Why are you pretending to be an officer of the law?" Lucky shot back in a childishly sing song voice.

The officer set his jaw and started around the front of the truck. Jersey turned towards his passenger and glared. He wanted to pummel him.

Lucky knew he had done something wrong. He sat up straighter. He was about to apologize but the officer had already moved around to his side of the truck.

"Let's have this conversation outside." He said, motioning Lucky to get out of the truck. The officer knew that he could find something in the cab worth an arrest if the guy was this edgy. He looked inside the cab but saw nothing but a can of Pepsi and a bottle of SoBe in the cup holders.

"When did you rent this vehicle?" The officer asked.

Jersey gave a deep sigh, trying to calm his nerves without sounding annoyed. Suddenly there was a loud bang from the back and he sucked in his breath.

~~~

Katrina had Richard by the throat. She had finally managed to catch him. Her anger was spilling out. Richard had his tongue sticking out of his mouth. He was trying to laugh more than he was trying to catch his breath. To him this was fun, a good way to use his newly limitless energy.

~~~

The officer looked down the length of box. "What did you say was in the back?"

Jersey answered quickly, "Watermelons. The longer we stay here, the more will pop because it's so hot back there."

The officer put his hand on the box to feel if it was as warm as the driver alleged. He left it there for a moment and he did feel heat pouring through.

Jersey was starting to sweat. He was lying through his teeth. The warmth in the back came from the charging car that produced no emissions except for heat. Jersey only knew about the watermelon problem from his early days when he worked in a grocery store. The trucks delivering watermelons always had some that had split open if the boxes weren't refrigerated.

As the officer paid attention to the warmth of the box he heard another pop.

~~~

Richard was climbing into the driver's seat but Katrina still had him by the neck.

"Stop it!" she whispered angrily "You are not driving!"

He wriggled his arm trying to get free and his elbow smacked the car's fuselage.

~~~

"See, I really have to get going." Jersey said.

"What's his story?" The officer gestured to Lucky.

"He's just learning my route. This is my last day and I only get paid for intact watermelons. I'm sure you understand." Jersey pleaded.

Another pop occurred in the box of the truck. "You sure you only have watermelons back there?"

"If you want me to open the truck, go ahead I don't care, but I really need to get going." Jersey pleaded again.

This time it was the officer who stepped back. He sighed and said, "Go ahead, get out of here."

Lucky scrambled back into his seat and Jersey released the brake to move through the curved roadblock.

Lucky still had sweat on his forehead. "I can't believe we got out of that. It was a good idea to get rid of all the crap in the cab especially the wrappers for the bandages. That was really smart."

Jersey leaned over and smacked his passenger really hard in the arm. Lucky crumpled under the pain.

"I should throw your ass out right here. Your smart mouth almost got us in serious trouble." Jersey reached over and smacked him in the arm again before he floored the accelerator. He knew that behind him, when the racecars got closer in line, there was going to be trouble. He wanted to get as far away from it as possible. Lucky pressed himself against the passenger side door, holding his sore arm.

The box truck was carrying a fair amount of weight and struggled to get back up to speed. He hoped that the stupid officer spent as much time with every vehicle that was passing through the roadblock as he had spent with them. If that were the case they might make it to California before the bullets started flying.

~~~

Pressure was mounting in the line of cars waiting at the roadblock. Eventually one of the racecar's drivers decided to take the chance and made a break for the sand. The other two racecars quickly followed. They peeled out of the line and took to the desert to avoid the roadblock. They went straight out to get away from the lights before turning to parallel the road but they were easily caught in the helicopters' search lights.

Cosgrove shouted into the booming PA system in his chopper. "Stop! We do not want to hurt you. Pull over or we will have to open fire."

The cars made no effort to stop. They headed farther out into the desert. The Apache Helicopters rose into the air to join those of the FBI and the Hummers took to the sands.

Other cars broke the line and ran off the side of the road. The people inside these vehicles took out weapons and pointed them up. The gang members were still looking to collect the million dollars. Some of the cars charged the police blockade. Shots flew from all directions.

The military helicopters turned away from the racecars and headed back to support the officers on the ground. The FBI choppers' side gunners opened fire.

~~~

Jersey shouted to Lucky as he stared into his side mirror. "Take out the walkie. Tell them they have to leave right now! We won't be able to stay ahead of the race while they are in the back. I can't get enough speed. Our truck is too heavy with the car in the back. They're going to have to make a break for it!"

Lucky took out the walkie he had tucked in his shirt pocket and brought it to his mouth.

~~~

376

Richard had managed to get himself fully into the driver's seat but Katrina still hand both hands around his neck.

"Get out of the driver's seat!" She yanked on him not caring if she tore his bandages.

When the walkie keyed up they both stopped to listen. Lucky's voice screamed out of the speaker. "You have to go now!"

Katrina strangled her driver even harder than before. "Get out of that seat!"

Richard didn't seem to mind being strangled. He calmly put on his seatbelt, released the emergency brake, and revved the engine.

"It's time to go. Get in," he said as if there were nothing wrong.

Katrina screamed in frustration. "If you kill us because you didn't listen to me, I'm going to haunt your ghost for the rest of eternity!"

"You can't haunt a ghost," Richard said with a smile. "Now get in and stop sounding like a wife."

Katrina screamed loud enough to startle Jersey and Lucky. They both looked back towards the box through the metal of the cab wondering what was going on.

Katrina pounded on the hood as she ran to the passenger side. She pulled herself up and slid in through the window. After she got her belt on she punched Richard as hard as she could in the arm.

"Go ahead if it makes you feel better," Richard said with a smile. "With these drugs, I can't feel a thing."

Katrina rammed on her headset and powered it up. Her angry scowl marred her pretty face.

"Are you ready?" he asked.

Agitated beyond belief, she screamed "NO!"

Richard stomped on the accelerator.

~~~

Jersey's plan to get the MIT team past the roadblock had worked perfectly. No one was looking for a truck delivering watermelons. All the attention had been focused on the three racecars that were trying to skirt the roadblock and the gang members who were still trying to collect on the million dollar bounty.

Flashes of gunfire filled the night. There was no way any of them could see what they were aiming at. The roadblock had become a war zone. The only exceptions were the gunners who were firing from the choppers. Per military regulation, which the FBI and the Air National Guard observed, all machine gun style weapons had a tracer bullet on every fifth round. These tracer rounds, in the night environment, looked like laser fire from futuristic weapons and made the sky look like a scene from Star Wars.

Overshadowed by all of the activity behind them, the MIT car exploded from the back of the white box truck. Richard had rammed the door with sufficient force to shear the pins that had been holding the ramp up. The MIT car was airborne for a second before landing on the still opening ramp. Sparks blasted from the ends of the ramp that were now rubbing on pavement.

As soon all four wheels were on the pavement Richard cut around the truck to pull up next to Jersey's window.

"Thank you!" Katrina shouted.

Jersey saluted her. "Good Luck!" He returned.

Lucky stuck his head near Jersey's so that he could be seen out of the driver's window and shouted "Call me!" before Jersey pushed him back to his side of the cab and then pulled over to attend to the open back door.

Richard sped off.

Everything looked good. The war was behind them for once and the road ahead felt inviting for a change. Richard turned to Katrina and said "See, I can drive normally."

Katrina gave him 'The Look' before turning her attention to her mirror to watch the flashes of light and the long arcing lines of the tracer rounds.

Out of nowhere, the other three racecars pulled back onto the road from the sand. Their sudden approach startled an overly wired Richard. He steered erratically for a second before realizing who they were. He let his heart calm down now that he knew that these were his compatriots.

The Caltech car pulled alongside Katrina and her dower face changed in an instant. The driver smiled at her. She beamed at him.

"I thought you guys were going to be stuck back there." Katrina yelled out her window.

"Na. Those fools gunning at us had no chance." He said with a smile. "I'm a great driver."

Katrina smiled even wider and said, "Well, we had a few problems. We lit up the town a bit on our way out, but we're good."

He laughed. Lighting up Las Vegas certainly meant something different in his mind.

Richard, hearing the conversation, leaned in and turned his face to show the bandage. "Yeah, facial burns not included."

Katrina slapped him and he returned his focus to driving. She leaned back out of her window to flirt with the man whose name she had still not yet learned.

~~~

Ahead of them, the car with the dune buggy look drove next to the split style car which was currently connected and running as a normal car again. The passenger of this odd car leaned out of his window and handed a package to the driver on his right in the dune buggy car.

"We got the okay to take the next step. No one else was able to get close enough to finish the job. Do your thing and we'll meet you at the end, as winners."

The dune buggy driver nodded as the split car drove ahead to separate himself from the coming altercation.

The driver handed the package to his weapons specialist who accepted it with a smile. When he unwrapped it, a pistol fell out into his open hand.

With a smile he said, "Finally, a decent weapon."

~~~

Katrina had her hand out the window to touch the fingers of the Caltech driver. She giggled. Neither of them noticed that she still wore her headset so that the weapon above her was pointed at the driver while they flirted. One misstep and she could have taken his eyes out.

Richard was still full of adrenaline from the drugs he had taken for the pain from the burn. One of the many side effects was that he felt hyper aware of his surroundings. Part of him was focused on Katrina's flirting, of which he obviously didn't approve. He was the one who had just saved her life. Another part was focused on why the split car had just disappeared and the dune buggy car had fallen back with their weapons specialist hanging out of his window while his arm was outstretched towards Katrina.

Richard assumed the worst and panicked. The outstretched arm looked like he was holding a gun. He floored the accelerator. The MIT car performed like a rocket and shot ahead of the dune buggy car on its passenger side. Katrina screamed as though she was falling out of her seat on a roller coaster. Richard grabbed Katrina, cupping the back of her head through her hair.

As soon as they had passed the dune buggy he swerved into their lane and slammed on the breaks. As he did this he turned Katrina around and pulled her in close, so close that their noses were touching, and then he kissed her.

The driver of the dune buggy car swore loudly and swerved instinctively to the left to avoid the imminent collision but did not turn far enough out to compensate for the man hanging out of his window.

When Richard turned Katrina around quickly, the weapon on the roof swiveled to follow her head. When he pulled her close she leaned on the fire button. The weapon turned on and lazed a line across the competitor's car as it passed by. Because the dune buggy passed so close to them the bulb of the laser knocked the pistol out of the outstretched hand of the would be murderer.

The laser ran down the side of the dune buggy and inside the rear wheel well. The tire was cut in an instant and started to lose air rapidly.

The gun had fired when it had been knocked from the dune buggy passenger's hand and had planted a round in the rear driver's side tire of the Caltech car.

Both cars pulled to opposite sides of the road within a hundred feet of each other.

Richard stopped the car in the middle of the road before pushing Katrina way from their embrace. Katrina slowly opened her eyes to stare into Richard's.

The kiss surprised her. She took both of her hands and lightly touched both sides of Richard's face, pulling him closer for another kiss. They looked into each other's eyes. The moment felt like a lifetime. Somehow she liked kissing her driver. Somehow it felt right. Yet they had talked recently about his sexual orientation and this wasn't the direction she felt at the moment.

Somehow everything that had been good in that moment went disastrously wrong. Richard cringed from her touch to his bandaged face and he turned away. This brought Katrina quickly back to the real world. What had just happened?

Katrina turned around to see both cars on the sides of the road. "What did you do?" she asked angrily.

Richard held the bandaged side of his face lightly and pointed to the dune buggy car. The weapons guy just tried to shoot us, or you. I just flattened..."

Energy like the burst from a solar flare erupted from Katrina. She screamed as loud as she could with her arms raised towards the heavens. Richard moved his hands towards his ears to protect them.

Katrina tore off her headset and pulled herself out of the car. She walked over to the laser head that hung limply without anyone to direct it. She nimbly removed it from its casing and carried it over to the dune buggy. On the ground she found the pistol between her and her destination. She picked it up. Now she had two ways to kill these bastards.

Somehow she thought that it had been these idiots who had ordered the bounty against them, the ones who had punctured their tires, the ones that had made their race experience hell, and that they were the ones responsible for burning Richard's beautiful face, scarring him for life. She was going to destroy them both.

As Katrina approached the passenger, dazed by her own apocalyptic anger, she raised the gun and pointed it at him. "You're both going to die!"

Their driver laughed.

Katrina fired the first round, somewhat wide, into the body of their car. "I'm going to shoot your legs and then I'm going to let my laser burn a hole through your eye until it goes out the other side."

They both realized that she was serious and struggled to get out of the car as fast as possible. The driver fell out and they both ran into the desert to put some distance between them and the crazy woman. Katrina placed the laser unit on the car over the area where she imagined a fuel cell might be hidden and turned it on. She casually walked to the other side and shot both of the driver's side tires. She fired off another round into the dash destroying the main computer screen.

The laser melted its way through the layers and the car shut down, all of its lights fading to dark. Katrina left the laser on and it continued burning into the skin. She wanted the car to burn. The fuel cells should ignite any minute.

The Caltech car quickly pulled over and the cute driver slid out his window and ran up to her. "What are you doing?" he asked.

"I'm going to have both of these bastards killed. They tried to murder all of us. I'm destroying their car so that the gangs coming up behind us will hunt them down." She turned towards the desert and shouted so the bastards could hear her. "You better hope the police find you first!"

"You think the gangs are coming?" he asked.

"Oh yeah," Katrina said. "This fire will help them find the car."

Suddenly the fire started as if on cue. It didn't take long to erupt from a small flicker to an inferno. Katrina had estimated the location of the fuel cell properly.

Katrina reached in to turn it off the laser and removed it from the car. "That's enough," she said. "I'm done. This race is over for me."

The Caltech driver looked at the growing fire and took Katrina's arm to walk her away from the car in case the fuel cell blew.

"You can't stop now. You can't let that splitting racecar win. They're the ones who gave these guys the gun."

Katrina looked at the ground as revelations opened in her mind.

"I have a problem though," the Caltech driver continued. "If the gangs come we'll be in the same situation as those idiots in the desert. I have a bullet hole in my tire and we're already driving on our spare."

Katrina looked back toward her car to offer some kind of help but didn't see Richard anywhere. She panicked. With his level of energy, he could be anywhere. She looked left and right but he wasn't anywhere to be seen. She took off at a run to investigate. When she arrived at the car she set the laser head and pistol on the roof and saw Richard lying on the seat holding his face in pain.

Chapter 25

    A war was being waged all around the helicopter that Cosgrove and Colliste occupied. Their side gunner's tracer rounds illuminated his firing path but they didn't light up the damage being inflicted on the vehicles below. Perhaps there was no damage at all.

    Cosgrove struggled with the idea of Jurisdictional Prudence. He knew that in instances where one agency was under fire they were obliged to help the affected agency as a priority higher than their own case. The problem that he struggled with was that all of the gang activity was directly under the state's purview and the amount of firepower right on the scene was more than sufficient to get the rogue individuals under control. Plus, the air National Guard was here to lend a hand.

    Now, if the gangs crossed over into California that would be a different story. Right now, all that he knew was that the racecars were getting away, again. If he successfully apprehended the drivers of the racecars, then the bounty would no longer be an option and the gang members would all go home; everyone would be happy.

    Cosgrove pointed to his traveling partner. "Get the other chopper on the line. We're going to pursue the racecars and leave this mess to the Nevada Highway Patrol."

    Colliste nodded and picked up a radio.

~~~

    Katrina watched Richard through the window of the car. She had no idea how to help him. Should they just let the police catch up or would the gangs get there first? The image in her mind flicked to police officers finding their dead bodies on the road. But how could they keep going? She was frozen in place, lost in her own thoughts.

The Caltech driver leaned in next to her and saw Richard lying across the seats. "Looks like he's in serious pain."

His passenger walked up and asked, "What are we going to do?"

They could hear the helicopters and it sounded like they were getting closer. They had to do something now or it was all over. He took the laser head from Katrina and handed it to his weapon specialist, whose name was Jeff. "Finish off our car. We're with them now."

Without question Jeff ran over to their car and set the laser to disable their car.

The Caltech driver turned back to Katrina, "My name is Ty, we're in this together now and we need to get going."

Katrina nodded absently as the power in the Caltech car went dead and Jeff ran back to them, handing Katrina back her weapon.

"Help Jeff reconnect the laser head so we can leave," said Ty as he walked around to the driver's side of the car.

Together Katrina showed her engineering peer how the weapon went together. He looked genuinely impressed. It helped Katrina focus. She began to explain the functions in more detail but Ty spoke to get their attention.

"Help me get Richard in the back so we can all fit in the car."

They ran over and slid into the windows. It was a tight fit but they tugged at Richard to get him behind the seats until he was curled across the back of their storage area with his head closest to the passenger side of the car.

He whispered to Katrina, "My burn hurts so badly. I can't focus."

Katrina reached back and touched the side of his face that was not covered in bandages. Her eyes filled with tears. She had no idea how to help him.

Ty took a minute to familiarize himself with the controls and then released the break.

Jeff twisted his torso to reach around the passenger seat to put his fingers on Richard's neck to check his pulse. "The pain medication needs a boost to keep him stable. He's not going to go into shock but the pain will only get worse."

"We have nothing to give him. What can we do?" Katrina asked.

Jeff had an idea. "Adrenaline could help. We just need to get him amped up."

"How fast can this car go?" asked Ty.

Katrina turned to him with all the seriousness she could muster. "Somewhere around 200 mph. If he needs the adrenaline, step on it!"

~~~

Back at the finish loop Grant Phyindress had a glass of booze in his hand waiting for the cars to get closer. The starting line girls, all wearing tiny bikinis, danced around him. Most everyone was half in the bag by now except for Ian Practor.

Ian stood in one corner of the room with a very sour expression on his face. His cell phone was in his hand and he kept glancing at it, expecting it to ring at any moment.

All of the lights around the loop were lit and the spectators of the Invisible Race were filling up the stands. A large LED screen sat atop a post over the finish loop. The screen showed the stats of the race in the center and in each of the four corners smaller sections showed the remaining cars. Lots of excitement energized the place.

One of the technicians interrupted Phyindress' celebration.

"Sir, we have lost all camera feeds for the race. The cameramen are all stuck at a roadblock and the racecars are gone. People are starting to get anxious, what should I do?"

Phyindress turned to his girls and said loudly, "Please excuse me, I have to go find some lost race cars." He had already had enough alcohol for his words to become slurred but he had spoken loudly enough for the whole room to hear him and they all cheered as he moved toward the cluster of technicians who were set up on one side of the room.

Phyindress became a completely different person as he walked toward the technicians. He was still half in the bag and his words were still slurred but he focused on the problem like a pro.

"The internet community must have information or they will stop watching. We must at least give them updates. Each car's fuselage has a built in GPS tracker. No one else knows about them except for the manufacturer of the skins. That was my backup in case all of the cameras went down. Have those trackers turned on and do it fast. We need to know where the cars are and get some cameras out there. Do it fast."

The technician made a quick phone call then turned to his computer and punched in the codes. Instantly the image of the roadblock disappeared and was replaced by a map of Nevada with two large red dots on it. Both dots were on the same road heading towards California, perhaps only fifteen minutes away from Death Valley.

It took a few seconds before labels showed up next to the dots. Phyindress leaned in to read through his blurred vision. He put both hands in the air excited. "Alright! It's down to our car and the MIT team. Bertrand will be so excited. His man Jenkins pulled it off. A worthy contender!"

Phyindress turned back to the party, bumping into Practor on his way to a small stage.

Ian watched the screen with the two labeled dots from the shadows of the open electronics center, fuming.

Phyindress stepped onto the small stage carefully. He raised his hands in the air.

"Attention everyone. We are finally down to the last two contenders! I'm sorry to say that our camera crews have been held up at a police roadblock and will not be able to film the last leg of this great race. If you'll direct your attentions to the screen, you can see the two dots that represent the two remaining cars moving toward the California border. One is my entrant, the other, the MIT car."

Cheers erupted throughout the room. Practor gave in and took a drink from a passing waiter. He didn't savor it. He kicked it back preparing to finish a job that apparently no one else could.

Phyindress shouted above the cheering. "Last chance to get a small wager in. I have a man going around taking information. Tell him how much you're putting down and he'll swipe your credit card."

Phyindress tried step off the stage gracefully but tripped and had to be helped back down into the crowd. Practor left the room in disgust.

~~~

The darkness of the desert felt omnipresent. Cosgrove and Colliste were nowhere and everywhere at the same time. Being in a helicopter flying low and fast did weird things to their tired minds. Colliste couldn't take the odd silence anymore. All day they had been so busy that they couldn't see straight at times. Now they were doing nothing but trying to catch racecars going full bore across the desert.

"Are Weaver and Brockton going to join back up at the end to help round up all the cars left?"

"No, they're out." Cosgrove said. "They're going to be okay, but after that explosion they are stuck in observation at medical."

Colliste nodded agreeing that they needed the recovery time.

The pilot's voice broke over the com. "We have a fire ahead, looks like a car is burning. And there's a second car off the road."

Cosgrove said to Colliste, "If there are two less cars in the race, then it should be easier to find the one with the weapon on the roof. Maybe that crazy weapon is what started the fire here too."

Finn took the microphone and spoke to the pilot. "Put us down nearby so we can see if there are any casualties."

The chopper put down on the highway near the cars. Cosgrove and his man jumped out, guns drawn, and with a strong flashlight lighting their aim. Both headed over towards the Caltech car. When no one could be seen, they lowered their weapons. Cosgrove headed over to the fire leaving Colliste to investigate the abandoned car.

The rotors blades made for hurricane type winds around the agents and it was difficult to see much of anything with all the sand flying around.

Colliste ran to the burning car to see what his boss had found.

"No bodies here." Cosgrove shouted out over the wind.

Colliste shook his head. "No bodies in the other car either but they have a bullet hole in the back tire and what looked like a burn on the hood of the car."

Cosgrove shook his head, irritated at not knowing what the hell it all meant. "Call in that two cars are down and where to find them. Also, they need to get some searchlights up here and see if they can find whoever was in these cars. They could be lost in desert and they may need medical attention."

~~~

Richard could hear the engine working hard, but it was still humming along like it was supposed to. He kept his eyes closed, lost in the pain. He couldn't see how fast they were driving but felt as though the G forces were higher than they should be. He could feel them pressing on him and knew that the car had to be going higher than a 100 mph. He was worried about the guy driving the car. He wondered what kind of training the guy had and if Katrina was paying attention to the charging system.

No one spoke and his worry grew. Finally he couldn't take it anymore and had to look. He opened one eye a sliver and saw the landscape rushing passed the windows. When he turned to see the speedometer holding at 160, both eyes popped open. Without realizing it, his fear pumped adrenaline into his system and the pain drained away.

"Pull over, pull over!" he shouted hoarsely.

Ty did as he was told. It wasn't his car, after all. As soon at the vehicle stopped, Richard scrambled over everyone to climb out of the car through Katrina's window. He ran towards the driver's side and told TY to slide over. Ty obliged without any argument and Jeff climbed into the storage area to get out of the way.

A second later the car took off again and this time it flirted with the 190 mark. Everyone in the car was nervous, except Richard. He appeared to be completely calm now and in his element.

"How close to California are we?"

"Five minutes or so at this speed." Jeff said quickly.

Richard and Katrina both looked at him surprised.

"This is an area of the country we know very well." Jeff added.

Ty nodded.

Ahead lights filled the road. It reminded Ty and Jeff of the roadblock but they didn't seem concerned.

"I think that's the California state line. You think there's another roadblock?" Jeff asked.

Ty nodded. "You might want to get off the road here and go around. That's how we got around the last one."

Katrina had only one question. "How did that split car get around?" She asked knowing that none of them knew the answer, but also placing in everyone's mind that if they could do it, so could their car.

Richard's mouth went into high gear. "Maybe the other car already went around."

"Well, what are you waiting for? Get off the road."
Katrina instructed.

Richard shut off the lights and went out into the
sand. They bounced around on the uneven ground.
Without their lights it was impossible to see anything.
There was a new moon that night and everything out
here was black. Richard used the lights of the roadblock
to judge his position and easily circumvented their
problem. The officers never even turned their lights to
try to find them.

Katrina wondered why they had set up the
roadblock at all if no effort was being made to stop those
who went around.

~~~

Cosgrove held the communication device to his
mouth speaking with the helicopter pilot. "How fast are
we going? Can we catch up to them if they're still
moving?"

"Normally we can go just shy of two hundred
miles per hour, but I have you two in the back and the
gunner. That slows us down to about 175. Can't change
the physics. I can't move any faster unless you get off."

Cosgrove looked over to the gunner.

The gunner looked surprised and said quickly.
"I'm not getting off."

The pilot began to speak again. "The roadblock on
the border of California should slow them enough to help
us catch up. Unless their cars can go 200 mph we'll catch
them."

Cosgrove killed the microphone. He was angry
that nothing was going right. He leaned back against his
seat hard. All he could hope for was that he got to them

before they finished the race. That had been the goal all along but they were running out of time.

~~~

Darkness engulfed them. They had turned the car's headlights on when they had returned to the interstate but they were the only car on the road. Their jaunt into the sand hadn't lasted long. On the distant horizon they could see street lights.

"That should be Death Valley Junction ahead where those lights are," Katrina said. "We're going to drop you guys off there. It should be a safe place for you to get in touch with your team."

Jeff nodded wearily, Ty on the other hand, began to object. "No. You can't let us out now. We can still help you, we can help you win."

At over a hundred miles per hour it didn't take very long to arrive at those lights and Richard slowed to a stop.

Katrina turned to look Ty full in the face. "I would love to have you stay and help us, but I know what we will find at the end of this race. The FBI, Homeland Security, California SWAT will all be there. We are going to be arrested, you'd be arrested too if you're still with us. We are going to testify against those bastards that tried to kill us."

Ty looked down into the dark floorboards of the car he still sat in seeking some argument that would change her mind. "What if Richard can't drive? I can be here to take over."

Richard glowered at Ty. Katrina could see him and tried not to laugh. Richard leaned toward Ty but she put her hand on his chest and pushed him back into the driver's seat.

"We have to go." Katrina stated, hoping this would be enough to get Ty out of the car. "You know it's best if you guys get out here."

Ty took a pen from his uniform's pocket and took Katrina's hand. He wrote on it and said, "Here's my number. Call me after the race."

"You mean when we get out of prison?" Richard asked sarcastically.

Ty and Richard locked eyes. Katrina turned from one man to the other ending on Ty. She moved her hand from Richard's and pulled at Ty to get him out of the car. "I'll call you, just go. We're running out of time."

Ty slid out and Jeff climbed out of the back over Katrina and out of the car. Richard didn't wait another second for goodbyes. He burned rubber, leaving their Caltech friends behind.

~~~

Colliste had his head leaning on the window staring out trying to find a racecar. He was so tired. The angle made his neck all tight and he knew he would soon have a large headache.

They had spotted several vehicles that had turned out not to be racecars. Apparently there were other people that lived in the world that owned cars and drove at night. The helicopter had crossed over the state line not all that long ago and the traffic had all been stopped at the roadblock. He hadn't seen any cars for many minutes now. He could see the faint lights of a small town ahead just as the pilot came on to announce that Death Valley Junction was ahead. As they approached, a distinct set of headlights were visible. Colliste was about to tap his boss on the arm to let him know that he had found something but decided that with all the false alarms he should wait to be sure. Damn he was tired.

In the moonless night in the desert, a set of headlights could probably be seen for a hundred miles. At least it felt that way. It's difficult to gage distance without other visual cues.

To Colliste these lights seemed very far away despite or perhaps because of the speed and height of the helicopter in which they flew. Tonight's pitch blackness hampered his visual acuity as well. He thought that the lights he was observing were pointing in the wrong direction and felt that this would be another false alarm. The streetlights up ahead would at least make identifying the type of vehicle possible. It was a real bitch trying to recognize a specific type of car on a dark road.

As they got closer he realized that the car had been stopped but had just sped off. Colliste swore under his breath because now they were going to be watching it in the dark again.

"Did you see that?" Cosgrove asked. "That might be our car."

Colliste sighed and said, "They just pulled out, I have them now."

Cosgrove pulled his binoculars to his eyes and focused in on the car. As it shot forward spitting sand and rocks, a street light glinted off the weapon attached to their roof. Cosgrove began to jump and down in his seat with excitement. The whole vehicle rocked under his moving weight. The gunner rocked wildly on his perch. Over the intercom system, the pilot yelled a warning.

Cosgrove shouted back in return. "Follow them!"

~~~

Katrina looked so tired as she lay slumped in her seat. Her headset sat askew on her head. It didn't matter that Richard had the accelerator floored and the car flirted with 200 mph. She was just tired.

Richard had both hands on the wheel when he spoke. "Do you think we can catch them?"

"Oh yeah." Katrina returned drowsily. "And it should be soon. Their car can't go this fast for any length of time, and any prolonged speed would just take away the fuel they will need at the end."

"Say, look behind us." Richard asked. "Does that light look like a star or a...?"

Katrina turned around slowly to gaze at it.

~~~

Cosgrove had the car in its sights through his binoculars. Suddenly the weapon turned and pointed at them as Katrina had turned in her seat. He panicked, knowing the power it had, and shouted to the pilot.

"Move away!"

The pilot asked why. Cosgrove didn't think they had time for an explanation and reached in the cockpit. He grabbed the pilot's coat and yanked him to the side. The craft tilted radically causing the aircraft to bank so hard that they turned almost ninety degrees off course.

~~~

Katrina saw the light streak sideway across the sky. She turned back and stated calmly, "Maybe a jet or something."

~~~

The helicopter pilot struggled to get the craft stabilized. The passengers rolled around attempting to better handholds. Colliste had one good strong hand on the gunner whose harness had brought him inside the aircraft when they had tilted. Finally the craft became level again.

The pilot turned the craft back on course, set the autopilot, and unbuckled himself. He tore into the seating area and punched Cosgrove in the face who fell backwards from the impact. The pilot withdrew a pistol from its holster and pointed it to Cosgrove's head as he grabbed his dress coat.

"You want to die, fine. Your choice is to have me throw you out of my chopper or I can just shoot you. Decide, because I will not allow you to down this craft with that kind of stupidity. You may outrank me on the ground, but I have the right to shoot anyone who tries to down an aircraft, endangering the lives of all of the other passengers. And, right now I'm inclined to do it. So what is it, do I shoot or throw you out?"

Cosgrove stammered. "But... But they were turning their laser weapon on us, I was keeping us alive."

"If the aircraft goes down we all die." The pilot grumbled. "I don't have all day to hear your excuses!"

Cosgrove raised both his hands in surrender.

The pilot shook him violently but let him go. He turned to the gunner. "Are you alright Jim?" he asked.

Jim nodded.

The pilot pointed to Cosgrove who was still lying backwards across the seat. "Stay inside and keep an eye on this idiot. If he reaches into the cockpit again, shoot him." He turned on the spot and disappeared back inside the dark cockpit without waiting for a response.

Colliste put his hand over his forehead. This needed to be over soon. They needed rest. Cosgrove was going to over the edge, they were both were.

~~~

Richard leaned into the steering wheel to focus on his driving. He had both hands on the wheel, at the ten and two o'clock positions, expertly controlling the most advanced automobile he ever driven, or that he had ever heard of. Companies around the world were developing vehicles that could drive themselves. This one left the pure driving experience in the hands of the operator, but it never needed fuel. Sure it had to go at lower speeds to recharge the battery, but it never had to be plugged in. He could floor the accelerator for a thousand miles and his only fear, aside from the police, would be running low on power for short periods of time. This car deserved to win.

At that moment the adrenaline from the rush of the high speed driving kept his intense pain from returning. He turned to watch Katrina for a second. She had actually fallen asleep. He knew that she was exhausted. His ability to stay awake had come from the drugs he had taken. She, on the other hand, had to be very tired to sleep at this kind of speed.

Suddenly he heard gunshots. Muzzle flashes of gunfire back and forth ahead of him in the street gave briefly seen images of two cars, then nothing.

Katrina woke up with a start as Richard slowed the vehicle down to a more normal driving speed. It felt odd. Every minute at normal speed now felt like they were crawling.

Headlights came at them from a vehicle that was straddling the center of the road. Richard pulled over as much as he could with two of his wheels in the breakdown lane hoping to have enough room to avoid any problems. He considered going off road next.

"What's going on?" She asked, after realizing that it had been gunshots that had woken her.

"Don't know yet. There's a car coming this way and I heard gunshots. I'm not sure of what to make of it." Richard rattled off.

Katrina straightened out the headset and prepared herself mentally for battle. The weapon reoriented itself as the headset became settled properly on her head.

The oncoming car was now close enough for them to tell that it wasn't a racecar. Richard was ready to turn into the desert at any second. The other car skidded to a stop in the middle of the road and four people disgorged themselves and began to cheer.

Richard slowed their car to a stop as the four people ran towards them in the street. He recognized them now. Dillon was the first one that he recognized, then Frodes. Kristin hooted and hollered as she came in front of their headlights followed by Professor Jenkins. He walked at a very quick pace as the others ran ahead. Katrina slipped off her headset and she slid out of her window with tears in her eyes. She was so happy to see them. They all patted her on the back as though they had just won the race.

"How did you know it was us?" Katrina asked.

Kristin pointed to the weapon and said, "That is just unmistakable."

Richard had been dragged out of his window, with barely enough time to pull the emergency brake. Frodes asked about Richard's burn and the thrilling tale began to unfold as they were now old friends regaling each other with their battle stories.

Katrina pulled out of a monster bear hug from Dillon as Kristin patted her on the back. Dillon let her go and gravitated towards Richard's great tale.

Professor Jenkins stood quietly awaiting his turn with Katrina. His quiet demeanor made him stand apart from the students. Katrina turned into him and hugged him as she would a father.

"I never knew this would be so hard." Katrina said into his button down shirt, her tears choking her up. "I killed people trying to hurt us. I can't believe I hurt so many people."

Jenkins patted her back. "You did what you had to do. Protecting yourself is not a crime. It didn't help that the others were the ones who had initiated the battles in the first place. And that should console you a little. They would be alive today if they stayed home and watched the race on the tv instead of picking up a gun."

Katrina squeezed him even harder. "Do my parents know what's going on?"

Jenkins nodded. "We're keeping them safe."

Katrina pulled back. "Are they in danger?"

"I'll fill you in about everything that been happening behind the scenes after the race"

"No, I need to know now, are they okay?"

"They're fine, but you have to finish what you started. You're so close. In thirty minutes we'll be able to have a drink and share a week's worth of stories." Jenkins smiled as he said this.

They could hear a helicopter in the distance and all eyes turned towards the sound.

Jenkins pushed Katrina towards the car. "Get out of here. That's the FBI."

Richard and Katrina both knew what that meant. They both ran to the car. Kristin shouted a few updates as they climbed in.

"The split car is running out of power. You should be able to catch them easily. We shot out one of their tires which means that they will have to finish the race as a motorcycle."

Dillon shouted after the MIT car as it began to roll forward. "We'll have your back!"

Jenkins shouted. "Just go!"

The MIT car flew out away from their friends as the helicopter drew closer. The four ran back to their rented Corolla and took off after them.

~~~

Colliste shouted excitedly, "That's them!"

Cosgrove pointed to Colliste. "Get the other chopper on the line and find out where they are." When he turned, he watched the car disappear into the night.

Cosgrove looked at the gunner then poked his head into the cockpit and asked, "Why are they getting away?"

The pilot didn't look back when he spoke. "That's a fast car."

"How fast can they be, this is a helicopter?"

The pilot began to repeat his earlier lesson on speed and the basics of flight. "This vehicle was designed to travel at almost 200 mile per hour. With the extra weight, our speed has dropped to around 175. If you want me to go faster, you'll have to get off."

"So you're telling me that the car down there can do 200 mph?" Cosgrove asked.

"Maybe more," he said thoughtfully.

Colliste shouted. "The other helicopter is at least ten minutes behind us."

Cosgrove got back in his seat. At the rate they were going, by the time they showed up at the finish line, the race would already be over.

~~~

Richard had the accelerator floored again. They were so close and the split car had a head start but was losing power. He had to catch them.
Katrina sat back in her seat using one arm on the window edge to help support herself as she looked into the blackness of the night.

The expression on her face was very different from the calm pose she had struck not long ago when she had slept through the high speed driving. She looked scared now but it had nothing to do with his driving. She knew the stakes. She also knew that the split car couldn't be too far away and that they may still have a gun.

The MIT car found them quickly. The split car began weaving in the road to try to keep them from passing. Kristin had been right about their power problem. The car was barely doing eighty and they could hear the flat rear tire slapping with each revolution.

Katrina set herself up to use the laser on the other back tire but their weaving didn't give her a good target. She turned on the laser a couple of times but it was so bright in the darkness of the night that the other car could easily move away.

Richard weaved to try to match the movements of the other car to help Katrina's aim. He was afraid to try to pass the car in case they had other weapons on board.

They were both so focused on the laser and trying to line up a shot that they didn't notice the passenger holding a gun out of his window until he had already fired it. The shot came through the windshield between Richard and Katrina. Richard automatically slowed to back off out of range.

"What are you doing?" Katrina shouted. "We need to get by them!"

"If you get shot then this whole thing would have been for nothing. I'm not going to let that happen, not for a stupid race!"

Katrina leaned over, muckled on to the steering wheel and yanked hard. She put her foot on top of his on the accelerator and the car shot forward. Richard did all he could do to keep the car on the road as the split car's passenger prepared to fire the pistol again. The MIT car spun around because of the hard acceleration.

Katrina lowered her head and forced the weapon to its lowest position. When the car began to spin she depressed the fire button. She bobbed her head up and down to create a weaving pattern for the laser beam.

The pistol fired another round. This time the bullet would have found its target, if she had been sitting upright. The bullet buried itself in the impression Katrina had left behind in the seat. Thankfully her body had been elsewhere.

The beam etched a wavy pattern across the side of the split car and across the arm of the man who was holding the pistol. He dropped it as he screamed in pain. The gun hit the ground and discharged, striking his own car's remaining rear tire.

The driver could immediately feel the loss of contact with the road as the car wavered slightly. The driver grabbed the wheel with both hands and struggled to keep the vehicle straight. In a panicked moment he depressed the brake. The MIT car launched forward out of its spin.

Katrina sat back up. She could see the hole in the windshield in her line of sight and said, "Well it's a good thing I was..."

Richard punched her in the arm so hard she fell against her door.

"Owww! What did you that for?"

"You could have killed us both and you almost got shot. You could have..." Tears choked off the end of his statement, he couldn't finish.

"But we're in the lead! Finally! We can end this!" Katrina said.

Richard turned away.

Katrina turned to face forward again and could see that they were about to miss their turn.

"Turn here!" She shouted.

Richard slammed on the breaks and cut the wheel hard. The car skidded sideways in the turn.

The sound of a missile coming at them whistled through the air and there was no time to react. A helicopter that had been waiting to ambush them had fired an air to ground missile at them but had missed. Richard's sideways spin out, because he almost missed their turn, had saved their lives. The ground on Katrina's side of the car exploded. The car sideways motion from the late turn, in conjunction with the concussive force of the blast, moved their vehicle sideways by at least thirty feet. They stopped and it rained sand for what felt like hours.

Inside the car both Katrina and Richard's heads pounded. Disoriented and shell shocked, they tried to get the world back in focus. The sound of the chopper turning to get a new line of fire sounded very distant.

Katrina turned to see if Richard was okay and saw blood dripping off the bottom of his bandages. His head lay back to one side. Immediately Katrina thought he had been hit. She grabbed his face and brought it in closer. She couldn't see any new injury but when she looked into his eyes, they were beginning to roll back in his head.

"Where are you hit?!" She shouted.

"My face is throbbing, like something is crushing it."

She realized that the concussive force of the blast had further injured his burn. She remembered that adrenaline would substitute for a drug in the short term so she let go of his face and moved her foot to the accelerator. The car shot forward spitting sand out from under its rear wheels. Richard put both hands on the wheel instinctively.

"Drive!" Katrina shouted.

~~~

The chopper had lost its chance to fire again when the car drove off. The pilot changed direction and began to pursue them. The split car turned off the road, racing across the desert to avoid falling into the large pit created by the missile. The gunner inside the helicopter manning a large caliber machine gun aimed at the split car but the pilot held him back

"Don't shoot," the pilot's voice shouted into his ear. "That's the car we're here to support."

The large machine gun lowered then took aim at the racecar in the lead instead.

~~~

At the finish loop all of the stadium lights still burned brightly. Two racecars were approaching finally. The members of the investors' party group were all hammered. The fact that a helicopter was shooting at one of the cars didn't seem to affect them in the slightest.

Those who had been sitting in the lower priced seats were crowding the exits trying to get as far away from danger as possible. They poured out of the stadium seats as fast as their legs could carry them as machine gun fire echoed off the buildings.

Harvard Bertrand wasn't drunk. He had only pretended to be joining along in the festivities. He watched as his son drove while the helicopter fired on them. In the corner of his eye he saw Ian Practor walk back into the party holding a rifle. He had stepped down into the technicians pit to take up a position at the window. The technicians all watched his progress into their area worried but no one said a word. They just watched him, perplexed.

Using the barrel of his rifle he broke the glass facing down onto track. Harvard heard the glass breaking and marched over to Ian. Harvard demanded to know what he was doing.

"I am protecting our investment." Ian said snidely.

"You're going to shoot down that helicopter." Harvard said with relief.

Ian looked away and sighted in the chopper with his rifle before moving his sight down to the MIT car. "Yeah, that's what I'm doing."

Harvard's eyes grew wide. He knew that the rifle's aim had changed to a target much too close to the ground to be one that was flying. Something inside Harvard broke. As Ian was about to pull the trigger Harvard dove on top of him, taking him to the floor.

"That's my son you're aiming at!" He shouted.

~~~

Large caliber machinegun fire peppered the land around the MIT car as Richard maneuvered them between the split car and the chopper. The gunfire ceased and he breathed a sigh of relief.

"What are we going to do! Can't you do something with that laser on the roof?"

Katrina looked completely exasperated when she responded. "I can't blow things up with it! All it can do is burn a little hole."

"Well, burn a little hole in the gas tank or something!" Richard shouted back.

The chopper rose higher into the air to change positions. The split car slammed on its brakes to get away from Richard and Katrina and suddenly they were alone on the track again, a prime target.

~~~

The split car turned towards the finish loop. When it got close, the car slowed and the weapons specialist slid out of his window. He ran towards the rear of their vehicle and removed the single ramp required to get them up on the dais. He ran to the dais and set the ramp in place. The split car drove backwards to create enough room to get their vehicle up to speed to climb the steep ramp. They were going to win. All they needed to do was to climb the ramp and go through the loop.

Suddenly, embedded lights came on around the perimeter of the dais.
When the Split car had gone far enough back it turned back towards the finish loop and accelerated. The sandy ground didn't help with acceleration and with his shot out tires he didn't have the traction to get up to speed. The rubber slapped the sand slowing him down. He had

very little power left. The driver leaned forward trying to will his vehicle to go faster.

<p style="text-align:center">~~~</p>

Richard could see the split car making a run for the loop. The chopper was nowhere in sight. Richard cut the vehicle hard and drove towards the ramp. The weapons specialist on the track ran in front of the ramp thinking that no one would intentionally run him down in front of all of the witnesses.

Richard didn't care. It would be a game of chicken, his car with its laser against a single pathetic man. He was pretty sure the man would move.

<p style="text-align:center">~~~</p>

The split car was coming in close. In the corner of the driver's eye he could see the MIT car coming at the ramp. If one of them didn't stop in time they would hit each other. The split car driver leaned in further towards his steering wheel and willed more speed.

<p style="text-align:center">~~~</p>

Richard didn't need to will more speed. He leaned back and pressed confidently on his accelerator. Katrina started to panic. The guy in front of the ramp wouldn't move. She screamed for Richard to stop. He still didn't care.

"If you want him to move, turn the laser on. Make him get out of the way."

Katrina turned the laser toward the man standing on the track. His eyes were wide but he held his ground. When the laser fired, all of the dust in the air illuminated the beam. Just before it touched him, the man dived away to the left. In another second Richard would have run him over.

In that second many things happened at the same time. The MIT car used the front push guard to knock the ramp away. The split car driver knew that if he didn't turn he would crash into the dais. He yanked on his steering wheel hard and banked to the right towards the man who was still lying on the ground. The weapons specialist rolled to try to get out of the way but his arm didn't make it in time. His driver ran over it, breaking it in several places. He screamed.

Then the chopper fired a missile at the MIT car as it passed the dais. When the sound of the missile could be heard, the slow whistling sound, Richard yelled something indiscernible as he cut the steering wheel. The missile hit the ground beside them and exploded. The MIT car rose into the air with all the sand below it and flipped high into the air.

The Corolla pulled into the finish loop area and its crew watched the events unfold before their eyes. Twice the MIT car rotated in the air in its arc to the ground before landing on all of its wheels in an upright position as sand rained down all around them.

After their team's car landed properly, it was back to business. Professor Jenkins captained the four wheeled gun boat by shouting commands to his crew. "Open fire on that chopper! Burn the barrels off your guns to bring it down. Dillon, keep us between the chopper and our racecar."

Frodes and Kristin both opened fire from opposing windows. The small vehicle rocked from each shot gun shot.

Richard and Katrina just looked at each other, stunned, as the car came to rest. Richard shouted to Katrina, "Are you okay?"

Katrina nodded. Her ears rang so badly it left a painful echo in the back of her head. "You're bleeding!" she said in return, pointing to his bandage.

"It's alright," He shouted back. "I have plenty of adrenaline now!" He turned to face the heavily cracked windshield and drove.

Katrina didn't know what he was planning to do but he was driving towards the split car again. She was afraid he was going to ram them with the front guard.

~~~

Cosgrove was chomping at the bit to catch up to the racecar. They were seconds from flying over the finish loop enclosure when a huge explosion rocked the air. Its light brightened the night beyond the track's lighting. The blast knocked Colliste out of his seat. Cosgrove found a lucky hand hold before he hit the floor. When things settled a second later Cosgrove pointed to Jim. "You might want to be on that gun right about now."

Jim nodded and resumed his original post.

As they flew toward the race track's enclosure they could see the guns being fired from the Corolla. All eyes followed their aim to see another chopper bearing down on them. This chopper had no markings, unlike the plane letters spelling FBI on each side of theirs.

The pilot of the unmarked helicopter had obviously been surprised by the appearance of the FBI and he banked hard to put some distance between the two aircraft. Cosgrove asked one question to solidify his decision making process. "How far out is our backup?"

The pilot shouted back. "Three minutes at best."

"We need to keep these people safe. Go after that chopper!" Cosgrove shouted.

The pilot turned and followed the unmarked helicopter.

~~~

Inside the party, everyone was still celebrating. The activity that was happening outside was more exciting than anything Phyindress had told them before they had chosen to attend this party. They cheered for the MIT car, they cheered for the split car, they cheered for the lone man running around on the track with a broken arm who was trying to reset the ramp. These drunks fools cheered for everything.

When the FBI chopper entered the arena and chased the other one away, they booed. They knew it would be more boring now that they were gone. There seemed to be no regret over the fact that their entertainment revolved around people trying to kill each other.

Harvard still struggled with Ian Practor. This may have been the first time he had ever fought for his son. He had been a fool to ignore Richard for all of those years and he knew that it was his fault that his son ever had anything to do with this race. He was also proud of his son's accomplishments, so proud in fact that he would have given his own life to save his son's. He wasn't a young man anymore but he had the strength of blinding love at that moment. He snuck in a punch and knocked Practor to the floor before diving over him again.

They both struggled for control of the rifle. It became more like a tug of war. Practor had resorted to kicking with his feet like a spoiled child. Harvard punched him in the face but Practor still wouldn't let go.

"You don't need to do this, my son's car can't win, they have no ramps to get up the dais." Harvard grumbled.

A lightbulb went on in Practor's mind. He forced himself up against the window so that he could see the cars. There were no ramps on the MIT car's roof. He had forgotten that they were supposed to be located on top of the car.

Practor smiled at the good news. They can't win without ramps to get up the dais. And the split car had one. At that particular moment he didn't consider that other options could exist. He didn't see ramps, to him the race was already over.

Practor turned to Harvard Bertrand and let him have the rifle. He pushed it with all his might, forcing the stock back into the other man's forehead.

Bertrand collapsed to the floor. He was out cold.

Practor took the tail of his shirt and rubbed the entire weapon down to erase his fingerprints, then he positioned the weapon beside his unconscious opponent. He took Bertrand's hands placing them in the correct positions to fire a weapon before walking away. No one else was paying any attention to them. Now he couldn't be accused of trying to change the outcome of the race, or intentionally hurting anyone. He left Bertrand to take the blame thinking he had the race in the bag now. The MIT car couldn't win, they had no ramps.

~~~

The pilot of the unmarked chopper chuckled as bullets flew past him. The rounds being fired from the gunner's side mount on the FBI chopper all missed as they arced around him. He had led the FBI helicopter away from the track but he only needed to turn back for one good shot. He had two missiles left and plenty of bullets. His only concern was the small unpredictable white car.

~~~

"Since there are no choppers shooting at us for the moment now would be a good time to figure out how the use that weapon on the roof to protect us when it returns." Richard said as he chased down the limping split car.

"What are you going to do?"

"I'm taking that bastard down!" Richard shouted at the top of his lungs, indicating the remaining racecar.

Katrina thought for a moment. "I have to lean out the window to make an adjustment to the head sleeve so it can point up at a better angle and..."

"I don't care, just do it!"

After unbuckling her seat belt, Katrina turned her head to turn the laser to her side of the car so that she could reach it and then shut down all of the power while it hung just outside of her window. She removed her head piece and reached out the window. She had to have half of her body out of the window to grab it. "You know it would be easier to do this when we're stopped. The bumps are really cutting into me."

Richard didn't answer. He only had one thing on his mind.

Katrina worked quickly. She detached the laser head and pulled it inside, carefully pulling on all the wires equally to ensure that they stayed together but something was caught and she couldn't bring the head into the car. She slid back out further and tried to find what was stuck.

~~~

The split car's driver could see the MIT car chasing him in his side mirror. He checked the power gauge on the instrument panel. It showed dangerously low power readings. He should have been through the loop by now. The driver slammed his fist on the dash hoping it would give him more power. It didn't.

His weapons specialist worked feverishly to pull up the ramp with his one functional hand. His other arm hung crooked.

Desperate times called for desperate measures. The driver leaned forward and picked up a pistol he had kept hidden under his seat for moments like this. This was his personal weapon and he was running out of options.

When he looked up to check on the distance of the other racecar, he found them right on top of him. He had misjudged their speed.

~~~

Richard knew they were close enough to get the job done. He reached over and yanked on Katrina's jump suit pulling her back into the car. "Hang on to something!"

Katrina wrapped her seat belt over her shoulder and braced her hands on the dashboard just before the front push guard slammed into the side of the split car. A loud crack thundered out in the night and the car's forward moment stopped suddenly.

~~~

The split car driver shook his head to clear his vision after the impact. He floored the accelerator and the car moved forward. There was a huge crack in the fuselage but it hadn't disabled the car. He cut hard to head back to the dais hoping the ramp was back up. He leveled his gun out of his window and aimed at a tire. If they got a flat they'd be stuck in the sand. He pulled the trigger.

The flash of light then the loud bang got Richard's attention. He knew that was the sound of a gunshot. The sound of the slug hitting the rim made Katrina and Richard think, what happened? Their faces reflected horror until Katrina recognized the meaning of the ringing of the aluminum rim. She laughed.

Richard stared at her until she answered his unasked question. "He shot the tire to slow us down. We have solid filled tires! He did nothing."

Richard laughed, however his anger increased. The idea that the bullet did nothing didn't help the fact that there was yet another person trying to kill them. He floored the accelerator and rammed the back of the split car.

The car spun sideways out of control for a second and then rolled onto its side. The split car had a mechanism built in to keep the car from falling over when it was in split car mode and it forced the car back upright in slow motion as though there were a magic rope that had pulled it upright. The spinning weighted disks inside the car's wheels always wanted to be perpendicular to the ground. Even though two of the tires were flat, the spinning disks still operated flawlessly.

Katrina's jaw dropped as she realized what had happened. Her mind went into high engineering mode trying to work out the specifics of what she just witnessed.

~~~

After the car popped back up, the driver of the split car knew that he was running out of chances. If he didn't win the race soon the MIT driver would run him over. He could see the anger on Richard's face. The driver threw his gun to the floor and drove off.

~~~

Richard pursued him again. Katrina still had a dumbfounded look on her face. He turned to his weapons specialist and said, "You may want to finish what you were doing. That chopper will be back any minute." Katrina nodded and went back to work.

~~~

Frodes had his head out of his window searching the sky for the chopper.

"Do you see anything?" Jenkins asked.

"No they're too far out. I can see the lights on the FBI chopper though. It looks like they're coming back around this way." Frodes said. "Maybe they chased them away."

"Stop the car." Jenkins shouted.

Dillon slammed on the brakes. The two racecars drove by, Richard chasing the split while Katrina hung out of her window to work on the weapon. Jenkins watched what Katrina was doing for a moment and then made a snap decision. "Dillon, pull up on Katrina's side of the car."

When Dillon got close enough to Katrina's side of the car, Frodes yelled to her. "What are you trying to do?"

"I'm flipping this sleeve so the laser head will point upwards."

Jenkins shouted, "Vincent, switch sides. Help Katrina pull the sleeve out. Kristin keep a watch on the sky."

Frodes switched sides and leaned out of the open window. Katrina yelled to him. "I'm at a bad angle. The sleeve keeps getting hung up. If you pull it straight out it should come out easily. I need to put it back in upside down so the angle of attack points upwards."

"You think that'll work?" Frodes asked.

"Yes, now hurry up. It will lock into place. Push hard enough until it clicks in."

Katrina turned away from Frodes who was trying his best to remain level. She slipped back in with the laser head. She disconnected all the wires and reset a few of the switches for a slightly different operation. Frodes shouted to her when he got it separated. Katrina eased the laser head out of the window again before sliding out herself.

She handed the head to Frodes. "Hold this a second."

She slipped back in and dragged the wires out. Carefully she wound them back inside the arm where they belonged.

Kristin shouted, "The chopper is back! Frodes I need you now."

Suddenly machine gun fire rain on them. The passing chopper was at the wrong angle to do too much damage but a row of bullets sprayed across their path just the same. The Corolla took several hits on the hood and the MIT car saw sparks across its push guard. Jenkins shouted at Katrina to hurry up.

Katrina was trying not to have a panic attack while she and her friend were hanging out of the windows as bullets flew. "As soon as I finish pushing these wires back up the tube, line up the head to fit in the slot. There is a red line on the laser head that matches a red line in the sleeve."

Frodes turned the laser head in his hands looking for the red line as Katrina pushed the wires as carefully as she could back inside the arm.

When Kristin began firing her shotgun into the sky, Richard turned the steering wheel suddenly and the two cars separated, the laser head still in Frodes' hands.

Katrina watched the laser head go in a different direction. She turned towards her driver and punched him in the arm. "What were you thinking? We almost had it all together!"

Richard screamed. "I was saving your life!" as a new round of machine gun fire erupted on the side of the car where she had just been a moment earlier.

Her jaw dropped open. She was stunned by the fact that Richard always seemed to have her back. Katrina turned away ashamed and finished putting wire back into the robotic arm. Not only was their weapon not ready to help protect them, it was riding around armed in the back seat of another car. One hit to the high power capacitor and it would probably explode, killing everyone in the car.

~~~

Jenkins gave new orders. "Frodes get back on your shotgun. Focus on the guy holding the machine gun.

Dillon, keep us between the helicopter and our car."
Dillon turned around and tried to match the speed of the
helicopter.

"What about the laser head?" Frodes asked
between shots.
Jenkins turned his head so fast something should have
cracked. Sure enough he could see the laser head on the
seat behind a kneeling Frodes.

"Oh shit!" He shouted.

~~~

The chopper cut hard to the right as the FBI
chopper got closer to them. The pilot called to his gunner.
"Hang on, cutting hard!"
The gunner found a hand hold as the helicopter
banked, straining his harness. It was a maneuver most
pilots would never attempt because it could down a
vehicle based on faulty aerodynamic values against the
blades that held them in the air. Luckily, the blades
didn't snap and the chopper was now facing the
oncoming FBI chopper. The pilot fired a missile at his
new target. The propellant lit, launching the cylindrical
bomb forward. The pilot laughed.

~~~

Frodes and Kristin fired their shotguns and
reloaded them so many times that they had to resort to
holding the muzzle with the socks off Frodes' feet
because of the heat. It looked funny but it kept their
hands from getting scorched. Their consistent efforts to
put buckshot into the air towards the chopper made a
cloud of tungsten steel. The hard pellets hammered

against the armed nose of the weapon as it sailed towards the FBI chopper.

The FBI chopper didn't react to the moving missile. The pilot's attention was taken with trying to keep up with the sudden movement of their prey. At the last second, when he saw the propellant of the missile, the pilot tried to reorient the chopper to avoid being hit. He pulled hard on the stick but in his heart he knew that they were dead. He couldn't avoid a missile that had been fired so close to them.

~~~

All of the small hits from the tungsten pellets built up on the armed sensors designed to trigger the explosives and prematurely detonated it mid-air. The explosion between the two choppers forced a concussive wave against both helicopters. Both pilots temporarily lost control but a moment later, the seasoned pilots regained control and righted themselves. The FBI pilot steered away to come up with a new plan of attack.

The other pilot was just angry. He shouted to his gunner to destroy the white Toyota that was causing them so much grief and he steered closer towards it.

~~~

Colliste was the first to get up off the floor. His seat belt had broken when the chopper had lost control from the blast. He went over to help his boss get up from the floor and put him back in a seat. Cosgrove moaned lightly. He had been the closest to the door and had absorbed part of the wave from the blast. Then it occurred to Colliste that if his supervisor had been knocked out from the blast then the gunner had to have been hit worse.

Colliste turned toward where Jim the gunner had stood on his perch but he was gone. His mouth fell open. He stuck his head out of the door and tried to see through the dust to the ground. He couldn't see anyone on the ground.

Colliste pulled up the safety harness' strap but theend in Colliste's hand was shredded. Anger bubbled up in his gut. He jumped out onto the perch without a harness and took the machine gun's handles. He quickly found the unmarked chopper and let lead fly in their direction screaming with a rage he didn't know he had within him. The machine gun hammered in his hand as the expelled brass flew into the wind.

~~~

The split car was ready to make another run at his re-positioned ramp. Richard's crazy driving scared the crap out of him. One more hit and their car would fold enough so that it wouldn't be able drive straight again. It was already difficult enough to stay straight as it was. His steering wheel had to be cocked severely to the right just to manage it.

He could see the Corolla trying to evade the helicopter. The stupid pilot was supposed to be protecting him from the MIT car and instead he was playing with the crazy people in the white Toyota. He turned the car towards the ramp and stepped on it. The energy gauge sank lower. He hammed on the steering wheel begging the car to go faster.

Ahead he could see the MIT car change direction and move to cut off his path to victory. It slowed in front of the ramp and when it took off again his ramp was being dragged away by the driver. His weapons specialist was running after them while cradling his broken arm.

~~~

Richard lost his grip on the aluminum ramp when he hit a bump and dropped it more than thirty feet away from the dais. He didn't care. If they set it up again he would go over and grab it again.

"We need to figure out how we're going to get through the loop without getting shot at," he said quickly as he changed directions away from gunfire ahead of them.

Katrina tapped quickly on a keyboard.

"Are you listening to me?" Richard asked.

"Yes, and I have this under control. Keep away from the bullets and don't let the split car on his ramp." Katrina turned her eyes up to look at him properly before typing more code.

Richard's eyes were on her fully and she could see that the bandage on his face was soaked with blood which had started to drip onto his uniform. She knew that their time was running out. If he lasted two more minutes without passing out they would be lucky. Adrenaline could only go so far.

~~~

Bullets raked the side of the unmarked helicopter barely missing the gunner. Colliste's aim was quite good under pressure. The pilot of the unmarked helicopter shuddered at the sound of the bullets hitting his aircraft.

He shouted to the rear. "Are you alright?"

"Yeah, that was close. Fly better or I'm going to get hit."

The pilot's anger flared, "Shoot better and they wouldn't still be shooting back!" he shouted.

Another round of bullets raked the side of the chopper and gunner got hit high in the leg. He fell over screaming in pain. The machine gun on the FBI chopper was military grade, firing a standard NATO 7.62 caliber bullet.

Being hit by the larger sized machine round meant that he might lose that appendage or even bleed to death. Either way he was more than injured, he was catastrophically wounded and he knew it. Another spray of bullets struck the chopper. The shooter threw himself back inside and inched his way to the pilot.

"Get us out of here," he pleaded. "We can come back with more firepower."

"Stop whining. It's just your leg. We almost have them. I've still got one missile left. One perfect shot and we're out of here." The pilot said, disregarding the pain of his friend.

~~~

Katrina pointed to the Toyota and waved them over. The enemy chopper had veered off to avoid more bullets from the FBI helicopter and that gave her a minute to work on the laser.

Richard watched the split racecar. At that moment their weapons specialist was trying to drag their ramp back towards the dais. He struggled under the pain of his other arm.

Richard and the Toyota approached each other from opposite directions then stopped. Both drivers took a moment to breathe.

Frodes switched out his shotgun for the laser head. Katrina placed her hands on the laser head as well so both of them could guide it into the sleeve. When it slid in and clicked into place, Katrina shouted to Frodes. "Take the small mirror off the arm and break it off."

Frodes looked perplexed. "What do you mean?" he asked.

"Take the small mirror tucked under the right side cowling and tear it out."

Frodes didn't question her directions, he pulled it off and held it out so that Katrina could see it.

"Good," Katrina said. "Place it just over beam's output on the laser head and wedge it into place so the beam will reflect back in."

Frodes struggled to get this part taken care of. It took a few seconds. Richard shouted. "Hurry up I can see the chopper coming back!"

Kristin began to shoot at it, the white sock still on her hand moved back and forth on the barrel.

Frodes let go and shouted "Done!"

Richard drove off without waiting for Katrina to respond. Katrina slid back into her seat and put her seat belt back on then her head set. She began to type furiously. Richard didn't ask any questions. He just tried to stay away from the enemy chopper. Although it didn't seem like they were shooting at them at the moment.

Katrina began to shout instructions. "I need you to align us parallel to the chopper at some point soon. Tell me just before you do, but then slam on the brakes for a second, and cut the wheel and turn away so that the back of our car is facing them."

Richard smiled. He knew that Katrina had a plan and he trusted her. Katrina finished typing and slid the keyboard away. She picked up the weapon's controller and began to watch out the window. The split car was making a new run on their ramp. They had managed to get it back in place. He turned the wheel away from the chopper and put Katrina's plan on hold to go take their ramp again.

In a repeat performance Richard took the ramp as the weapons specialist with the broken arm watched him take away their ability to finish the race.

~~~

Finn Cosgrove was slowly coming back around. He could hear Colliste rummaging around the cabin looking for something.

"What are looking for?" he asked.

"Ammunition. We're out," he said. "I think I hit their gunner but I can't finish the job without more bullets."

"Where's Jim?" Cosgrove asked.

"He's gone. He was blown off of his perch by the explosion."

Cosgrove suddenly got an influx of memory. He remembered the explosion and his eyes opened wide. "We lost Jim?"

"Yes! Now help me find some more bullets!" Colliste angrily demanded of his boss.

The pilot shouted into the cabin. "Tell Jim that we have six hand grenades in the back. Our back up will be here in less than a minute. I'm going in for another run. Get ready."

Both men looked at each other before scrambling to the rear of the chopper to find the hand grenades.

~~~

Katrina pointed out the window. "He's coming around."

Richard dropped the ramp and turned around. He passed the weapons specialist who swore loudly at them as they passed. Richard just laughed at him in return.

"Remember what I said about the lineup?" Katrina asked.

"Yeah, I got it." He turned to face Katrina with a smile, confident that something great was about to happen.

All Katrina could see was how bloody the bandage on his face was. She couldn't believe he had lasted this long. Katrina nodded and turned her gaze down towards her firing control to hide the tears that were welling up in her eyes.

Richard drove their car towards the enemy chopper. They were going head to head. The chopper lowered until it hung only ten feet from the sand. They were playing chicken now. The gunner must have run out of bullets because no lead rained on them. Closer and closer they approached. Richard had a plan and he wanted to be close enough to see the rivets before he executed it.

The FBI chopper bore down on the enemy helicopter from the side. The pilot shouted out, "Hang on, it's going to get rough for a moment! Don't throw a grenade yet, wait until my signal!"

Cosgrove and Colliste both found something to hold onto with one hand so that they could each hold a grenade with the other.

Carl, the pilot counted down the seconds in a whisper. "Three, two, one... "

~~~

The enemy pilot smiled for the first time in many hours. The MIT car raced towards him and he lowered his weapon almost level with his target. When he felt comfortable he placed his thumb over the missile launch switch attached to his steering control and prepared to press it. This last missile was going to finish off his target and then they could disappear into the night.

~~~

Carl's speedy approach at the enemy's blind side gave him a slight edge and that was all he needed. He had to pour on the power to catch up to the cockpit then turn in while staying under the rotors. One wrong move and their blades would become entangled.

Carl watched his gauges to determine his altitude as he turned up the accelerator as high as it could go. Quickly his craft lurched forward. He turned his gaze up to watch his rotor distance and pressed forward. He broke out in hives knowing how close he was to the other chopper. This was it.

When the FBI helicopter moved fast enough to match cockpits together the enemy pilot looked surprised to see a determined FBI pilot close enough to spit on him. Instantly, he moved his thumb off the firing button and grabbed his control stick with both hands hoping to pull up.

Carl growled as he tipped his vehicle's vertical axis towards the enemy's choppers left shoulder side. His rotor blade tips touched the enemy cockpit's plexiglass. The entire side of the clear windshield exploded like a bomb.

Shards embedded themselves into the enemy pilot causing him to lose his focus. The rotor strike pushed his aircraft's axis tilting it out of the strike zone. His blades came in fast and the FBI chopper nosedived to get away but the ground was so close that didn't have much room to maneuver. Carl throttled back the accelerator as hard and fast as he could and spun the craft so that the open doors would face the now open cockpit of their enemy.

Carl shouted, "NOW!"

Colliste and Cosgrove both tossed their grenades. The other helicopter tilted up and away as the FBI craft bottomed out into the sand and slid sideways.

~~~

Richard couldn't believe what had just happened in right in front of them. He was driving at full speed into the disaster. He had been anticipating their spin to allow the laser to do its job. Now the FBI chopper had crashed into the other helicopter and then hit the sand directly in front of him. Katrina screamed at the top of her lungs.

Richard cut his wheel to the left, stomped on the clutch several times while changing gears at the speed of sound. The car expertly avoided every obstacle while Katrina continued to scream at the top of her lungs.

As the MIT car raced around the spinning blades, one of the grenades exploded against the aluminum fuselage of the enemy chopper followed by the second one that had landed near the open cockpit. More shrapnel embedded itself into to the pilot, not enough to take him out, but enough to have him lean back pulling flight stick with him. The chopper rose up faster than the aircraft was designed to move.

Richard could see the chopper rising. Their one shot was disappearing. He tried to shout over Katrina's screaming but he couldn't get her attention. Instead he cut the wheel one last time positioning the rear of their vehicle toward the rising chopper and slammed his hand down on the firing button in Katrina's hand. The pneumatic cannon buried deep inside the robotic arm fired the laser head. It flew towards the enemy chopper and stuck to the side of the engine above the open door.

~~~

The wounded shooter was sprawled on the floor. His pulse was weak. The helicopter rose quickly but not in a straight line. He knew that the pilot must be in bad shape. Their craft wobbled as he dragged himself over to the second seat and pulled himself up into it. He didn't bother with a seat belt. He just took the stick to try to help control their flight path. When the helicopter leveled out he turned towards his friend. Blood oozed down his face and neck where chunks of skin and muscle were missing from the grenade blast. At that moment he did feel lucky that he had only been shot in the leg.

He took over and turned the chopper at the MIT car as it sped out towards the outer edge of the track. Friction against the flight controls slackened. His friend had slumped over in his seat and his hand had fallen away from the stick. The shooter turned the craft and aimed their chopper towards the MIT car as he flipped up his firing control's cover in anticipation of firing their last missile.

~~~

Katrina stopped screaming to catch her breath. She worked hard to regain control of her breathing. She could see that they had successfully negotiated around the crashing helicopter. Richard had managed to keep them alive and fire the weapon at exactly the right moment. She suddenly felt like a slacker.

"I'm going for the win." Richard shouted. "The ramp is already up and the split car is making another run."

Katrina shouted "Go!" sure that everything was good. "You have to get to at least fifty-three miles per hour for our ramp to work."

"What ramp?" Richard asked. "I was going to use theirs and go up one sided."

Katrina and Richard both looked at each other for a second.

"One sided up a single ramp?" Katrina asked. "Are you crazy?"

"What do you mean our ramp? We don't have one!" Richard said. "And why hasn't the laser finished off that helicopter yet?"

Katrina put both hands to her temples. "It's not like a laser from a science fiction movie. It takes time for the power capacitor to over..."

Richard cut her off. "How long is it going to take?"

"I don't know. Maybe a minute."

"A minute? We don't have a minute!" Richard shouted.

~~~

The split car limped along almost out of power. This was his last run. If he didn't get through the finish loop this time they would have to push it through.

~~~

The enemy chopper leveled off just outside the overhead lights of the finish loop. The lighting inside the loop made everything perfectly visible for the shooter. He turned the craft around and pointed it towards the finish loop waiting for the right moment to fire their last missile. Now that the FBI chopper was down he had nothing to fear. He could stay in that position for as long as they had fuel.

He could see the car that they were supposed to protect making a run towards the ramp. If he fired his missile to hit the MIT car, he could damage the split car. He wasn't sure that he cared anymore. Judging by how fast it was moving, he didn't think it would make it up the ramp anyway. The only thing he cared about was destroying the MIT car. He waited until just the right moment, timing was everything.

~~~

"I can't see the helicopter. Did it crash?" Katrina asked.

"I don't think so. Keep an eye out."

Katrina stopped searching the sky for a moment to reach under the dash. She pulled out a long wire with a bundle of black electrical tape at the end. She yanked the tape off and threw the ball out the window.

Richard had no idea what she was doing. "What is that?" he asked.

"That's our ramp. Remember back at the Cadillac dealership when I was working with the techs? Well this is the solution. This is how we're getting up on the dais." Katrina explained.

"Are you kidding me?" Richard said back. "How is that supposed to work? I can use their ramp and do the same thing."

"No you can't!" Katrina said. "At this speed you'll have to run over the other car, not to mention the danger of balancing the car on one ramp on the sand."

"How is your way better?"

"I have an airbag deployment charge at the end of these wires. Once I connect these two wires the charge will go off and it will open our folded ramp, Just hit fifty-three miles per hour and I'll do the rest. You have to trust me."

Richard tried to process their options. He knew that he could run up the ramp on two wheels. He had done many times in driving school. It was a breeze. But the split car being in the way could cause a problem if they arrived at the same time aiming for the same ramp. Their cars didn't have metal bodies and the push plates were only on the front and back. He couldn't just push the other car out of the way from the side. The plastic body panels would either shatter or end up melted together. And where was that helicopter?

~~~

The shooter watched the two cars racing toward the single ramp. He had no idea why the MIT car thought they even had a chance with only one ramp. He almost wanted to hold back to see what they were going to do. Though the split car was moving pretty slowly it should still make it to the ramp before the MIT car. Maybe he didn't have to do anything at all. The split car was going to win anyway.

Even if the split car were to win, he still wanted to kill the driver of the MIT car. The shooter positioned his thumb over the firing switch and prepared to fire.

~~~

Richard decided that Katrina was right. She was right almost as often as he was when it came to maneuvers. As he sped towards the ramp, positioned in front of the loop, he could see that the split car would arrive before him. He just hoped that they were going fast enough to make Katrina's contraption work. Then something else occurred to him.

"Which air bag did you use to make this thing?" He asked.

Katrina ignored him.

Richard repeated his question with more intensity. "Which air bag did you use to make this thing?"

"It's the passenger side airbag from this car."

Richard didn't say a word. He knew that if they made it through the loop, win or lose, they would come down hard.

~~~

Cosgrove stepped out of the crashed helicopter. His head was a ball of pain. He turned to look toward the finish loop and saw the enemy helicopter hanging in the air pointing at the two cars. He knew that he could do nothing further to alter the outcome of the race.

He pulled his pistol from his belt and pointed it at the chopper. He knew that he would never be able to take out the pilot but he could at least distract him. Carefully through the haze in his head he pointed his weapon and squeezed the trigger.

~~~

The shooter was counting down to his last shot, five, four, three... when a bullet hit the rear control blades causing the entire aircraft to shift his aim out of lock. He had to reposition the aircraft. The shooter yelled in frustration. He had missed his best opportunity. He realigned and began to depress his thumb on the firing switch.

The laser head attached to the chopper's engine casing glowed red hot. Suddenly it blew up. It produced a spectacular explosion causing the engine to partially disconnect from its mount, turning it sideways over the body of the helicopter. The rotors were turning at an opposing angle to the central axis of the body in crazy arcs as it spiraled out of the sky.

~~~

Richard could see the explosion out of the corner of his eye but had to ignore it. He was concentrating on his direction towards the dais and his speed. The sand slowed his acceleration and it was difficult to imagine reaching fifty-three miles per hour before he crashed into the back of the split car. The gap between the two cars was closing quickly.

Fifty, fifty-one, fifty-two miles per hour. With his right hand he released his seatbelt clasp.

Katrina was completely focused on the job ahead. She silently counted down until she reached zero and then touched the wires together.

The deployment charge detonated when both wires came together. Their single ramp, which had been reconfigured back at the Cadillac dealership, blew off the underside of the front bumper area, planted itself into the sand and lifted the car off the ground. At the frame's main cross member, under the firewall, the other side of the ramp pivoted launching the MIT car into the air. They flew over the split racecar as it drove up the ramp in the traditional way. The MIT car was still gaining speed from their momentum and the boost from the ramp's launch.

Richard dove from his seat position to cover Katrina. He didn't care if they won. If she died, he would lose his only friend. He didn't care what happened to him.

The two cars moved into the loop, one on top of the other. The MIT car's only drag was the air that pressed against it. The split car was fighting to climb the ramp with failing power and flat tires that dragged against it.

The lights that were embedded in the concrete loop changed colors from white to blue indicating that someone had won the race. The MIT car landed partially on top of the other car, dragging it through the loop and off the other side of the dais. Both cars flipped over before hitting the ground. Both vehicles had been reduced to clumps of smoldering metal and plastic. Nothing moved except for the smoke pouring from each engine.

~~~

The Corolla stopped and its passengers watched in shock. They had no idea who might have won and if anyone would be left alive after the crash.

Dillon sputtered almost incoherently. "We were all in the same shop when we built that car. When did they install a device that would make the car fly?"

No one answered him as they all abandoned their car and ran to try to help Richard and Katrina.

Chapter 26

In a hospital far away from the desert, Katrina sat sleeping in a chair next to the bed that held Richard Bertrand. His entire face had been bandaged leaving only one eye visible and small openings for his nose and mouth. One of his arms lay at his side in a cast and the opposing leg hung from a cradle connected to the bed.

Katrina showed no visible signs of injury. She was no longer wearing her racing uniform. She wore a pair of faded jeans and a t-shirt showing Snoopy on his doghouse pretending to be the Red Baron from WWI. Beneath the doghouse was printed "MIT students can make anything fly".

Finn Cosgrove walked into the room in a suit and tie accompanied by a plainclothes officer. Katrina awoke to the sounds of footsteps and the movement caused by Cosgrove's light kick to the bed post.

Katrina's eyes popped open and immediately scolded him for trying to wake Richard. "I hate it when you do that. Stop trying to wake him up. Let him sleep."

"You know I can't move this case forward until I speak to him."

"That burn on his face says it can wait. He's on Morphine and he's allowed to sleep as long as he needs to," Katrina said as she rose from her chair.

Her stiff movements showed that she hadn't escaped all injury in the accident.

"Why won't you tell us anything about what happened after we went through the loop? We deserve to know."

Richard's parents strolled through the door with their lawyer in tow. "You don't have to say a word," Mr.

Brenant said to Richard, not realizing that he was still asleep.

Harvard added, "He must wait until my son is ready to talk without being influenced by medication. They can wait outside." He said nodding toward Cosgrove and the officer.

Harvard sported a huge bruise from having the butt of the rifle rammed in his face but he wore it proudly.

Cosgrove turned towards Katrina, answering her question. "Because I need my information more than you need yours."

Cosgrove then turned towards Harvard. "Just so you know, you're not off the hook either. We still have not cleared up why you participated in the race as an investor in the first place, or why you were holding that rifle."

The lawyer didn't say a word, he only wheezed. He waved his one free hand to move the FBI agent along towards the door as though he were dismissing a servant.

Cosgrove turned to leave and said, "I'll be outside," then he left the room.

Cosgrove went to the nurses' station where Colliste was waiting. He too sported injuries from the crash. A bright blue cast on his left arm had a few signatures on it and when he looked up at his boss his black eye reflected the fluorescent lights. "I just got word that Carl is going to be fine, he won't lose his leg. He has one more surgery to get through and he will be grounded from now on, but he'll live."

"He's tough." Cosgrove said. "Besides, his wife will make sure he never sees a cockpit again even if he could pass the physical. She's a scary woman, when she says no he doesn't stand a chance."

Behind them Professor Jenkins, Frodes, Kristin, and Dillon snuck down the hallway. They slipped into Richard's room closing the door behind them softly.

Katrina saw them enter and smiled. She closed the shades on the glass walls between Richard's room and the hall and turned to hug them all in turn, Jenkins last.

He looked down on her to ask, "Are you alright?"

"Yes, if you don't count some nightmares every once and a while."

"Well, I've brought news." Jenkins said.

Katrina turned and woke Richard. She shook him lightly. He stirred before opening both eyes. In the room he saw his parents first, it was the first time he had seen his father since the second day of the race. He couldn't decide if he had the strength to be angry now or if it could wait until he was well enough to storm out of the room if he had to.

Professor Jenkins cleared his throat to get everyone's attention as he pulled a small piece of paper out of his pocket.

"Well, I have news. I expect all of you think that you know everything that transpired over the last five days, but I assure you that you do not. To help fill in the gaps I have secured a copy of the entire race as it was recorded by the organization who was broadcasting it. Of course there will still be a few gaps since I had our team stay away from their camera crew for a while. For that I will defer to Mr. Bertrand and Ms. Meservier to fill in the blanks at a later time."

Katrina burst out, "We want to know who won."

Jenkins smiled. "Your fancy flying stunt made you winners by three millimeters. There was a camera located on the finish loop to film the cars going through. The race was supposed to be decided by the sensors in the cars but since both cars went through at the same time we had to defer to the camera's version of events.

Cosgrove and Colliste entered the room and Jenkins immediately fell silent. The students all stared at the floor trying not to make eye contact with the agents.

"I see that Mr. Bertrand is finally awake and the professor is filling you in. I would like very much to hear this as well," said Agent Cosgrove.

No one spoke.

Cosgrove shook his head. "Now, now… It will be much easier to do this here, as a group than at our offices, individually."

Still no one spoke.

"Alright, let's try this a little differently." Cosgrove said before leaning against the wall as if he were willing to wait them out. "I am not here to enforce the laws regarding illegal street racing. I am here to put a dangerous man away for his mob activity, which included participation in this race. His name is Mac Killington. And I'm pretty sure a member of your team is in my custody because of his actions."

Frodes, Katrina, Kristin, and Dillon all looked at each other with surprise. They had no idea who Mac Killington was, or what team member could possibly be in custody.

Jenkins could see their surprise and sighed before he said. "Alright, I'll tell you what I know as long as you release Silvia."

All eyes turned towards the professor. He bowed his head before he began his story. "I had been working on my special engine for more years than I care to count. Grant Phyindress contacted me about this race as a way to build and test it. I was excited so I said yes. Harvard Bertrand, Richard's father, was to be our investor. I assembled a team and we created the finest machine ever to roll on any street in the world. However, I learned early on that there were other forces in play that were trying to influence the outcome of the race.

"So I did a little digging and found that the investor of the winning team would receive over a millions dollars and the contracts to use the winning technology. That could mean billions. When another teams' car was sabotaged before the race even started, knocking them out of the race, I knew that we could be in trouble.

"I decided to try to figure out who was behind it because we needed to keep our team safe. Part of the race included a way to disable other racecars in a way that wouldn't cause bodily harm. The laser head was designed to burn through the body's skin so the two layers hidden inside would melt together and shut down the car.

"It was a way to possibly trim down the number of cars that reached the finish loop but I think it was more to add enough drama for people to want to watch the race. Ideally all of the cars would make it to the end and they would just drive up and one would be declared the winner. The lasers would just keep the drivers a little more on their toes. But that didn't work out so well.

"When I found out that we had to build a weapon to disable an opponent. I had two young ladies designed an ingenious weapon delivery system. From what I witnessed during the race, my staff had indeed designed the winning concept in both car and weapon designs.

"One of the weapon's designers had to be in the racecar because we had no time to train anyone else to use the weapon properly, and it certainly couldn't be operated by the driver. The other designer, I talked her into working as a spy in the enemy camp.

"Silvia was really motivated to be doing something important for the race."

Katrina lowered her head. She thought that she had been chosen for her talent, not by default.

Jenkins continued without stopping. "So we made up a cover story about Silvia leaving the team because she didn't get the position of weapons specialist.

"I thought that she could do the job that I sent her to do and then just leave after it was complete. That didn't work out so well either. Poor Silvia. I was trying to keep my team safe and in doing so I put her in even more danger."

Cosgrove stood upright and interrupted the professor's description of the events. "What do you mean it didn't go so well for Silvia?"

"Well, she did her job, too well. Killington decided that she could be useful to him for more than just the one job. She almost got killed. I feel horrible for putting her in that position."

Katrina's hands went to her mouth.

Jenkins continued. "We were lucky your team pulled her out of there."

Cosgrove nodded. "It was a close call..."

Jenkins pushed on not wanting to hear the details. "She uncovered enough information while she was there to help another team of mine, but.... I'm getting ahead of myself here.

"I knew that I needed to provide back up for Richard and Katrina. Kristin and Dillon were more than happy to be their armed guards. They did a spectacular job. If it wasn't for them, I have no idea how the race would have turned out. And then we got to Las Vegas."

Cosgrove raised a hand to stop the confession before turning towards Katrina. "I want to know why you started a fire that burned an entire neighborhood."

Katrina looked defiantly at Cosgrove. "We were defending ourselves. There were hundreds of people shooting at us. The only weapon we had was the laser. We knew that it was powerful enough to injure people and maybe catch their clothes on fire. I had no idea the houses would catch fire."

"Those houses were nothing more than kindling in the heat of the desert." Cosgrove said.

"How was I supposed to know that?" Katrina shot back. "I didn't have time to consult Wikipedia about building materials used in Nevada. And what about people being allowed to own rocket launchers? No one is saying anything about that. That idiot burned half of Richard's face off while he was trying to protect me."

All eyes in the room turned towards Richard.

Cosgrove hadn't put much thought into how Richard had avoided the RPG, only that it had almost killed two of his agents.

Katrina took Richard's hand thinking back about that moment. Richard squeezed her hand in return.

After a moment of reflection Cosgrove got his energy back. "How did you get out of there without going through the roadblock?"

Katrina let go of Richard's hand in exasperation. "We found a place to stop and rest but Richard started to go into shock. That's where Jersey and Lucky caught up to us again. Jersey's an EMT so he cleaned Richard's burn and put a bandage on it and gave Richard some kind of pain medication. He's the one that told us about the bounty and helped smuggle us out of Nevada because he knew it wasn't safe for us to stop or even go to a hospital until the race was over. There were so many people with guns ready to kill us we hitched a ride for a bit to rest and stay safe. The drugs Jersey gave Richard amped him up so we could keep going."

Cosgrove piped up. "We were trying to save you. We traveled across half the country to stop the race before anyone else could get hurt. We thought Phyindress had rigged the race since it was his two cars that were supposed to win. But all of a sudden we were at war. We went from trying to stop the racecars to trying to take down all of the other people who had been hired to stop you. We lost a lot of agents in Nevada. Killington has a lot to answer for."

Professor Jenkins spoke again. "We were very lucky in the end but our best decision was choosing Richard as our driver in the first place. He pulled them through so many tight spots; no one else would have survived."

Frodes, Richard Bertrand's biggest fan, started clapping. It quickly grew to everyone in the room. Even the agents clapped.

Harvard wiped a tear from his eye. "You know, sometimes it takes a terrible event like this to put things in their proper perspective. I think Richard and I have a lot to talk about."

Katrina turned towards Professor Jenkins. "So it was Phyindress all along? He hired Mac Killington?"

He shook his head. "Turns out it was Ian Practor, a guy who worked for Phyindress. He made all the transactions though the company so that it would look like Phyindress was behind it. He hired Killington, but there were others too and we're still working on that. He wanted Phyindress to take the fall for all of it so when his boss was locked up he could take over the business and keep all of the money."

"The drivers of the two racecars were supposed to win, they were getting their orders from Practor?" Katrina asked.

"Yes." Jenkins answered.

"You're the one who sent that email?" Cosgrove asked, pointing at Jenkins.

"Well, technically Silvia sent it," he began.

"You arranged for Silvia to send every member of the FBI an email telling us Practor was behind this mess while she was inside our offices? Did you plan for her to be held in protective custody as a witness?"

Jenkins bowed his head. "Her safety was paramount, but yes, she knew that she could end up having to testify. Did you find Practor?"

"Yes, he was arrested at the airport attempting to leave the country in the company jet." Cosgrove said with a smile. "He wasn't so smart after all. But I have one more question. If Richard is the driver that you say he is how did he end up looking like this when his passenger is fine and they were both in the same car the whole time?"

Katrina turned to the agent with angry tears in her eyes. "He is every bit the driver they think he is, and the only reason that he's the one in the hospital bed is because he spent more time protecting me instead of saving himself."

"I used my airbag charge to create the ramp that got us into that finish loop. He threw himself over me as we went through the loop. He broke an arm and destroyed his leg to save me from going through the windshield. And I can't even count how many other times he protected me. He only got burned by the RPG because he was pushing me out of the way."

Silence filled the room. Richard Bertrand had turned out to be far more than the spoiled playboy that he had embodied at the beginning of the race.

A stout nurse came in and announced that everyone needed to leave. Her voice carried authority with every syllable and not even the FBI agents objected.

The members of the team said their goodbyes to Richard before leaving the room. His parents left after assuring Richard that they would be back soon. Finally Professor Jenkins and Katrina were the only ones left. The nurse pressed a button on the morphine drip next to her patient's bed and in seconds Richard was asleep.

"I don't want him up again for at least four hours." The nurse said before she left.

Jenkins put both his hands on Katrina's shoulders and asked one last question. "Are you coming back with us?"

Katrina shook her head. "No, Richard protected me through the entire race even though I wanted to kill him half of the time. I owe it to him to stay. When he is well enough to travel, I will take him home to finish his recovery. He's going to need a good long break."

Professor Jenkins smiled and hugged her one last time before leaving the room.

Katrina watched him walk down the hall before resuming her post in the side chair in the corner of the room. She picked up the magazine she had already read at least twice when she heard her name softly spoken.

She rose quickly to be at Richard's side. "What's wrong? Do I need to get the nurse?"

"No."

"No?" Katrina asked softly.

"No, I can't go to Maine with you." Richard said.

"Why not?"

"I should go home with my parents for a while. You have no idea how horrible I look under all of these bandages." Richard said as he closed his eyes ready to let sleep take him again.

Katrina shook him awake, annoyed that his presumption. "I don't think so. You don't need to hide yourself away. So what if you have some scars. You saved my life..." The emotion of the moment caught in her throat, "I can never repay you for that. You will come home with me and meet my parents and..." Katrina's voice trailed off as she realized that he was asleep again.

She leaned over and kissed him. "We'll have plenty of time to talk later. We'll talk about everything. It's my time watch over you now."

Thank you for reading The Invisible Car Race
I hope you enjoyed this title
Please leave a comment as to how you liked this book
where you purchased this title
Or drop me a note at
toscribble1@gmail.com

www.ingramcontent.com/pod-product-compliance
Lightning Source LLC
Chambersburg PA
CBHW030329120726
47901CB00007B/1733